Tangled Up in Christmas

Tangled Up in Christmas

LISA RENEE
NEW YORK TIMES BESTSELLING AUTHOR
JONES

Entangled Publishing, LLC
2614 South Timberline Road
Suite 105, PMB 159
Fort Collins, CO 80525
rights@entangledpublishing.com
Visit our website at www.entangledpublishing.com.

Amara is an imprint of Entangled Publishing, LLC.

Edited by Liz Pelletier
Cover design by Bree Archer and Liz Pelletier
Photographer: VJ Dunraven/Period images
Cover images by Leembe/GettyImages
Interior design by Toni Kerr

MMP ISBN 978-1-64063-762-7
ebook ISBN 978-1-64063-763-4

Manufactured in the United States of America

First Edition November 2019

[illegible]

[illegible]

Manufactured in [illegible]

ALSO BY LISA RENEE JONES

THE TEXAS HEAT SERIES

The Truth About Cowboys
Tangled Up in Christmas

THE INSIDE OUT SERIES

If I Were You
Being Me
Revealing Us
No In Between
I Belong to You
All of Me

THE CARELESS WHISPERS SERIES

Denial
Demand
Surrender

THE SECRET LIFE OF AMY BENSEN SERIES

Escaping Reality
Infinite Possibilities
Forsaken
Unbroken

THE DIRTY MONEY SERIES

Hard Rules
Damage Control
Bad Deeds
End Game

CHAPTER ONE

Hannah...

I sit next to "Joe from Houston" on my flight to Dallas. Joe, a midthirties guy who might be nice enough if he didn't use the gap between his teeth as a resource to spew inappropriate remarks in my direction. In the hours since we boarded the same flight in Los Angeles, his efforts to acquire my phone number have gotten less and less restrained, his crude remarks making it quite clear that's not all he wants. I'm not sure what that says about where I'm at in my life right now—probably not much—but starting over at twenty-eight, well, that's another story. One I don't wish to live, but I am.

The wheels hit the runway, and I stare out the window, wondering if Texas still smells like queso, margaritas, and hot cowboys to me, as it once did. I fear not, though. I know not. The day I moved away to Los Angeles, I stepped beyond those distractions and others. Distractions like Roarke Frost, the man who ripped out my heart and shattered it, and did so at a time when I needed him more than ever.

But I didn't need him, I remind myself. I made it on my own and quite well, at least until now. *Now* my plane has just pulled up to the gate, and as soon as the pilot winds down the engines, I'm in knots, wishing I were back in Los Angeles. Maybe that makes me a coward, hiding from the past, but nevertheless, that's what I feel. Only there's nothing back there for me. My famous photographer boss is in trouble, and I'm blacklisted right along with him. My dream job is no more. And since the cost of living in L.A. is more nightmare than dream, and my studio apartment above his studio is now under siege by the bank, home sweet home is all there is for me.

It's time to deplane, and my heart thrums in my ears. Joe from Houston is speaking to me, but I don't hear many of the words coming out of his mouth. "You make cowgirls look good," Joe says, and yes, I heard that and what follows. "How about that number? I can show you how good over dinner."

This will be my first time on Texas soil in six years. I'm not spending one night with this man. "I'm on my way to Whataburger," I say. "And that's a religious experience that requires I go alone."

He blinks. "Religious experience?"

"Joe from Houston, if you're from Texas and don't know that Whataburger is a religious experience, you and I should break up before we ever get together." We're now deplaning, and he stands up. I do the same, grab my purse, and dart forward in front of him, praying I can escape him as we exit.

Nervous energy overtakes me, and I slide the strap of my purse across my chest because I do. Because it's something to do as I wait my turn to exit. Soon, too soon, and somehow not soon enough, I'm walking up the ramp and darting in between people to avoid Joe from Houston. This mission actually aids in my mental state, keeping it focused on the task at hand, not the past, not the return to a home that is no longer home. I clear the waiting area and turn left with one goal: the bathroom, but I make it a few more steps and stop. My camera. Oh my God, I left my camera on the plane. A really expensive camera. My only really expensive camera. I can't afford to launch an event-planning business, as I hope to, and replace that camera.

Panic ensues, and I race back toward the plane, running right into Joe. "She came back. I knew she would."

"Move, Joe. Move now or I swear I will knee you for every woman who you ever talked to the way you talked to me on that plane, and I am so not joking right now."

His eyes go wide, and he quickly releases me. I take off running, rounding the corner, dashing through the gate seating area where I find myself bumped and cursed, but I've lived years in Los Angeles. Crowds don't bother me. Bumps don't bother me. Losing my camera, my way of earning income, *that* would destroy me right now. Finally, I manage to work my way to the entryway to the ramp. "My camera," I announce at the door. "I left it on my seat."

"Which seat, honey?" says the flight attendant, a nice Texas woman with a big blonde hairdo and a vocabulary of "y'all" and "fixin'" that I know all too well.

"11A," I say. "Can I just go look?"

"No, I'm sorry, it's against regulations. But I'll go check." She retreats down the ramp as I'm left there to wait.

I all but lose my patience, but thank God, the attendant returns, walking toward me with my camera. My relief flows out with appreciation, and it's not long before I'm back on my way to baggage claim, wondering where my head is that I'd leave my precious camera, one that had taken me years in L.A. to afford, behind. "Back in L.A." is the answer. I want to be back in L.A., working my way through and up the fashion world chain of command.

But I'm not, so I refocus on an old mission that, minus Joe, is now one-dimensional. I hunt for a bathroom while my cellphone rings, and I don't have to look at the number. I answer with a greeting. "Hey, Linda," I say, knowing this will be my best friend from college who is now a rather accomplished photographer in her own right. She's also my ride.

"You're here! I can't believe you're here. You're home, honey, and just in time for the holidays to ramp up in three weeks. Though good gosh, it's going to be a hot season. It's still ninety outside today."

"Three weeks from now is Halloween, and yes, my birthday, neither of which is a holiday, and home is not Dallas, it's Sweetwater. And just to be clear, it gets cold for about a day or two the week of Halloween every year in Texas, if you can call the first time it gets to fifty degrees for the season 'cold.'"

"You're from Texas, which makes this home. Furthermore, your parents don't own the ranch in Sweetwater anymore. They moved to Indianapolis, but you chose to return to Dallas because it's familiar. Just another reason you're home. End of topic. Next up. Your birthday most definitely *is* a holiday, as is Halloween. Good grief, woman. I have work to do on you. It's a good thing you *are* home. I'm out front," Linda continues, "and a really rude police officer just threatened to tow me, so you need to get here now."

"Oh God." I hustle my pace. "You, woman, are always getting in a fight with someone."

"You don't get in enough fights as far as I'm concerned, or you wouldn't have been blacklisted along with your boss for his mistakes."

"He was blacklisted for something that didn't happen."

"He should have protected you."

"He can't even protect himself right now." *And*, I add silently, reminding myself to stay focused, *I have skills, not just with a camera*. I coordinated many a huge event through him. I can put those skills to use.

"Oh God," Linda groans. "I have things to say about your boss, but the jerky officer is at me again." There is the sound of what I believe to be knocking on her window. "I have to go. Hurry! Get to me quick!" She disconnects, and ugh, so much for the bathroom. I see the sign but pass it by. I can't have Linda getting towed or, worse, spouting off like she does and getting in bigger trouble. Thankfully, Dallas Love Field is rather compact, and the walk is short—or it was, way back when. It's remodeled, and nothing is as it was or where it was. I navigate here and there and pass through the security exit to find Linda standing there, her red hair piled haphazardly on top of her head.

"He directed me to a parking spot," she says, hoisting up her boobs, which might not be bigger than mine, but she bravely displays her assets today with a deep V of cleavage cut into her T-shirt. "These helped."

We burst into laughter and then launch ourselves at each other, hugging fiercely before she pulls back. "I only have ten minutes. Let's get to baggage claim." She tugs me forward, and I groan with how full my bladder is.

"I have to pee, like, now. I have to. This is non-optional."

She grabs my arm and drags me forward. "This way. I know where a bathroom is."

This motivates me, so I step up my pace all too willingly, and it's only a minute before her phone is ringing and she stops. "This is important. It's about a job. I have to take it."

"Bathroom?"

She points. "That entrance on the left. They just changed the signs, and they're hard to see, but that's the women's restroom."

That entrance is not nearby, and I really can't linger to wait on Linda. I hurry forward, and my phone rings now, too. Afraid it's the real estate agent who's supposed to show me rentals, I dig for my phone, grabbing it only to find it's Linda calling. My brows furrow, and I look behind me to find her motioning wildly, but I don't have time for this. I have to go to the bathroom. I round the wall to the entrance as she'd directed and smack hard into a body. A man's body. A man in the women's bathroom.

"Wrong bathroom, woman," the grumpy man snaps, giving my well-filled-out T-shirt a once-over.

"Are you serious right now?" I demand.

"Get out of the way." The man literally grabs my arms and sets me against the wall.

"Are you crazy?" I demand, ready to call security, but he's already walking away.

I drop my bag that's killing my arm, push off the wall, and face the bathroom, looking for a sign, certain that man was a jerk to hide his embarrassment for going into the women's restroom. Instead, the sign reads Men, and I want to crawl into the hole my embarrassment is digging in the floor.

I turn to make a rapid departure, grab my bag, and proceed to run into another hard body. "Oh God. I'm sorry. I—" My gaze lifts, and I gasp at the familiar man now holding my arms, touching me for the first time in six years. I'm touching him, too, my hands curled on the black tee that stretches over a chest that proves to be more impressive than ever. He's a man now, but then Roarke Frost was always all man. "Roarke," I whisper, as if the name in my mind isn't enough confirmation. I need it on my lips, the way I once needed him on my lips.

"Hannah," he breathes out, his voice low and rough. His brown eyes are still that warm milk chocolate, but I was always the one who melted in the heat of any moment spent with this man.

"Oh my God, I'm so sorry," Linda gushes, appearing beside us, huffing and puffing. "I was stuck on the call, and I couldn't reach you and, well, as you know, I directed you to the wrong bathroom." She's rambling, her attention turning to Roarke, who is still holding onto me. Who is still focused on me and me alone. "Sorry," Linda repeats. "Sorry—she went the wrong way because I told her wrong."

"I'm not sorry at all," Roarke says, his eyes warming with the words. "I can't believe you're here."

"In the men's bathroom?" I joke, trying to get off the topic of why I'm in Dallas. "It's a game we play in L.A." I cringe at the stupid comment.

His dark brows dip. "Game?"

"That was a joke that's going nowhere. There is no game."

The air thickens between us, memories pushing and pulling, pushing and pulling. I want to push him away. I want to hold on to him and pretend nothing ever went wrong. "You look good, Hannah," he says finally. "Your hair is longer, and I swear your eyes are a little greener."

Anger bristles inside me. My hair. My eyes. That's all he has to say after—well, everything that happened? "Why are you here?" I ask.

"I'm on my way to Kentucky to work with a horse," he says, which isn't a surprise. His family always trained horses, but he's taken that to a whole new level. He's now a YouTube sensation, the Horse Wrangler. Which I know because I've been watching the videos that I will never admit to watching. "Are you home to visit?" he asks. "Aren't your parents in Indianapolis now?"

"I'm here for work," I say, because it's not a lie. I am here for work and for a place to live, but that's beside the point. "A fast in-and-out trip."

A man clears his throat, and Roarke grabs my bag and motions me toward the wall, and when I nod, he catches my hand the way he used to catch my hand. It's familiar. He's familiar. So is the heat rushing up my arm and across my chest. No one makes me feel what this man makes me feel, and this makes me angry. He betrayed me. He hurt me. *He hurt me.*

"I get back Friday night," he says. "We need to talk. We've needed to talk for a long time. Can I see you?"

Of course he returns Friday, I think. Of course he wants to talk now when he hasn't tried once in six years. "I leave Friday morning."

An announcement sounds for a flight, and he grimaces. "I'm late. That's my flight, and I have to head through security. Damn it. We need more time." He scrubs his jaw, a good three-day dark shadow there, dark like the hair on his chest where my fingers used to play often. But that was then and this is now. "There are things I've wanted to say to you for a long time."

"It wasn't meant to be," I say. "Let's just leave it at that, Roarke." And the truth is that there is nothing he can say that would change anything.

His gaze lingers on mine and then lifts skyward before lowering. "I have to go. Hannah—"

"Go, Roarke. That's what you told me years ago.

That's what I'm telling you now. Go. Because it's what's right for you and me. And you're holding my hand."

"Yes, I am, and I don't want to let it go."

"But we both know you will. Just like you did before." The words burn out of me, anger in their depths.

His jaw clenches, and he lifts my hand, kissing my knuckles. "Goodbye, Hannah." He turns and walks away, bypassing the bathroom by necessity, no doubt. He's leaving. Even when I left, it was because he'd checked out. I lost him before I lost him, or what went down would not have gone down.

Linda steps in front of me. "You know the Horse Wrangler? Oh my God, I need details." She glances over her shoulder. "That man's butt in jeans. That's part of what makes him an internet sensation, you know? Women love him."

I grimace. Yes. Yes, they do. Just one of the reasons I'm not going to share details of a longtime crush on my next door neighbor that became a summer engagement gone wrong.

"The way he was looking at you," she continues. "Did you and he—" She joins two fingers. "Did you—"

"Bathroom," I say. "I need a bathroom before I can properly decline to share details. Now all you get is a grunt."

She grimaces and motions me forward. "After the bathroom."

I grab my bag, and we start walking. And yes, I get my bathroom escape, but Linda gets nothing on

Roarke. That's a closed subject, just as it's a closed chapter of my life, and yet, when I lay down in her spare bedroom that night to sleep, I can almost smell that man's cologne: an earthy, rich scent that is all man. The wrong man for me.

CHAPTER TWO

Hannah…

Two weeks later…

"Hannah!"

At the shout of my name, I rush out of my newly minted office and into the lobby of Linda Moore Photography where I'm now renting a space (okay, borrowing an office) to find Linda on the floor. "Oh my God," I gasp, rushing toward her. "What happened?"

"I fell off my own heels," she groans. "I know. I'm stupid, but I think I broke something." She starts panting. "I think I might be sick."

Pain so bad she's going to be sick. That's not good. "Let me call an ambulance."

"No." She grabs my arm, peering at me through a crazy mass of red curls, the rich red color a dramatic contrast to my light-brown alternative. "I have to be at a photoshoot for the Rangers today," she announces.

I blanch. "As in the professional baseball team?" I ask, certain that can't be the case. Granted, despite being old friends, I've only been back in Dallas for two weeks. I've shared this office with her for a week of that since I officially opened Spring Event Planning.

"Yes. Yes, I do all their photography. I can't miss this event." She rises up on her elbows. "Jason

Jenks, their new pitcher, is launching a kids camp. That's why I'm in heels on a Saturday. It's a high-profile event. And Jason is a really big deal right now. He just returned from retirement to pitch again."

I know who Jason is all too well, but I keep that to myself. "You have to be seen by a doctor first. Where do you think you've broken something?"

"My hip. It hurts too damn badly to be bruised, but I can just push through this." She sucks in air and tries to stand, only to cry out. "Okay, this isn't happening. My doctor lives next door to me. Can you grab my phone from my purse on the reception desk? I need to see if he can come here."

"Of course." I stand up and run my hands down my black jeans, even as I rush to the desk, find her cell, and return to squat next to her. "Let me get you some Advil."

"Thank you," she says. "The stabbing pain is easing, but it's still bad. I can tell it's bad." She punches in a number, and I hurry to my office, grab a bottle from the drawer, and snag a water from the fridge in the break room.

By the time I return, she's leaning against the receptionist's desk, and there's a white ring around her lips. Pain. She's in pain. I rush forward and kneel in front of her, setting the water down to pop the bottle open and shake four pills onto my palm. "Take these. Did you reach your neighbor?"

She accepts the pills and downs them with the bottle of water I open and offer her before answering. "He's on his way. I need you to do this job for me. I have a team of shooters meeting me here in fifteen minutes to head to Globe Life Park. That's where the event is taking place. It's an announcement and then a party. I'll introduce you to our team, and you can take charge of the shoot."

My eyes go wide. "What? Me?"

"You worked for a fashion photographer in L.A. A famous photographer."

"Right up until he got caught up in the Me Too movement and went down for it," I remind her. "I'm attached to his reputation. I don't want to do that to you, especially with a big-league operation."

"No one is going to know."

"Not a normal everyday person, but this is the big leagues, quite literally."

"You're amazing. You've shot some of the world's biggest celebrities."

"Yes, but—"

"Please. I'm begging you. I can't lose this contract. I need them to know that when I couldn't make it, I sent someone better."

I swallow hard. She's been generous enough to offer me an office for half the rent anywhere else would cost. She even found me an apartment two blocks away. The truth is that right now, with this job for the Rangers, she's delivering all over again, by way of an opportunity to build credit outside the disaster that stole my career in L.A. I owe her. I owe her big-time.

"Look," she says, still making her case, unaware that I've already made it for her. "Jason is a super-nice guy and—"

"I know," I say. "You don't have to tell me."

She blinks. "You know?"

"We grew up together, as in he babysat me. We lived on neighboring ranches in Sweetwater."

She blanches. "How did I not know that you're that close to Jason Jenks?"

I wave off the connection. "We haven't spoken in years," I say.

"Did he become a big-shot snob?"

"Jason?" I laugh. "Oh good gosh, no. Jason is not that way. Life just got in the way of our friendship." And so did his best friend, Roarke Frost, but I'm not going to talk about my dirty laundry and Roarke. "We aren't close," I add of Jason and me, "but country family is always family. And you're family now, too. I'll shoot for you."

"Thank you so much. This is great. This is going to soften the blow of my not making it. I'll call now and tell them you're coming."

"I'll go pack up my camera," I say, pushing to my feet and heading to my office.

I'm not going to run into Roarke, I tell myself as I pack my camera bag. *I'm not*. Roarke will not be at an event at the Rangers' clubhouse. Besides, he's probably traveling again or in Sweetwater.

I grab my purse and my camera bag and glance down at my black jeans, boots, and T-shirt, which, as an outfit, works just fine for crawling around and taking good shots. I'm not changing. I have no one to impress with anything but my photos. I exit into the lobby to find a man in his midthirties, with dark hair and glasses, kneeling next to Linda. "This is Mark," she announces. "He's a newly minted doctor who lives next door to me. We have no chemistry, but hey, I'll fix you up with him if you like."

Mark laughs and gives me a quick inspection, his eyes warming with approval. He's cute. Actually, he's really good-looking, but I feel nothing. Nada. Nope. It's not happening. But then, the name Roarke always has had a way of destroying any warm fuzzies I might feel for anyone.

"I think the first thing you need to do," I say, "is get better." I glance at Mark. "What's the prognosis, Doc?"

"I'm going to get x-rays," Linda replies before he can. "Right after I send you and the team off to play with the hot ballplayers in tight white baseball pants. Lucky you."

Lucky me.

As long as the only person from my past I see today is Jason, not Roarke, then yes, lucky me.

• • •

Linda's team consists of four shooters, two who are highly experienced and two who aren't, none of whom require much supervision. Once we're at the stadium offices, we're set up in a private room that is decorated for some sort of Christmas photo op even though Christmas is still a few months away. We sit down on chairs dressed like Santa Claus, where we each set up our cameras. We're then handed maps while being briefed about the party in the clubhouse and the speech to follow on the field in roughly an hour.

As we're left to our jobs, I divide up my team, motioning between Liz and Mike, both college-age photography students. "I need you to just randomly shoot whoever and whatever you can get on film. I don't want one thing at this event not on our film." They both nod eagerly. "Weave and shoot," I add. "Follow the crowd but become shadows. Don't make anyone feel uncomfortable. If they don't want to be in a photo, quickly move along. I'll walk down with you."

My attention turns to Mary and Kate, both experienced shooters. "Head out to the field. Shoot there now. I don't want one second missed out there, including the setup. I'm going to walk the party and then meet you out there." I open the door, and they eagerly head out.

Liz and Mike follow them out, and the three of us head to the club, which isn't a short trip at all. We travel a long hallway and finally find ourselves showing press passes at the entrance, the packed room just beyond security. Once we're past the entry point, the room is bustling with people in casual wear, drinks in hand, the swell of voices, and clinking glasses all around us. I split Mike and Liz left and right to begin to shoot.

I'm about to start working the room myself when suddenly I'm standing face-to-face with Jason. He blinks down at me. "Hannah? Holy hell, Hannah. It's really you."

"Yes. It's really me."

He pulls me into a hug, a bear hug. "I can't believe how long it's been." His hands go to my arms, and he gives me a keen inspection. "Beautiful as ever. Are you here to stay?"

"Yes. I'm back."

"And you didn't call me?"

My cheeks heat. "I just got back."

"You mean you were avoiding Roarke. I'm not Roarke, woman."

"Jason?"

With the female query, a pretty brunette has appeared by his side, and he quickly wraps his arm around her. "Jessica, baby, this is Hannah. She grew up in Sweetwater. I used to babysit her, believe it or not. God, I feel old. Hannah, this is Jessica, my fiancée, who runs the new Flying J bakery with my grandmother. My grandmother is here somewhere."

"The cookies being served are the new launch cookies for the Flying J bakery," Jessica adds before shaking my hand. "And nice to meet you."

"I heard Martha had cookies and a cookbook," I say. "I saw her and you, Jessica, on the news. And you, too, Jason. I'm so glad to see you back on the mound." I leave out any comment about what drove him away: the plane crash that killed his parents.

"It's all been loads of fun," Jessica says. "Martha and Jason deserve this attention."

"What about you?" Jason asks. "I remember you went to L.A. to work for some big-name fashion photographer. I'm surprised you came back to Texas."

"Who was the photographer?" Jessica asks eagerly. "I love fashion." She glances at Jason and gives him a smile. "And ugly cowboy boots these days." They both laugh at what is clearly an inside joke before she glances back at me, eagerly awaiting my reply.

"Tobie Manning," I supply reluctantly, and considering I'm here professionally, I steel myself for any knowledge she might have of the scandal.

Her eyes go wide. "*The* Tobie Manning? Oh my God. He's ridiculously famous. What a dream job."

"It was," I concede and decide it's best to address this head-on when I can direct the content of the subject. "But then," I add, "he got caught up in the Me Too movement and I got blacklisted with him. That's L.A. for you."

"Oh no," Jessica says. "Did you get harassed?"

"No, he likes men, but honestly, he's not guilty, or I wouldn't have stayed with him so long. There were plenty of guilty people that deserved to be booted, but he just wasn't one of them. This is all about him firing a group of models who were causing havoc on a set. It's pretty brutal to see this happen. They used a good cause for the wrong reason."

"So if he beats this, will you go back?" Jason asks.

"No," I say. "It's time to do me. I coordinated so many events for him in L.A. that I've opened an event-planning service in Dallas. I'm sharing an office with the photographer for this event, and she got hurt, so here I am."

"Event planning?" Jessica asks. "Wait. Wow. I'm looking for an event planner. We're holding a Christmas event to launch the kids camp we're announcing today. It works out perfectly because it's during Jason's off-season, but truly, with only a month to go, we have nothing worth mentioning done for this thing. We need you. Please. Say you'll help."

I blink. Me? She wants me? I'm still trying to

get my head around this idea when she insists, "You have to do it. It's a great opportunity to establish your new business, and we need someone Jason doesn't feel will use us for the press." She eyes Jason. "A friend who's worked with celebrities. She's perfect."

"You *are* perfect for the job, Hannah," Jason agrees as a man appears by his side, leaning in to whisper in his ear before hurrying away. Jason refocuses on me. "I need to go deal with a few things here, but you and Jessica should exchange numbers. We'll get you a check and details tomorrow." He hugs me. "Glad to have you back." And then he's gone. He walks away as if this is settled. I'm doing this job for him.

"I need to run, too," Jessica says, holding her phone in her hand. "What's your number? I'll call you tomorrow."

I recite my number, and she hugs me. "We're a friendship in the making. I know it. Talk to you tomorrow." And then she's gone, too. I inhale and tell myself this is good. This is great. I'm launching my business in a big way. This isn't my past. It's my new future, and if Roarke somehow shows up in the middle of the event, it doesn't matter. He means absolutely nothing to me anymore. He can't hurt me. He can't touch me. My dread is simply about dredging up a past long ago forgotten. So why is my heart racing?

I turn and start walking fast, really fast, without even seeing where I'm walking. I blink, and I'm in the hallway, walking back toward our setup room. I stop and eye the bathroom sign, darting inside. I'm halfway to the stalls when I spy the urinals to my left. Holy crap. This time, I really went into the men's bathroom. I turn and all but run for the door, rounding the entry hallway only to plummet into a hard chest. Again. Good Lord, what is happening to me, besides Texas?

"Sorry. I'm sorry, I—" My words falter as I find myself staring into the warm chocolate stare of Roarke Frost.

His fingers flex on my arms, the swell of heat between us instant, burning me alive. I don't want to feel this, not with this man. "Roarke," I whisper, hating how good his name tastes on my lips.

"Hannah," he says softly, his voice somehow silk and sandpaper on my nerve endings, and his mouth, that damn mouth I know on my mouth all too well, quirks at the edges, amusement in the depth of his stare. "Why exactly are you in the men's bathroom again?"

CHAPTER THREE

Hannah...

Why am I in the men's bathroom? I bristle with that question, which should embarrass me but really just angers me. Really, truly, I bristle with just about everything to do with this man, and I'm not a bristler, and yes, that's a word. Look it up in the awkward ex dictionary; it's right there with about ten other words and/or phrases that I can't speak out loud. But back to bristling. It's *not* me. You can't bristle in the fashion industry in L.A. without getting run over. You can't bristle over your ex jerk of a fiancé without getting run over, either. You certainly can't think about all the times you were intimate and naked with him without just being plain stupid. I'm not going to be stupid with this man. Been there, done that, which brings me back to why am I in the men's bathroom? Inside the very stupidity of that action is a bit of a poetic explanation and a warning.

Roarke is every reason I've ever been stupid.

"I blame you," I say, pushing away from him, his hands falling away from me, and I tell myself that's what I want. Away from Roarke, with him no longer touching me, but I'm cold everywhere I was hot seconds before. "You're the reason I'm in the men's bathroom."

"You thought this was the place to speak alone?"

"There is no place for us to speak alone, Roarke. I ended up here, in the wrong bathroom, with the wrong man, because I was flustered, and you know why I was flustered? Because I just saw Jason. I just agreed to do some work for him, and while that's great and generous of him, I couldn't revel in the career opportunity he gave me because I knew, *I knew*, that job leads to you. And here you are."

"Hannah." He takes a step toward me. I rotate and walk away, exiting the bathroom into a group of four stunned men about to enter. I don't explain why I'm in the men's room. I use them, darting around them even as they block the bathroom doorway. They're my shelter, my escape, and maybe that's cowardly and everything my father—a man as tough as nails—would hate me to be, but I can feel the build of something cutting and vulnerable inside me. Something I don't want to feel. Something I can't afford to feel and be here in Texas. Something that I haven't let myself feel since Roarke tore me apart years before.

I dash down the hallway and all but trot to avoid a full-out run, thanking the Lord when Mike rushes toward me, assuring there will be no alone time with Roarke. "We have a problem," he announces, panting as he reaches my side. A problem I can handle. Well, any problem that isn't Roarke. "What's happening?" I ask.

"Nikki Miller, and yes, I said Nikki Miller, the movie star, is *here*. I thought that was camera-worthy, so I shot photos of her. She got pissed and took my camera. Like, literally yanked it from my hands, and then her security people took it."

Roarke steps between us. "I know Nikki. I'll get your camera back."

Of course, he's here to be Superman. He's always Superman for everyone around him but me. Of course, he knows Nikki. For all I know, she's his girlfriend, the kind he wanted when I wasn't enough. And, of course, he's followed me to relieve some nagging guilt from his shoulders. Or maybe he was just walking this way. Why would I think he has a nagging anything where I'm concerned?

"You're that Horse Wrangler, aren't you?" Mike asks, and with that, I'm done.

"I'll let the Horse Wrangler help you," I say. "We have one camera shooting right now with Liz. I need there to be two." I walk around Mike and away from Roarke, and this time, Roarke doesn't follow. This time he's forced to let me go to offer his promised aid to Mike, but then, he's good at letting me go. The past proves that and proves it well.

Hurrying forward, I make my way back to the party and waste no time getting to work. I start shooting, wondering when Roarke will reappear, but he doesn't. I try to be pleased about this—I *am* pleased—but damn him, there's a clawing sensation in my chest, right where my heart he'd once shattered beats a little too rapidly.

• • •

A good forty-five minutes later, Roarke is nowhere to be seen, and I'm shooting the banners for today's event when Jessica appears beside me. "We're about to head down to the field." She hands me a badge. "They added an extra level of security. Make sure your team is wearing these." She hands me three more badges. "I have extras, and if I see them before you do, I'll make sure they have them as well."

"Okay, thanks." My brows furrow. "Is there a security alert of some sort?"

"Jason returning to baseball has the press going a little nuts. I'm sure you know he's a private person."

I nod. "Yes, he always was," I agree, and it's ridiculously comforting to recognize at least one person from my past as the person I knew then and now, but then I never knew Roarke. I only knew his public persona. "And I get it. It's a personality trait but a necessity in his high-profile lifestyle."

She squeezes my arm. "We know you get it. That's why we're both feeling lucky that you're back and available to help us with these projects."

I open my mouth, about to ask about the plural nature of that statement, assuming she means today and the Christmas event, but I never get the chance to clarify because someone calls Jessica's name. She lifts a hand. "I need to find Roarke. You know him, right?"

"Yes," I say tightly, wondering why I can't escape that man tonight. "We grew up together."

"Of course, you did. That was a stupid question. Can you help me find him and get him to the field? Jason needs him, and I'm being pulled in a million directions right now."

"Happy to help," I say, and I am. I just need to get past this Roarke thing, and perhaps exposure is the best way to desensitize myself where he's concerned.

"Thank you for helping." Her eyes light up. "I can't wait to talk about the camp's holiday event. Text me if you find Roarke before me, will you? And I'll do the same."

"You bet," I say, and already she's swooping in to embrace me with a quick hug before she fades away into the crowd.

I press my hand to my face. Good Lord, I just promised to go hunt down Roarke, the very man I justified running from less than an hour ago, but that wasn't exactly a mature move. Desensitizing is my new strategy. The control is mine. I own my emotions. I own how I allow them, and him, to affect me.

Settling my camera across my chest, I start weaving through the crowd, and it's fully five minutes before I break through a cluster of a half dozen people to spy Roarke, but he's not alone. There are not one but two stunning women, one blonde and one brunette, both angling in his direction, to ensure he's suffocated with the view of their boobs. Their very big, perfect boobs that make my what-I-sometimes-feel-are-pretty-decent boobs look like a chalkboard with two thumbtacks. There you have it. Just another reason I'm not with this man. He can't even ignore me with one other woman anymore. It's two.

I grab my phone from my front pocket and text Jessica: *I got him.*

Great, she replies. *Tell him to hurry and come with you. I have Mike, Liz, Kate, and Mary. You might want to grab a jacket. It's chilly. It's finally starting to feel like the holidays!*

It's sixty outside and that's chilly? Not that L.A. was much better. I sigh and stick my phone back inside my purse as yet another woman joins the entourage Roarke is forming. Of course, he's all tall, dark, and a Horse Wrangler, so what did I expect? He's good-looking and charming, always has been. The guy every guy wants to hate but can't because he's so damn nice and lives to save needy animals. Right. Saver of animals. Breaker of hearts. I might break his toe with my heels if I were wearing them. But fear not, all those with miserable exes, Fashion Week in New York City, and a creepy B-list actor did remind me of the value of a well-placed knee. Wisdom I might have to share with Roarke and soon.

Empowered by this thought, I close the space between him and me, stepping to the open spot in front of him. A flicker of surprise touches his handsome face, and when our eyes lock, the collision of the past with the present is a wicked hard jolt. A jolt that fades into white space as the room, the people, fall away, except for him, my ex-fiancé. My ex–best friend. My ex-everything. I revolt against the memories assailing me and open my mouth, which is never a good idea.

"I'm supposed to take you down to the field," I say flatly, and then that open mouth speaks for itself, "but clearly you have escorts who can help you better than my camera and I ever can. Jason is waiting on you." I turn and start walking, my heart racing despite my desire to remain unaffected by that man and his women.

I *am* unaffected. Screw him and his horse-wrangling, womanizing self. I looked him in the eyes. I handled him and me. Perhaps the comment about his escorts wasn't perfect, but it's done. We've been done for a long time. Nothing about a few bathroom and boob-infested meetings changes this at all.

Exiting to the hallway, I head down the stairwell I'd been directed to take to reach the field, letting the heavy door slam behind me, slamming a mental door on Roarke as I go, visualizing, as a yoga instructor told me some years back. In hindsight, though, if I'd gone to more than one class, maybe I wouldn't hear the door above open and assume it to be Roarke. Yoga was just too much posing when I'd rather be behind a lens, letting someone else pose for me.

"Hannah, wait."

At the sound of Roarke's voice behind me, I don't freeze. I've decided to desensitize. I've decided to face him, and us, and take control, when up to this point, I've done the opposite. "It happened. It's been years. I don't need you to talk me off some cliff I'm not on. We both have lived lives outside of each other."

"We lived a lot longer in a world where we were together."

"We were friends. Everything else was fast and over."

"We still are friends," he says.

Friends. I can't be his friend. Friends are people

you trust. I don't trust Roarke. "Jason's waiting on us."

He walks down a few steps, and I could back away, but that wouldn't be taking control. That would be giving him control. And so, this time, I don't run. I stand my ground and let him approach. I let him because that says *you don't scare me*, while every encounter since my return with this man has said the opposite.

It seems like a smart move until he's standing right in front of me, towering over me, which would be easy to do no matter what, considering he's six foot two and I'm five foot two. He's also close, so very close that the scent of him rushes through my senses, stirring hate and lust, and I don't even know what to do with those things. "What are we doing right now, Roarke? What are you doing?" And why am I not turning and leaving?

"Those women up there ambushed me. I don't know them. I don't want to know them."

"You don't owe me an explanation. I'm not yours. You're not mine."

"There's a lot about that statement I could argue with."

"I don't even know what that means," I say. "There's nothing about that statement that can be argued."

"You're wrong," he assures me. "You know it. I know it."

The door from below opens, and Jessica shouts, "Roarke, we need you now! You, too, Hannah."

At the sound of Jessica's voice, Roarke grimaces, and this conversation is over. She steps to our sides and looks between us, her eyes narrowing with a keen appraisal. "Everything okay?"

"Yes," I say, and I mean it. I look at her and add, "Being home is good." I look at Roarke. "I'm not leaving this time."

His brown eyes narrow, and where they are normally warm, now they burn with something I don't understand, but then, I never understood this man. I just thought I did. "Good," he says. "This is where you belong."

"Yes, it is," Jessica says, and just when I'm feeling in control, really in control, she adds, "This is really rather kismet. Jason and Roarke, the baseball whisperer and the Horse Wrangler, together for one camp, with you back to help us find its full potential. Let's get to it."

The floor falls out from underneath me. Jason and Roarke are doing this together? As in, I'm coordinating the festival for Jason *and Roarke*?

"Hannah," Jessica continues, "can you get some shots of Jason and Roarke together and alone after the announcement for promotional material?"

"Yes," I say, trying not to sound like I'm not presently suffocating in a big bubble of Roarke overload. "Yes, of course."

She laughs. "Great, and I'd say shoot Roarke first with his horses before they have time to create a new poop mound on the field, but I think getting some shots of him riding right here on the baseball field could be amazing. We'll need to do that last after the field is cleared."

In other words, I'm working overtime, alone with Roarke.

CHAPTER FOUR

Hannah...

It's not long before the field is filled with famous personalities, with Jason and Roarke in the center of it all. And the horses. Roarke has four magnificent stallions with him, their coats glistening with beauty. And as angry as I am with him, even I can admit there is something magical about that man and his horses. I send my team to the outer edges of the field, capturing the crowd and the panoramic views. I take the field, the close-ups, and do so despite my reservations about how close this places me to Roarke. He doesn't get to push me into the shadows. I shoot the horses and resist my desire to touch them and talk to them. They're in a crowd, and I don't know their temperaments, but shooting them takes me home again, back to the ranch, back to that summer with Roarke.

Jessica begins testing a mic at the podium setup in the center of the field, and one of the horses is not pleased. I'm close, and I know what fidgeting like that means. "Roarke!" I shout, backing up, but he's already there, pulling me behind him as he soothes the beast.

"Easy, Mr. Rogers."

I'd laugh if I wasn't still feeling the sting of his touch, and "sting" is a loosely chosen word. It doesn't sting. It's more like a tingling warmth that has spread up my arm and across my chest and might now be climbing my neck. The horse jumps in the air, and my God, Roarke gets close, too close for comfort. I shake myself and pull my camera into position, trying to stave off my fear for him by way of staying busy. The camera becomes my outlet, and with it, the shots are incredible. Roarke works the horse, and Mr. Rogers settles down. Two men who I assume work for Roarke rush forward, feed Mr. Rogers a carrot, and then lead him toward an exit. The crowd erupts in cheers. I lower my camera, and Roarke isn't looking at his admirers. He's focused on me, quickly closing the space between us, and then his hands are on my shoulders. "Are you okay?"

No, I'm burning alive with your hands on me, I think, but what I say is, "Outside of you scaring me? Screw this Horse Wrangler junk, Roarke. You got too close. He could have killed you with one kick."

"You of all people know I know how to handle a horse."

"I know a lot of things about you, Roarke," I say, and I can't stop the crack of a whip in my voice. "Too much."

His hands fall away, his jaw sets hard. "Not as much as you think." He steps around me and walks toward the podium. Clapping erupts again, and I rotate to watch him raise his hand to acknowledge the crowd, my camera automatically lifting, the shots coming fast and furious, but even so, his words stay with me: *Not as much as you think*.

Asshole. I get that. I found that out. I thought he was the greatest man I'd ever known. That's what young love does to you. It makes you stupid and romantic. I'm not that girl anymore.

Jessica tries the microphone again but not without checking with Jason first. Once he waves her onward, she announces Jason, who joins her, now wearing his team jersey. "Welcome, everyone. I can't wait to talk about a very special kids camp, and who knew Mr. Rogers—that's the horse—would have allowed me to show you why this is so special?" He motions to Roarke, and Roarke joins him. "Did you see how calm this man was, how cool? Well, let me tell you, those are the batters who every pitcher, myself included, hates to face. Those are the pitchers who batters fear. Together, Roarke and I are going to teach these kids how to focus, how to stay calm, how to embrace the moment instead of fearing it. Skills that reach beyond the baseball field. And yes, we'll have some animals on board to help, with supervision, of course." He pats Roarke's arm. "This man is more than the Horse Wrangler. He's an amazing vet, with a zoo of animals the kids can enjoy."

My mind travels through a history of witnessing that man save animals, and it's one of the things I always loved about him. It's one of the things that made him seem too good to be as bad as he was to me. I shake off that thought, and for the next two hours, I follow the event and take photographs, checking in with my team and staying busy. There are occasional brushes with Roarke, but for the most part, we keep our distance. Until we can't.

The crowd begins to dissipate, and Jessica catches up with me. "Do you need any shots of the group together?"

"I got plenty," I say. "I got some incredible action shots outside with Jason and Roarke."

"Let's get Roarke and the horse and then game-plan on what you need for Jason. We need to get the horses off the field." She waves at Roarke. "Roarke!"

Roarke looks up from a conversation he's having with a man I don't know and waves back before saying something to the stranger and heading this direction. "What's up?" he asks, joining us, and while I can feel his eyes on me, I stay focused on Jessica.

"We need to get some shots of you riding and training the horses. I'm about to clear the field for you and Hannah. I'm going to let you two talk it out while I handle the clearing."

Roarke gives her an incline of his chin, and she squeezes my arm before hurrying away. Roarke shifts his stance to give me his full attention. Now I have to look at him, and the impact is pretty much like a wrecking ball. This man's stare slams into me, and I can barely catch my breath. "I'm all yours, Hannah," he says softly.

It's the wrong thing to say to me. "For now," I reply and motion to the horses. "I need you riding whatever pretty thing over there you want to ride."

He grimaces. "Hannah—"

"Don't say whatever you want to say," I warn. "It will piss me off, and I'm not as gently pissed off as I was back in the day when you initially pissed me off. Go ride, Roarke."

He doesn't go do anything. He just stands there, staring at me. I think he's going to speak. I *want* him to speak. I want him to yell and give me a reason to yell, but that's a safe fantasy because that's not Roarke. Roarke is Mr. Cool and Calm. That's who he is, and clearly, that hasn't changed since I left. I used to like that about him. I used to think it spoke of a man in control, a man who couldn't have his buttons pushed by anyone. Now, it's irritating. I want him to react. I shouldn't, but I do, and I tell myself that's called being human. It's also called looking for self-worth in a man, and that's a problem. And if he stands here one more second, I'm going to say something we both might regret.

Almost as if he read my mind, he turns on his heels, and I ready my camera, which may or may not have the lens land on his butt. I may or may not notice through said lens that said butt still looks perfect in jeans. Okay, I do, but it's a fashion thing, from the fashion industry now inbred in me. I must assess how clothing looks and fits. The butt, and the man attached to that butt, stops beside a black stallion with a gorgeous mane. He reaches up and strokes the stallion's neck, all long and luxuriously, something he does in the intro to his videos, not that I watched more than a couple here or there. I wonder how many women—not me, of course—have seen that intro and thought about him stroking them. At least they weren't stupid enough to let him actually do it, like I did.

He climbs onto the horse's back, and I fire away

with the camera, but not without a pinch in my chest at the memories of my youth that man on a horse delivers. God. This isn't home. Dallas isn't home, but this man, *he* is home. He was a part of my life from birth until I left for L.A. Shoving aside such thoughts, I race forward and lift my hand, motioning with my finger for him to ride. He waits on me, and when I'm close enough to run with him, he begins a trot—that's how easily we're in sync. We begin what is a game of him performing with the horse and me following along, lines, circles, prances, and poses, until I send him on a fast run away from me to return. Once he loops back, I step directly in his path, gobbling up every moment with my camera. I don't even realize how in his path I am until, suddenly, he and the horse are right in front of me, but I don't get run over.

The horse, at the man's direction, bows in front of me, bringing Roarke eye level with me. I'm standing there with two magnificent beasts in front of me. My eyes meet Roarke's, and I see the message in the depths of those brown eyes that I know so well. This is the apology I wouldn't listen to earlier. The problem is that I can forgive, but I can't forget.

CHAPTER FIVE

Hannah...

I'm still captured in Roarke's stare and in the spellbinding moment of him on that horse, kneeling in front of me, a prince before his princess. I was, but I'm not now, and I can't ever be again. I share another look with Roarke, understanding what he wants. This is a piece of our past. This is a routine I helped him with, so I give in because the horse worked so hard to give me this moment. I bow to him now and stroke his nose. He neighs and stands at the same moment I do.

I don't know how it happens, but some of the ice around my heart melts, and Roarke and I smile at each other. And my God, I feel that moment. I still feel him. No wonder I have no social life. I never got over this man, and that statement has so many layers, and they aren't the kind that keep you from eating a cake. They're the kind that drag you into the mud and you can't stop sinking.

That's when the sudden explosion of what looks like white snow all around us, followed by the flash of cameras, jerks me out of the world where, for a few moments, it was just me, him, and the stallion. "Did you get that?" Jessica shouts at someone. "Tell me you got that."

"I got it!" Liz shouts. "That snow was brilliant!"

"Me, too!" Mike chimes in. "That's a great

Christmas promo shot for the camp! What a great idea, Jessica."

Jessica steps to my side, glowing with her brilliance. "They had it in some party room," she says, "and I thought: we're having a festival at the holidays. A Christmas festival would be magical. That means we can't pass up a shot with snow on the baseball field." She laughs. "Who cares if it's Texas and it barely ever snows? It's all about the kids and the holidays."

I glance around at the little beads of white all over the field and then at her. "I think the idea was to get the shot with Roarke, though. Is there more of that material I can use to shoot with him alone?"

"Are you kidding me?" she asks, moving closer. "That was incredible, too magical for a do-over. Did you and Roarke train the horses together back in the day?"

"Yes," I say. "We did."

Roarke dismounts and joins us. "Old habits don't die," he says, giving me a nudge.

"I had no idea you two knew each other this well," Jessica says. "I mean I guess I should have. Sweetwater is a small town."

"He babysat me and made me clean horse poop," I say. "Needless to say, I have a lot of shit memories." I glance up at him. "But I still like the horses."

Jessica glances between us. "Well, you two are pretty magical together. I couldn't stop watching you. I think this is all going to come together beautifully."

Someone shouts for Roarke, and he glances

over his shoulder and back. “Are you done with me?” he asks. “I need to manage the horses.”

“Yes,” I say without looking at him. “I am.”

“Me, too,” Jessica says. “Dinner tonight, Roarke. Eddie V’s. Eight o’clock.”

“Got it,” he says, giving a nod and disappearing from our little circle. He doesn’t speak to me. It bothers me, and I hate that it bothers me.

“Can you join us for dinner?” Jessica asks. “We can game-plan the campaign and then set up a time for you to come see the camp and shoot there?”

Dinner and more Roarke. No. No, I can’t do that. I have to say no. I can’t say no. “I, ah—yes,” I say. “Sure. Dinner. Great.”

She narrows her eyes at me. “Is the ‘shit’ between you and Roarke a problem?”

My eyes meet hers, and I breathe out. “No. I’ve shoveled enough shit in my life to know how to put it in a box and leave it alone so that it doesn’t stink things up.”

“Good. I’m super excited about your involvement.” She hugs me. She’s a hugger, which is fine. This is Texas, not the L.A. fashion business, where a touch became a grope far too often. It’s interesting to be back in the world of old but not the old me. “I’ll text you the restaurant address,” she says, and with that, she hurries away. I can’t help myself—I turn, my gaze seeking the man who might have been my husband, just in time to watch him disappear off the field with a horse. My heart squeezes just thinking about those shared moments with him today. Maybe we can be friends or maybe that would kill me, but I’m an adult. He’s an adult. We can make this situation work. I hurry forward toward the exit, and suddenly, my foot has squished in something, something extraordinarily gross.

I look down, and my foot is in horse shit, Roarke's horse's shit. Somehow, this feels like a teaching moment. I need to remember the past. I need to remember that even gorgeous beasts have a shitty side.

CHAPTER SIX

Roarke...

I manage to get away from the stadium without questions I'm not in the mood to answer, but they're inevitable. They're coming. Which is exactly why I enter the hotel I'm staying in and head for the bar, a cozy dim-lit spot with lots of leather and wood, otherwise known as my safe place. There's also a staff member putting up a tree in the corner, because apparently no one believes Halloween is a holiday, like I do. It's also Hannah's birthday. And obviously, the Irish whiskey in my hand intended to whisper sweet nothings in my ear and calm my nerves isn't working. Hannah's on my mind, and the past is burning a hole in my belly. All I see is her beautiful face framed by all that long brown hair, while her bright-green eyes bleed from the pain I've caused her.

"Somehow I knew I'd find you here."

At the sound of Jason's voice, I glance to my left to find him claiming the stool next to me. "I thought you'd be with your fiancée at that fancy apartment you rented for the season."

"It's next door," he says. "You didn't really think you'd escape me by hiding out here, did you?" He motions to the bartender and points to my drink, holding up two fingers, before he adds, "I didn't even bother to go to your room."

"You didn't get enough of me at the announcement?"

"Nope," he says, accepting the drink set in front of him and taking a sip, while I down the rest of mine to be ready for the refill. "You were occupied by Hannah." He glances over at me. "What did I miss? Because when I left for college, she was a kid, and there was nothing between you two."

I cut my stare and sip from my whiskey. "The summer I finished med school, I came home and so did she. At that point, she was twenty-one and I was twenty-seven. She was all grown up."

"And?"

I glance over at him. "We came together hard and fast, no looking back, or so I thought. She was trying to launch her photography career while helping me with the animals. She traveled with me. She took every opportunity to fill her portfolio with damn good work."

"Of the horses?"

"Of everything, but the animals, the horses, they were her ticket to success, I thought. Of course, she ended up in fashion of all things." I cut my gaze. "We were engaged."

"Holy hell," Jason says, knocking on the bar. "How the hell do I not know any of this?"

I shrug. "You were having that shit season you had and on the road. I would have told you when you got a break. I just never got the chance. We ended badly."

"Define badly?"

"I loved her."

"Holy Mother of God," he says. "That's not an

answer, but it's a wake-up call for me on where we're at on this. You've never said that about any woman."

"Because they weren't Hannah."

"And yet you let her go?"

"She thinks I cheated," I say. "I didn't. She wouldn't listen."

"Why?"

"Too hurt. Too emotional. Too ready to run."

"Sounds about right for Hannah. She recoiled when things went badly for her. Not to mention, she was always stubborn."

"Yeah," I say, offering nothing more, even though there is more. There's a reason I didn't fight harder to prove her wrong, and Jason's father was involved in ways Jason doesn't know about, and I'm not telling him, either. His father is dead. His mother is dead. It's taken him three years to get back on the mound and start living again. I take another drink.

"I didn't know, man," he says, "or we wouldn't have set her up for this job, but I hate to pull it from her. I get the impression she really needs this launch for her business. Hell, I think we need her to launch this camp. She knows us. She knows our town."

"She does and we do. I don't want her to lose the job," I say. "I'll keep my personal business with Hannah personal and at a later date."

"You're going to have to talk this out and clear the air."

"And I will. When the time is right. There are things I need to say to Hannah and some things I'll never say to her, but I won't risk making things worse. It's waited years. It can wait a little longer. Hell, maybe it can all wait forever. She hates me."

"She doesn't hate you. I could see that even from a distance. She's hurt. She's not recoiling any longer, but she's still protecting herself. Don't wait. Fix it."

Fix it.

If only it were that easy, but it's not. Because this is about more than me being set up with Hannah to look like I cheated. This is about my father's connection to her father and how her family ended up in ruins.

CHAPTER SEVEN

Hannah…

I part ways with Linda's staff at the stadium and hit a drive-through nearby, where I order a large fry and a chocolate shake—comfort food—which is necessary at the moment. It's also a perk of being out of the fashion industry, where everything that went into one's mouth was judged. I hated that part of that world. Honestly, I hated a lot of that world, except for learning from an amazing photographer. And the clothes. I did love the clothes.

While waiting on my order, I try to call Linda, who doesn't answer. Why did I agree to dinner tonight? Why? Eddie V's is ridiculously expensive, and that's not the only thing expensive tonight. The emotional baggage I lug with me while Roarke is around comes with a price, and it's not cheap.

My order is ready, and I pull onto the road, throwing enough salt on the fries to salt a small town before testing my shake. It's vanilla. *Ugh.* I do not need anything new that is vanilla in my life right now. That's pretty much the excitement level of where I've landed: vanilla. Some might find a vanilla existence a safe, comfortable one, but I don't. Roarke sure doesn't, either. He's gone from veterinarian to Horse Wrangler and baseball coach. There's nothing vanilla about that man, and clearly, one woman was too vanilla to fit his lifestyle.

Thanks to the Dallas traffic, I have an hour on the highway to think about that fact and every moment with Roarke at the event today. He made me perform with him, and that was all about trying to remind me that we were good together. Or I think it was; I feel it was. He wants to just forget the past. That's not going to happen. I might be vanilla, but I am not a fool. I was never a fool, which is why I walked away.

By the time I head into my new loft-style apartment a few blocks from my new office in Linda's space, I'm starting to worry about her. What if the break was bad? What if she needed surgery? Because I only have about forty-five minutes to shower, dress, and get back on the road, I leave her an urgent message and climb into the shower.

Thirty minutes later, I've managed to shower, dry my hair, and do my makeup. Another ten minutes later, and I've tried on five outfits. I'm back to just my underwear and a bra when Linda calls. "I've been worried sick about you."

"*Ugh,*" she murmurs, sounding drugged. "I broke my leg, and my blood sugar and blood pressure are off the charts. They say it's the pain, but I don't know. I might have diabetes. I'm trying not to be depressed. No chocolate? No cake? No donuts? I think I might rather die."

"Does it run in your family?"

"Yes, it does. I'm screwed, which is why I panicked and why they drugged me and I've been knocked out. I'm going to be here at least overnight. I'd ask how the shoot went, but I can't seem to care right now."

"It went well, and I booked a job organizing Jason's new kids camp, which I can explain later. I got the job because of you, so we can split the fees. I'm meeting them for dinner, or I'd be there with you."

"Nonsense," she says. "You take care of business and you keep the business. You saved my ass today, and I want you to stay in Dallas. Keep the job to launch your company." She groans. "I'm hurting. I need to go. I'll torture you with questions at some point, I'm sure. Just not now. Kisses." She hangs up.

I grimace, worried about her, and decide I need to be at the hospital first thing tomorrow morning. For now, I refocus on the outfits on my bed. The burgundy dress is pretty, but it feels like I'm trying to impress Roarke. I am most definitely not trying to impress that man. The black dress pants and emerald green tank win.

• • •

I arrive at the restaurant just on time and check in with the hostess, who immediately leads me through the dimly lit space. Our destination is a private room in the back of the dining area with sliding wooden doors, allowing privacy. The hostess opens one door for me, and I slip inside, only to have the entire room pause in conversation to stare at me, but I see just one person. Roarke is directly across from me, next to an empty seat. My seat that will be between him and Jessica.

"She's here!" Jessica exclaims. "So happy you

made it." She pushes to her feet, looking lovely in a pink dress. In a few steps, she's hugging me, and Lord help me, my eyes meet Roarke's over her shoulder. The connection punches me in the chest, and I quickly lower my lashes, fearing he'll spy my reaction. Fearful I'll hand him that power.

"I hope you're hungry," Jessica says, pulling back to look at me. "Because the food is so darn good here."

"Starving, and I haven't been to Eddie V's in nearly a decade."

"Well then, let's order," Jason chimes in. "Welcome, Hannah."

Jessica releases me, and I suddenly realize that the table is for four. There are only four of us. Jessica and Jason and Roarke and me. My God, how had this happened? Jason and I exchange hellos before I head to the opposite side of the table. Roarke stands to pull out my chair, and I let him. What am I supposed to do? Kick him in the shin? That would be satisfying but unprofessional. I'm not unprofessional.

Once I'm settled in my seat, my purse on the arm of the chair, the waiter is immediately by my side asking for my drink order. "We opened a bottle of wine," Jason offers. "Help us indulge?"

"Yes please, but a small glass," I say. "I have a decent drive home, and I'm not what you would call a good drinker." It's a statement that slips out before I considered the first time I slept with Roarke was after consuming a bottle of wine.

I swallow hard and focus on the waiter, who fills my glass, a long pour that should be short. I need the long pour, though. I'll take it. I sip the sweet red liquid and then drink deeper. I'm aware that I haven't looked at Roarke. I'm fairly certain we're all aware that I haven't looked at Roarke. Jason's cell phone rings, and he glances at the caller ID and then leans in to whisper to Jessica.

Roarke leans closer to me, a spicy masculine scent teasing my nostrils. It's not the same cologne he used to wear. Good. I don't need any more reminders of the past. "Is this how we're going to do this?" he asks softly.

I inhale a small breath and then set my glass down. "I'm certain I don't know what you mean."

"You haven't even looked at me since you sat down, Hannah."

Steeling myself for the impact, I cut my stare and meet his eyes, the punch of awareness between us trembling through me, but it means nothing. It's not a mutual feeling. It's simply his impact on me and who knows how many other women. "Happy now?"

"Not for a very long time," he says, and before I can question that statement, the waiter returns to take our orders.

I try to get away with a salad and potato, but Roarke isn't having it. "I know how you love a good steak." He eyes the waiter. "Rib eye, well done, no pink or she'll send it back."

I want to reject the order, but I can't. I don't eat meat that has any pink at all. Jason laughs. "Because she got so damn attached to the animals," Jason teases before he and Jessica order, but that distraction doesn't last. Jason comes right back to the topic at hand. "There was this one cow," he tells Jessica.

I wave a fork at Jason. "Don't go where you're about to go."

"Bessie," Roarke supplies. "She named her Bessie and—"

I whirl on him. "You need to stop. Stop talking about Bessie. That has nothing to do with how I eat my steak."

Roarke laughs, a deep rumble of sexy laughter. "We better stop, Jason," he says, but he's looking at me. "She didn't eat meat for a year after naming that cow."

He's trying to remind me of just how well he knows me, but he knows less than he thinks he does, just as I knew less of him than I thought I did. "You save animals. How does it not bother you to save one and eat it the next minute?"

"I don't eat the animals I save, and animals help us understand the food chain."

"Okay, no steak for me," I say. "Seriously. That will be wasted money." The waiter pokes his head in the door, scanning the table to check on us. I lift my hand. "Can you cancel my steak? Just a salad and a potato." I have a quick conversation about my order, and as soon as that's behind me, I down a big swallow of wine. "Tell me about the festival," I say. "It sounds exciting."

"Yes," Jessica says. "Let's talk about the festival. I think it has to be a one-day event because Sweetwater can't handle a crowd of overnight visitors. In general, that's an issue. We're building cabins for the campers on the ranch."

"Wait," I say, my voice coming out rather choked, while my pulse is now thundering in my ears. "The festival is in—it's in Sweetwater?"

"It is," Jessica confirms, "and why did you just turn ghostly on us? Is that a problem for you?"

Yes, I think. *Yes, it's a problem*. It's the place that used to be home. It's the home that doesn't exist anymore. It's good memories. It's bad memories. It's everything I ever was and wasn't with Roarke, but if I let him or the past drive me away, he wins, and I lose the opportunity to restart my career. That can't happen. "No problem," I reply, lifting my glass and finishing off most of my wine before adding, "planning a festival in Sweetwater is a dream come true."

CHAPTER EIGHT

Hannah...

My statement hangs in the air, and to Roarke's good credit, he bites back a reply, or maybe Jason just beats him to it. The two men share a look and Jason snorts. "A dream come true," he replies dryly. "Come on, Hannah, this is Roarke and me you're talking to. We've had our share of crap at the ranch. No one dreams of a festival in Sweetwater, especially when they grew up in Sweetwater. I call foul."

I ignore Roarke's burning stare to my right and scowl at Jason. "They do when that festival is high-profile and can launch their new business," I say. "So you strikeout on that call of foul."

He laughs. "You can't strikeout on a foul."

"I didn't say you were striking out on a foul," I counter. "I said your call of foul was a strikeout. Or perhaps you'd rather me just say *wrong*. It was wrong."

He laughs all over again. "You still got that quick mouth, don't you?"

"I was thinking the same of you," I retort, without missing a breath.

Two waiters appear with the bread to be dispersed, saving me from further battle but not from the man sitting next to me, not from Roarke. The truth is, over the past few years, it's become pretty clear that where Roarke is concerned, I can't be saved. Every man is compared to him, and considering what he did to me, they should win, but they never do. Maybe it's time that I stop trying to be saved. Maybe that's my problem. Maybe I need to just accept the past as exactly that: the past, and then leave it there instead of using it to define the future.

As if he's just heard that thought, Roarke leans in close, his voice low, for my ears only. "Sweetwater misses you."

Sweetwater misses me. I hate that I want that to mean that he misses me, and even if it does, I remind myself that it doesn't mean much. We all feel nostalgia at times, and as for Roarke and me, we're a part of that town, a piece of each other's history. We were all friends, a part of a small community, an extended family, that in the case of Roarke and me, became so much more, too much more. "It's been a long time," I say softly, daring to look at him. "It's exciting to see the town come to life in new and exciting ways."

"It needs new life," he says. "After an extended drought, the locals are hurting. We need to help them, and we need you to help us do that. We have good ideas about the camp and the festival, but we're stretched too thin to realize our potential. And that doesn't just mean the town's potential. It means the potential of the kids attending the camp. We're going to help those kids face their fears."

My brow furrows. "I thought you were helping them chase their dreams?"

"Fear is the primary reason that people don't chase their dreams. You were meant for this project. Not only are you from Sweetwater, trusted by all of us, but fear didn't hold you back. You got on a plane and went to L.A. You were brave. You chased your dreams."

He thinks I was brave? Is he really that clueless, that checked out of how badly we ended? I got on a plane because I was running from heartache he created, and even now, just thinking about the moment I stepped on the plane guts me. "It wasn't easy to leave," I whisper, reaching for my wine, but my hand doesn't make it to the glass. Roarke catches it, and I might as well have fire searing my skin. Shock and heat rush through me, and I jerk my stare to his. "Roarke," I whisper, tugging at my hand.

He holds it easily. "This town and every kid in it, they're us, Han," he says softly, using his old nickname for me. "They have the world at their fingertips, and we can show it to them. Sweetwater turned out pretty well for all of us. It can for them, too. Don't let what happened between you and me stop you from being a part of this."

In other words, he does know how broken I was when I left. I pull my hand from his, and this time, he lets me. "Some might say that leaving Sweetwater is what made it all turn out for us. I left. You left. You traveled the world. You still do." It's out before I can stop it, an accusation in those words, my knowledge of his history that didn't include me. He left all right, and that path never led him to me. He never came for me. He didn't fight for me.

He leans closer. "It's not that simple. You know it. I know it."

"They both travel too much," Jessica agrees, "but no worries there, Hannah."

With my name, I lean back in my seat and as far away from Roarke as possible. "We do need them for the festival," I say, following where she's leading, eager to redirect the conversation to work.

"They both cleared their schedules until the camp sessions are done for the year," she assures me. "Of course, Roarke does have emergency medical care he provides, but we'll work around that. The animals come first."

"It's off-season for me," Jason brags. "The team is backing the program, and with the recent good fortune of all involved, all of the proceeds are now going to the children's hospital."

This perks me up and excites me. Not only is it a great way to market the festival, it's an amazing project to take part in. I reach for my wine again and begin eagerly asking questions.

"When does camp start?" I ask as we pin down details on who I should speak with for support at the charity itself.

"We have several camps planned," Jason says. "The first is three weeks in November. The second is two weeks in December."

"And two weekend camps in between the other two," Roarke adds.

"We can't really launch the camp with a festival in two weeks," I worry, setting my fork that I barely remember picking up back down.

"We had the idea of the festival come about a bit late," Jessica concedes. "We're aware of the timeline challenges."

"It's a challenge," Jason says, "but I heard Roarke explain the economic situation in the town. We need to make this happen now and in the future. Our hope is that the festival can become more of an annual event than just a camp launch."

No one understands the struggle to survive in a small town more than my family who didn't, in fact, survive. I already wanted to help, but my eagerness just notched up higher. "If we do this November first," I say, "we won't be able to do it right."

"Which is why, as I mentioned at the field, we're thinking about a Christmas festival on December first with the launch of the second camp," Jessica replies. "Unfortunately, this is an idea we came up with so late in the game that we couldn't announce it at today's event."

"Two days ago," Roarke says dryly. "And the only thing we know for sure is there will be cookies." He lifts his wineglass. "To the new cookie empire that's already creating jobs in Sweetwater even before the camp and festival. We have Jessica to thank for that."

Jason and I follow suit and lift our glasses. "Ironically," Jessica says, lifting her own glass, "we have my jerk of an ex to thank for that," she says. "Had he not cheated with his secretary, I wouldn't have left my law career behind and taken a sabbatical in Sweetwater." She laughs, and one by one, she clinks her glass to ours. "To lousy exes who lead us to bigger, better, and sweeter places." She turns her gaze to Jason. "Like you."

The two of them huddle up, and I just sit there watching them, refusing to look at my ex. My ex who isn't lousy. He's a good guy. He saves animals. Animals love him. He just didn't love me. I down my wine and set down my glass.

"Hannah," he says, easing closer. "Let's go take a walk."

Thankfully, the doors to our private dining area open and the first of our food arrives. My hero this night isn't a man saving me from heartache. It's a side salad, but even it wants more. It's begging for dressing, which is set beside me before the waiter, strategically it seems, steps between me and Roarke to fill my now-empty wineglass. He's given me space to breathe, and I change my mind in that moment. A man *is* my hero tonight, and per the tag on his shirt, that hero's name is Ralph. I think I love Ralph right up until the moment he leaves, but I'm strategic as well.

I pick up my fork and shove a big bite of salad in my mouth, only to realize that Ralph's hero skills do not include replacing glasses in proper places. My glass is right at my elbow, and it's too late to stop what comes next. It tumbles in Roarke's direction. I drop my fork and reach for it, but I end up catching it too late. Roarke turned to grab it as well and, in doing so, made the glass in my hand a target. I try to pull it upright, but the wine splashes forward and all over him, almost as if I'd intended to throw it at him.

CHAPTER NINE

Hannah…

The wine splatters onto Roarke's face and pretty much plops onto his lap. "Oh god," I say, setting the stupid glass down and grabbing a napkin. "That was an accident." I don't think. I react. I wipe his face. "I would never do that on purpose. You know that. You know me. I wouldn't do this."

"I know," he says, my hand and that napkin landing on his leg. The muscle beneath my palm—his muscle—flexes, and suddenly, I'm aware of my legs pressed to his legs, my hand on his powerful thigh. Our faces close. His brown eyes staring into my eyes.

"I don't—"

"I do," he says softly.

I want to ask what that means. I need to know what that means, but I don't get the chance to find out.

"How bad is it?" Jessica asks. "Do you need to go to the hotel and change?"

Roarke takes the napkin from me and glances at his pants, while I quickly scoot back, placing distance between him and me. "I'm wearing black jeans," Roarke replies. "No harm, no foul." He glances at me. "Let's drink the next round." The waiter reappears, quickly attending to the mess, and a few minutes later, it's as if nothing happened.

"Back to our salads," Jessica says. "And not to tease you, Hannah, but considering all my mishaps since leaving the city for the country, it's nice to know a born country girl can have a few mishaps herself. You have no idea how many I've had."

She goes on to tell me about how she came to Sweetwater, fell in the mud, fought with Jason, and generally became a perfect mess of the perfect woman for him. We are all laughing when the waiter delivers more bread to the table, and I've decided I adore Jessica. Her story was to make me feel better about the wine because she doesn't know how many mishaps I've had around these two men, and they me. We grew up together, and I settle into those memories with comfort instead of pain. I want to be a part of this festival. I'm the right person to make this special.

"We can make December first work for the festival," I say, bringing us back to that topic. "It's going to be tight, but that would make for a fun holiday event, too. I'll need to work around the clock and hire some help, but we can do it."

"This is great news," Jessica says, motioning to the table. "Everyone eat. The main course will be here, and our salads will be untouched."

Obediently, we all grab our forks, and somehow, my leg collides with Roarke's again, the force of that connection jolting me. I suck in a breath, and while I don't look at Roarke, he's looking at me. I can feel his stare, but fortunately, Jessica saves me. "Bread, Hannah?"

Setting my fork down, I reach for the bread. "Yes, please." Unfortunately, the table is wide, and

I can't quite reach the basket.

Roarke solves that problem by snagging it for me, setting it between us. My eyes meet Jessica's, and there's awareness in the depths of her stare. She knows about Roarke and me, or at the very least, she feels the push and pull between us. "Thank you," I say, glancing at Roarke.

His lips hint at a smile, and I can't help but remember how they feel on my mouth, on my body. I've never been kissed the way this man has kissed me, and if I were asked to explain what that meant to someone else, I think I'd decline. It's simply too personal. "I remember how much you love your bread," he says softly, and while this comment, about bread of all things, shouldn't feel sexual, apparently his knowledge of my love of bread feels that way to my body because I'm warm all over.

"Let's talk about the parade," Jessica says.

That kills the mood. My gaze whips around and lands on Jessica. "Parade?"

Roarke chimes in with, "Wait. A parade?"

"That's right," Jessica says. "A parade could allow each town store to have people camped out at their location." She perks up. "What if we had an elf at every store?"

I need to reel her back, make this more doable. With that in mind, I say, "We have a short window. What if we hold the festival at the campgrounds with vendor booths? Then there's some sort of prize for going to each participating store's booth. We could launch a parade next year if that feels important after this year. Maybe have the old camp members be a part of the parade."

"Okay, that's brilliant," Jessica says. "Really brilliant. When can you come to the ranch?"

When can I come to the ranch? Of course I knew that had to happen, but nevertheless, butterflies explode in my stomach with the promise of memories, so many memories, both good and bad. "When do you want me?"

"Tomorrow!" Jessica laughs. "But that's not realistic for any of us. How about the day after tomorrow?"

"I can do that," I say as more food arrives.

The four of us chat about what the festival might look like, and the conversation and laughter flow as easily as the wine. I don't mean to drink as much as I do, but every time Roarke and I share a laugh and a smile, the pinch in my heart has me lifting my glass. It's not something I do often, drinking liberally, and at some point, I resolve to just enjoy the wine and Uber to my apartment, but that's okay. It's the responsible thing to do, and I pride myself on being responsible.

When it comes time for dessert and coffee, I happily order a brownie ice cream sundae, eager to soak up the wine with the starch in the brownie while restoring my wits with caffeine. It's also a treat a dinner in the fashion world would shun, but screw them. I'm not in L.A. anymore. I'm sitting next to my ex, who cheated on me, and I'm going to eat the sunday. I dig in and enjoy every bite. I eat it all, and I don't care who might judge me, but that's the thing about these people, about being home; no one even thinks about judging me.

We've all finished up our desserts when I feel the calling of wine and coffee driving me to the bathroom. "I better find the ladies' room," I say, pushing to my feet and sliding my purse over my shoulder.

"I'll join you," Jessica chimes in, standing as well.

"Good thing," Roarke teases. "I was about to offer to escort her to the proper door."

The wine gets the best of me, and I sit back down and turn to face him. "That was your fault."

He leans in closer. "I made you go into the men's bathroom not once but twice?"

"Yes," I say. "You did."

"You didn't even know I was around the first time at the airport."

"Obviously I sensed you were near because I only do stupid things when you're around."

"It's all my fault?"

"We both know it's your fault, Roarke."

His expression tightens. "Hannah—"

"Don't say whatever you're about to say." I stand up, and that's when I realize that Jason and Jessica are staring at us. I try to think of something brilliant to say, but I have booze and Roarke on the brain. "I walked into the men's room not once but twice in a couple of weeks and not by intent, which might or might not make that sound more reasonable. Of course, Roarke was present to witness both occasions." I look at Jessica. "In light of this information, considering I'm well wined and in Roarke's presence, I'll accept an escort to the ladies' restroom, if you're offering."

Jessica glances between us and smiles before

stepping to the end of the table and offering me her arm. "Girl trip."

I accept her arm, and together, we head for the door. I don't look back at Roarke, but damn him, I hear and feel the deep rumble of his laughter. I scowl but head out into the main restaurant with Jessica. "Would you like to talk about you and Roarke?" Jessica asks as we walk toward the bathroom sign.

"Not unless you're worried about our past affecting the festival."

"I'm not," she says, and once we round a corner and then cut down another hallway to wait for the sealed bathroom door to open, she halts and turns to face me. "I know you're a professional. I know you care about the town, and I don't know what happened between the two of you. I promise. I know nothing, but matters of the heart I do know. I just—I know. If you need me, I will be there for you, and if I need to kick Roarke's pretty little ass, I'll do that, too."

I laugh. "Oh no. You don't get to take that fun from me. If he needs it, I'll do the kicking."

She smiles. "Or we can do it together."

The bathroom opens, and a woman exits. I motion Jessica forward, eager to gain a few minutes to myself. "I'll be fast," she promises, hurrying into the one-person room. My head spins from the wine that just won't be defeated by chocolate and coffee or sheer will. I plot my escape, eyeing the exit sign. I'll go to the bathroom again as we all part ways and have an Uber wait for me.

Jessica exits the bathroom. "All yours," she says.

"I'll wait for you."

"That's okay," I say. "I'm good. I'll be right back to the table."

"You're sure?"

I nod. "Positive."

"Okay then. See you in a sec." She hurries off, and I dart into the bathroom. Locking the door, I pee and wash my hands. I check my makeup and don't allow myself to think about how I might look to Roarke. My lipstick isn't on my nose. Good enough. I open the door and gasp as I find Roarke standing there. "Wrong bathroom," I say, recovering quickly. "Do you need an escort?"

"No," he says, pushing off the wall and stepping in front of me. "But you do. I know you. I know how you reacted to the wine. I'm not letting you drive back to Dallas tonight."

"I'm fine, and Jessica and Jason—"

"Left. I sent them on their way. We need to talk." He catches my hand in his. "Come with me."

Heat rushes up my arm, over my chest, and settles low in my belly, and that's when I know I've made a mistake. An Uber can save me from drinking and driving, but it can't save me from Roarke.

CHAPTER TEN

Hannah…

I don't know what part of me is reeling more, my emotions or my body. Either way, the friction Roarke's touch is creating in my body isn't helping. I tug at my hand. "You can't grab me and order me to go with you, Roarke."

"I'm not ordering you around, Hannah," he replies, releasing my hand as if burned. "You know that's not me." He catches the doorframe, holding it instead of me, and I hate that part of me wishes he would have held onto me a little longer. "You know me."

"I don't know anything where you're concerned."

"You know me like no one else but Jason knows me."

"If that was the case, we wouldn't have ended the way we ended. No. We wouldn't have crossed the lines we crossed."

"Is that what you call being engaged to marry? Crossing a line?"

"It's the line that left us here." I fight the urge to push him out of the way, which would require touching him. "You're blocking me in the bathroom."

"Blocking? Where the heck is that coming from, aside from your need to run, and you can't run right now?"

"Run? I'm here tonight. That's not running."

"After running to another state."

"At the table, I was brave," I fire back. "Now I was running? You're still standing in front of me."

"Because we still need to clear the air, for us and everyone else involved in this project."

He's right. Of course he's right, but I'm suffocating from this man right now. "What are you going to do? Tell me everything I think I know about the past is wrong?"

He cuts his eyes, seeming to struggle a moment before he levels me in a stare. "There's a lot you don't know, Hannah," he says, "but right now, right now we need to focus on now. We need to find out how we move forward, and that won't happen if we're living in the past." He takes several steps back, offering me space I both crave and despise. "But this is your decision. Start a new future or live in the past and torture everyone around us, as we do."

I force air into my lungs and slowly push it out. "You're right. You're completely right. So—back to the table?"

"No," he says softly. "We need to be alone, Hannah. To my hotel. I'm not letting you drive home."

"Your hotel?" My heart is officially beating too fast. "Roarke—"

He presses a hand on the doorframe next to me but only one hand. He's close again, but he hasn't blocked me in. I wish he would. I wish he'd piss me off. "I'll get you another room if you don't want to stay with me."

I blanch. If I don't want to stay with him? What

is he saying? "Is that an invitation?" I ask before I can stop myself. I turn to him and hold up a hand. "Don't answer. I don't want an answer. I'll get a room, my own room."

"As long as you don't drive, Hannah." He offers me his hand. "Come with me." He pauses for effect. *"Please."*

The please gets me, and not because it's out of character for Roarke. It's not. Roarke isn't a man who backs away from that word. He's not a man who demands unless we're naked, and that's a different ball game. That's the balance that is this man. He's an alpha. He's in control, and yet, he makes me feel like *I'm* in control. He makes the animals he works with feel they're in control when it's him with the control. That's what he's doing to me right now, both giving and taking my control. He's given me a choice to go with him or to refuse, but in truth, if I accept his offer, he's won. No. No, that's my anger at him talking. He always makes sure everyone wins. That's the balance part of this man again. We both win if I say yes because we get to the other side of us in a more positive way.

And now comes my move, my choice.

I could withhold my hand, but I think about his words, about stepping out of the past into the future. If I hold back, if I act as if I'm afraid to touch him, then that past owns me. He owns me. And he'll know it. He'll know how much he affects me. A man who didn't even come after me doesn't get to own me.

I press my palm to his palm, the connection tingling up my arm, and it's not just sexual chemistry, though we've always overflowed in that area, a volcano of pure, hot lava. This now, though, is far more scary, far more impossible to control. This is like sliding back into a second skin, into a familiar feeling, and that feeling of belonging with this man I can't fight and I don't even try. We do belong together; we're a part of each other's lives, just not as husband and wife. That was where we went wrong.

My gaze lifts to his, and we stare at each other, those intelligent eyes of his searching my face the way I'm searching his, looking for answers, though I wonder if he knows what answers any more than I do. "I'm parked near the back door," he says, pushing off the wall and straightening. "We can get your car in the morning. If you're agreeable."

I nod without argument. It's all logical. It's all a smart choice. "Yes. Yes, that works." He gives my hand a small tug, urging me forward, but he turns as I near, laces his fingers with mine, and guides me toward the door.

I'd call our handholding inappropriate if the floor didn't feel unsteady, and I think he knows this. I just hope he believes it's all about the wine. I wish that was the case.

We exit into the parking lot, into a dark, humid Texas night, no signs of fall this October evening. There are no stars in the sky, but the restaurant is smart and safe, with plenty of artificial lighting. Roarke motions to the right. "That's me," he says, and I'm not surprised when I see a sporty black pickup truck waiting on us. Roarke is comfortable in life. He was even before his recent fame, thanks to his veterinarian skills, but he's not a man who laps up luxury. He'd rather buy a horse a stable it might not have than buy himself a BMW. Every man I dated in L.A. would have picked the BMW. I'd rather watch him care for a horse than ride in a BMW. We made sense right up until the point that we didn't.

Roarke leads me to the passenger's side of the truck and opens the door. It's a big step up, and I know a truck and know it well, but I also dress for the country when I'm in the country. This truck is country. This man, he's far more complicated. Right now, we're complicated, and considering how complicated, I thank the Lord that I wore slacks. I place my high heels on the ledge and hike myself up, but my heel catches on a hole somewhere, and it's not pretty. I start to tumble, yelping as I do, only to have strong, familiar arms catch me. "I got you," Roarke murmurs, and the thing is, there was a time when I believed he did, when I believed he always would.

That time is now gone.

In this moment, with his hard body holding me, I don't remember anything but need and pain. It's a powerful feeling. It's every question I've wanted answered since I left, that only he can answer. It's an ache that seeks comfort, one no other man has soothed. And yet Roarke is the reason it exists.

He inhales, drawing in the scent of my hair, I think. He always loved my shampoo, and I want to scream at him to stop. I want to scream at him to never stop.

He sets me down on the ground, one of my heels staying behind. Roarke turns me and allows me to grip the door. He's close, his body big, hard, heat radiating off him and smashing into me. He leans down and pulls my shoe from a hole between the step and the truck itself. "Sorry about that, Han," he says softly, setting it down on the ground next to my naked foot. I quickly slide it into place, but when he stands up, towering over me, I'm aware that I'm naked in almost every possible way with this man. That's a problem I need to fix. That's a vulnerability I need to erase, and there's only one way to do that.

I have to prove to myself, and him, that he's no more to me than I was to him. And that's never going to happen when I want to be naked with him this badly.

CHAPTER ELEVEN

Hannah…

"Obviously it's time to break out the cowboy boots again," I say.

His lips, his really beautiful lips—I've always thought his lips were beautiful—curve. "And get back on the horse. There's more than a few waiting on you in Sweetwater. How long has it been?"

"Too long," I say, "it's been too long," and this time, I'm not just talking about a horse. I'm talking about so many things. It's time I get a grip on every part of my life that's been causing me pain, affecting who I am and how I interact with others. And the truth is that Roarke and Sweetwater represent those things. This festival is a blessing.

He offers me his hand again. "Need a hand?"

I don't hesitate this time. I'm taking control and that means of everything, including what's going on between the two of us. That means I don't melt at the idea of touching him. I place my palm against his, and before I can even weigh my body's reaction, it sways; I sway. Okay, I'm taking control after the wine stops taking control.

He catches my waist, his touch scorching. Lord help me, my nipples pucker. When was the last time I was that sensitive to a man's touch? The answer is simple: the last time I was with him. We stand there, our heads low and together, our breathing the only sound between us, but there is so much more expanding in the thick Texas air: history, so much history. And friendship. This man was my best friend, and it would be a lie to say that I don't miss him. Control isn't lying to myself or even him. It's owning what I feel and how I respond to what I feel. So yes. I miss him. I miss the him I knew before the him who hurt me.

"Let's get out of here," he says softly.

"Yes. Let's." I rotate and face the truck again, stepping up on the ledge, but not before I check my heel. The minute I hike myself upward, Roarke is right there, holding onto me, making sure I get inside this time.

Roarke doesn't linger. He shuts me inside. Maybe he needs a breather, too, because Lord only knows, I'm suffocating from him and all the history, all the damn feelings. Control is my goal, and suffocating does not get me there. He's slow to round the truck, but finally, he opens the door and climbs inside. The air thickens, and the cab light slowly dims. There was no slow dim for us. There was no slow start for us. It might have seemed that way to some. We were friends. We were neighbors. I was too young for him, six years his junior. I always had a crush on him, but then I was home for a summer, and college just seemed to erase the years that divided us.

He starts the truck, the sound jolts me back to the present, and that's a good thing. I was about to go down a rabbit hole of locked lips and passion with this man. No. I was about to go down a rabbit hole of emotion. Sex is not emotion. He taught me that lesson.

"Where's your hotel?" I ask.

"The Ashton, a few miles up the road." He doesn't look at me. He doesn't say anything more.

I sink lower into my seat, and I wonder now if he's regretting the decision to take me to his hotel. If he dreads the confrontation he's invited? He probably does. He probably thinks I'm still that into him. My behavior has said nothing less. I've shown him that he still has that much control over me. And he's right. Or he was. He did. Tonight, that ends. Tonight, I get my closure, and so does he.

It's not long before he pulls the truck into the hotel parking lot. I don't sit there all awkward. Maybe it's the power of wine, but my leash is off. I open the door and climb out of the truck, and my heel doesn't even think about getting stuck this time. Trucks are my history, and no pair of high heels, and certainly no man, no matter how hot, no matter how sexy all his dark hair and dreamy eyes are, gets to take that or anything from me. Even my damn boss took my career. Maybe I should have stayed and fought harder. Or maybe I just needed an excuse to come back home.

I slam the door shut, and Roarke is already standing in front of me, his handsome face hidden by shadows. He catches the fingers of one of my hands and walks me to him, the charge between us electric, just like it always was. Even before we were an us, before we were engaged, in love, and planning a damn wedding, when we still denied we were more than friends, the current between us was alive. This time, though, I'm not looking for a Prince Charming. This isn't another Cinderella story.

"When we go inside," he begins.

"Let's just go inside," I say, because I want him to know that I'm not running as he accused. I don't need to run from anyone or anything.

His eyes narrow, his expression unreadable, but his reaction is without further delay. Still holding my hand, he folds our arms at the elbow, aligning our bodies and placing us in motion. There is no question that we are, in this moment of time, ex-lovers, still burning alive for each other, but there is also no question that for me, this is about burning it out. No. It's about burning it out my way, not his. Whatever happens when we walk in that hotel, I'm going to own it when I walk out; it will be my decision.

We enter the lobby, and Roarke doesn't even pause, nor do I want him to pause. His pace is steady, our pace is steady, and he leads me to the elevator. I find that I'm not nervous. Why would I be? I've known this man my entire life. In fact, I'm more alive right now than I have been in a long time. Anger begins to take shape, a ball in my belly that grows and flows through my body. Yes, I'm angry. I'm really angry with this man, and I realize now that I have never allowed myself that emotion. I felt pain after his betrayal. I felt hurt, but I never let myself be mad. It's a liberating emotion, rather than defeating like everything else I've engaged in since our breakup. It's freedom, too. I'm not to blame for the past, and while he might owe me answers, why would I ask for them? What do answers solve? Nothing. Nothing he can say will change what happened. Nothing he can say will turn back time. Nothing he can say will make me put a ring back on my finger. And that's okay. For the first time since I left, that's really okay.

We reach the elevator, and he jabs the button. The doors open, and he doesn't let go of me, like he believes I'll run away. The more I think about that accusation on his behalf, the more that anger bubbles inside me, a kettle of built-up thoughts and feelings, waiting to boil over. He simply turns us and walks me backward into the elevator. He swipes his keycard and punches in a floor. I don't know if I want to yell at him or push him against the wall and kiss him. I don't do either. The doors shut, and we face each other, our hands and elbows still joined. And we just stare at each other, and that's when I feel the push and pull of emotions, his emotions. He wants to try to explain the past. He *needs* to try to explain. But that's not what I need. That's not what I want. That is not where I find my zen, whatever that really even is—my center, I guess.

The elevator halts, and as we wait for the doors to open, I feel the tension rising inside me. I don't want to hear his reasons why. I don't want to revisit what I felt back then. I will not listen. I pull my hand away from his and turn to the door. It opens, and I'm in the hallway in an instant. Roarke steps to my side and motions down the hallway. I'm going to his hotel room. I could ask for my own. I could ask, or even insist that we go downstairs, but those things don't work for me. I know what does.

We reach the door, and he swipes his card, pushing open the door. Without hesitation, I enter the room, and I don't even see the space before me. I whirl around to face him, and when he shuts the door and locks it, I'm right there waiting. The minute he turns to face me, I'm standing in front of him, pushing him against the door. "I don't want to hear why. Ever. Do not open your mouth and give me a reason because it will only piss me off. It's done. That part of us is done. We are—"

He catches my hips and turns me. Now my back is against the wall, and his powerful thighs cage mine, his hands cupping my face. "We are anything but done," he says, and then his mouth is on my mouth, his tongue licking past my teeth, caressing deep.

I moan with the taste of him, wicked and wrong and yet oh so right. I want this. I want him, but this has to be on my terms. I shove on his chest, tearing my mouth from his. "This means nothing. You aren't forgiven. We aren't us again. We aren't—"

"We never stopped being us, Hannah. If that's not obvious to you, it is to me. I'll show you."

"Don't show me. Just—just kiss me."

"I don't need to be told twice. Not where you're concerned." And then he's kissing me again, and I don't stop him this time because if I do, I'll think too hard, and that's not an option. I don't want to think. I don't want to talk. I just want to feel this man close, one last time. That's all.

One.

Last.

Time.

A proper goodbye.

The one I never had.

The one we never had.

CHAPTER TWELVE

Hannah…

I have never wanted anyone the way I want this man. If I have ever questioned the truth in that statement—and I did, of course—I don't now. The taste of him, the feel of him next to me, his hands sliding up my back, molding me close, is fire while the past is ice, and that somehow only makes me need that heat all the more. I don't hold back. I need this. I need him. No, my body needs him. Because that's what this is. Sex. It has to be sex because sex is all there is for us. I will not love this man again.

I tug at his T-shirt and press my hands beneath it, the feel of hot, hard muscle beneath my hands, almost punishing, he feels so good.

"Take it off," I order, letting the purse on my shoulder fall to the ground.

He doesn't argue. He pulls his shirt over his head, and before it hits the ground, before I can study the stallion etched on his arm, his hand is under my hair, at my neck, dragging my lips to his. "I didn't think I'd ever kiss you again," he says, "and that was torture."

And yet he didn't come for me. That's my thought. "Don't talk, Roarke," I order because I'm angry again. I'm hurt again. I need to stop thinking. I push to my toes and press my lips to his, and when his hand comes down on the back of my head, when his tongue presses to mine again, it's heaven. It's relief and fire and passion. It's forgetting. It's memories. I can't explain what kissing him feels like, but I just need more of it, of him.

"I missed the hell out of you, woman," he murmurs against my mouth, ignoring my command for silence, but his tongue strokes deep, and that counteraction to his words drives everything else away.

I make the decision right then that I'm not going to fight wanting Roarke. I want him. I have always wanted him. He's right. I ran, and denial is what will make me run again. I'm done with that. I'm not hiding from this or him anymore. I'm not giving him that power. I want. He wants. That's as real as it gets. That's as honest as we ever were or ever will be again. I don't hold back. I sink into the kiss. I let my hands slide over the hard lines of his body.

He catches the hem of my blouse and tugs it upward. I don't even think about stopping him. It's over my head and gone in a blink, but I'm focused on him and him on me. His gaze rakes over the swell of my breasts beneath black lace, my skin heating, sex clenching. Already his fingers are snapping open the front hook of my bra and skimming it off my shoulders. "God, woman," he whispers, his lips brushing my neck, finding my ear. "You're beautiful," he adds, and no man saying those words to me has ever mattered, but they do now. They do with Roarke. He's always mattered, too much. He's always mattered too much, as proven by the power I gave him to hurt me.

I can't do that again; I won't. His hand is on my breast, and I cover it with my own as if that somehow makes me in control, but there's an explosion of my senses that rules my body right now. And Roarke is the reason for that explosion. As if proving that to be true, his teeth nip my bottom lip, and no sooner do I yelp than he's licking the offended lip, then cupping my backside and lifting me.

My legs wrap around his waist, heels falling to the ground, fingers diving in the long silk of his dark hair. My fingers have always loved his hair, and why wouldn't they? I spent years of my life fantasizing about doing just this before that summer when I finally could, when we finally stopped fighting what was between us.

Roarke settles me on my back on the bed, the mattress caving with the weight of our bodies together, the sweet weight of his body on mine. I can't breathe and yet, somehow, I can finally breathe again. His lips press to mine again, his kiss deep, drugging, consuming, and I both hate and love him. My fingers remain in his hair, and I'm rough, tugging, pulling, that anger inside me burning a hiss of energy through me.

I catch his leg with my leg and arch into him. His hand slides under my backside, molding me to him, the thick ridge of his erection pressed to my belly. I moan, and his lips are gone, his mouth traveling down my body to my neck, my shoulder, and my nipple. My leg falls from his leg. His hands find my hips, his mouth, my belly.

Roarke's eyes collide with mine, and Lord help me, I feel him inside and out; I feel him all over. My heart squeezes with emotions I don't want to feel. "Why are you still dressed?" I demand, trying to return to someplace safe, someplace that's just sex. He kisses my belly again, and then he's unbuttoning my pants, the zipper following. His hands, God his hands that have not touched me like this in so long, slide under my waistband, and he carries them down my bare legs. I'm panty-less, a habit I developed in L.A., where panty lines were sins that might get you fired. His mouth finds my sex, kissing my clit before he gives me a lick. I arch into the gone-too-quickly touch of his tongue. He's gone, too, now, dragging my pants down my hips and legs.

He tosses them aside, and I sit up. He's already pulling off his boots. My eyes go to the stallion on his arm—Mercury—the horse that was his everything growing up, the half sleeve that is so a part of this man, and yet I've only seen it once, the night I left him. He got it that day. I was with him.

I shut my eyes, trying to block out the past, but my mind starts to replay that day. He lost Mercury the month before. That tattoo was a way to heal. I drew it. I created the image. I was always sketching him and his horse. And I was his best friend. At least, I thought I was, but—

"Hannah," he says softly.

The minute he says my name, I rotate and scoot to the edge of the bed. This is crazy. It isn't giving me back control. It's cutting open a wound to let it bleed out again.

I stand up, and he's there, in front of me, completely naked, thick and hard at my hip, his fingers splayed between my shoulder blades, his other hand in my hair.

"Don't do this," he orders softly. "Don't make this about then. This is now."

I'm angry again, damn him. "Why aren't you kissing me?"

"Hannah—"

"Kiss me or let me get dressed," I whisper fiercely.

He kisses me, and when our tongues touch this time, I'm not the only one angry. He is, too. I taste it, lying there on my tongue, and this infuriates me. What does he have to be angry about? But just as sure as I taste that anger, there's a desperate quality to him, a possessive need that is so raw and real that I can't deny it or him. That's my trigger. That's the pop of restraint that is no more.

Suddenly, we're wild, kissing, touching. We've been lost. We're found right here, this night, and it doesn't matter what that means or where this goes. There is just now. I don't even remember how we got down on the bed or how our legs got wrapped together, the thick ridge of his erection pressed between my thighs. We don't talk about birth control. He's the only person in this world who knows that I can't have kids. For just a moment, that stirs up thoughts again, about talks of adopting, about that small window of time when I wanted so many things. But he presses inside me, stretching me, filling me, and this moment is all there is. The new wave of wildness between us.

We kiss. We touch. We arch into each other. We have these moments where our lips part, but we just breathe together. Then we unleash again. I don't want it to end, but his hands and his body and—I can't stop the burn that builds, the edge that becomes a ball of tension. He drives into me, pulling me against him, arching my hips against his, and with a swipe of his tongue for added effect, I tumble into orgasm. I bury my face in Roarke's shoulder and the wave of pleasure trembles through me.

He cups my butt and my head, and with another thrust, he lets out a guttural moan, one that I feel like a vibration throughout my entire body. He quakes into his release, and for a few moments that feel eternal and yet so very fast, the world doesn't exist. There is just the two of us. Every imperfect moment evaporates. There is just how perfect we are right now.

We collapse into each other, and we don't move. We just hold each other, but the longer we lie there, the more reality seeps back into the picture, the more I don't know what to do next. How does one act after sex with your ex-fiancé? It all seemed so simple when my pre-sex bravado was in place, but it's not easy to find your bravado while naked.

It's Roarke who moves, pulling back to look at me, stroking hair from my face, and there's such tenderness in his touch, in his eyes, that my chest tightens with emotion. "I've missed you," he whispers, which is everything I want and everything I don't want from him.

"It's not that simple," I say. "This isn't—"

His cellphone rings, and he grimaces, his forehead touching mine. "You know—"

"That your patients matter. Yes. They matter to me, too." It's an easy statement to make. I know how much the animals mean to him. It's part of what makes him a special human being. It's part of what made me love him. It's part of what still makes me like him as a person. "Take the call."

"I'll be fast," he says, kissing my temple and then pulling out of me to roll away.

I grab the tissues on the nightstand and manage to wrap a throw blanket around me when I hear Roarke say, "Banamine, Trental, and Amoxicillin. I'll be there as soon as possible. Call me in an hour with an update."

He has to leave. There it is. This is over. It's that easy. He disconnects his phone and grabs his underwear, pulling it on before grabbing his pants. "I have a horse I'm caring for, for a high-profile customer, that is showing signs of placentitis. She might lose her pregnancy. I need to get back."

"Of course," I say, hugging the blanket to me. "I spent a lot of time hanging out with you and your father, helping with the animals. I know what that is. You know I do."

He closes the space between us, his hands coming down on my arms. "Come with me. I need you to come with me. I've got a vet student at the ranch. She's administering drugs. We have time to go by your place."

"You don't need to risk an extra hour, which is what that would take. You need to go. Save that foal and its mama."

"Come with me."

"You need to get dressed and leave. I'll be there the day after tomorrow, with holiday cheer to spread."

"Hannah—"

"You need to leave."

"I don't want to leave. We didn't talk at all."

"We didn't need to talk. This wasn't about talking. We're not going back. We just—we needed this out of our system."

He studies me a long moment, his jaw hardening. "Are you serious right now, Han?"

"Yes. Clearly we needed to do this. We did. And we worked off all the anger and steam. We can work together. I'm not angry. I'm not going to act like you're my enemy. That horse reminds me that I actually like you."

"You like me."

"Yes. You're a good guy and—"

His hands fall away. "A good guy." His tone is crisp and hard. "A good guy." He scrubs his jaw and turns away. He doesn't say anything else. He grabs his boots, sits down with his back to me, his impressive shoulders and arms flexing beneath the stallion tattoo as he pulls them on. I just stand there. I don't move. I don't speak. I want to go with him. That's how stupid I am. I want us to be what we once were, no matter how big of a lie that perfect couple turned out to be.

He stands up and walks toward the living area, which is the first time I even realize we're in a suite. He disappears around the corner, I assume to grab his shirt. I hold my breath, waiting for what he will do next, and I'm shocked when I hear the door open and close.

I walk forward into the living area and stare at the empty room. I walk to the closet by the door, and there's no bag there. He left. He's gone. The burn in my eyes and chest promise an eruption. I turn away, afraid he'll come back in and see what's about to happen. Hurrying forward, I dart into the bedroom, then the bathroom, and shut the door. I lean on the wooden surface and wait and wait. I wait some more. He doesn't come back, and now I'm naked but for a blanket, in a hotel room, where I just had sex with Roarke. I slowly sink to the floor, where I do what I swore I would never do for that man. I cry.

CHAPTER THIRTEEN

Roarke…

I had to get out of that hotel room before I told Hannah everything, and that would be a mistake. If it wasn't a mistake, I'd have told her before now. So I do what I can't do in Sweetwater.

I go to Whataburger.

I mean, how the hell else do you deal with being kicked to the curb by the only woman you've ever loved? It doesn't matter that I just ate. I order a burger, onion rings, and a strawberry shake, and then I hit the highway. If I tell Hannah I didn't cheat, I have to tell her about a vicious battle between our families that left her father determined to keep us apart at all costs, including framing me for cheating. And since Jason's father was involved with it all, too, telling Hannah means telling him, and Jason doesn't need to hear this shit about a father he's recently lost. And it's not like telling the story saves me with Hannah. Either she'll hate my family or her own. There's no win for me in this because there's no win for her.

I lost her years ago.

I won't get her back now.

No matter how much I love her.

As insane as it is, it's because I love her that I won't tell her that I didn't cheat on her. It's because

I love her that I let her go, but now that she's back, saving her might just kill me.

• • •

Hannah...

I don't stay in the hotel room. Funny how sex with your ex, followed by tears, will wipe out the effects of wine, especially when it wasn't that much wine. Instead, I grab an Uber to take me to my car and do what I couldn't do in L.A. I climb in my car and drive to Whataburger, where I order a burger, onion rings, and a strawberry shake. With my feel-good order in hand, I hit the highway and drive toward Dallas. I start eating and do so heartily, hungrier than I realized. The truth is, other than the brownie at the restaurant, I didn't eat much today. Besides, every self-respecting Texan knows that emotional distress is made better by Whataburger. I concentrate on every bite and use my onion rings as an escape from any other thought. I will not replay any kiss, touch, or intimate moment with Roarke. I will eat Whataburger. There is only Whataburger seducing me right here, right now. It's a strategy that works for about ten onion rings and a bite of the burger.

Then it's all over. The mental hammering begins; the revisiting of my time with Roarke takes over. I replay it all, every minute with him in that hotel room, and when I arrive at my loft-style apartment, it's with an empty bag, a full stomach, and a heavy heart. I undress and fall into bed. I don't cry again. That's the thing about Whataburger and emotions. It fills you up and weighs you down. I need to sleep, and somehow, I do, which I only know as fact because I shut my eyes to darkness and wake to sunlight trying to burn holes in my retinas. There is also a sound.

I jolt and sit up, looking around the bedroom that is only a bed and not much more, to realize that sound is my phone that has now stopped ringing. I grab it from the nightstand to find Linda's name on my caller ID. Swinging my legs over the edge of the bed, I punch redial. "How are you?" I ask the minute she answers.

"Going home tomorrow," she says. "Dying anyway. I need Starbucks. I need it like I need my next breath."

I laugh. "I'll come bring you Starbucks. I need to talk to you anyway. Wait. What about being diabetic? Can you have Starbucks?"

"Shut up," she says. "Bring the damn coffee or die. And what do you need to talk about? Did something go wrong?"

"No," I say quickly. "No. Nothing is wrong, but I want to talk to you about that job I booked. I'll tell you all about it over Starbucks. I'll get sugar-free syrup."

"Don't be a bitch. If you walk in here with sugar-free—"

I hang up. She's getting sugar-free. I'm about to set down my phone when it hits me to change my L.A. number to a Texas number. The way my L.A. boss made me change my Texas number to an L.A. number. I'd resisted. I'd known that once my Texas number changed, Roarke could no longer call me.

In the end, my new L.A. number brought me relief, regret, and finally, peace. Relief that I could stop waiting for Roarke to call. Regret that I wouldn't know if he finally did. Peace that I'd finally stopped waiting on him. That had been four months after I'd moved. Four months that had been all about waiting for Roarke, not living for me. Last night wasn't a return to the past. It wasn't about him. It was about me. I did what I said I would do. He walked out, but he did so knowing that this time, I just needed closure.

Why doesn't it feel like that's what I have?

I hurry to the shower, and I swear, as I step under the warm water, I can still smell Roarke's cologne, and I hate the regret I feel as it fades into perfumed body wash. An hour later, I'm in the used piece of junk Ford Taurus I bought when I got to town, dressed in jeans, a tank top, and sneakers, with boots on my mind; I need a pair before I head to the ranch tomorrow. I force myself to think about shopping, and that leads me to the budget for this project. I'm just arriving at the hospital when Jessica calls.

"Hey, you," she says. "How are you?"

"Good," I say, pulling into a parking spot and killing my engine. "My mind is swimming with holiday ideas. I actually think I might put on a few holiday tunes on my way to Sweetwater tomorrow."

"And jingle all the way here?" We both laugh, and she murmurs, "Oh God. That was a bad joke."

"It was pretty bad, but I still liked it."

"Good. We're going to get along well then. I'll fall on my face. You can laugh."

"Or we'll fall together and laugh together."

"Even better," she says warmly. "I was talking to Jason this morning, and we know you'll have to basically be here for a month to make this happen. I'm going to send you a proposed budget and what we'd suggest as your payment, which I hope you feel is generous and appropriate, considering the commitment. We also recognize that while here, you can't be growing a new business, which is an accommodation we're making in your pay."

"This job will single-handedly be the reference I need to get new jobs."

"We hope it will be," she says. "And listen, we're redoing the plumbing in the cabin. It's a long story, but there were pipes running from the orchard that caused widespread flooding and other issues."

"Orchard? There's an orchard there now?"

"Yes. Jason's dad tried to transition from cattle to apples. Ultimately, it's going to be profitable, but it was launched on a small budget and poor construction. Anyway, I talked to Sue at the Sweetwater Bed and Breakfast. She has a room for you for the next week on us. After that, we'll have a couple of options here at the ranch. Does that work?"

"Yes, of course. I love Sue. She and my mom were friends back in the day." It's the first time that I think I might have to tell my parents what's going on. Word will get back to them, and I don't want them to be upset. Well, they will be upset that I'm back in Sweetwater, but the burn will be more bearable if the news is delivered by me.

Jessica continues. "Sue told me you're lovely,

just like your mom, which I knew already. Can you confirm the email for the proposal and a bank account for a wire?"

We exchange the needed information, and Jessica says her final goodbye. "Give me an hour and check your email. I'll get the wire complete right away. Talk soon." She hangs up, and I frown. She's sending the wire before I read the proposal? My phone buzzes with a text, and I glance at my Apple Watch to read: *Starbucks withdrawal is real.*

I laugh at Linda's message and climb out of the car. A few minutes later, I'm sitting in her room listening to her tell me all about a male nurse with a "beautiful butt." "Seriously," she says. "It's a work of art. I'd stay a day longer to ask him on a date, but I'm not up to the rejection right now."

"Who says he'll reject you?"

"He's married."

"Oh." My eyes go wide. "Oh. You want to ask him out?"

"No. Yes. No. Of course not. It's a bad joke. All the nice butts are married. Tell me about the project for Jason."

I give her the full rundown. "I'll be gone a month, though. Will you be okay?"

"Honey, you're renting an office, not in business with me, outside of saving my ass by taking the photography job, which I'll pay you for."

"You paid me by giving me the chance to get this job."

"I still can't believe you're friends with Jason and the Horse Wrangler," she says. "Can you introduce me?"

My stomach knots, and her eyes go wide. "Oh my. What nerve did I just hit?"

Leave it to Linda to miss nothing. "He was the only man I've ever loved, but now I hate him, so sure, I'll fix you up. In fact, he's single, and he has quite the nice butt. I can attest to that. In fact, I can attest to that quite recently. As in last night, but that's okay. It was a blast from the past. I was testing him for you. My best friend and my ex. My two best friends, one from the past and one from the present. The perfect couple. You would—"

"Stop right now," Linda orders. "Stop what you're doing right now." She points at me. "Breathe. Deep breath and then start again. What did that asshole do to you?"

CHAPTER FOURTEEN

Hannah....

Why did I just open this Pandora's Box? Why? "Can we just forget I said all of that?"

"Ah, no. And no." She sits up straighter. "Talk to me. Why do I not know any of this?"

"I always had a crush on him, but he and I never really happened until after college."

"You never said a word about him, at all."

"He was like a rock-star crush. That's what he felt like until the summer after college. You and I lost touch for a while back then. And besides, it happened, and then it was over."

"Clearly not," she says. "Talk to me."

"I told you what there is to tell. We were all close growing up."

"Now, see, you didn't tell me that part." She motions me on. "Keep going."

"I was close to Jason, too. We were like siblings, but I crushed on Roarke. I was too young for him, and he treated me like a kid sister. Then I went home the summer after college, while I was sending out portfolios and résumés, and we fell in love. We were engaged. We ended."

"You were young, honey. He was young. Time heals and time matures. Maybe now—"

"He cheated."

Her eyes go wide. "With who?"

"Cindy Lou Phew."

She laughs. "No, really."

"That was her name. She's a model. Look her up."

She grabs her phone and does just that. "Oh, Phew, like phew—oh God. Forget the cursed name. She's gorgeous."

"Right." I stand up. "I need to go."

"Honey, don't run from me. I didn't mean to take you down Avenue F for fucked-up. How did he know Cindy?"

She didn't mean to take me down Avenue F, but here we go. Down Avenue F. I grab the rail at the end of her bed. "The whole Horse Wrangler thing. He did that kind of thing before it was ever on the internet. He was hired by Macy's for the Christmas parade. He was managing the horses for a group of models riding them."

"Were you there?"

"I was, which made it worse, or maybe it made it better because I found out the truth. I don't know. Either way, he disappeared for a couple of hours."

"Disappeared?"

"He told me he was meeting with Macy's executives, but then I got an anonymous video of him with Cindy hanging all over him."

"Hanging on him? What does that mean?"

"It doesn't matter," I say, not going down a path that offers excuses for Roarke. Been there, done that, didn't save my heart from destruction. "I'm done talking about this," I add. "I really need to go. I have to pack and make arrangements for the trip."

"So a holiday festival, huh?"

"Christmas festival," I amend.

"Christmas festival," she repeats and points to the chair next to her. "Talk to me about the event, nothing more, I promise. Yes?"

I hesitate, but I don't push back. I actually need to talk to her about this. "Yes," I agree, sitting down in the spot she requested I sit. "And depending on the budget, I'd like to have your team handle the photography. If you're up to it?"

"Hell yeah, I'm up to it," she says. "That kind of event belongs on my résumé. And I love the holidays. Please tell me you're putting Santa hats on Roarke and Jason and standing them under some mistletoe. That will get people to the event." She grimaces. "Sorry, Hannah. I guess Roarke and mistletoe don't mix for you. That was so stupid of me. I blame the drugs. They gave me lots of drugs. I'm a horrible friend."

"You are not a horrible friend." I have a flashback to kissing Roarke last night, and my cheeks heat. "You're in business mode, thinking smart. Roarke's a single man. He can kiss whoever he likes under the mistletoe, and since Jason isn't a single man, he can't. In other words, a campaign with Roarke under the mistletoe might be exactly the right way to get the women to town."

"Hannah," she says softly. "Don't—"

"I am. It's a great idea. I might need to use some of your contacts in the press."

"What about mistletoe and the cowboys at the ranch? And a few hot baseball players from Jason's team? Not Roarke."

"Roarke—"

"Hannah—"

"Linda."

She glares, and I start rambling about a bachelors auction to bring people to town, going with what works at the moment but getting excited about the idea as I talk. Linda perks up, and she lets the topic of Roarke pass us by. Or I think she does. Once my purse is on my arm and I'm headed to the door, she calls out, "Did he admit to cheating?"

I don't have to ask who "he" is. Of course I know. I turn to face her. "He denied it, but he didn't fight for me. He let me walk away."

"Maybe your distrust hurt him?"

It's not a thought I haven't had myself, but it still doesn't feel right. "Maybe. Get some rest. I'll call you later." I turn and disappear into the hallway, feeling the knife of the past twisting in my heart. So much so that I'm parking at the mall to shop, and I don't even remember how I got there. My email alerts me to a new message from Jessica, and I pull it up: *Hey, you! The wire is sent and the budget is attached. Let me know your thoughts. If the money isn't fair on your end, don't hold back. Talk to me. See you tomorrow!*

I pull up the paperwork and about fall over at the size of the budget. This is going to be the best holiday festival imaginable, even in the short time window allowed. I tab to my income page, and this time, I about choke. I'm quite certain there's a typo and an extra digit in front of the total. I quickly pull up my bank account and find the pending transaction for the same amount. I dial Jessica.

"Hey," she greets. "You got everything?"

"Yes, but I think there's an error. You paid me too much."

"No. No, I don't think so."

"Jessica, you paid me twenty-five thousand dollars for a month of work."

"You'll need to hire staff. You'll need to be here for a month and—"

"This isn't an error?"

"No. We trust you, and you know we're requiring a confidentiality agreement so—"

"Wait," I say. "You're paying for my silence? I thought Jason and Roarke trusted me?"

"They do. Of course they do. They just have legal terms and—"

"I'll sign the agreement, but I'm not taking that much money. I don't need to be paid to be silent. I'm a friend, family, even. Or I thought I was. Maybe I'm mistaken on that. I'll see you tomorrow, Jessica." I hang up, throw my phone in the seat, and grab the steering wheel. How was I so wrong about my life back then?

I decide the mall is not going to happen. I'll just buy some boots at the country store in Sweetwater. I need to go home and pack. Home. Sweetwater was always home, but that's like saying Jason and Roarke were always family. And yet, they need to buy my silence?

I pull out of the parking lot and make the short drive to my apartment. I've just stepped back inside my place when my phone rings again. I stare at the number because even by memory, I know it.

It's Roarke. My God, is Roarke the one who now gets to fire me for hanging up on Jessica? I inhale and answer the line. "Calling to tell me why you want to pay me off?"

"We gave you what we'd give anyone else. Do you want us to cheat you?"

"Anyone who needs to be paid off to ensure your privacy is cheating you. I don't need to be paid to keep your secrets."

"You need to be treated fairly."

"I thought—" I stop myself from saying, *I thought I just needed to come home*. I don't know where that comes from, but it's on the tip of my tongue.

"You thought what?"

"I thought we were friends, damn near family. I thought—"

"You and me, we're a hell of a lot more than friends, and you know it. You pushing me away last night doesn't change that."

"We're—"

"Us," he says. "And that means something."

"It means nothing. Not anymore."

"Hannah," he says, his voice low, rough. "You know what I regret?"

"I don't want to hear this."

"You not coming with me last night."

Me, too, I think, which only serves as proof that sleeping with him was a mistake. I'm not done with him and that was the idea—to feel done. "I'm going to donate the money," I say, changing the subject.

"Talk to me before you do that. Come see me when you get here."

I don't want this request to please me. It's business, and yet nothing about this man is business to me. "I actually need to talk to you about some ideas for the festival, so I'll catch up to you."

"We need to talk before you donate that money, Hannah. Promise me."

"Fine. I mostly promise."

"Mostly?" he challenges.

Once again, I change the subject. "How's the mama horse and the foal?"

"I had to operate on her uterus, but we saved the pregnancy. She's confined. She could use some love. The kind you give to the animals. Another reason to come see me."

Memories of helping him with the animals suffocate me. Those were good times, special times. I've missed the animals. Damn it, I've missed him. "I'll see you and her soon." I hang up.

CHAPTER FIFTEEN

Hannah….

I spend the evening on my bed with a pizza big enough for two (which reminds me that I'm one person), while thinking through the festival and actually drafting a plan, including staff, timelines, and marketing. I have ideas and obstacles, one of which is simply the age of the kids. I have no idea if I'm catering to college-age students or ten-year-olds or both. We have motels nearby, only about ten minutes from town, a nest of hotels, in fact, with a big rest stop as the centerpiece. But will they be enough? Anyone coming in from Dallas will have to stay the night and there certainly aren't five-star hotels for anyone to enjoy.

We.

I just said *we* like Sweetwater was still my place.

It is right now, I remind myself. *It is for this festival.* I want it to go well. I can't blow this. This isn't even about my career. This is personal, no matter how much I might want to say otherwise. This is a good thing that Jason and Roarke are doing. It's good for the kids. It's good for the town, and that town was my home growing up. My family lost everything they had there, and while I really don't know how that happened because it was after I left, and to this day, my parents get upset when I try to talk about it, I have to believe more industry would have helped. Maybe my parents would have expanded into something beyond the crops that were susceptible to everything from weather to the economy.

I set my MacBook aside. I have to call my parents. I dread telling them I'm going back to Sweetwater, and I'm not really sure why, aside from I think the loss they felt there is quite embarrassing and emotional. I debate if this call is better made to my mom or dad and decide on my mom. She is always positive while my father is quite intense. I dial, and after a few rings, I get her voicemail. Great. I need to do this, what with my visit to Sweetwater being tomorrow. I try my dad. He doesn't answer. This really shouldn't surprise me. They both hold high-level positions at the Future Farmers of America, and the FFA convention is in two weeks. They lead exciting and busy lives. I'm not sure this Sweetwater stuff really matters anymore, but then, I'm not sure why they won't ever talk about it, either. I try my mother again and leave a message this time.

My cellphone beeps with a message, and I glance down to find a photo of a bunch of hot firefighters in Santa hats: *Use your imagination. Make this a Christmas festival no one forgets.*

It's Linda, and I text her back: *You do know this is for kids, right?*

Kids have moms, aunts, cousins, and grandmothers, she replies. *And moms need motivation to drive to Sweetwater.*

I laugh. She forgets that the kids are the moms' motivation, but she's not wrong in a broader view of the public and general attendance, but I still don't know enough about the vision and goals, I realize, to make these kinds of decisions. I really think that a bachelor auction, an adult event, the night before the festival could be good, though. My phone beeps again, and Linda's still pitching: *What about an adult night at the end of the festival? I'll come check out the goods and spend money at the festival if you promise me a hot man at the end. A hot cowboy sounds good to me.*

Aren't you injured and in pain? I type. *How are you thinking of hot cowboys?*

Because I need a hot cowboy to come kiss it and make it feel better.

The way I thought Roarke would kiss it and make it feel better last night. And he did. I felt really good until it was over. Now it feels like I stirred a witch's brew, and the pot is filled with trouble and heartache. Unbidden, my mind goes back to that conversation with him earlier:

"You know what I regret?"

"I don't want to hear this."

"You not coming with me last night."

I wanted to go with him, I think, but I can't go down this rabbit hole of stupidity. I won't. I'm not falling for that man again. He cheated. The end. He will not come back from that. We will not come back from that. For all I know, the man has a girlfriend right now, and I'm reading into things anyway. With a twist of my gut at that idea, I scoop up my work, pack it all up, and get ready to leave early tomorrow. I climb underneath the blankets, including the comforter my grandma made for me when she was still with us, and then plug in my phone and turn out the lights. My phone buzzes again instantly, and I cringe. I completely forgot Linda. I grab it, expecting to find a message from her. Instead, I find a shot of a gorgeous white horse: *That's her. She's uneasy. She needs someone to sing to her.*

It's from Roarke, who clearly got my number from Jessica or Jason, and why wouldn't he? He's now one of my bosses. As for the text, he's talking about me singing to the horses, to all of the animals he was treating. I did it even before we were a couple. It was my thing. I always came to his ranch and sang to the sick animals. I miss that. I miss the animals. I don't even think about holding back on this. I type my reply: *I would love to come sing to that beautiful girl.*

My phone rings instantly with his number, and I swallow hard against the nerves and ball of emotion in my throat. "Hey," I say softly.

"Hey," he says, and my God, his voice, that deep resonating tone of his, does funny things to my belly. "When are you going to come sing that song?" he asks.

"I'm leaving early in the morning. I'll be there by lunch."

"Good," he says. "You'll make Snowflake and me happy."

Snowflake is the horse. I don't even ask for confirmation. I know how his mind works. The horse is white as a *snowflake*. How very Christmas of him. Emotion balls in my chest. "Roarke," I whisper. "You know we—"

"I know a lot of things about us, Hannah, and it's time you know, too."

"I don't know what that means."

"Yes, you do, but put that aside for now, and only now, because we need you for this festival."

"I'm coming. I'm not backing out if that's what this call is about. You don't get to make me back out."

"Good," he says. "That's the right answer."

I don't know what that means. He's talking in code, which isn't Roarke, but then, I'm not asking for details, either. I change the subject. "I forgot to ask how old the kids are at the camp?"

"Middle school and high school. Why?"

"I'm just trying to frame the festival. I need to know who I'm catering to."

"I think it needs to be about the town, not just the camp. Something people look forward to that has nothing to do with the camp."

"Right." I think about the kids. I think about Roarke. "You're going to be good at this. I've seen you online. You're good with kids."

His voice softens. "You've watched my videos?"

I'm busted, so busted. "There was one of you when you were with a group of kids that went viral on Facebook," I say, and it's the truth. It's the video that made me go to his YouTube channel. "That one at a rodeo. I saw it. The world saw it. You'll be amazing at this." My mind starts to play on the past, on him as a father, to some lucky woman's kids.

"I thought of you that day, filming that video."

"Me? Why?"

"Because a little girl sang to one of the horses,

right before she poured her drink all over her and me."

I laugh because this is a memory. I was eighteen, and he was twenty-four, home from vet school for the holiday, hotter than ever, but we still weren't a couple. It was in the air, so in the air then, but it was years later before it really happened. For a moment, I'm back in time, climbing out of his truck at his ranch, a huge fountain drink of Dr. Pepper in my hand, after a run to the store. I'd rounded the truck, and one of his dogs raced to greet me, knocking me over and into him. That Dr. Pepper flew open, and somehow, it all came together in the wrong way. I'd turned to try to protect the drink, and Roarke had grabbed me. The drink exploded all over him. And he'd just laughed. We'd laughed until we cried while Maxwell, the pup in question, had licked the soda off him. I loved that, all of it. I'd known I loved him that day. I'd finally admitted it to myself.

"How is Maxwell?" I ask, of the German Shepherd.

"Lost him last year." His voice cracks with those words, that sensitive side of him I love ever present.

I tear up. "That hurts my heart."

"Mine, too, but he was an ancient old boy at that point. He needed to rest."

"Yeah. I guess so, but it still hurts. I wish I could have said goodbye."

"Me, too," he says. "I didn't know how to reach you. I wanted to tell you."

I swallow hard. "I better go. It's an early morning for me."

"What time will you be here?" he asks. "I'll

meet you in town at the B and B where you're staying."

"You don't need to meet me. I don't know what time."

"Call me when you pull into town."

"I'm not calling you when I get into town," I say.

"Then I'll wait for you at the bar next door."

"Roarke—"

"See you tomorrow, Han." His voice is low, rough, familiar in an intimate way, and then he hangs up.

CHAPTER SIXTEEN

Hannah...

My drive to Sweetwater starts with Starbucks, as should all drives. I've stopped for a second coffee and a muffin, which becomes three cake pops when the muffins are sold out, halfway to Sweetwater. I've just stuffed half a vanilla cake pop in my mouth when my mother calls. I answer with a choke. "Hey, Mom. Sorry. Hold on." I manage to swallow without getting into a wreck with the help of a slug of white mocha. "I'm back," I say. "You love to catch me with food in my mouth."

"Easy to do, since you always have food in your mouth."

"Mostly healthy food," I say, though the past two weeks that hasn't been true, but all good reunions require food for the senses.

She laughs. "How many times have you been to Whataburger?"

"Four times. I can't seem to convince myself this is my new normal."

"I might have to come see you just to have some myself. I miss it. We don't have it here, either. How is Dallas, honey? How's the new business?"

"That's what I wanted to talk to you about. The craziest thing happened. My friend Linda, who I told you about, the one I'm leasing a space from—she got hurt and sent me on a job. Guess where?

Or with who? It was the Rangers, and Jason was there."

"Jason. Oh my. That's a blast from the past. How was that?"

"Good. He and Roarke are doing a kids camp in Sweetwater. They hired me to put on a town festival. Would you believe I'm headed there now? It's going to be a great credit and launch of my business." She's silent. And silent some more. "Mom?"

"You're going to Sweetwater?"

"Yes. Yes, it's—"

"I can't believe you're going to Sweetwater." Her tone is pure disbelief, and not in a good way.

"Why is this a problem?"

"For starters, Roarke broke your heart."

"We're adults. We can handle this."

"And sometimes the past is better left alone." Someone calls her name. "I need to go, but please rethink this."

"I'm on my way there. This is a great opportunity, and it helps kids and the community."

"Right. I need to go." She hangs up.

My father and I are not close, but my mother never just hangs up on me. We're close, but then that has always made the Sweetwater secrets bigger and more confusing. Roarke will know what happened. He'll tell me, and my mother has to know this, but it's time I know. It's past time. I shove another cake pop in my mouth. I wonder if cholesterol is an issue at twenty-eight. It probably is. I should eat healthier, which should be easy to do at the ranch. There are always lots of fresh veggies. I sigh. Okay, that was at my family ranch where we grew veggies. It's going to be hard to ride into town and see our place owned by someone else, and right now, I don't even know who.

I turn up the radio and try not to think about the ranch that was one half a farm that is no more. Or maybe it is. It's just not ours. Instead, my mind flashes to me naked with Roarke last night. My God, he'd felt good, and right, so very right. *What are you doing, Hannah?!* I turn up the radio and start singing, practicing for Snowflake the horse. I'm going to sing her a concert I've organized right here in this car.

• • •

I'm just outside the rest stop on the outskirts of Sweetwater when I finish off a rendition of "Sucker" by the Jonas Brothers and dive into Luke Combs' "Beautiful Crazy" when my car starts making a sputtering sound. My eyes go wide. This can't be happening. No. No. No. I'm so close to Sweetwater. So very close to my final destination. The sputtering doesn't stop. I turn down the radio and eye the exit that gets me to the rest stop. I might make it, but I didn't check my fluids before leaving, and I should have in a car I don't know well. If I have a leak, I could bust something expensive. I pull over to the shoulder of the road, kill the engine, and watch smoke come from the hood. This is a horse poop moment. Is someone telling me I don't belong in Sweetwater?

Nevertheless, I'm here. I grab my phone, and the

internet has one bar. I have two numbers: Jessica and Roarke. I dial Jessica. "Are you here?" she answers.

"Sort of. I'm on the side of the road by the rest stop. My car broke down."

"Oh no. Oh gosh." I hear a voice in the background and smile in spite of the situation. It's Jason's grandma, Martha. "Is she here? Is she here? Tell her I have cookies going in the oven."

"Her car broke down," Jessica says, speaking to Martha.

Martha worries for me, and as I listen to her fret through the line, it warms my heart. This is the part of Sweetwater I love. The way everyone knows each other and cares for each other. "We'll be right there to get you," Jessica assures me.

I describe my car and location and disconnect; the Texas heat that needs to let up already—it's October—has me opening my door and getting out. Just breathing this air, this Sweetwater air, has emotions rushing through me. I cover my eyes with my hand and consider walking to the rest stop. Yep. I'm gonna do it. I can't stand here in the heat with only my own head to swim around inside. I start walking and dial Jessica.

"I'm walking to the rest stop. It's hot, and I can't use my air."

"Got it. Help is on the way, I promise."

"Thank you, Jessica."

We disconnect. I grab my purse and roller bag and start walking. I've made it to the exit when a truck pulls up behind me and stops. I turn to find Roarke getting out. Oh God. Roarke, looking all hot in jeans, boots, and a black T-shirt that hugs the same hard body I was hugging last night. All my girl parts start to melt. I'd like to say it's the heat, but fooling myself isn't taking control. Last night was about control and owning the past and present. He's hot. He has bedroom skills that I've experienced firsthand. Of course, he makes me melt.

But that reaction doesn't rule my world.

He steps in front of me, that spicy scent of his circling me like a tiger going in for the kill, and then the tiger does go in for the kill. He takes my bag, sets it behind him, and cups my head. The next thing I know, he's kissing me, and I'm not stopping him. His tongue is just so damn good at everything it does, and when his hand slides to my hip and pulls me closer, I'm without resources to resist. I moan and try to pull back, in my mind at least. I'm pretty sure my body snuggles closer to his. I kiss him back. I can't help it. I really have no desire to even try to help it.

His lips part mine, though, and that tongue of his is no longer next to my tongue, and logic slams into me. "You can't just come up to me and kiss me. Last night—"

"I didn't properly kiss you goodbye." He releases me. "I owed you. Next time, I'll ask. Or maybe you will. If I'm lucky." He brushes the hair from my face behind my ear. "But I was going to lose my mind without that kiss. Come on. Let's get you to your room and take care of your car." He turns and starts walking toward his truck.

I stare after him, stunned, confused, and frustrated that he made me want him again. Anger is the result. I charge after him, walking to the passenger door, and I'm about to open it when he opens it for me like he's a gentleman and all. Which he is, except when he's cheating on his fiancée. I turn to face him. "I'm not going to ask. And the answer, in advance, to a future kiss is no." I climb in the truck and face forward. He doesn't fight me. He shuts me inside, but when he rounds the vehicle and joins me, he doesn't drive, either. For a good two minutes, we both face forward, the charge of all that is and has been between us filling the small space.

"I'm going to change your mind," he finally says, and I feel him look at me, compelling me to look at him, and I can't stop myself. I do. My head turns, my eyes meet his. "Because there are—"

He doesn't finish that sentence. He scrubs his jaw and faces forward again, turning on the engine and placing us in drive.

CHAPTER SEVENTEEN

Roarke...

Because there are things you don't know.

That's what I'd been about to say to Hannah, but with what end? She'll either want to know what that means, when I have no answers, at least not yet, or she'll think it's an excuse for cheating, which I didn't do. Why would I cheat on the woman who was my everything? With the road before me, her taste on my lips, and by my side, this is my dilemma, but it's one I have to solve. Hannah is here now. I can't let her go again, I won't. I just have to figure out how the hell I do that without destroying everyone else.

"Shouldn't we wait on the tow truck?" Hannah asks as I pull us onto the highway.

"It's Nick Wright doing the towing. I told him where to look and what to look for."

"Nick," she says. "Oh wow. I thought he vowed he was never going to end up in this"—she roughens her voice up and imitates Nick—"Godforsaken small town for the rest of his life."

"Apparently the city was a 'rat trap of humans,'" I say, quoting Nick. "His words, not mine. His father retired and moved to Florida. He came back and took over the garage."

"His father left? I'm in the Twilight Zone."

"There's a lot that's changed," I say, solemn now

because of the recent losses that hit close to home for me and for her.

"Jason's parents," she says. "I didn't know about the plane crash when it happened, or I would have come back for the funeral. I did call him when I found out."

"He told me." I glance over at her. "It mattered to him. He went through a rough patch after they died." I turn us down the country road leading to Sweetwater. "They didn't have life insurance, and they had a pile of debt. He was just coming off an injury, and he hadn't been in the big leagues for long. He used all of his money to pay off the bills and then stayed to protect the families that count on the ranch. The good news is that Jessica helped him see a path to play ball and take care of the ranch."

"Which is fabulous, but there was no life insurance? And debt? That doesn't seem like his father."

There's so much about our families that none of us knew or understood, I think, but that's part of that story I can't tell without consequences.

"Welcome to Sweetwater," she says, reading the sign as it comes into view. "I can't believe I'm back."

I can't believe I let her leave in the first place, and as much as I'd like to say there's no looking back, only forward, I can't. If our path was that simple, I would have chased her down and married her years ago. I pull us into the Sweetwater Bed and Breakfast parking lot, which is basically a historic house painted white with a massive porch that sits next to a restaurant, which is also a bar.

Parking, I kill the engine. “Sue is going to be elated that you’re here, but I’m telling you right now, if you don’t go see Martha and try her cookies, she’ll hunt you down.”

“I’m not ready for that,” she blurts without further explanation, but she doesn’t have to give me one. Jason’s grandma baking for us all is a part of our past, a part of the history she left behind when she left me. She looks over at me. “Can you take me to see Snowflake first?”

Animals always gave her comfort, as they do me. It was one of the things that drew us together. I know this woman, and there’s so damn much heartache in her, heartache I failed to save her from, that it cuts me. “Yeah, baby,” I say softly. “I can take you to see Snowflake. She would like that.” *And so would I*, I add silently. “You want to check-in first?”

“Yes. Yes, let me check-in. Of course, this is the beginning. This first day back in Sweetwater, I’ll be all the gossip of the small town.” She opens her door and climbs out. By the time I’ve grabbed her bag, I’m at her side of the truck and she’s holding up a hand in stop sign fashion.

“I just realized that if you go in there with me, I’m not the gossip. *We’re* the gossip. Everyone will think that we’re back together.”

“And just to be clear,” I say, stepping closer to her. “That’s a bad thing?”

“Yes, it’s a bad thing. For all I know, you have a girlfriend I could piss off, too.”

“I don’t have a girlfriend who isn’t you.”

"I'm not your girlfriend."

"No. You graduated to fiancée before I lost you." I don't give her time to reply. I ask the question that's tortured me, on and off for years. "And you, Han. Do you have a boyfriend? Someone who replaced me?"

"No one," she says without hesitation. "You made sure of that, and I don't like it."

"I'll try not to be as pleased as I am about that comment, considering you did the same to me. Actually, no, I won't. Let's go register so you can meet Snowflake."

"No, Roarke. No. I don't want you to go in there with me."

"Everyone is going to talk about us anyway. This is Sweetwater, remember? Population of less than ten thousand. We just drove into town together. We'll be spending time together. Do you really think we're going to avoid that speculation?"

She sighs. "No. Of course, we won't. We're already the talk of the town. Let's just go inside."

"Look at it this way. Sue's good practice for my grandmother."

She groans. "Oh God. I love her, but she's going to try to marry us off again, isn't she?"

"Yes," I say, and not unhappily. "She will."

"Is she the fireball she always was before?"

"Times ten. She's doing Pilates now with Martha. She says it's taken years off her attitude and body."

"Wait. What? We have Pilates here now? Seriously?"

I don't miss how she used the word "we" like

this is her place again, her home. The way it should be. "We do indeed, and I promise you, you'll be recruited. Jessica now goes with Ruth and Martha."

I crinkle my nose. "I'm not Pilates material. I don't bend."

I arch a brow. "Am I being goaded to comment or should I keep my mouth shut on that topic?"

"Keep your mouth shut because aside from it getting you in big trouble, the kind you know you don't want, you've now made me feel like I can't go see Snowflake. Martha and her cookies are with Jessica, and both are waiting for me."

"They'll give you a pass to see Snowflake." I motion to the bed and breakfast. "Let's get this done so you can start singing."

She smiles at that, a warm smile, and we fall into step together. The walk is short, free of locals, thankfully, and we climb up the wide wooden steps and enter the house directly into a huge living room with a desk, just to the right of the door, where Sue is sitting. Sue, who is a robust sixty-year-old, hops to her feet, which isn't much of a hop, since she's barely five feet tall. "You're here! I can't believe you're here, honey!"

She rounds the desk, and I watch as Hannah is embraced, followed by a head-to-toe inspection. "My God, you're more beautiful than ever. You look like Angelina Jolie. Don't you think so, Roarke?"

Hannah looks nothing like Angelina Jolie. For one thing, Hannah's shorter with more curves. She's got brown hair a shade lighter. Her green eyes brighter, sweeter. And her face isn't long and thin, it's heart-shaped with adorably full cheeks, but I agree on one point. "She's more beautiful than ever, yes," I say, glancing at Hannah. "You are."

Those adorable cheeks heat. "Thank you, Roarke."

Sue claps. "You two are just too perfect together." She hands Hannah a key. "But I get it. The town is small. People talk. Staying here, instead of his place, gives you some privacy." She winks. "I won't tell anyone if you're never in your room."

"We're not back together," Hannah explains quickly. "We're— " She struggles for words and looks to me for help. "We're— "

I cross my arms in front of my chest. "Go on. We're what?"

She scowls at me. "Not getting along."

Sue laughs. "Oh God. I miss the way you two get on." Her phone rings. "I better get that." She squeezes my arm. "I'm so excited about a Christmas festival right here in our town. I have ideas. More later. You two go on up to the room if you like." She grins. "It's a king-size bed for a couple who's always been into king-size fun."

CHAPTER EIGHTEEN

Roarke…

Hannah pales and turns to me, reaching for her suitcase. "I'll go drop this in the room."

Now both our hands are on the handle of her case. "I got it. I'll help. I promise not to be inappropriate unless you ask. That was our deal. I'll stick to it. Unless you're afraid you'll ask and you don't have the willpower to be alone with me."

Her eyes meet mine. "Stop teasing me."

"Ask and I won't have to."

"Roarke," she pleads softly.

"I'll behave, Hannah. I promised. I know you don't believe me, but my word matters. It always has. It always will."

"I always believed you were honorable."

"I am, and I have opinions on why you decided to forget that so easily, but I won't share them now, here. This has to go up there." I motion to the winding steps leading to the guest room. "I'm not watching you struggle with it. I'll take it myself if you like, and you can stay down here."

"No. No. It's fine. Come with me. And thank you." She glances at the key, and together, we head toward the stairs and then up them.

We reach the second level of the old house and turn right to stop at the door at the end of the walkway. Hannah opens the door and enters. I follow her inside, but I don't shut the door. I'm not forcing myself on her, and the truth is, the more I think about how easily she believed the worst of me, the more I revive a big load of pissed off. I set her bag on the bed for easy access, the way I used to when we traveled, the way she likes her bag.

Somehow, she moves for the door, and I turn at just the right moment to bring us toe-to-toe, her hand landing on my chest. My load of pissed off becomes a burn to hold her in about three seconds flat. Heat radiates from her palm straight to my cock. I'm hard. I'm hot. I'm in love with this woman, so why the hell wouldn't I be hot and hard?

Her gaze goes to her hand on my chest and lifts, but her palm doesn't move. "I didn't mean to do that."

"I'm not going to kiss you or pull you down on that bed," I say. "I'm just going to think about it, but maybe you should move your hand."

"Right," she says, but she doesn't move her hand. "Roarke—"

"Hannah," I warn. "If you don't move your hand, I'm going to shut the door, and I'm going to kiss you again."

"It's just that—"

I move to shut the door. She grabs a handful of my T-shirt. "No. No. Stop."

I turn to face her again. "What are you doing?"

She yanks her hand back. My jaw sets hard. "Let's go see Snowflake." I move to the door and wait for her. She stares at me for a good three seconds before she hugs herself and walks past me and into the hallway. Side by side, we walk down the stairs, and while I left her bag upstairs, our baggage is a load that hasn't been left behind.

We manage to escape without another encounter with Sue, but of course, the one we had will carry far and wide in the town. We exit to the front of the house, and I walk with her to the passenger's door and open it. She turns to me, and I stop her before she starts. "Don't tell me not to get your door. My mama might be gone, but she remains with me, and she brought me up right."

Considering she was also close to my mother, who passed when I was a freshman in college, her lips purse, but she doesn't fight me on my manners; she climbs inside the truck. I shut her inside and round the truck. I've just settled in beside her when my cellphone buzzes with a text message. I pull it from my pocket and read it before I glance at Hannah. "Nick said he ate your cake pops. He was hungry. He's not charging you for the tow, but—" I hesitate with the blow that follows, "your engine's blown."

"No," she says, turning to face me. "No. Please say no. I just bought that car." She presses her hands to her face. "This can't be happening."

I want to pull her to me and comfort her, but right now, I have no right to do any such thing. I can't just touch her. I want to touch her so damn badly. "God works in mysterious ways, Hannah. There's a reason you got that extra money for this job."

"To pay me off. I don't want it. I'll handle this."

"That money is not to pay you off," I counter.

"You have to know that."

"I'll suck it up and finance a car," she says, as if I haven't even spoken. "Thanks to this job, if I do it well, and I plan to, I'll have a steady income."

I have about ten questions about what went wrong in L.A., but Jessica told me enough to stave off my urge to be too pushy too soon. I turn on the engine, and my cellphone rings again. I grab it and glance down to find Martha calling. I show the caller ID to Hannah. She groans. "Let's just go see her. I'm starving anyway. I'll eat her baked goods and sing better for it."

"You sure?" I ask, still cognizant of her earlier discomfort.

"I need to make this festival the best Christmas festival ever. It has to be wonderful for everyone involved. I need to dig in, and meeting with Jessica and Martha will help."

My phone has stopped ringing and has started again. I glance down and sigh, answering, "Hi, Grandma," as I return my gaze to Hannah.

"Is she okay? I heard she broke down. Is she with you?"

"Yes," I confirm. "She's okay. She's with me. And before you ask, yes, we're headed to Jason's place. We had to get her checked into her room."

"Are you still in love with her?"

"Grandma," I warn.

"That's a yes. Oh, honey. I hope it works this time. Hurry. We all want to see her."

"We'll be there in ten minutes." I disconnect and shove my phone back in my pocket. "Maybe we should have a little whiskey after the cookies."

She laughs. "Then I'll be singing something like 'Happy Birthday' to Snowflake. You know I don't drink well."

I place the truck in gear. "And that's a problem, why? You do remember what we're about to endure?"

"Right. Whiskey and 'Happy Birthday' it is."

I laugh and back us up, and it's not long before we're turning down the country road that leads to my place and to Jason's. It also leads to the fork that connects to her family ranch that isn't her family ranch anymore. That's a dangerous emotional tightrope I lead her away from before this homecoming. "I built a veterinarian hospital."

"What?"

"We have a full hospital now. I have three vet students at all times and another full-time vet."

"Wow." She turns to face me. "That's a big operation. Just for horses?"

"The majority of what I treat personally is horses, but the vet I have on staff works for Sweetwater and other nearby locations. Plus, I don't turn away special cases for any animal. You know that." We pass through the Flying J entrance to Jason's property.

"I can't wait to see the hospital. And meet Snowflake," she says as I pull us up to Jason's house, where my grandmother is waiting on the porch. "And drink that whiskey."

"She loves you," I remind her. "You're family."

She turns to look at me. "If that were true, I wouldn't be paid for my silence. If that were true—" She stops herself. "Never mind."

She reaches for the door, and I dare to touch her, to gently catch her arm. "Wait. Please. Look at me."

She inhales and turns those beautiful green eyes of hers on me. "I've been gone for a long time."

"Too long," I say softly. "Too damn long, Han. You *are* family. And time and distance didn't wash that away. The money isn't about paying you off. It's about family taking care of family. I might not deserve you, but you don't get less than everyone else. You deserve more than everyone else." I release her arm. "You'll feel it. I promise you. They'll make you feel it." I open my door and get out, willing this big family to make her see that she's a member of it. And nothing and no one will change that, but even as I do, I feel like a damn hypocrite, because family is what drove us apart—just not this part of our family, I remind myself.

Hannah gets out of the truck, and my grandmother, all five feet one inch of her, with her long silver hair, comes flying down the stairs to greet her. In about sixty seconds, I'm at the front of the truck, watching my grandmother embrace Hannah, and I hear her say, "Welcome home, granddaughter," only to have Hannah burst into tears.

CHAPTER NINETEEN

Hannah…

The minute Ruth calls me granddaughter, my heart swells with emotions, the tears flowing of their own accord, and I know why. My grandmother died when I was five. Ruth was always next door; she was my other grandmother, the only one I really know at all. Marrying Roarke would have made that all the truer. Losing Roarke meant losing her, too, only right now, it doesn't feel like I lost her at all, though I know I have. It's not fair to put her in the middle of me and Roarke. I wouldn't do that to her, but for now, it feels good to have her back, if only for a little while.

"Why are you crying, honey?" Ruth demands, pulling back to inspect me, her crystal-blue eyes so like Roarke's, beautiful, intelligent, kind. They also see way too much. "This is supposed to be a happy homecoming," she adds.

"It is," I promise, swiping at my eyes. "It is happy. These are happy tears."

"They better be," she chides. "We're thrilled you're here and part of the festival, and if you ever go silent on me again, I'll hunt you down. That's a promise. Let me get a look at you." She inches back a bit farther to give me a once-over, while I note that she's still slender and fit. I think I need to try Pilates. She looks good.

"You are beautiful, honey," she declares, when she's the one who is beautiful, inside and out, her long silver hair and elegant features having aged like a fine wine. Her inner light, still so ever present. "My boy was a fool to lose you," she declares.

My cheeks heat with that awkward comment. Roarke seems to respond, stepping to my side, the place I used to believe he'd always stand. "As you can see," he says, "Grandma still knows how to get right to the point."

Ruth points at him. "And how to keep you in line, boy." She takes my hand. "Now, you go away. We're going to do some girl talk and catch up."

She means she wants to drill me about me and Roarke. "I'd love that," I say, at least about the time with her, not the talk about Roarke. "But," I add, "I need to talk to everyone about the festival, and I think Roarke needs to be a part of that talk."

She crinkles her nose. "Fine, then. He stays for cookies and coffee and leaves for the girl talk. I'll take you to my little cabin behind Roarke's house if that's what it takes to get some alone time."

"You're still there?"

"You betcha, honey," she says. "Till the day I die. A perfect girl hideout."

In other words, I'm not getting out of that girl talk, even if I dodge it today. She wants to know what happened between me and Roarke, and she won't stop until she gets answers, a conversation I'd avoided years before, and with reason. What do I say? Do I tell her he cheated? No. No, I discard that idea immediately. I won't do that to Roarke. I loved Roarke. God, I still do. I won't hurt him or talk badly about him ever. "I'd love to have some time with you and Martha, Ruth. It's been a long time."

"I'm really not sure how I feel about being left out of the girl talk," Roarke comments, "but Hannah promised to help me with Snowflake. You know how good she is with the forlorn animals."

"Oh my, yes," Ruth says, looking at me. "You used to sing to the sick animals, and you just have this way with them that soothed them, like another Horse Wrangler! You two were going to be Mr. and Mrs.—"

"Ruth," I say softly, warning her to stop, and it's enough. She gives me an understanding look, purses her lips, and wraps her arm around me. "Let's get you inside and get you fed. What have you eaten today? You look thin."

"Today? Coffee and two cake pops, since Nick ate the other two. I'd get mad at him, but he towed my car. I owe him a million cake pops."

"I'll have Martha bake him some goodies for helping. We need to get you some real food before we feed you cookies."

"No, that's okay. I'll take the cookies. Last night I ate most of a pizza by myself. I feel like I'm having theme days. Yesterday, I lived on pizza. Today, I live on cookies. It's really a fantasy feast to be envied. Tomorrow, however, I'll live on vegetables. It all evens out. It's all about balance."

Roarke laughs and opens the door to the house for us, his eyes lighting with mischief. "Vegetables make everything better, right, Han?" he teases, and it's an inside joke that has my cheeks heating. It's about me and him in a field of vegetables. It was after a fight. We were no longer fighting once we left that field. It's not the kind of story you share with anyone, but it *is* one that you remember.

"The problem is that vegetables come with a short shelf life," I reply. "The benefits only last so long."

"It's true," Ruth says. "You have to feed your body with good things every single day." She nudges me. "And cookies and cake pops."

"And pizza," I add, and as she tugs me forward into the house, my gaze catches Roarke's with a warning in my stare, one that I forget as soon as I enter the living room of Jason's house; only when I was here before, it belonged to his parents. This realization, the finality of their deaths, steals my joy at the scent of Martha's baked goods permeating the air.

"I can't believe they're gone," I whisper.

"I know," Ruth says, squeezing my arm. "It never feels right, but Jessica has brought new life to the place and to Martha."

Roarke steps behind us, and I can feel his presence pressing against me, the past that is lost, heavy in the room, in every possible way. "Come," Ruth says, taking my hand and leading me forward, down a hallway.

It's not long before I'm walking inside a large, beautiful kitchen where Martha and Jessica stand behind the center rectangular island with icing bags in hands and cookies in front of them. "Oh my God!" Martha exclaims, dropping her bag to run toward me, spry like she's years younger than her seventy-something years, her gray hair much shorter and more old-fashioned than Ruth's.

I'm swept into a hug by my "other grandma," and this time, it's Martha who cries, and her emotion pounds into me. She's still living with the loss of Jason's parents and her daughter. I'm a piece of the past connected to them, and suddenly, any past I have to overcome feels like nothing.

Before long, I'm hugging Jessica, too, and hearing all about the Flying J bakery that Martha and Jessica have made hugely successful with cookies in a major restaurant chain and a series of cookbooks.

I'm also recruited to help ice their new carrot cake cookies, as is Roarke, and the two of us end up at opposite endcaps, facing each other with icing bags in hand. "Is Jason around to talk about the festival?" I ask.

"He's at the new field throwing balls," Jessica says. "He spends a couple of hours a day out there, but shoot your ideas at all of us."

"This is for the town with the camp as a press point, right? And maybe the bakery? We want adults and kids at the camp, correct? And I assume opportunities to donate to the charity benefiting from the camp?"

"Exactly," Jessica says. "Exactly." Her eyes light. "What if we could become like the Christmas festival in the state? Or even beyond the state. Like Santa's Workshop has nothing on us. I know that's a big order for this year, but a girl can dream, right?"

"We can make it pretty special," I say. "We'll get

booths and snowblowers. We'll decorate like crazy. The big thing is getting people here, which means using our assets."

"My baked goods?" Martha asks. "I can donate."

"Baked goods by the famous Grandma Martha is good," I say. "But what if we hold a bachelor auction and recruit baseball players, and even firemen from local stations, even from Dallas, to be a part of it? Of course, we'll make them all wear Santa hats."

"We have to have Santa hats," Jessica laughs.

"Yes," I agree primly. "We do. And we also have to act fast to make this happen, but I believe this would bring in big money for the charity. And if the players don't want to agree to go on dates, they could auction off a dance, a kiss, or lunch. They could pick some prize that is their choice. We could also ask them all to donate an item to the auction—a ball, a signed shirt, or whatever." I don't breathe. My mind is working fast and I keep going, changing topics only slightly. "I'm already thinking about agreements with nearby hotels." I laugh. "I'm talking a million miles an hour. Feel free to hate the idea but—"

"I love it!" Martha says. "How about one winner gets to bake cookies with Jason and ask him questions?"

"They might rather do that with just you," I say. "You're becoming a star in your own right."

"Agreed!" Jessica and Ruth chime in.

Roarke's eyes warm on me. "Agreed."

"Oh, you all," Martha says. "I'm no star, though the Food Network did ask me to be a judge on

Cupcake Wars. It's very exciting!" She waves it off, though. "Enough about me. Getting back to Jason. We could let the person who wins try to hit a pitch Jason throws, or play ball with him, or just have coffee. We'll have to get Jason in on it. Roarke," she continues, looking at him, "no date for you, but you could introduce the winner to your horses or take a lady on a horseback ride." She then glances at me, and I have a feeling a bombshell is coming, even before she says, "Of course, you could supervise, Hannah. That's why I said he's not up for auction for a date." She glances between Roarke and me. "Because you two are a couple. We all know it, even if you two aren't saying it yet."

CHAPTER TWENTY

Hannah...

Roarke arches a brow at me, challenging me to reply to Martha. I do so without hesitation. I pick up a cookie and stuff it in my mouth. The sweet taste hits my tongue, and I spontaneously moan, which really isn't the best reply to a question about Roarke. I try to fix this. I point to the cookie. "That moan was for the cookie, not Roarke."

Everyone laughs, including Roarke, which is one part good and one part bad, because I think I've made it seem like I might moan for Roarke. Which I did.

Just.

Last.

Night.

I try again. "Roarke and I aren't a couple. I'm not even sure we're really friends."

"You look at him like you want to gobble him up, like the cookie," Martha teases.

"I do not!"

"I think you do," Roarke interjects.

"I do not." I lean on the island to face off with him. "I do admit that you're still hot, but that means nothing but trouble in my book. However, you're really sweet to animals, you even save their lives, so we might, and that 'might' is a big one, get to the friend marker." I pick up another cookie and look at Martha. "And these cookies are the best thing on planet earth." I then look at Jessica. "How do I go about talking to the team about the auction, or would you prefer to do that? This part of the process will be urgent. We need to get the auction lined up to start advertising for it. And how do you think the guys would feel about posing in Santa hats for the marketing material?"

Everyone laughs again, and Jessica says, "Why don't we spend tomorrow together, getting everything moving?"

"Roarke will do it," Ruth says.

"Shirtless," Martha adds.

Roarke holds up his hands. "Oh no. I keep my shirt on. The horses and I will do the hats. That's where we draw the line." He takes a bite of a cookie and eyes Martha. "And I agree. Your cookies are the best. Every new creation is better than the last."

"Thank you," Martha says. "I'm thinking I'll launch a gingerbread cookie for the festival. It seems Christmas appropriate. What do you think, Hannah? We could have an area for kids to decorate them, too?"

"I love it," I say. "Can you bake a batch so I can shoot some photos for the advertisements?"

"I have to come up with the cookie," Martha says. "But I'll start working on it this evening and get something baked, even if it's not the final recipe."

"Perfect," I approve. "Now, let's talk about rides, booths, events, as well as a scavenger hunt. Oh, and the town decorations. Is the mayor involved?"

Roarke's phone rings and he pulls it out of his pocket, eyeing the number and answering the call. "What's up, Amanda?"

Amanda isn't a name I know, and I hate the way my stomach knots at his familiar tone with her. I don't even know who this person is. Why am I reacting this way?

"I'll be right there." He disconnects. "I have an emergency that I need to attend to at the hospital." He looks at me. "When you're ready, call me. I'll either come get you or send someone to pick you up."

"I'm not bothering you during an emergency," I say. "Go, Roarke. Save a life."

"I'll take her where she needs to go," Jessica says. "No worries. Go. Go."

Roarke's eyes linger on me, and I feel his hesitation before he gives Jessica a nod and turns and heads for the door. I hate the torment I just felt in him, and the idea that he's distracted by me, yet again, while caring for an animal, bothers me. "I'll be right back," I say, and without looking at the room, I hurry after him.

I step onto the porch as he's reaching his truck. "Roarke." He turns to face me, surprise etched on his handsome face.

"You coming?"

"Not now, but uh, saving animals is sexy. You know that, right?" It's out before I can stop it, my gut driving me to say what it feels like he needs to hear, what lets him know I support him. And it's not flirting. I'm just speaking the truth.

My reward is a rumble of his deep, masculine

laughter, the tension I'd sensed in him fading away. "I'm glad you think so."

"I'm going to come and sing to Snowflake when I'm done here. Okay?"

"I'll hold you to that," he says, giving me a wink, before he climbs in his truck and starts the engine, a man headed out to be a hero, like he is most days.

I watch him back out and drive away, wishing I was with him, which isn't new. I've wished I was with that man for years. Maybe it's time to be friends. Maybe that's how I reconcile that need. We were, after all, best friends. I lost a future husband. I lost a friend. Having one of the two back would be pretty wonderful. It's a growth thing. It doesn't have to be all or nothing for us.

The door opens behind me and then shuts as Jessica steps to my side. "You still love him."

I could deny the truth but why? "Sometimes love isn't enough."

"Nothing is enough when you're thousands of miles apart. I've gotten to know Roarke, and I wondered why he was alone. Now I know. He looks at you like you're his beginning, middle, and end."

But I'm not, I think, and not just because he cheated. He didn't even fight for me. He didn't come after me. I swallow hard and remind myself of Martha fighting to survive the loss of a child. My problems are nothing. This festival is important. It's about helping those who need help, about a charity for kids. "Let's go talk to the mayor," she says. "In answer to your question, yes, he's involved. He wanted us to stop by today. I think you know him. Luke Kilmore."

I turn to look at her. "Luke's the mayor?"

"Yes. He said you two were friends."

"We're more than friends," I say. "Luke grew up here, too. He also became a rodeo star, and we crossed paths in Vegas a few years back."

"Oh," she says. "Is this a problem?"

"Nothing happened, but not by his choice. That was mine. He felt too close to Roarke. I just couldn't do it."

Her lips curve. "Because you love Roarke. I think that's pretty special. Years and miles apart and you were loyal to him. Let's grab a cookie for the road and go see the ex-rodeo star. Seems we should auction him off, too, don't you think? Find him a nice hot mama who isn't you."

I laugh. "Yes, I do believe we need to auction him off."

She opens the door and glances back at me. "We'll save you for Roarke and Roarke for you." With that, she goes inside the house, leaving me to think about that premise.

Roarke.

Me.

Us.

God.

I want him. I want to forget the past and just be with the man I love, wrap him up for the holidays and make him mine, but I know me. I will never let go of the betrayal, and yet, I can't seem to let go of him. I should put a Santa hat on the man and auction him off, but I won't because it's not just the betrayal I can't let go of. It's him.

But I go back to where I was a few minutes ago.

Maybe we need closure, the kind I was looking for on some level by sleeping with him last night. I missed the mark, though. The closure we need is about forgiveness. I don't have to forget. I do have to forgive, and that's what leads us back to friendship.

CHAPTER TWENTY-ONE

Hannah…

I follow Jessica into the house, and just the scent of baking cookies has my stomach growling. I really do need food, real food, but for now, I hurry back to the kitchen and enter to make an announcement. "I have an urgent need for cookies. Can I get some for the road?"

Martha and Ruth laugh, and once I have a bag filled with cookies in my hand, the women sandwich me in a hug. "We're so glad you're back!" Martha explains.

Ruth turns me to face her, her hands on my arms. "You're my granddaughter. Don't forget it." She kisses my temple and sets me away from her. "Now, go plan this festival and then sing to Snowflake. That's an order." She winks. "And feel free to kiss Roarke for me if you want to."

My cheeks are, once again, heating. These women are so good at making me blush, but then they always were. It's funny how those things you hated in your youth, you endure with fondness when you grow up.

A few minutes later, I'm in a sleek black BMW with Jessica, both of us stuffing our faces with cookies. "She's really a brilliant baker," Jessica says, starting the car. "I'm so lucky I have the opportunity to allow the world to taste her food."

"It's amazing the way you came in and turned her skills into a business."

"From divorce attorney to entrepreneur," she says, backing up. "I blame her cookies for inspiring me. Now you're an entrepreneur, too. I love that this little town manages to become an opportunity for so many. I hope we can keep that going, use the festival to create more great things for more people."

I know now why Jason loves her and Roarke approves of her place by his friend's side. She's really a generous, good soul.

"You know," she says, glancing over at me. "I'm pretty excited about the festival. It showcases my two favorite people in the world: Jason and Martha."

Funny thing is that I would have said Roarke and Ruth were my two favorite people. They were family. Right now, they still feel like family.

"Do we need to talk about this thing with you and Luke any further before we get to the courthouse?"

"There's nothing more to tell."

"Did you date when you were in Sweetwater?" she asks, and I suddenly wonder if this is about Roarke or me. I do believe she's protecting him, which could bristle my nerves, but it doesn't. I like that she's protective. I'm envious that he has that in his life. That he has this place in his life.

"We didn't," I say, and while there is more to add, it comes back to one place. "I was always all about Roarke." I glance over at her. "And that story, the one of Roarke and me, is Roarke's to tell, not mine."

"It's your story, too."

"But this is his place and his people."

She huffs at that. "Oh please. This place and these people are yours, too. That's quite obvious to see."

"Nevertheless," I say, not about to argue this point, "Roarke and I were engaged. Now we're not. The rest is his story."

She glances over at me, presses her lips together in an obvious effort to stop herself from asking more questions. That must not be working because she grabs a cookie and shoves it in her mouth. I laugh and do the same.

The rest of the short drive is cookies and talking about the town decorations. We pull into the courthouse with a vision of candy canes and Christmas trees to present to Luke. We find the tall, blond, and quite good-looking ex-rodeo star in his office, scowling at the paperwork in front of him. "Why the heck are you the mayor of this town?" I demand.

His gaze jerks upward, and he stands. "Holy hell, I don't know, and get your sweet ass over here and give me a hug."

We meet at the end of the desk, and he looks like himself in faded jeans, a button-down rodeo-style shirt, and boots. The office says otherwise. "Come here, girl." He hugs me, which was wholly brotherly in the past, but then he adds, "You need to sing to me and get me all worked up again." I grimace and push away from him.

"I didn't sing to you." I poke his chest. "I sang to the bar."

"But damn, baby, you got me hot under the collar."

"Tequila got you hot under the collar. You were drunk."

"Your point?" he challenges. "I knew what I was doing. Is that why you walked me to my room and tucked me in like I was a two-year-old who needed a blankie, not a man?"

"Oh good Lord, Luke," I say. "Stop talking. What happens in Vegas is supposed to stay in Vegas, remember? You told me that enough times that night."

In Vegas, where he was drinking his way past his girlfriend cheating. The cheating part is what almost won me over. I related to his pain. He pulls back to look at me. "Nothing happened to stay in Vegas, though it should have. You're as pretty as sunshine on a rainy day, and that was a rainy day. As is today, because believe you me, me behind this desk is a damn thunderstorm."

I twist around to motion Jessica forward. "Nothing happened between us. Don't read into this."

"I already said that," Luke chimes in behind me. "I told her you tucked me in like I was a two-year-old. That doesn't exactly say we were knocking boots, babe. You were too hung up on Roarke despite him breaking your damn heart just like Karen did mine." He eyes Jessica. "Hi, Jessica."

"Hi, Luke," Jessica says. "Always interesting when we meet."

"Seriously," I say as he shakes Jessica's hand. "Why are you here, in this town, and mayor of all things? What's happening? Are you still drinking tequila?"

He doesn't laugh. He scrubs his jaw and motions to the seats in front of his desk. "Let me tell you two pretty ladies a story. And for the record, I might need tequila before this job is done with me."

We claim our seats, and he rests his arms on the desk that is a big ol' wooden thing but looks small compared to him. He's big, tall, and muscular from wrestling bulls. "I thought your parents moved to Dallas and you were a rodeo star? I'm living in the Twilight Zone."

"My dad hated the big city. He came back here and took over as, you guessed it, mayor. He then proceeded to rupture a disc in his back. I was on a break, six months off until I go back to the circuit as a judge this time. He made me acting mayor, which yes, that can happen in Sweetwater. It did." He rubs his hands together. "So, let me get to mayor duty for this town and doing what good I can while I'm here. We're having a festival. Do I get to ride a damn bull for this festival or is it all just gingerbread men and candy canes?"

"You," Jessica says, "get to be auctioned off for charity. You do not have to kiss your date, but you do have to smile real pretty at her."

He groans. "Old Lady Misty will buy me. I'm screwed."

We both laugh because Old Lady Misty is also the cat lady who has lived here for as long as I have walked this earth. She's eccentric but sweet. "This is for the children's hospital, right?" I ask.

"Yes," Jessica says. "A good cause."

"A very good cause," I say. "And if she wins you, you get to play with kittens." His eyes light, and I point. "Don't make a bad joke about another kind of kitten."

He holds up his hands. "I'm innocent. Don't make Jessica think I'm a dirty cowboy."

"I went to school with you. You are a dirty cowboy."

"Not anymore. And fine. Fine. I'll do it because Lord only knows I'm still the single-est bastard in this town." He eyes me. "Next to Roarke, but then you're back. You back with him?"

"Roarke and I are none of your business," I say because I'm not inviting a proposition. And the truth is, part of me wants to scream at the idea of Roarke being single and free. I want to claim him, and that's a scary reaction.

"Let's talk about those gingerbread men and a whole bunch of candy canes."

Jessica and I chime in and find out that the town has pretty much no budget. Luke does, though, and he donated ten grand to be used for the festival or the charity. We leave in a happy place and end up at the diner down the road, where I have my first meal of the day at six o'clock.

"He's a good guy," Jessica says, once we've ordered.

"He's always been a good guy. This town is pretty good at making them that way, I think."

"You didn't tell him that you're not with Roarke."

"Luke and I are not a future couple. Luke, however, has been burned by a woman, and I think he just doesn't want to be alone anymore. I don't need him making me his backup plan."

"He's gorgeous and smart. He's a rodeo star. What's wrong with him? Why is he alone?"

"He's jaded, I think, after his girlfriend cheated on him. And I know he has a lot of groupies on the road, which is great at first, but those people don't really care about you. I imagine much like Jason must have experienced in baseball."

"That's true. He did. Buckles Bunnies. That's the groupies, and don't even get me started on that. Bottom line. He was cold and guarded when I met him, but you and Luke—"

"Never happened. Won't happen. I've already told you, he even told you, that I've always been all about Roarke." The waitress fills our coffee cups, and I grab the creamer. "Even in L.A."

She links her fingers under her chin. "Did you date?"

"I did. I even had a few who stuck around a bit, but my heart just wasn't in it. Roarke ruined all men to follow." I want to ask what she knows about Roarke's recent history, but I bite back the questions.

"You can't hold a torch for him all these years. You have to be with him or let him go. The same goes for him. This isn't healthy."

"I have no idea what Roarke has been doing all these years."

"He wasn't falling in love with another woman, I can tell you that. What is wrong with you two? Why aren't you together?"

I inhale and let it out. "I'm sorry. It's— I can't

talk about this. It's complicated. It's between me and Roarke."

She flattens her hands on the table. "Good grief, we hired the right person to keep things private around here. I'm in the inner circle, and even I can't get any gossip."

I laugh. "How about some fashion world gossip instead?"

"I'd love some fashion world gossip, but damn it, woman. I can tell how much you love Roarke. Life is short. Don't lose each other again. And one way or the other, you have to free your hearts for each other or someone else."

She's right. I realize in this moment, with Jessica, that she is absolutely right. "You think Roarke has held on, too?"

"Honey, I know he has. I've talked to Jason about this. You're it for that man."

I pick up my coffee and sip, drinking in her words with the warm beverage. "We lost each other a long time ago," I say, glancing at her, "but being back, being with him again, I meant what I said earlier. Maybe we'll find friendship again."

"I don't know what happened between you two, but I'm here if you need to talk." She pulls out a folder from her bag. "But now, let's cheer up and get all wrapped up in Christmas even though I'm going to secretly hope that you get all wrapped up in Roarke."

I did, I think. *Last night.* The problem is that I'm still all wrapped up in Roarke.

CHAPTER TWENTY-TWO

Roarke...

I get Old Man Levor's poor pup, who was hit by a car, stabilized and resting well before I leave him with Nathan, one of my interns, and head outside for some air. I step outside the vet offices that have been a part of our operation since long before I took over five years ago now, back when my father was the king here. A blessed cool breeze lifts around me, the hope of fall finally showing itself rather than pretending to be summer, the hint of a holiday season arriving with it. A holiday with Hannah present. I didn't think I'd ever see that day again, but I wanted to, damn straight I wanted to. But being here and being with me are two different things.

I walk toward one of the gated areas where a beauty of a stallion, who just arrived and hasn't been broken in, is grazing. The owner, who hired me to train him, named him Warrior, and it's fitting. He's regal and abrasive, but we'll fix the abrasive part when he learns how much love his beauty will get him. I've just reached the enclosure when the sound of an approaching vehicle has me turning. The minute I eye Jason's truck, I grimace and turn away. Hannah still hasn't shown up, and damn it, I want her here. I need her here. She belongs here, with me, and in ways she doesn't even know, not yet, ways I intended to make her believe in me again; only her showing up, before I could go to her, complicates that presentation.

Jason joins me, and we both stand there, studying the horse for several minutes, before he says, "You're still so fucking in love with her."

"Was that ever in question?"

He turns to look at me. "No. But I didn't see it, and I should have. I was too wrapped up in my own bullshit to see beyond that shit."

"I wouldn't have talked about it anyway."

"Bullshit," Jason murmurs. "I would have made you talk about it just like you made me talk about the crap that almost ruined me with Jessica. I let you down."

"You didn't let me down, man. You're—you're family."

"So is she."

"Yeah," I say. "Yeah, she is." I turn away from him, feeling the punch in my gut at how right he is and how wrong this has all gone.

Jason faces the enclosure again with me, both of us silent a few moments, before he adds, "I would have made you do something to get her back or made you move on a long time ago."

"I didn't want to move on, and now that she's back, I still don't." I look over at him. "I have to get her back."

"Then let's talk about that. She thinks you cheated. Make her believe you when you tell her you didn't."

"It's not that simple, man. There are things you don't know. Things I'm not ready to talk about."

"Fair enough, but why did she think you cheated?"

"The *why* doesn't matter," I say, not about to get into the topic of the video, which came from a source that will only set a fire I'm not ready to light. "She believed it. She didn't even consider listening to what I had to say. Even now, after all these years, every damn time I've been with a woman, I've wished I was with Hannah."

"Then whatever the complication is, whatever you won't talk to me about, find a way to simplify that shit. You're good at that. You do it for the animals all the time. You do it for the people you teach to handle the horses. You do it for the interns. I've seen you. Do it for yourself. The way you're going to do it for those kids who come here and learn from you." He knocks on the wooden gate. "I need to get home. I promised my grandmother I'd spend some time with her tonight, and I've learned that we don't always get a tomorrow. You should remember that, too." Leaving me with the lesson he learned after losing his parents so damn tragically, the one driven home by my father's stroke, he turns and walks away.

He's right, of course, he's right, but his lesson is double-sided for me. Our parents, all of our parents, got into a nasty war that ultimately led to Hannah's family losing their land. It also led to some nastiness between families that included framing me for cheating. I can save myself by telling Hannah everything, but then Hannah and Jason would find out how shitty their parents are and were. And I'm not sure Hannah can forgive me for what my father did to her parents any more than she can forgive her parents for what they did to us. What I am sure of is that Hannah coming home is like the hand of a clock that's been stuck but now moves. It's time for change. It's time for resolution. It's time for me to fight for Hannah. It's past time for me to fight for Hannah.

I can't live another day without that woman.

CHAPTER TWENTY-THREE

Hannah...

Once we set the topic of me and Roarke aside, Jessica and I huddle up there in the diner and do some major brainstorming. It becomes apparent that we really do get along so very well and our shared excitement for the festival feeds that connection. Jason calls somewhere in the middle of our third cups of coffee and promises to have at least a couple of guys for the auction in the next twenty-four hours. When we're wrapped up and walking out to her car, I groan. "I haven't even checked on my car. I need to get a rental, which is going to be about an hour drive. Maybe Nick can take me."

We climb inside her BMW, and Jessica is as generous as always. "I can take you into the city tomorrow. No worries at all."

I shake my head. "No. I'm not asking you to do that."

She waves that worry away. "You didn't ask at all. What are friends for if not to help? And we need you mobile. Come on. I'll take you to sing to Snowflake. I'll let Roarke get you home. Or not."

I scowl, and she laughs, but I let it go. I could avoid an awkward moment with Roarke by seeing Snowflake after I get my own transportation again, but Snowflake needs comfort. And I need to see her. And Roarke. Lord help me, I need to see Roarke.

I sink into the leather of my seat and think about last night; every touch, every kiss, every moment is suddenly back with me. I didn't want it to end, and the abrupt way that it ended was like reliving the past. One minute I was with him, and the next minute, I wasn't. I've never felt like we had closure.

Jessica pulls up in front of the veterinary office that sits on Roarke's property, and I realize that I haven't even asked about his father. "How is his father?"

"He had a stroke, and from what I hear, it was rough. He moved to a retirement community down in Georgetown."

"A stroke," I whisper, and I know, I know how badly that must have affected Roarke. And I wasn't here, but I have to remind myself that wasn't my doing. I shake myself and look at Jessica. "Thank you for the ride. I'm excited to get started on everything."

"Do you want to come to the house and work tomorrow?" she asks. "We can get your car and then hunker down together."

"Yes. Great. What time?"

"How about ten? I'll pick you up."

"Perfect," I say, exiting the car and settling my purse across my chest to securely hang at my hip.

Jessica pulls out of the drive, and I turn to wave before facing the office again. Roarke's truck is right beside me. He's here for sure. My gaze lifts and finds the stable to my left, and I know that's where all the sick horses are housed. Snowflake will be there. I start walking, motion detectors setting off lights on a designated path that leads me straight to the door.

I reach the stable and enter the well-lit building to find a horse to my left, with Roarke on one knee next to a pretty redhead, giving her instructions. The horse shuffles slightly. "You're nervous. It's making him nervous."

"I don't want to get kicked."

"You're going to get kicked by acting nervous," Roarke warns. "The animals sense your emotions."

"I'm clearly better with small animals." The redhead stands, and Roarke follows her to her feet. "You need to just deep breathe, Allison."

Allison's gaze shifts and lands on me, and my God, she's gorgeous. Really, really gorgeous. "Hello," she says, and she's not even a little standoffish. She's friendly. She's a nice person, I just feel it, as silly as that might seem. And she's working with Roarke, who has a thing for redheads, or he did when we were growing up. He dated a girl in high school and—

Roarke turns to find me there, and his eyes light. "Hannah."

My instinct is to protect myself from this man, to run before he can hurt me again, but he's completely and instantly engaged with my presence, and already he has closed the space between us. His hand reaches for me as if it will land on my waist, but he catches himself and curls his fingers in his palm. Leaning closer, he lowers his voice and says, "Now would be a good time to ask."

"Ask?"

"You're killing me here, woman," he murmurs, and it's then that I realize what he means. He's not thinking of the redhead. He's thinking about me. He wants me to ask him to kiss me. He wants it to be okay to casually touch me. And Lord help me, I want him to touch me. I want things that will only lead me to heartache. I want everything I lost to be found and never lost again. If only that were possible. If only—

"Can we talk? You know," I lower my voice, "alone?"

"Take the night off, Allison," Roarke calls over his shoulder and then refocuses on me. "Come with me, Han," he murmurs, and this time, he doesn't resist touching me. He catches the fingers of one of my hands with his, and while it's a barely-there touch, that "Han" along with the connection about undoes all my reserve. Han might seem like a silly name to many, but it's not to me. It's what he's called me all my life, what no one else calls me. It's a joke that became an endearment to me. It's memories and love and passion. It's everything we were, which was everything.

He leads me past Allison, deeper into the stable, which is large with a long walkway. I might follow him if he were anyone else, but he's quick to ensure that we're side by side, like we're together. He's not pulling me. He's not leading me anywhere. His touch is pure heat, warmth spreading up my arm and across my chest. I could pull back, I could tell him not to touch me, and I know that Roarke would let me go, and he'd hesitate all the more in the future, too. I just can't seem to want him to let me go, and yet, too soon, he does.

He motions to the right, to an opening on my side of the walkway. We step inside an empty stall well away from Allison's hearing, and the scent of the stables, hay, and horses is all about history, memories, family. I stop just inside the doorway and turn to face him, but our fingers are still joined. He steps into me. I don't step back.

"I'm struggling with so many memories and feelings," I whisper. "I want to pretend we're us again."

"We don't have to fucking pretend. I love you, woman. I have always loved you."

I'm not stunned by these words. I just don't know what they mean to him anymore. "And I love you," I say, comfortable in the honesty of those words, far more so than I was in the fake flippancy of last night. "But we both know that I'm never going to get over you cheating."

His jaw clenches and his fingers slide away from mine, he withdraws, just as he has for years, and that cuts. Instinctively, defensively, I fold my arms in front of me and take a solid step backward.

He runs fingers through the longish strands of his dark hair, leaving it a rumpled, sexy mess before his hands settle on his hips. "I didn't cheat."

Anger comes hard and fast. "Is that why you didn't come after me? Because your mind was on me and not her?"

"I didn't even know that woman. I don't know that woman. I didn't cheat. And as for why I didn't come after you, aside from having a family situation here that I didn't know about until you ran off—"

"I didn't run off. I left. There's a difference."

"Actually, you're right. You left. You made that decision. You didn't even think about hearing me out. You didn't just leave, Hannah, you got on a plane and went to L.A., without so much as telling me. You made it pretty clear that there was more going on than a foolish accusation."

"What does that even mean, Roarke? What more was going on?"

"You wanted out. You wanted a reason to take a break."

"I did *not* want a reason to take a break. I was dying inside after I received that video. You didn't even come for me. You and that woman—"

He steps closer to me again. "*I didn't cheat.* Why would I want that woman? I've dated since you left. I've tried to move the fuck on. I haven't been celibate, Hannah, but no one was you. I don't know why I'm saying this. You don't believe me. Why the hell were you going to marry me if you had so little faith in me?" He holds up a hand. "Don't answer. I don't need my heart ripped out of my chest yet again. Do you still want to meet Snowflake?"

"Roarke—"

"Not now, Hannah. If you know me at all, you know when I hit a wall, I've hit a wall."

"If I know you at all? Me coming back, all I did was open our wounds, so we can bleed together, right?"

He inhales and steps to me again, and I can't

even believe how much relief I feel with that move on his part. He lifts his hand and brushes hair behind my ear. "If I could bleed for you, if I could take all the pain for you, I would, but maybe that's the problem. Maybe that was my mistake."

"I don't understand."

"I know, and the truth is, Han, I don't know how to make you understand. Just know this: if I could turn back time and have a do-over, I'd find a better way. I'd make sure we ended up together. Do you want to meet Snowflake?"

"Yes, please."

"I'll show you where she is."

I nod, and this time, he doesn't reach for my hand, the absence of his touch leaving me cold and wanting. He steps out of the stall and waits on me in the walkway. I step to his side, and we walk three stalls down to the corner, the final door, and stop. "She's drugged and resting. She's been uneasy."

He opens the door, and I step inside to find the white beauty laying down, which is a true sign of just how drugged she is. Most people don't know that horses do sleep laying down, at least that's their deep REM sleep, but they rarely get caught on the ground. As animals prey upon them in the wild, they're hypersensitive to noises. They're up before we know they were down.

"Poor girl," I whisper, moving toward her and kneeling.

For the next few minutes, I talk to her, and yes, I start to sing, a soft country song: "Bless the Broken Road" by Rascal Flatts. A song about choices, about a path that was broken. No. It's really about finding your way back home, whatever home means to you. I have no idea why this song always comes to me when I'm with the animals, but it just feels like it speaks to their plight of feeling lost in the moment. It hits a little too close to home, to me and Roarke right now, though, but I'm committed. I keep singing. Soon, I'm sitting next to Snowflake, stroking her nose, and now I've changed songs. I've decided to get into the festival mood, and I launch into "Rudolph the Red-Nosed Reindeer."

Roarke laughs and sits down next to me. He even joins me in a few Christmas carols for Snowflake's benefit, and I don't know how long the two of us just sit there with Snowflake, but I never did in the past, either. "I need to check on a dog I operated on earlier," Roarke says. "I'll be back. Unless you want to come with me?"

"How bad is the dog?"

"Pretty bad."

I stroke Snowflake's nose. "I'll be back tomorrow, girl. I promise." I kiss her, and Roarke is already standing. He offers me his hand, and all the tension between us has faded. I slide my palm into his, and he helps me to my feet.

The heat between us is instant, the history filling all the empty spaces between us. "I know after what happened earlier this is crazy for me to say, but Roarke, it's good to be back here. It's good to be here with you."

"It's good to have you back, Hannah."

Hannah, not Han. His guard is up, and I want to tear it down, proof that I'm a conflicted mess where Roarke is concerned, but in this moment, I don't care. "I'm going to make my homecoming special. I'm going to make this Christmas festival special. And I'm going to be here to sing to Snowflake every day until she gives birth."

"Snowflake and I are going to hold you to that." He lifts my hand and kisses my knuckles. "I guess I just broke a promise. I kissed you before you asked."

"The hand doesn't count," I say, my voice raspy with emotion.

"Careful now. I'll take liberties and decide I can kiss other places, and it won't count."

"I'll let you know if you cross a line."

"Roarke!"

At the sound of a panicked male voice shouting his name, Roarke tears away from me and bursts out of the stall. I follow him, sealing up Snowflake, and when I exit the stables on his heels, it's to a helicopter landing near the hospital. A few minutes later, I'm watching as a horse is being wheeled into the building, and the magnitude of how special this man is, of how much he does for animals overwhelms me. He was always bigger than life, and a part of me, when faced with that on a real level, when I was his partner in life, was intimidated. For just a moment, I consider his accusation that I ran. Did I run? Was I scared? Was I so intimidated that I felt I wasn't good enough?

As I stand there with that question in the air, Roarke screams my name. "Hannah! I need you!"

Hannah! I need you! The words radiate through me, and I take off running, but this time, it's not away from Roarke. I'm running to him.

CHAPTER TWENTY-FOUR

Hannah…

I reach the hospital, and Roarke is waiting on me. "I'm short an assistant," he says. "I called in staff, but I can't wait. Are you up to scrubbing in for me?"

"Yes. Yes. Of course." It's something I've done in the past, to the point that it was once second nature. To the point that he wanted me to go to vet school, but the idea of failing an animal was just too much for me. "What's the situation?"

"Bella's a prize-winning racehorse who now has what is likely a career-ending fracture." His lips thin. "But I could give a shit about her career. I care about her life and her pain."

And he does. Like his father before him, he hates horses being used for sport, but rather than that driving him away from caring for them, it pushes him to want to be there to ensure someone takes proper care of them. "I know you do. I'm here to help. Let's do this."

He turns for the door and holds it open, and in a matter of minutes, I'm standing with Roarke and several people from the helicopter crew who've graciously stayed to offer us aid, watching as they further sedate the horse, a beautiful black beauty. Once the horse is stable and prepped for surgery, it's just me and Roarke in the operating room.

For the first time in years, I stand beside him, handing him any tool he needs, when he needs it, and watching him work. I'm once again in awe of his skills, his calmness, his focus. It's a good half hour into surgery when two of his crew, both unknowns to me, quietly join us, but I hold my position. Roarke is focused. We all work to help him, not to distract him.

This animal is his life and his world when she's in front of him. There is nothing else, and this surgery is an example of at least part of my reasoning for staying behind in Dallas when he returned for Snowflake. I was emotional, and I would have delayed his return, distracted his attention, even, and being here for Snowflake when she needed him was what mattered.

It's hours later when the surgery is complete and I've officially met the staff that helped us with surgery, while Roarke works through a care rotation for Bella and Snowflake, taking the first shift himself. While he's talking with his team, I join Bella in the stable where she's resting.

Easing down beside her, I sit, stroking her nose, singing to her softly. Roarke joins me and sits down next to me, and this is not an unfamiliar scene. Even in our youth, we'd nurse the animals his father cared for. We look at each other, and there is a world of history and love between us right now. All the bad is gone. Funny how animals heal us, even if it's only for a short while. We sink lower against the wall, and somehow, at some point, my head settles on his shoulder, my lashes heavy. I don't even remember when I fall asleep.

The next thing I know, Roarke is kneeling beside me, caressing my cheek. "Hey," he says softly.

"Hey." I sit up and check on Bella, who's sedated and sound asleep. "She's okay?"

"Yes. One of my crew is going to take over. Let's let her rest. It's almost four in the morning." He stands and pulls me to my feet. "Let's get you to a bed."

Realization comes hard and fast. "I have no car. I have to get a rental tomorrow but right now—"

"Stay here." His hand comes down on my hip, and he steps into me. "Stay with me, Hannah. We're both exhausted, and I *want* you to stay."

There are so many reasons to say no, but none of them seem to matter. Not tonight. Not now. "Yes, but—"

"Don't finish that sentence." His hand settles on my face. "Ask me," he says, and somehow it's both an order and a question, which is so Roarke. He's strong, demanding, even, but in the right ways, at the right times.

But I don't ask, not with words. I push to my toes and press my lips to his. He leans into the connection, and his tongue presses past my lips. The taste of him isn't sex or demand; it's tenderness, it's love. It's friendship. It's all the things we once were and so much of me wants us to be again.

He draws back, strokes my hair behind my ear, and then, wordlessly, laces the fingers of one hand with mine. Together, side by side, we walk toward the main house. "I heard your father had a stroke and moved away."

"Yes to both. I took over the house about a year ago. My old place is now where the interns stay."

His place being a much smaller house on the other side of the property. "I can't believe your father left. Why? Where is he? I'm confused. He loved this place."

"He officially retired and moved to Georgetown with some woman he met."

I glance up at him in disbelief. "Some woman he met? You didn't know her?" They were close, too close for that statement to make sense.

His lips thin, and he wraps his arm around me. "As I said, he had a stroke, and therein lies the answers you're asking for. He wasn't the same afterward."

"That still tells me nothing."

"He couldn't operate. His hand wasn't steady, and he just got angrier and angrier. He rented a place in Dallas, and the next thing I knew, he was buying a house with some woman he met."

Some woman he met. Those words again, and they say so much. Roarke is not pleased by this development.

We reach the giant winding porch of the blue ranch house and head up the stairs. I want to ask more about his father, about how this makes him feel, but there is a weariness about him tonight. He's exhausted from the surgery. I know him. Now is not the time. Will there ever be a time that it's right for me to ask? Do I want there to be? I think yes. I think it's time I admit that this man is still important to me. He's still so very important to me.

We enter the house that was remodeled not

long before I left for college, and it's as beautiful and modern as I remember, with hardwood floors and leather furniture and towering ceilings. We walk the stairs toward the upper level and then down a long walkway toward the master bedroom that had once been his father's.

Entering the large room with a steepled ceiling, it's odd for me to be in Roarke's space. He sits down on the end of a massive oak bed with huge posts, which wasn't here before, that exhaustion I'd sensed downstairs now radiating off him. I sit next to him, and he falls back on the mattress. "We both need showers, but holy hell, I need to just lay here a moment."

I lie back with him, and we both stare up at the ceiling for several long minutes before, in unison, we look at each other. His fingers brush my cheek. "It was good having you here tonight and not hating me."

I catch his hand, emotion welling in my chest. "I don't hate you."

"No, tonight you didn't, but tomorrow's a new day."

I curl up next to him, on his shoulder, and he folds me close. "I don't hate you, Roarke," I whisper. *I can't hate you*, I add silently. I love him too damn much.

He doesn't reply. We just lay there, and I know we have to get up and clean up, but right now, it's us, it's right. He's warm and wonderful and holding me when I thought he'd never hold me again. For now, I just want to live right here in his arms, and I silently will him to wait a little longer to get up. He gives me that wish, and I snuggle in closer to him, my hand on his chest, his heart steady beneath my palm, my eyes heavy, my lashes lowering. And for the time being, I block out the bad, and all is perfect in my world; having Roarke in my life again is perfect.

CHAPTER TWENTY-FIVE

Hannah…

My eyes pop open as a voice calls out, "Roarke! Roarke!"

"Ruth," I whisper and sit up straight, as does Roarke, sunlight trying to burn my eyeballs from my head through the parted curtain.

Ruth's voice lifts in the air again. "Roarke!"

"My grandmother," he says, as if the voice has just started to process in his mind.

"Obviously we fell asleep and never showered."

"Are you up there, Roarke? Don't make my old ankles walk the stairs."

"Oh God, she's coming up here."

"Easy, Han," Roarke says, his hands coming down on my shoulders. "We're dressed. It's not like we're naked and rolling around in the sheets, though I wouldn't complain if we were."

"We're in your bedroom. She's going to think that we were."

"And that matters why?"

"Because everyone is trying to make us a couple again."

"Right," he says, releasing me. "We wouldn't want that. I'll catch her before she gets up here."

I grab his arm. "I didn't mean that the way it came out."

"There you are!" Ruth exclaims, entering the

room, and while perhaps I shouldn't feel a burning need to make what just went wrong with Roarke right, I do. God, I really do.

"Roarke," I whisper, my hand still holding onto his arm.

"Oh, Hannah, we've been worried sick."

At this announcement from Ruth, I release Roarke and turn around to face her. "Worried?" My brows furrow. "I don't understand."

"Jessica went to pick you up, and you weren't at your hotel, and you're not answering your phone."

I blink. "Right. I have no idea where my purse and phone are right now."

"You must have left them at the stable," Roarke suggests.

"What's going on, you two?" Ruth asks, looking between us. "Because you're both a mess. You sure don't look like it's been a night of hot loving."

"Grandma," Roarke chides, while I urgently cross my legs with the need to pee like a Russian racehorse, and having actually met a Russian racehorse, thanks to Roarke, I'm one of the few people who understands that statement. When a horse pees, get out of the way.

"I'm just keeping it real, honey," Ruth replies, plucking her tongue at Roarke and looking between us. "You two are a mess." She waggles a finger at me. "And you, missy. We weren't sure if you were in danger or Roarke ran you off."

"I don't run off that easily," I assure her. "But I'm so very sorry for scaring everyone and letting Jessica run around looking for me. Roarke had an emergency case last night, and I stayed and helped.

I came up here to shower, and we sat down to talk, and that was it. We were asleep."

I can almost feel Roarke's anger at my explanation. I came up here to shower. No. No. I came up here to be with him. God. Can I make this any worse with him? I'm confused. I don't know what I want or what I feel.

Ruth's cellphone rings, and she grabs it from the side of the big bag at her hip, answering and then quickly saying, "I've got her. She helped Roarke with surgery and fell asleep. All is well." She glances at me but keeps talking to the caller. "Yes. Yes. I'll bring her for gingerbread cookie tasting, but she needs a shower and some sleep first. Let's make it after lunch. Yes. Right. We'll handle it." She disconnects. "I told Jessica I'd take you to get a car."

Not Roarke, I think. Of course not Roarke. Roarke has things to do, like sleep and be pissed at me.

"How did the emergency turn out?" Ruth asks.

"Racehorse with a broken leg," Roarke says. "She'll recover, but she won't race again."

"It was tough surgery," I add quickly. "Roarke was incredible."

"He always is, honey," Ruth agrees. "You of all people know that. I always thought you'd end up a vet yourself."

"I'm better behind the scenes and behind the camera." I glance at Roarke, but he doesn't look at me. "I don't have Roarke's calm confidence."

He doesn't comment. He glances at his watch. "I need to get down there and check on Bella."

"I'll come, too," I offer. "But I have to pee first. I'll meet you down there." He nods and heads for the door. "Don't you need to pee, too?"

He glances over his shoulder at me. "I don't do such things. You know that." He pauses beside his grandmother, kisses her, and heads out into the hallway.

I'd laugh at his joke, but it was dry and stiff when he's never dry and stiff. "I'll be right back, Ruth," I say, heading to the bathroom.

"I'll make coffee," she offers.

"Fabulous. Thank you." I hurry into the bathroom, wasting no time doing my business and cleaning up. One look in the mirror and I decide I pretty much look like raccoons have settled under my eyes and then played with my lipstick. I quickly scrub off the mess and open a drawer to find the toothpaste. There's a new toothbrush, too, and I put it to use. A dash of Roarke's cologne and all is well. At least for now. I grab the sink. I don't know what I'm doing with Roarke. He has a good reason to be pissed. I let him feel like I'd opened the door to more, then I'd shut it in the bedroom, but really I didn't. I just need time. I need time that's about me and him, not me, him, and this town, and I don't know if that is even possible.

I push off the vanity and head downstairs, following the scent of coffee to the giant kitchen, with a giant wooden island framed in navy-blue wood. Ruth pours me a cup of coffee, and I join her at the pot, gratefully accepting the brew. I begin to mix it the way I like, adding creamer and Splenda, while Ruth just stands there, watching me, studying me. "Your eyes light when you look at him."

Of course they do, I think. *I love the man.* "I had to pee."

"Your eyes didn't light because you had to pee. That's a silly explanation."

She's right, of course. How did that even come out of my mouth? "I love him. That hasn't changed."

"Then why aren't you together?"

"What did he tell you?" I counter.

"He won't talk about it," she says.

"It's his story to tell you, Ruth. You have to know that."

"He loves you."

"I know that," I say. "I do. I just—I don't know that we love the same way."

Her brows dip. "That's nonsense. You two are amazing together."

"Hi."

We look up to find Allison holding my purse. "Roarke thought you might need this."

And he sent her. Of course he did. She's so pretty. She must be the first person he thinks of for everything. "Thank you," I say, somehow managing a cordial reply when my emotions officially want to explode right here in this kitchen. No, they want to explode outside, standing in front of Roarke. I cross the room and accept the purse. "How are Bella and Snowflake?"

"They're both doing well," she says, shoving red hair from her pretty face.

"Good." I turn to Ruth. "Do you mind taking me to my hotel?" I need out of here before I really do explode on Roarke. What good will that do? And why am I even letting Allison get to me?

Ruth studies me. "Hannah," she warns softly.

"Yes?"

"Are you being objective right now?" she queries.

I blink. "What?"

She purses her lips at me and looks at Allison. "What's Roarke doing right now?"

She laughs and shakes her head. "Would you believe he's suturing a pig's leg? Who'd have thunk it, right?"

Ruth turns her attention back on me. "I repeat. Are you being objective right now?"

God, this woman reads me too well. "No," I admit, with the realization that Roarke was just trying to take care of me and an animal, as well, but there is a lesson here. I'm not being fair to Roarke in all kinds of ways. "And on that note," I add, "I'm going to go check on Roarke. I'll be right back."

She nods, approval in her eyes. I slide my purse across my chest and turn to find that Allison has already gone. I hurry through the house, and when I step onto the porch, Roarke is walking up the steps, urgency radiating off him. "Hey," I say. "What's wrong?"

"I have an emergency case I need to fly out to take care of."

"After Bella just got here?"

"There's some sort of horse sickness that's taken down ten horses." He steps onto the porch. "I really don't have a choice."

"Oh," I say, and I manage to be both disappointed at his departure and proud of the fact that he's the one people come to for complicated cases such as this. "It's kind of incredible and amazing the way you can help with such things."

He studies me a long, hard beat. "What happened in the bedroom—I was wrong."

I blink, stunned by this whiplash change of topic. "What?"

"I'm pushing you too hard," he says. "Me leaving is probably a good thing right now because if I stay, I'm going to keep pushing. I need to give you space."

I close that space between us now, and I dare to press my hand to his chest. "I don't need space. I need to figure this out with you, just you, Roarke, not this entire town. I can't do this while we're the town soap opera."

"You need to think about what you're saying right now and what you really want. You need space."

My hand falls from his chest. "*You* need space."

"No, I don't need space. I've had years of space, but you're a little too good at giving it to me for my comfort right now. I can't do hot and cold with you, Han. Not with you. I'm not wired that way. I *can't* do it." He repeats himself, which he doesn't do, but then he says nothing more. He steps around me and enters the house.

CHAPTER TWENTY-SIX

Roarke...

It's an hour after I leave Hannah on my porch, and I reach for the bag I've packed on my bed when I pause, my jaw clenching. I kneel and pull out the clear plastic sealed box under the bed and set it on the mattress. It's Hannah's. It's all the things she left at my place that I kept finding in random spots for a year after she broke my damn heart. I squat down again and pull out a pair of red boots that we'd bought for her on a trip to Dallas together, not long after I'd proposed to her at the ranch. I'd sat there in that store and watched her light up trying on those damn things. She'd wanted them for under her wedding dress. I'd lit up watching her because, apparently, that's what happens when you fall in love. Everything about the person becomes endearing. The idea of her as my wife sure as hell lit me up.

I open the plastic box and pull out the velvet case inside, lifting the lid to stare down at her heart-shaped ring I'd had custom designed. I'd told her I picked it because she had my heart. Fuck. I'd been so in love with her. Who am I kidding? I still am, but she's never going to forgive me for something I didn't do. That's clear. I shut the lid on the ring, and I stuff the case in the boots before I slide the box back under the bed, the boots beside it. While Hannah is supposed to be beside me in this bed, but I don't know now, any more than I did in the past, how to make that happen.

A few minutes later, when I should be on my way to the airport, I pull over to the property next to ours, the one with the Private Property sign with grass overgrown—wasted land. Land that used to belong to Hannah's family. I've tried to buy it. I've tried to buy it for *her*, but the government owns it, and they won't let it go. They still want that damn highway to come through here one day. I can't buy it. I can't beg for it. I can't get anyone to listen to me, and I've been trying since the day I earned enough money to make that happen. That damn highway that started a war between families, driven by Hannah's family and finished by mine, is my nemesis. In the middle of it all was Jason's father, who was already damn near bankrupt at the time. At the root of every problem between me and Hannah is this property.

No.

No, I stop myself with that. If Hannah and I were as strong as I thought, she wouldn't have left me over a fake cheating allegation. There was a problem there between us that I don't want to believe existed, but it did. But I can't even begin to fix it as long as that damn sign sits on this property, and I'm the only one left who knows why and how it turned so damn bad for three families who were the best of friends until they became enemies.

• • •

Hannah…

Ruth is truly the best. She studies me with a keen eye when we settle into her Buick, which I swear is an older version of the same Buick she had when I was growing up, but she says nothing. She takes me to the B & B to shower, and she and Sue gossip while I dress.

Lunch is a drive-through, and Ruth tells me all about the empire that is now Martha's cookies, and it's fun to listen to her excitement. "I'm helping her now. It's good to have a purpose. We're even coming up with some healthy treats to market. You know I've really learned to take care of myself."

"I love that you do."

"We're going to Hawaii next summer," she says. "I need a beach body to catch me a man."

I laugh, but I'm also aware that Ruth lost the love of her life before I ever left Sweetwater. She's been alone for a long time. I'd love to see her marry again. In fact, I think I should include a few senior hotties for the auction. I love that idea, and I can't wait to share it with Jessica.

It's not long after we eat that I have my own car, and I promise to meet Ruth at Jason and Jessica's place in an hour. I have an overdue stop I need to make—a dreaded stop but also overdue. Forty minutes later, I get out of my rental and stand next to the overgrown gates of my family property. KEEP OUT and PRIVATE PROPERTY signs are stapled to wood and driven into the ground by more wood. Overgrown grass and weeds overtake the property. The government owns it, and I still don't know what happened. I dial my mother, but she doesn't answer. I dial my father, and he doesn't answer. I tell myself that it's about their work demands, but I know I'm wrong. I know it's about me being here. I need to talk to Roarke.

A movement to my left has my gaze lifting and finding a deer, and the apprehension of moments before fades into a smile. A reindeer, I silently jest, because it connects to the holidays and the holidays are always filled with hope and healing. Jessica was right. One way or another, it's time to heal, and maybe if I heal, I'll be better equipped to help my parents do the same.

CHAPTER TWENTY-SEVEN

Hannah…

Amazing how that deer has lifted my spirits.

By the time I'm in Martha's kitchen with Martha, Ruth, and Jessica, sampling gingerbread cookies and looking at holiday decorations to order for the festival, I'm quick to laugh and smile. There is a warmth to the room, to these people who I've missed. I've seen my parents, of course, but only a few times in the past three years. They've been busy, traveling, removed in a way they never used to be. I wish they were here. They were happier here, I think. I was. I was happier. I need to get them back here for the Christmas festival. It would perhaps heal them, as this return to Sweetwater has me.

With that idea expanding and taking root, I throw myself into making the event perfect.

The four of us—Jessica, Martha, Ruth, and me—spend hours planning the festival. One major accomplishment: we nailed down a healthy list of donations and bachelors for the auction. Martha and Ruth literally squeal at the idea of a few hot seniors, chatting about their own highest bids while Jessica and I share a smile.

When Jason shows up near sunset after another pitching practice, he's dressed in baseball pants and a cowboy hat. He glances around at the kitchen walls plastered with photographs and plans. "What the heck happened in here?" he asks, missing the hook on the wall with his hat as he examines our masterpiece.

Jessica rushes forward, scoops up the hat from the floor where it landed, and sets it on her head. "It's every wonderful thing we're doing for the festival and for this town. The holidays will be special here in Sweetwater."

Jason drags her to him and kisses her. "Beautiful," he says, and the warmth in his voice stirs emotions in me, and really, my God, can I stop feeling so many emotions? Roarke is instantly on my mind, but then, he's never far away from my thoughts. The truth is, he's *never* been far from my thoughts.

"I better go," I say. "I want to swing by to check on the horses Roarke just operated on, and I plan to be up early tomorrow to work on the hotel partnerships and really, so much more. I'm going to set my room up as an office and just get a ton done." I take a bite of the newest gingerbread offering and give a thumbs-up. "This one. It's delicious."

Martha beams. "Thank you. That's my favorite, too."

"Why don't you use one of the offices at Roarke's place?" Jessica suggests. "He doesn't use the downstairs at all. You'll be more comfortable."

I give her a reprimanding look, and she just smiles. "Do you want me to call him for you?"

"No, I don't want you to call Roarke for me." I gather my things. "I'll be fine in my room, away from distractions like beautiful animals."

Ruth smiles. "You do love those animals."

"I do. I missed them." And I dare to add, "I missed all of you."

"Prove it and stay around," Martha says.

"I'm with Martha," Ruth chimes in.

"As am I," Jessica adds, giving me a big ol' grin.

"Let me walk you out," Jason offers, rounding the island to take the box of things I've gathered today, from samples of breads to random magazines we've used for inspiration.

"Thanks, Jason."

I'm graced with a round of hugs from everyone before Jason and I make our way to my car. He sets my box in the backseat and then joins me at the driver's door. He stands there looking at me, seeming to want to say something. He opens his mouth and then shuts it, running his fingers through his dark brown hair and then settles his hands on his hips. Whatever this is has me holding my breath, waiting. God, is this where he tells me something I don't want to hear? What could it be?

"He loves you," he says, the light of a full moon illuminating his handsome face. "He loves you," he repeats. "If you have any doubt, don't. That man loves you."

I should feel relief at his words, but Jason's so darn on edge, I can't feel anything but on edge, too. "Why does this seem to distress you so much, Jason?"

"I don't know the details—I didn't know anything at all until a few nights ago—but I do know that that man didn't cheat on you."

Cheating. That's the topic. That's why he's on edge, why I'm now on edge. I don't want to talk about this. "It's complicated."

"No," he says. "No, it's not. It's not complicated at all." He's unleashed now, no more holding back. "I don't know what evidence you had that convinced you he cheated, but I'm telling you right now, he wouldn't lie to me. He *did not* cheat on you. And furthermore," he adds, his voice strong, "there's no one but you for that man. I mean, yeah, he tried. He had women. He dated. He fucked around. That's what we men do when we want to convince ourselves a woman doesn't own us. You know how we know we're owned?" He doesn't give me time to reply. "It doesn't work."

"And it—it didn't work for Roarke?"

"Hell no, it didn't work. You have that man's heart. No one had even a little bit of a chance because he loved you. He loves you." He throws his hands up. "And that's all. That's it. That's everything. That's what I had to say." He starts to turn away and stops. "No, that's not all. You belong here. You weren't even at my damn wedding. And you know why? Because I didn't have an address to send an invitation."

Guilt stabs at me. "I should have stayed in contact. I would have loved to have been there."

"And I'm not paying you for your silence," he continues. "I can't believe you even threw that crap out there. I'm paying you what you deserve. This is a big job, and having someone I love and trust here to do it matters. Keep the money or I will beat your ass like the big brother I am. Got it?"

I laugh. "Got it. But just for the record, little sisters always find a way to pay you back."

"As you've taught me many times growing up. Seriously. Glad to have you back to do it again." He pulls me to him, hugs me, and then he's heading up the stairs, and I swear, I'm thinking of that deer again. Hope. Friendship. Home. I left all those things behind. I left Roarke behind, but I'm back now.

I climb inside my car and think about Jason's words: *He didn't cheat.* Was I young and insecure to the point of being foolish? I was insecure. I know that. I was young, only twenty-one, the girl who'd had a crush on the older boy who became a man, and she finally got the man. And what a man he is, so damn gifted. The funny thing is, now, I don't feel like I did then. I don't feel too young, too inexperienced, too different from him. And yet, I feel like Roarke and I are the same in so many ways. We were always connected.

But did I let insecurity influence how I dealt with that video sent to me of that woman all over him? I don't like how real this feels, how much I now question myself, how unfair I might have been to Roarke. That would explain why he didn't come after me. I'd thought it spelled guilt, but maybe it was anger and hurt.

My cellphone rings. Hope stirs again, that this time the call might be Roarke, and I'm ready to ramble, but it turns out that it's Linda. "How's the little town of Sweetwater treating you?" she asks.

"Better than expected." I start my engine and insert my headset to free my hands. "How are you feeling?"

"Like I need a hot cowboy to come and kiss it better. How is that bachelor auction looking?"

"Quite nice. I'll send you a list of hot prospects tomorrow, but you better start saving money."

"Oh God. I'm dying now. Give me a hint or ten."

I laugh and give her a few names, listening as she practically overheats on the phone when I mention the Rangers' catcher, "Mad Man Madison" to everyone but his mother, who calls him Max Madison.

"I'm going to take out a second mortgage on my offices to get that date." She then goes on to describe this date, and the woman has me in tears by the time we hang up just in time for me to arrive at Roarke's place. I pull through the gates, and I don't stop at the office that's dark now. I park in front of Roarke's house.

Climbing out of the car, I stick my phone in the waistband of my jeans and glance down at my sneakers. I really need to make time to buy a pair of boots tomorrow. For now, I move on to dealing with a night chill that suggests we might really be three days to Halloween. Grabbing the hoodie I'd left in the car earlier, in case I needed it, I pull it on and walk toward the stable. Once I'm there, the motion detectors flicker to life, and the very fact that no one is here is good news for the horses. Bella and Snowflake must not need around-the-clock care.

I hurry through the stable to find Snowflake standing and appearing so much better. I spend some time with her, singing and talking before I leave her for Bella. Bella's laying down, and I have to wonder if the big blue cast on her leg is bothering her or if she's in pain. Either way, she's clearly sedated. When I sit down next to her, I end up with her head right beside me, her eyes watching me. I sing and stroke her nose, and it's hard to explain to someone who doesn't know horses, but I feel her relaxing. I feel myself relaxing with her. Very few people understand why my comfort with horses is so incredible, but Roarke knows. He was there the day I decided I could tame a stallion, too. I'd snuck into the enclosure and ended up on the ground, trampled.

Roarke and his father had pulled me to safety, saved me, and taken me to the ER.

That was the day I lost my ability to have kids, and I was still a kid at sixteen, while Roarke was a man of twenty-two. A month later, with Roarke's help, I'd ridden that very stallion with him on top with me.

I shut my eyes, thinking about that ride, about how I'd started over with his help then. I wonder if that's really possible now. I can feel sleep overtaking me, but I don't care. Being here with Bella reminds me that I can get back up. She's helping me, and I'm going to help her. Darkness overcomes me, and I let it happen. I'll get up soon. I just need to doze off.

• • •

"Hannah."

I blink and sit up to find Allison squatting in front of me. "Hi."

"Hi." She holds up her phone. "Call for you. I guess you're not answering your phone."

I blink wide awake, worried now about what is going on, and take the phone. "Hello?"

"Han, baby, it's two in the morning."

At the sound of Roarke's voice, I warm all over. "Roarke."

"Go to the house. Stay the night. Get some rest."

"Where are you?"

"Houston. Give Allison her phone and call me when you get to the house."

There is no hesitation in me. Not only am I staying here, in Roarke's house, I'm eager to call him back. I need to talk to him. "Yes. Okay. I'll call you back." I disconnect and hand the phone to Allison. "Thank you."

"Of course."

We both stand, and she smiles. "You're good with the animals. And Roarke. One day I hope someone looks at me the way he looks at you."

I feel a pinch of guilt for being jealous of Allison. It wasn't fair to her or Roarke. "You will. You're beautiful and talented." I think of the advice Roarke had given me that day when we rode the stallion that hurt me, the same advice I've let guide me when I'm behind a lens. "Relax into what you're doing. That's when your magic will show. Let the animals, or even the people you're dealing with around the animals, feel your kind soul, not your nerves. Your calm feeds calm. Your nerves feed nerves. Your trust breeds trust."

"Good advice. I think I think too much, instead

of just living in the moment."

"As do I," I say, and with that, I hurry out of the stall and toward the house, Roarke's house.

I want to live in the moment with Roarke. I just hope the moment isn't lost.

CHAPTER TWENTY-EIGHT

Hannah…

I grab the few things I have with me from the car, and without hesitating, I walk up the steps to the house, with a motion detector setting off a splay of light. I know where the key is hidden. Roarke knew I'd know where the key was hidden. I walk to the statue of a stallion in the corner of the porch by a rocking chair, pull open a hidden compartment, and remove the key.

I waste no time heading inside, flipping on lights, and locking up. I grab my box that is now on the ground by the door and find myself staring at the living room, where I've spent so many days of my life. I was always here. Jason, Roarke, and me. Our parents had all been best friends. We'd been best friends.

Eager to talk to Roarke, I head up the stairs and go to his room. Once I'm there, I set my box by the bed, run to the bathroom, and when I finish up there, I kick off my shoes and climb onto the mattress. I dial Roarke, and he answers on the first ring. "Silly woman. What are you doing sleeping out there alone? Sick animals can act out. You could have been hurt."

"You're right. Sorry. I shouldn't have fallen asleep out there. I guess I didn't want to go back to my room. I wanted to be here."

He's silent for several beats. "Where are you right now?"

I swallow hard. "Your bed."

He breathes out. "Ah fuck, Han."

"I, uh—if you don't want me to be—"

"You know I want you there. I just want you to be there with me. Or hell, maybe you don't know. Maybe you never knew. If you knew, you'd have been in my bed all these years."

"I've been thinking about that." I settle back against the headboard.

"What about it?"

"Maybe you were right. Maybe I ran. I was young, and I felt in over my head with you, Roarke. Maybe I didn't let you explain because I just always thought I wouldn't be enough, so if you didn't cheat, then you would."

"That's what you think of me—that I'll cheat? That it's inevitable? That's what you thought of us?"

"I was a girl, not a woman. You'd been my crush my entire life. I'm not a girl anymore, but the girl ruined it for the woman. I miss you."

"But you don't trust me."

"I was a girl," I repeat, "and I was wrong not to listen. I don't know what else to say besides that I'm sorry. And I wanted to say this in person, but you're there and I'm here and I couldn't wait."

"Why the change, Hannah?"

"Being with you woke me up. That's why. I missed you and us, but I'm getting the feeling that you won't get over me judging you instead of trusting you."

"I'll answer that this way. I've been doing some thinking, too."

I inhale and breathe out, terrified of what he's going to say next. "And?"

"I was angry that you didn't trust me, but not once did I look at myself and ask why. Not once did I ask what I did to allow you, the woman who was everything to me, to doubt me. I thought we were so damn strong, that we were shatterproof."

"You didn't cause that in me."

"I don't believe I caused it. I've thought about that as well. I loved you beyond all else. There was no way I could love you more, but that doesn't mean I couldn't have done more. I didn't notice your insecurity. I should have seen it, but damn it, you should have talked to me, too."

"I don't think I realized how strong it was, how insecure I was. Honestly, Roarke, I'm only now admitting to myself how I felt. But it was me, not you. I think it was the wrong time for us. Maybe I needed to find my own place in the world, to stand next to you in yours."

"And now?"

"I'm a damn good photographer. I have a reputation. I left because my boss got in some trouble, but I could have stayed. I'd have had some discomfort for a short window, but I would have made it. I was close to stepping out of his shadow, but I didn't really like that world. It's not me. I'm not high fashion. I'm Sweetwater chic. I'm animals and horizons and people's faces, not their dress sizes."

"That never felt like you, but why event planning not photography?"

"Because I love making everything come together into something beautiful. It's like my form of surgery. I'm having fun. I haven't had fun in a very long time. And as for my photography, at my core, it's my passion, yes. I have some ideas about where I want to go with it, and I'd love to tell you about them, but the point is, I know who I am now. That changes a person. I wish you were here."

"Me, too, Han. Me, too."

"How are the horses?"

"I believe it's a food-borne illness. We're running tests, and I'm treating a good half dozen horses. I called my father. He's joining me here tomorrow."

"Your father? I thought he retired."

"I hope this shows him that he has a purpose beyond a scalpel. I think you inspired that call."

"Me?"

"Yes. At some point, I'll explain why, but not now. Not on the phone."

"When do you think you'll be back?"

"I don't have a timeline."

"What about Bella and Snowflake?"

"One of my staff additions who you haven't met, Javier Vasquez, has been on a humanitarian trip to Mexico to help deal with a cattle contamination. He's back tomorrow. Javier is damn good. You'll like him."

"I like you here better."

"And I will be soon. We both need to rest."

"Yes. I suppose we do."

He's silent a moment. "I wanted to know where you'd go when you got to the house. I wanted to know if you'd go to my bedroom."

A hotspot starts in my chest. "And I did."

"Yes. Yes, you did. Goodnight, Han."

"Goodnight, Roarke."

We disconnect, and I lie back on the mattress, his mattress. The man I love, and yet, even here, on his bed, in his house, we're worlds away, and not just in miles. We just opened a door. Now we have to find out if it can stay open.

CHAPTER TWENTY-NINE

Hannah…

I wake to sunlight and the ding of my text messages. I grab my phone to find a photo of about twelve wild horses running across an open field. Of course it's from Roarke, and I text back: *Beautiful.*

Yes, he replies. *And two of them fell sick this morning. It's not the food supply, or they wouldn't be affected.*

Has your dad arrived? I reply.

My phone rings and I accept the call to hear his answer. "Not yet. Hoping like hell he has some insight."

"What are you thinking?" I ask, sitting up, hearing the frustration in his voice.

"Poison. I think it's poison."

"Intentional?"

"I don't know. I just don't fucking know."

"You'll figure it out. You always do."

"But how many more horses suffer before I do?" He doesn't wait for the answer I can't give him. "I need to go into surgery, but look in the box under the bed. I'll call you later."

"Okay. Good luck in surgery."

We disconnect, and I'm officially curious about what's under the bed. I throw away the blankets and climb out of the bed, but not before I inhale that wholly masculine scent of Roarke clinging to the sheets. I go down on my knees and pull the box from beneath, lifting the lid and sucking in a breath at what I find. He kept my clothes? I have no idea why this feels significant, but it does. Perhaps because it's as if he never let me go, even when I thought that's exactly what he did.

I pull out my old brown cowboy boots with blue flowers on them as well as my old favorite jeans and a black T-shirt with a stallion on it. I even have socks and a bra and panties. This is perfect. I set it all on the bed, and I'm about to get up when I notice something else under the bed to my left. I reach for it and pull it out, sucking in a breath at the sight of my red boots, the boots I planned to wear under my wedding dress.

I stand up and set them on the bed, my heart thundering in my ears. These boots are special. This man is special. Suddenly, I want them on my feet. I want to wear them like I do this life with Roarke. I sit down in the corner on a big overstuffed brown chair, and when I go to pull on the right boot, I hit something. I reach inside and pull out a velvet box. My heart is now exploding. Oh God. My ring. He kept my ring. I open the box and stare down at the heart-shaped diamond, and I'm back under the big oak tree where we carved our names, the river flowing beside us, two horse tied up nearby.

Roarke goes down on his knee in front of me. "What are you doing?" I ask, laughing, in a fabulous mood after a fabulous ride.

"Hopefully not screwing this up." He reaches in the pocket of the jacket he's wearing and produces a box, which he opens. Inside is a stunning heart-

shaped diamond ring. "I had it custom made. A heart because you have my heart. I love you, Hannah. You as my wife will complete my life. Will you marry me?"

My tears are instant, streaming down my cheeks. "Yes. Yes."

He stands up and slides the ring on my shaking hand before he kisses me, and I'm the one who feels complete.

I come back to the present and stare down at the engagement ring. I love this ring. I love this man. God, how I wish I could turn back time, but even as I have that thought, I think of my words to Roarke last night. I was young, too young when we were together. I wasn't ready. We weren't ready. I close the box, and I set it and the boots on the ottoman in front of the chair. I could put the boots and ring back under the bed, but I'm not going to do that. I ran before. I hid from everything, including Roarke. I'm ready to talk about the past to live in the present more fully. When Roarke gets back, I'm going to be right here, waiting on him, and so are those boots and that ring. I don't know if that's where we're headed again, but I no longer want to shut that door any more than I want to force it open, either.

I shoot Roarke a message: *I know you won't read this until surgery is over. I'm thinking about you. That's all I wanted to say.* I hesitate and breathe out, and I think about Jason's insistence that Roarke didn't cheat. I don't know what happened, but I know Roarke cheating on me never felt right. That's why it was so completely devastating. I glance at the clothes I've left on the bed. He kept my things. He didn't let go. I glance down at the message and dare to put myself on the line by adding, *I was really always thinking of you.*

With that, I head to the shower, his shower, and what's telling to me is that I don't feel fear. I don't feel like I've just set myself up to be hurt again with Roarke.

CHAPTER THIRTY

Hannah…

An hour later, I'm dressed, and with what products and items I can scavenge in Roarke's bathroom, I dry my hair and apply the makeup from my purse. As far as a place to work, I think I might just use that big brown chair in Roarke's bedroom. I want to be in this room. It feels like him. It feels like home. It doesn't matter that my parents' place is gone. The truth is that Roarke, and the animals, and this place, just feel like home.

First things first, I make coffee, and then head to the stables to check on the horses. Once I'm through the double wooden doors, I find Allison standing with a tall, good-looking, dark-haired man and a horse.

"Hannah!" Allison greets. "Bella and Snowflake are on their feet and doing well this morning."

I light up. "Marvelous. Wow. That is such great news."

"You must be the infamous Hannah," the man says, crossing to offer me his hand.

I accept his hand. "And you must be the infamous Javier," I reply to the man I guess to be about thirty-five. He's also tall, fit, with thick, wavy dark hair and friendly brown eyes.

He laughs, a low masculine laugh that is as friendly as his eyes. "Indeed I am. Roarke told me to expect you around the stables."

"And Roarke told me how magnificent you are at saving animals. I'm honored to be around the stables with you." I look between Javier and Allison. "I made coffee if either of you wants some. Just walk on into the house. I left the door open. I'm going to say good morning to the horses."

If either thinks it's strange that I'm in Roarke's house, they don't react as if they do. I head toward Bella's "bedroom," as I like to think of their stalls, and Javier calls out, "There are two horses joining the retirement farm today. Roarke thought you might want to greet them on arrival."

I stop walking and smile with both the opportunity and the fact that Roarke told Javier I'd want to be involved. I turn to look at him. "What time?"

"Late. About six o'clock. I can call you when they arrive."

"I'll be here," I say. "And thank you. I want to go visit the retirees anyway. How many are there now?"

"Twenty here. He bought a property sixty miles south that has fifty horses."

This warms me. Roarke saves animals. It's so damn sexy. "That's a lot of horses that need attention. I'm looking forward to helping give it to them."

He smiles, a very nice smile, and I don't miss the way Allison is watching him with intense eyes. She didn't look at Roarke like this. She likes Javier. I might just have a little matchmaker in me, because I like them together. With that thought, I turn and head toward Bella, and I decide right then that I need to go to my room and get my camera. I'm itching to do what I once did: photograph the animals, capture the special moments that show how perfect they are when we as humans are so damn imperfect. Those shots will be my prize-winning, career-making shots, because they're my passion shots. That's what my life has been missing. Passion. No. A love for life.

It's midmorning when I walk into the bed and breakfast and become a victim of the Sue Avalanche. Her comments and questions include:

"I noticed you weren't here last night."

"I told Debbie over at the country store how cute you two are together."

"What was the emergency that got flown in the other night?"

"Where's Roarke?"

"Are you two planning a wedding again?"

That last one punches me in the belly. "I don't know about a wedding, but we're planning a Christmas festival with Martha's new gingerbread cookie being launched during the event."

Of course, I know this reply will have her calling Martha, but that's fine by me. As long as I don't have to answer any questions. When I leave with my suitcase, she's all smiles. Of course, I haven't been officially invited to stay at Roarke's place more than last night, but my gut says I need to be clear on where I stand, and I'm pretty sure my suitcase and me in his bedroom makes my point.

I stop by the store, shocked and pleased to meet no one I know there, and it's not because I don't want to get reacquainted with people. It's about what I said to Roarke. I need to figure this out just him and me, and that's the one negative to Sweetwater: everyone is always watching. There is no privacy. For now, though, I get my privacy, and with popcorn, fruit, and veggies, I'm stocked for a healthy few days of work. With the holidays coming, it's eat well now, and eat junk later with no guilt. By noon, I've made myself what my mom used to make me: biscuits and tomatoes with salt and pepper. It's a whole lot of heaven in my mouth.

I'm done eating, and I haven't heard from Roarke, but I don't read into that at all. He's got his hands full. He needs to stay focused on those sick horses. Instead of fretting about his silence, I hunker down with coffee in the big chair in Roarke's room and start working. Priority number one: I need hotel partnerships. I figure that out quickly. Priority number two: I need a website to host the auctions. Finding someone to do this takes me a few hours, but soon, the work is in progress.

It's about four o' clock, and I'm starting to get anxious about that text to Roarke. Have I misread him? Am I taking this to a place he didn't want to go? I mean, I did dive right into sex. Maybe that's all that's comfortable to him with our history. My mother's many warnings about not being too available to men and keeping my legs shut claw at me. I head down to the kitchen and make another pot of coffee when my cellphone that, yes, is attached to my palm, rings, and this time, it's Roarke.

"Hi," I say. "How are—"

"I never stopped thinking about you. I can't

talk. I just wanted to say that on the phone."

I smile and tear up. "I'm glad you did. Go. Take care of the horses."

"I'll call you tonight. I can't promise when."

"Don't worry about me."

"Where are you?"

"Your kitchen. Is that a problem?"

"No. No, that is not a problem. Bye, Han."

"Bye, Roarke."

We disconnect, and I set the phone down. I'm terrified. I still love him so damn much. He could hurt me. I turn and glance out the window, and I'm in disbelief. There's another deer. It feels like a sign, it feels like more of that hope. There is hope in the air. There is hope for me and Roarke.

CHAPTER THIRTY-ONE

Roarke…

I've barely hung up with Hannah when my father's truck pulls up to the house where I'm staying, just north of a ranch owned by the Native American reservation that called me here to help. I haven't seen the old man in six months, and I'm not sure what the hell to expect. The last time we were together was in Dallas, at one of Jason's baseball games. He'd been more himself than he had been since the stroke, and unlike today, his woman, Becca, a pretty brunette in her forties and ten years his junior, had been on his arm.

Today, he looks fit and younger than his fifty-five years, and I hope like hell he stopped smoking those damn cigarettes they suspect caused his stroke. He doesn't have one in his hand, and that's a good sign. He walks toward the porch, and I step out of the shadows. His face lights up, and I hurry down the stairs to be embraced.

"Damn Horse Wrangler." He eases back to look at me. "I can't believe you're a YouTube sensation."

I scrub my jaw. "You and me both. You and me both."

"Yeah, well, it suits you." He imitates me and scrubs his jaw. "Not as pretty as me," he adds, "but the camera does you wonders."

I laugh. We do look alike. He's tall and fit with

thick dark hair sprinkled with the salt and pepper I, no doubt, will one day have myself.

"Why don't you do this week's edition with me? We'll let the viewers tell us who's prettier."

"Oh hell no. I'm not letting my boy's feelings get hurt."

This is the father I grew up with. This is the man who I know battled to save animals and taught me to fight for them like family. "Now," he says. "Let's get serious. Talk to me about the poison and these horses that need to be saved."

We head down to the stables, and he examines the animals as I share my suspicions as well as the lab work I've run. "I know a guy we need to call in." He pulls his phone from his pocket, and a few minutes later, he announces, "He's catching a chopper in Wyoming. He helped me with a case back when you were about ten, I think. Read a lot like this one."

"That's good news because I had another horse fall tonight."

"You think someone's targeting the reservation?"

"No one is ready to go down that rabbit hole right now, but we can't close any doors."

"Any animal need urgent care now?"

"They're stable. I need to talk to you about something else. How about a good cup of strong coffee? It's the only way this place makes it."

"I need some more hair on my chest." He pats my shoulder, and a few minutes later, we're at an old wooden table with cups in our hands.

"I'm not coming back to Sweetwater if that's

what you want, but I'm feeling back to me. My savings is plenty enough to live on, but I'd like to see the world. I'm looking at doing some jobs that will help me make that happen and let me get back to helping animals." He winks. "I'll even work for the Horse Wrangler."

I chuckle. "You working for me? That'll be the day."

"I miss my son." He narrows his eyes. "This isn't what you wanted to talk about now, is it?"

"It's part of it, but there's more."

"I'm listening, son."

"Hannah came back to help with the camp Jason and I are running."

"Hannah," he breathes out. "I see. Does she know?"

"No, she doesn't know. I'm the only one who was home when this happened. Jason was playing ball, and I didn't even know until Hannah was gone."

"How important is she to you now, present day?"

"I love her. I have to find a way to make the past right."

"Do her parents know she's back?"

"I don't know."

"Well if they do, I can tell you right now, they will lash out. They will end you and Hannah again just like they did before."

"And we both know who bankrupted her family. That was you. I just don't know how I tell Hannah you drove them to bankruptcy."

"I had no choice." He leans forward, tapping the

table. "You know this. They sold out the portion of their ranch for that damn highway the state wanted to run through Sweetwater and just about had Jason's parents convinced to sell the entire ranch, or at least his father. I don't believe his mother ever knew. His dad made rash decisions because of his gambling issues. That highway was going right in front of the sanctuary, and that meant we would be shut down. The animals would be homeless. I did what I had to do to stop that."

"Right." My lips thin. "You hired someone who found an endangered insect of some kind in the right territory to use the protection laws to shut down the highway."

"It's not my damn fault Hannah's parents spent the down payment the government gave them before it ever hit their account. It's not my damn fault the government kicked them out for not paying it back. That didn't have to happen. I offered to help them with the payments. They declined my help and lashed out at you. You know what I believe. Her father told me that you would never marry his daughter."

He believes Hannah's father was behind that video that was sent to Hannah. "I know what you believe," I say. "I need some air." I stand up and leave the room, walking outside the porch and grabbing the railing. I should have told Hannah everything when it happened, but I was just so damn stunned by how easily she believed I'd betray her. And what defense did I have but to demonize her parents? Would I do it all over again the same? Maybe. Maybe not. I'm a different man now. She's a different woman. All I know is that my father is right. It's time to make this right.

A plan starts to take shape, and I walk in and talk to my father. "Are you willing to tell your story?"

He stands up. "Damn straight. You want me to talk to Hannah?"

"No. I'll talk to Hannah, but I have a plan to fix this mess that's going to take teamwork."

"Tell me how to help."

I pull my phone out and dial Jason. "Hey, man, how are the horses?"

"We're working on a solution. We need to talk, and I'm going to ask a favor."

"I'm listening. What's up?"

"In person. This needs to be in person. Can you come here?"

"That sounds serious."

"It is. I need you, man."

"Then, I'm on my way. Tell me where I'm going."

CHAPTER THIRTY-TWO

Hannah…

I'm just heading out to greet the new members of the horse family when Jessica pulls up in her shiny BMW. "Hey, you!" she greets, climbing out of the vehicle. "I heard I'd find you here."

"Hey!" I say, hurrying down the stairs to meet her. "What's going on?"

"Jason had to go out of town. I thought maybe I'd stay with you, and we could have a girl slumber party to plan the Christmas festival here at Roarke's place. I can even help with the animals."

"That sounds wonderful," I say, truly pleased with this idea. I want to get to know Jessica, and having a new friend here would be welcomed. Of course I might not stay, but I shove aside that idea the minute I have it. I want to be here, and even if things don't work out for me and Roarke romantically, that man is still the best friend I've ever had. I need to keep him in my life.

"I even bought vegetables and popcorn," I say. "We can feast."

"Seriously?" She crinkles her nose. "That's the best you can do? Vegetables and popcorn?" She gives me a sly look. "But I must say, grocery shopping is very intimate. It didn't take you long to move in here."

"I don't know that I have moved in. I'm just—

I'm watching the animals while he's gone."

"Because he doesn't have a staff to do that?"

"Okay, smartass," I chide. "They have their hands full. And right now, I'm on my way to welcome the new horses to their retirement home. Want to come?"

"I'd love to." She dangles her keys. "I'll drive. I know where we're going."

A few minutes later, we're greeting the two new horses with Javier by our side. It doesn't take long for me to decide that Javier is intelligent, good-looking, and kind. He's really impressively skilled as well, as I determine when one of the horses is acting oddly, and he takes immediate action.

"He's a good addition to the team, don't you think?" Jessica asks, watching him work.

"He is. How long has he been here?"

"About a year, I think. From what Roarke and Jason both told me, Roarke was really feeling the loss of his father, and he needed help. He and Javier get along well. Javier is really all about the medicine. Roarke is more the surgeon with a magic way of taming and calming animals."

"A gift Roarke inherited from his father," I say. "I still can't believe his father left."

"He was gone before I got here," she says. "I've never seen anyone but Roarke in action." She glances over at me. "That man was a rock for Jason when his parents died. He helped us come together. I value his friendship. I value him as a man who gives and protects. And that man loves you."

"I love him, too," I say softly but without hesitation, my heart squeezing with the words.

"But it's complicated," she supplies.

"Yes, it is, but it feels less so every moment that I'm here."

"That's a good thing," she says, wrapping her arm around me, and the two of us grab a bushel of carrots Javier provided and head out to the field to feed the horses. Just thinking about the fifty additional horses at the other facility brings tears to my eyes. They'd all be dead if not for this sanctuary, if not for Roarke.

It's hours later when we sit in the kitchen with wine-filled glasses, cheese, and veggies. "You're a good influence on me," she declares.

"Because there's no Whataburger here. Beware if there is. I'll eat your meal and mine."

She laughs and holds up her glass. "Whataburger is good eating."

Her phone buzzes, and she looks down. "Roarke posted a new video."

"I can't quite get my head around Roarke posting videos."

"Well, he doesn't. Would you believe it's Mick, one of his warehouse guys? This tall, brawny, good-looking black guy who looks like he's been lifting weights with Arnold Schwarzenegger. He's a complete YouTube fanatic and was some sort of tech genius in the army."

I sip my wine. "Army. Interesting. I'd like to meet him. Seems we have all kinds of heroes running around here."

"I think he really is a hero. He was in combat, and I've heard stories about some sort of Special Operations. Anyway, he's the one who loaded the video that started the whole Horse Wrangler thing. He started it all and, of course, he gets a cut of the money. Roarke wouldn't have it any other way." She scoots over close to me. "Let's watch the new video."

"Yes, let's," I say, and for the first time ever, I'm going to do so without denying I'm doing it, without denying my pride in Roarke, without feeling any anger.

"Oh my," she says. "That's—" She looks at me. "Is that his father?"

"Yes," I say, watching as the two of them work with a horse that's basically losing its shit. "Yes, it is. He looks good."

"He does," she says as my phone rings.

I grab it from the counter to find Roarke calling. "That's him," I say. "I'll be right back."

She smiles. "Take your time."

I wave at her and answer the line. "Hey," I say, walking out into the living room and settling onto the comfy brown couch.

"Hey, baby. How are you?"

Baby. The endearment spoken in a soft and tender voice does funny things to my belly.

"I'm fine," I say. "How are you? I just saw the video you loaded with your dad. That seemed pretty special."

"It is. It damn sure is. He's better, Han. I read articles and talked to doctors about how strokes can change a person's personality, sometimes permanently. Thank God, it now looks to have been temporary in his case. He's even taking on contract vet work."

"That's such good news. Was he able to help with the case you're on now? Did you find any answers to your problems? Why are the horses sick?"

"My father has an expert he's worked with coming in tomorrow. We'll see. I had another horse go down today. I hope like hell we can stop this before we add to the numbers."

"Have any died?"

"Not since I got here."

"Where are you exactly?"

"A Native American reservation just outside of Houston. I'm in what amounts to a cabin that they call a house. What about you?"

"I hope you don't mind, but Jason went out of town, and Jessica showed up here to help greet your new horse retirees. We ended up at your house for a sleepover."

"Did you now?"

"Yes, I mean—Roarke, do you mind?"

"I mind that I'm not sleeping over with you. Of course I don't mind, Hannah. Damn it, woman, you know—" He curses under his breath. "When I get home."

"When do you think that will be?"

"Right now, I have no end date for this hell." His father calls his name.

"I heard. You need to go. I'm just getting drunk on wine and the scent of you all over this house. I'm good here."

"Hannah," he whispers. "I'll see you soon."

We disconnect, and for the first time in weeks, I realize that Saturday night, Halloween, is two days away. It's also my birthday, and the only thing I want this year is to be with Roarke, and, ironically, considering I'm in his house, I don't think I'll get that wish. I think of the holidays before me and wonder where I'll be on Thanksgiving Day, aside from in a panic preparing for the Christmas festival only days away. Will I be with Roarke, or will the past be just that—the past—and us with it?

CHAPTER THIRTY-THREE

Hannah….

The next morning, I wake to a text message of an amazing spotted horse, followed by a call from Roarke. "Morning, sunshine," he murmurs, his voice etched with exhaustion and worry.

"You don't sound good."

"Every horse has lived. I'm damn good, baby. I'm damn good. Just tired and ready to find a solution to this problem rather than managing the results of the problem."

Someone calls his name, and he curses. "I need to go. I'll try to call you later."

"Don't worry about me. I'm here. I'll be here."

He's silent a moment, and then he says, "Make sure you mean that when you say it." And then he hangs up.

I sit up and think about that "baby" endearment that feels so much like our past, but the past isn't on my mind as I shower and dress. The present is on my mind. The future is on my mind. The jeans, boots, and pink T-shirt I pull on were once my uniform, and I slide into them now with ease and comfort. I slide into this life like it's my life because I've lived in this world more than any other. Which is exactly why when I pull up to Jason's house, I open the door without knocking. I've been here a million times. This is what we do in these parts between these families.

I'm greeted with coffee and Martha's fresh cinnamon rolls that are so big and delicious they successfully void out the vegetables I ate last night, but they're so worth it. While pigging out, I settle in with the team—Martha, Ruth, and Jessica—and get to work. As the day progresses, we're all excited about how well the Christmas festival is coming together. I end the night alone in Roarke's house, in his bed, wishing he were here. I'm laying there, staring at the ceiling, thinking about him, when he calls.

"Hey," I murmur. "How's it going?"

"We're making progress. We think we found a contaminated pesticide. Tomorrow is going to be a good day filled with answers. I know it."

"That's great news." We chat for several minutes about the horses here and there, and finally, he asks, "Where are you right now?"

"Bed," I say. "I was about to go to sleep when you called."

"What bed, Han?" His voice is low, rough, almost demanding and, somehow, not demanding at all. More urgent, a question delivered as if he's hanging on a limb, waiting for my reply.

I don't want him to fall. I don't want to fall, either, but I climb out there with him anyway, because there is no option but to take a chance with this man, no other option at all. "I've decided I'm house-sitting for you. It's easier to check on the horses."

"And when I get back?" he asks, his voice velvet smooth.

Heat rushes through me. "I guess we'll figure that out when you get back."

"Yes. Yes, we will. Goodnight, Han."

"Goodnight, Roarke."

We disconnect, and I slide down onto the pillow with a smile on my lips. When he gets back. "Hurry, please."

• • •

Another morning comes, and I'm up early, this time dressed in nice jeans and a lacy top, with good reason. I'm on a mission in town today to put together the scavenger hunt. The hunt is simple: each participating store will have a different version of Martha's Christmas cookies somewhere to be found along with a ticket. The hunter who finds the ticket will get a prize. If the participants get all the tickets from each store, they can enter to win a grand prize.

I spend hours explaining this to two dozen stores, and more than half ask about me and Roarke.

"When's the wedding?"

"What happened, honey?"

"What did he do to win you back?"

"What did you do to win him back?"

"You lucky girl. He's so crazy hot."

"When's the wedding?"

It's a little bit of torture because it's dodgeball, and dodgeball is not a gentle game.

By noon, I've eaten a candy bar and headed on to meetings with our hotel partners. Come late afternoon, progress is made, and Jessica calls.

"Coffee?"

"Food. I need food. I'm pulling back into town. Can you meet me at the diner?"

"You bet. I'm hungry, too. I'll be right there."

I pull into the diner parking lot, and a number I don't know registers on my caller ID. I kill my rental car engine and answer. "This is Hannah."

"Hannah, if you don't come and talk to me about your car, I'm going to require something more than cake pops. Perhaps a meal cooked by Martha."

"Nick," I say. "Oh God. I'm sorry. I can't even believe I forgot my car. It's dead, right?"

"It's going to run you about two grand to fix."

"Can I sell it for parts or anything like that?"

"What are you going to do for a car?"

Good question. "I guess I'm sucking it up and buying a new one. I shouldn't have bought a used car that was that old anyway. Actually, sell it and keep the money for your trouble."

"I'm not going to keep the money," he says. "When I sell it, you have Martha invite me to dinner."

I laugh. "I'll get you the invite. I can't believe you're back."

"Back at you, Hannah. Hear you're back with Roarke."

"The town is singing. No comment on that. How are your parents?"

"They moved," he informs me. "I'm here alone for Thanksgiving. That's a hint."

"Dinner. Thanksgiving dinner. That's what you've

been hinting at?"

"Yes," he says, "and for a city girl, it didn't take you long to figure it out."

"Because I'm not a city girl. I'll confirm that Martha's cooking and get back to you."

"And I'll get the car sold."

I laugh again, and we disconnect. A few minutes later, I have a piece of cornbread on the table with butter, lots of butter, slathered on it. I just couldn't wait on Jessica. I've just stuffed a huge bite in my mouth when Luke sits down in front of me. "There she is." He grins his pretty-boy grin. "Stuffing her face like always."

I about choke on the bite in my mouth. "Gee, thanks," I say, reaching for my water. It's like we're back to the old days, when we were kids picking on each other, only he's not looking at me like a kid sister anymore. "That's how I want to be remembered."

"You know I remember all kinds of things about you."

My brows dip. "Stop being flirty. I don't like it, and you're not even doing it well. You're acting like the guy who used to pick on me while undressing me with your eyes."

"I'm here!" Jessica announces, joining us.

"Thank God," I say. "Luke is being creepy."

"Not the mayor of our little town," she says, motioning for him to get up. "I need in, and you aren't staying."

He stands and lets her get in. "I'm not being creepy. Jesus, you women. I'm just being friendly." He sits down in front of me again. "I know you're with Roarke."

"Yes," Jessica says, meeting my stare, "she is."

My cellphone rings, and I look down to find Roarke's number. "I need to take this." I answer the call. "Hi," I say, standing up only to have Luke step in front of me.

"Hannah," he says.

I scowl. "Luke, move. I told you I need to take this."

"Luke," Roarke says, and he doesn't sound happy. "I heard you were with Luke."

"Oh my God. This town." I walk toward the bathroom. "I'm not with him. I was waiting on Jessica, and he sat down."

"Acting like you were lunch."

I head into the single-user bathroom and shut the door. "Acting like a creep, as I just told him. Ask Jessica."

"Are you trying to get me back for something I didn't do?"

"What? Oh God. No. No. No. Roarke, don't do this. I promise you, *I promise you* that is not happening. I just want you. I want you here with me."

"Fuck, woman, if you ever loved me, cut me loose if that's where this is going."

"I don't even know what that means. I was with Luke for about three minutes until Jessica saved me. How anyone even had time to call you, I don't know."

Someone yells his damn name again. "Damn it to hell," he curses. "I need to go. I'll leave you to your lunch."

"With Jessica. Call Jessica. Please call Jessica."

"I've got to go." He hangs up.

I press my hands to my face. "We're too broken," I whisper. "I can't fix this."

I inhale and force out the air. I need to go back out there. I have to do my job. I'll deal with this emotionally when I'm alone. I rotate and open the door, walking toward the table. Thankfully, I find Jessica alone. "Please tell me he's really gone."

"He is." She leans forward. "What's wrong?"

"Roarke. Someone called and told him I was with Luke." And as much as I mean to, I can't hold back. "I thought he cheated, and now—now, I don't think he really did, and he just accused me of trying to get even."

Her eyes go wide. "Oh God." She grabs her phone. "I'll call him."

I grab the phone. "No. No, he's working. I can't clutter up his work with this. It's too important."

"That's mature of you, but someone already did that for you. If he called in the middle of his work, they upset him. He's distracted. Compromise. I'll send a text. Okay?"

She's right. Roarke was needlessly distracted. "Whoever did this to him, to us, pisses me off."

"Me, too. Let me help fix it."

I nod. "Yes. Okay. Thank you." I release her hand.

She types a message and hits send before reading it to me: *She called him a creep and thanked God when I showed up. She loves you. She's really upset right now because you were worried about this when you have animals to protect. I promise you,*

Roarke, she did nothing even a little wrong, and you know I'd tell you if I thought otherwise.

I tear up. "Thank you. Thank you so much, because the thing is, I deserve what I just got. I didn't give him the benefit of the doubt."

"You want to talk about it?"

"Yes. But not here. I'm angry after what just happened."

"Agreed. Why don't we go see the new retirees again? We can talk there."

"Perfect." I flag down the waitress.

An hour later, we're sitting on a bale of hay, watching the horses roam, and I hurl all of my junk at Jessica. "And there you have it," I say after I tell her everything. "My biggest mistake."

"You were young. He was your idol. That wasn't healthy."

"He was my best friend."

"You hadn't gotten past the idol part. That was youth."

"Well, whatever it was, it may have been too much to overcome."

"Nonsense," she says, but there's been nothing from Roarke in reply to her message. She squeezes my hand. "You are the first to remind us all that he's working. And his work is all about focus. He'll call you, not me."

Only he doesn't call. Hours later, many hours later, I lay in the bed, staring at those red boots, and watch the clock turn to midnight in silence. It's my birthday, and I'm celebrating with Roarke's silence.

CHAPTER THIRTY-FOUR

Hannah…

I stay at Roarke's place again. I decide that if he wants me to leave, he'll have to tell me to my face. I need him to know that I'm in this, wherever it takes us. So I stay, but I don't fall asleep with a call from Roarke. I also don't wake up to a text or a call the next morning. I wake up to the doorbell and knocking. Afraid something is wrong, I pull on a robe and rush downstairs to the front door to find Jessica standing there, already dressed, with bright-pink gloss on her lips.

"We have to go to Dallas. Every Halloween the team has a huge party for charity. It's a perfect time for you to meet everyone who will be involved with the auction."

"Dallas?"

"Yes. I booked you a room at the Ritz, which is where the party is taking place. We're paying. We're staying there, too, despite having an apartment in the city. Drinking and driving don't mix, and we figure we'll drink."

We. We. We. She and Jason are a great "we." My heart hurts just thinking about being at some party while Roarke is gone. "Jessica—"

"He had an emergency last night. They were out on the range somewhere dealing with it. I heard he fell asleep a few hours ago. He's not avoiding you."

"Right," I say. "That makes sense." Only it doesn't because he'd normally tell me about it, but then, that was the past. This is the present, after the mess between us.

"Stop looking like you're being punished. I promise you, you will love this, and it's good for the festival."

That snaps me out of my negative attitude. "Right. The Christmas festival. When do we leave?"

"The minute you're ready. It's a long drive, and I want us all to have time to rest."

"All?"

"Well, you and me. Jason is already up there. He had a team meeting." She waves her hands at me. "Go. Dress. I know a Whataburger on the way."

I laugh and rush toward the stairs. A girl trip will be good, and I can check in on Linda before I come back. Actually, I need to just buy a car while I'm there so I don't have to keep paying for the rental. I hurry up the stairs and grab my phone from the nightstand. I've missed a call from my mother. I dial her back. "Happy birthday!" It's both of my parents singing to me.

"Thank you both," I say to them, as I'm on speakerphone. "How's the annual event coming together?"

"Horrible," my father grumbles. "If we had you here, you could organize it for us instead of some Sweetwater Christmas festival." He grunts as my mother has obviously elbowed him. Her famous move to shut him up is easy to pin down.

"Why don't you come to that festival and see my good work?"

"I don't think we can do that, honey," my mother says. "But send me pictures."

"We have a gift for you," my father says. "But we don't know where to send it."

"Bring it to the festival," I say. "It's a great way to celebrate Christmas early. You can sit on Santa's lap and ask for a bottle of that whiskey you like to land under the tree."

"You don't give up, daughter, do you?"

"I wouldn't be your daughter if I did."

"You come here for Christmas," he counters.

Christmas. Where will I be for Christmas? "We'll talk at the festival."

My father laughs. "Ah, daughter."

A few minutes later, we hang up, and I check my phone. Nothing from Roarke. It's as if the idea that I might punish him turned a switch. I'm on, and he's now off, and it's letting me see how easily he could hurt me. He still has too much power over me, and I don't know how to fix that. I don't even know if I want to try.

• • •

I enjoy the ride with Jessica, and during our travels, she tells me all about meeting Jason and her ex cheating on her. It's a story that has me in knots because I felt all the things she felt, but more so because I love Roarke. She didn't love her ex. There was no better man waiting on me. There was only Roarke, left behind. It's fairly early when we arrive in Dallas, only two o'clock, and both of us are tired. We head to our rooms to rest.

"Oh, by the way," she says as we both step away from the registration booth. "It's a costume party. I had a bunch of options sent to your room. I like the nurse for you. You're Roarke's nurse to all the animals. Now you can be his naughty nurse. It's kind of hot, you know?"

I laugh, but Roarke isn't here, so he doesn't need a naughty nurse. My room is of course luxurious, and I collapse on the bed, willing my phone to ring. It does. With Linda's number. "Happy birthday!" she exclaims. "Tell me how happy!"

"Very last minute, I'm here in Dallas for a Halloween party," I say. "I thought I'd invite you to breakfast tomorrow."

"What? Oh no. I'm not there. I'm in Houston for a photoshoot."

"Well, that kind of sucks," I say.

"It does, and I have a present for you. I need your Sweetwater address."

My Sweetwater address. That's a complicated topic. "Come and bring it to me at the festival."

"That sounds perfect. It's good. You'll love it."

We chat a few more minutes, and when we disconnect, I toss my phone on the pillow and curl on my side. I need to sleep and forget that today is my birthday. Roarke knows it's my birthday, and his silence makes a point. He can't do this. We aren't doing this. Why did I let myself try to believe otherwise?

CHAPTER THIRTY-FIVE

Hannah...

I can't rest, so I get an Uber to the mall and buy a black dress and black cowboy boots and decide that's my costume. The dress has a flared skirt and a good amount of cleavage, and I buy it despite this. If ever I needed to feel like a woman, it's on my birthday after being dumped. If anyone asks, I'm a country witch. I've just finished flat-ironing my hair and applying stay-on pink lipstick when there's a knock on the door.

I slide the strap of a cute sparkling lipstick purse across my chest, to rest at my hip, and answer the door. I find Jason and Jessica standing there. Jason in his baseball uniform and Jessica in a Catwoman jumpsuit. I wait for Jason to wish me happy birthday and Jessica to feel bad that she didn't know, but he doesn't. "What the hell kind of costume is that?" he asks.

"I'm a country witch, and if you give me a hard time, I'll curse you on the mound."

"Whoa. Whoa. Whoa." His hands are in the air. "I surrender. You don't joke about that shit."

I look at Jessica. "You're looking hot, mama."

"Thank you. I have to compete with all the groupies who want him."

Jason wraps his arm around her and pulls her close. "No competition. You win every time, baby."

He kisses her soundly on the mouth, and my heart squeezes. They're an adorable couple. I'm really happy for them both. I hate that I feel their happiness as a reminder of my loss of Roarke.

Together, the three of us make our way to the party. "Each player picked a playlist of songs for the DJ," Jessica informs me. "So, before every song, they announce the player, and every time a player's song is picked, he donates money to the charity. There's going to be all kinds of music. It's fun, right?"

"Yes," I say. "Fun."

And it is. Soon, we're inside a room with music, food, booze, and even stages all around the event space for people to get up on and dance. There are goblins, zombies, fairies, and much more. And of course, lots of baseball players in uniform. The songs range from Jason Aldean, NSYNC, Taylor Swift, Brett Young, and even Billie Eilish. I meet the team, including Max Madison, the Mad Man catcher, and he's a hottie—big, fit, with pretty green eyes and a strong jaw—who I aspire to introduce to Linda. When he flirts, I tell him so, too. "I have the perfect woman for you," I say. "And she's not me."

Jessica laughs and links her arm with mine. "She's Roarke's woman."

"Oh, fuck," Max curses. "Sorry. Roarke's a badass. Love that guy."

"I need a drink," I murmur and pull away from Jessica to find the round bar in the center of the room with an empty spot with my name on it. I order myself champagne. Jessica joins me and says, "Two tequila shots." She nudges me. "We aren't driving. Let's do what I never do and drink."

The shots are set in front of us, and I look at them and her. "You're a bad influence."

"No one says that to good girl me. I kind of like it." She laughs. "At least when we have a hotel room to walk to and Jason to protect us."

We pick up the glasses, downing the shots, and oh God, it burns a path down my throat, warmth spreading over my neck. "One more!" Jessica yells.

"No," I say. "I'll be drunk in about three minutes if we do that."

The bartender fills our glasses. A baseball player by the name of Jack Jackson who I met earlier, a black guy with biceps that could be globes, steps to my side. "I heard you're Roarke's woman."

"I'm just a girl, standing at a bar, drinking too much tequila. I'm also the girl who'll auction you off in garters for the children's hospital if you're not careful."

He laughs and holds up his hands. "You win. No more questions." He rotates and disappears into the crowd.

I grab the shot and look at Jessica. "Are we back in Sweetwater with the gossip or what?"

"I know, right?" she says, lifting her glass, and together, we down the tequila.

"Come on," she says, taking my hand. "There's something I've always wanted to do, and now that we've drunk too much, we can. Come with me." She tugs me forward into the crowd and onto the dance floor, but she doesn't stop there. She heads to the steps leading to a packed stage and turns to me. "No one can ask you about Roarke if we're up here." The song "Con Calma" comes on, and Jessica gets all excited. "I want to dance."

My head is spinning, and I really want to escape the way that spinning is starting to take me in circles with Roarke and my forgotten birthday. I eagerly let her lead me to a corner where we're alone, and no one can talk to me again and ask if I'm Roarke's woman. I start dancing, and Jessica and I are laughing and having fun until the stupid music changes. It's Brett Young again, and this time, it's a slow song—"Mercy."

The words start to play, and in them is a plea from one lover to the other. Basically, please don't break my heart. Please step away and leave what is left of my heart. They resonate. They hurt. I blur out with the emotions this song brings and the lyrics go in and out. I turn to Jessica, and I think my face must be a mess because she pulls me into a hug. "Oh, honey. What's wrong?"

"I lost him. He hates me. I hurt him just like the song, and I still love him so much."

We talk like that the entire song, and she tells me how wrong I am. She tells me it's the tequila talking. "I shouldn't have given it to you." The music breaks as it has here and there for short announcements, though I don't hear this one. I'm just glad the emotional drug that is that song is over.

"Jessica! Hannah!"

"That's Jason," Jessica says. "He must know you're upset." She strokes my hair and pulls me to the side of the stage, where we squat in front of Jason.

"What's happening?" Jason asks. "What's wrong?"

"She's missing Roarke. She just needs him to be here already."

"I'm here."

At Roarke's voice, I look up to find him standing next to Jason. "You didn't think I'd miss your birthday, did you?"

CHAPTER THIRTY-SIX

Hannah...

Jessica leans in close and wraps her arm around me. "It was killing us not to tell you happy birthday!"

"Happy birthday, little sis," Jason says.

"Thank you," I murmur, but all I see right now is Roarke, standing there in a black T-shirt hugging his perfect chest. No fancy costume. Just him. And that's all it takes for him to be perfect to me.

I stand up, and Roarke grabs my waist and pulls me off the stage, catching me with his body, my hand on that perfect chest. "I thought you were done with me after the Luke thing."

"I will never be done with you, Han. Never." He eases me to my feet, and then he's kissing me, this deep, drugging kiss, and I don't care who sees. It's everything. That one kiss is just everything. "I love you," he says. "I have never stopped loving you."

The music starts to play, and the DJ says, "This one is from Roarke to Hannah." "Girl Like You" by Jason Aldean begins to play.

"You requested this?" Which is, of course, obvious, but there's tequila and Roarke involved, which means my brain is not exactly operating well right now. My body, however, is in overdrive.

"I did a lot of things to make tonight special for you, baby."

My heart squeezes with the message in this song, and Roarke hauls me onto the dance floor more fully, and we sway together. "I need you to know I've had tequila," I warn as my feet feel unsteady, "but that's your fault."

His lips curve. "Like you going in the men's bathroom?"

"Exactly," I assure him, hyperaware of his hands on my body, but then I've always been hyperaware of this man touching me.

"I see," he says. "All my fault."

I give an incline of my chin. "All your fault."

He gives my dress a once-over. "I like the costume." His gaze lands low on my cleavage. "A little deep, isn't it?"

"That's your fault, too."

His gaze lifts. "How is it my fault?"

"It just is."

"All right, then. As long as I'm the only one enjoying the view, I'll happily take credit for this one."

My cheeks heat, as if he's never flirted with me. "And what's your costume supposed to be?"

"Horse Wrangler, of course."

"You have no hat. A Horse Wrangler needs a proper hat."

"A hat gets in between you and me. That doesn't work for me."

The song lifts in the air again, and he leans in and sings along with it in my ear. I can't breathe, and every part of me is warm. He nuzzles my neck. "God, I missed you, Han." His voice is low, rough, affected.

"I missed you, too," I whisper, and when I pull back to look at him, I don't have it in me to protect myself with Roarke. "Every day in some way."

He strokes my hair behind my ear, sending a shiver down my spine. "Me, too, baby. Me, too."

The DJ comes on the microphone again, and the music cuts. "Now it's time for a special song. One for Hannah, who is coordinating the Sweetwater Christmas festival. Happy birthday, Hannah. Let's sing it to her, everyone!"

Suddenly, the entire room of hundreds of people is singing "Happy Birthday" to me, and I'm staring up at Roarke, fighting tears. He molds me close, kissing me, before he turns me toward the room to show me the giant cake being wheeled in. "Oh my God," I whisper, looking over my shoulder at Roarke. "I can't believe you did this."

"Watch," he says. "It gets better."

Now I'm intrigued. I face forward and gasp as Martha pops out of the cake, seventy-plus years young, in a fairy costume with rainbow wings. I rush forward and hug her, only to have Ruth sideswipe me and pull me into a hug of her own. Jessica and Jason show up to the hug party as well, and when Roarke and I are handed plates with the cake Martha created for me, it doesn't get any better than this. There's a warmth between us that I've never experienced with anyone but him, just him. The music starts to play again, and this time the song is "Rumor" by Lee Brice.

I start singing the words, about a small town gossiping about a new couple, much like this town is gossiping about me and Roarke. Roarke leans in and whispers, "Let's make the rumors true. Let's get out of here."

"Yes. Please." My entire body heats just thinking about being alone and naked with this man, this time without any emotional barriers. He kisses me, a slow slide of his tongue before he laces the fingers of one of his hands with mine and leads me toward the door.

The minute we're outside the party in the corridor, his arm is around my shoulders, pulling me in close to him. We don't speak during the walk, but that's the thing about me and Roarke; words aren't always spoken, but they're felt. We enter the elevator, and it's no different. He holds me close, and we endure the crush of a full car. Roarke places me in front of him, that big, perfect body of his cradling mine. That's the thing I can't believe I forgot all those years ago. Roarke was always there to have my back, to hold me up, to support me.

When we're finally on my floor, I hand him the key. He takes it, leans down, and brushes his lips over mine. He swipes the card and shoves the door open. I hesitate, but not with regret. With the sense that this is a new beginning, with the certainty that I will never be the same once I walk in this room. But then who am I fooling? The moment he kissed me the first time, it changed me. I was never the same. That's the power this man has over me.

CHAPTER THIRTY-SEVEN

Hannah...

I don't care how much power he has over me, because I don't believe that Roarke would ever intentionally use that power to hurt me. That's love, and I will never let insecurity or someone else's viciousness make me forget the power of love. I walk inside the hotel room and gasp. The luxury room, which I've barely noticed until now, is filled with vases of my favorite flowers—while lilies—mixed with red roses. They're everywhere, at least a dozen vases of a dozen flowers in each one. The door shuts behind me, and I turn to find Roarke right there, pulling me to him.

"I can't believe you did this." My voice cracks with the force of my emotions.

"Because I was such an asshole to you?" he teases, closing the space between us, his fingers catching my hip and walking me to him.

"No, I—"

"Thought I walked away because of Luke hitting on you?"

"You were pissed." My fingers curl on his chest. "I know you and you—"

"You do know me, Hannah. Don't forget that this time."

"I won't. I won't forget. Roarke—"

"Not now, Han." He cups my head with his

hand, his forehead finding mine. "Right now, let's just enjoy each other. We won't lose each other again." He pulls back to look at me. "Say it. We won't lose each other again."

His voice is rough, intense, full of demand that I happily answer. "Never again. We won't lose each other again."

He leans in to kiss me, and I press my hand to his chest. "I wasn't flirting with Luke. I would never try to get back at you."

"I know that, Han."

"You were pissed. I know you."

"Then you know I mean it when I say I'm *not* letting you go again."

There's a part of me that screams with past pain. He's not letting me go *now*, but he did in the past, yet he doesn't give me time to reply or to wallow in that pain. He's already kissing me again, his tongue a long stroke of velvet that I feel everywhere, every nerve ending in my body on fire. "I love you," he murmurs, and that's all that matters. Him. Me. Us. Love. The past doesn't matter.

He sits down on the stool at the end of the bed and drags me to his lap, and oh God, he feels so good. His hand slides over my back and down again, and there is nothing but this man who matters. Nothing. He has always been that missing piece of me. My fingers tangle in the thick strands of his dark hair as I sink into the kiss.

He moans, a low, rough moan, and tugs down the zipper at the back of my dress before he stands and settles me in front of him, turning me, my back to his front. Deft fingers unhook my bra, and his hands slip under the lace at my shoulders, but before he slides it down, he leans in and kisses my neck, scraping the delicate area with his teeth. My sex clenches, and I know how slow and well this man can make love to me, but I can't take the wait. I just need him, now, right now.

I rotate in his arms, letting my dress and bra fall to the ground, leaving myself in nothing but panties and thigh-highs. My heels are gone. They must have fallen off when he pulled me into his lap. Funny how I didn't notice.

Roarke's hot gaze slides over my body, and then I'm in his arms in seconds, his mouth on my mouth, and he tastes tormented, like I torment him. I want to end that in him, in us. I feel that in him, too, the need to drive us to another place, a better one. One of his hands cups my backside while the other cups my breast, teasing my nipple, the assault on my senses leaving room for little else but him. So much so that now, I'm the one who moans, tugging at his T-shirt as I do.

He tugs it, too, over his head, and I'm already caressing all that hard muscle by the time it hits the ground. From there, there's a whole lot of kissing and touching as we get his boots and pants off. The minute he's naked, he takes me down to the bed, my back settling on the mattress, but he isn't far behind. We end up facing each other, legs entwined, the thick ridge of his erection between us. "I didn't think I'd ever touch you again," he murmurs, molding me closer.

"Me either," I whisper, and then his mouth is there, lips brushing my lips, a full-on kiss following, and the heat between us is burning me alive. He presses inside me, and suddenly, I'm so very naked, we're so very naked, beyond the absence of our clothes, the vulnerability of wanting each other after hurting each other is there, present. But the funny thing is that yes, the past is here, it is, but somehow, it's more a glove that fits around us and draws us closer, where we huddle together to weather the storm rather than push each other away.

Every kiss and every touch is tender and somehow erotic, a slow, sexy dance of our bodies that begins to burn hotter. He nips my lips, then licks the offended skin. He repeats the action at my shoulder. It's almost angry, but it's good. I'm angry, too. I'm angry at everything that went wrong, and that becomes a part of the burn. Our need becomes frenzied, and he's thrusting and pulling me to him, our faces pressed close, our mouths parted. I don't want it to end; I don't want to ever end anything else with this man. But it does end. Release comes to me hard and fast, and I cling to Roarke. He shudders right over the edge with me, a low, guttural groan sliding from deep in his chest.

And then we're there, on top of a Ritz-Carlton mattress in a room of lilies and roses, holding each other the way we didn't think we'd ever hold each other again. We don't speak. We just lay there together.

Roarke is the first to move. He kisses my temple. "Let me grab you a towel." He pulls out of me, and I lay there with wetness clinging to my thighs, the insecurity that I know was a part of our breakup coming back to me. He's back in all of his naked, perfect glory in less than a minute, pressing the towel between my legs. I'm not shy about such things with Roarke, and yet I find myself sitting up and scanning for my bag to grab my robe.

The instant I turn away, he catches my arm and brings me around to face him. "Don't pull away. Don't shut me out again like you did the other night."

"I'm not. I'm not shutting you out."

"Tell me what you're thinking," he says. "Say it."

"I can't have babies, and you need to be a father. You'd be an amazing father."

"I'm a father to hundreds of animals, Han. You know this. And we can adopt if we decide that's what we want. It fits us. We rescue those who everyone else leaves behind."

"This was part of why I felt insecure. This was brewing inside me back then, and then that video just ripped me to shreds. I thought: he needs her. I bet she can have babies."

He drags me down to the mattress, catches my leg with his, and stares at me. "I didn't cheat."

"I believe you. I'm just being honest. I'm saying what I didn't say back then."

"And I'm listening. I should have listened closer. I should have known where you were on this, but, Hannah, baby, I'm with you. That's the only place I am on this. Never once did I consider another woman and kids as an option for me."

I suck in a breath and let it out. "I don't know how to get by this."

"We'll go talk to someone together." He strokes

my cheek. "We'll get by it together."

"I should have given you a chance to explain the video, but I think some part of me thought that I was letting you off the hook. But you won't move on. You won't let me let you off the hook."

"You belong with me, and I belong with you."

"But you didn't come for me. Some part of you—"

He cups my face and forces my gaze to his. "Don't say what you're about to say. It's not true. I love you. And I meant what I said. I'm not letting you go again. Ever. You run this time, I will follow."

CHAPTER THIRTY-EIGHT

Hannah...

Roarke and I order room service, and we get ready for its delivery by dressing. I grab a robe as he pulls out a pair of sweats from a suitcase. "Your suitcase is here?"

"Is that a problem?"

"Not at all. Just wondering how you pulled all of this off."

"I arranged the room and the party yesterday. I wanted to call you, but I knew I'd tell you I was leaving my father in charge of the problem in Houston and coming back."

"Really? Well, how are the horses and your dad?"

"His friend found the toxin, and he's tending to the horses and doing a damn good job." We sit down on the couch in the corner, and he opens the champagne I didn't notice for all the flowers, filling two glasses. "I really think he needed me gone. He needed to know something went well because of him."

"I think that was the perfect thing to do. Tell me about the toxin and the horses."

He's about halfway through his story when the food comes, and we barely miss a beat when he grabs the food. We keep talking, with so much to talk about and catch up on, that we eventually move to the bed, while I tell him all about my life in the fashion industry. I don't even remember falling asleep. I do, however, remember waking up because I'm on my stomach, and Roarke is kissing a line down my spine. I moan with the pleasure of it and look up at him. "You can't do what you're thinking about doing. I have to pee."

He smacks my backside. "Then go pee. I'll meet you in the shower."

And so he does. For the first time in years, we shower together, and it's not a quick shower. I end up in the corner, with him inside me, his mouth on my mouth, and it's truly the best way to wake up. I'm in the shower with Roarke. I'm starting a new day and a new life with Roarke.

A good hour later, after a call from Jessica and Jason, we're dressed to meet them for breakfast. Roarke is in jeans and a stallion T-shirt, and since I just happen to have my own stallion T-shirt, I pull mine on as well. I paint my lips pink, slide my purse over my shoulder, and exit the bathroom to find him sitting on the couch, on a call. "We'll be down in ten," he says, standing up and giving me a once-over, his gaze landing on my shirt. "You found your things under the bed."

"Yeah," I say. "I did." I think of the boots and the ring, wondering if he'll ever dare propose again.

He closes the space between us, his hands settling on my waist. "Move in with me. Let's do what we need to do while we're here to get you moved. If you want to keep your apartment until you're sure, I'll pay for it, but come home with me. Be home with me. I want—"

"Me, too. Yes. Yes. I don't care about the apartment. I just want to be back home with you."

He smiles, this brilliant smile that lights me up inside, and then he kisses me. "Home it is, then." He brushes my hair behind my ear, an intimate and familiar move that I missed beyond words. "What do you need here? Can I just have someone pack you up?"

"I can get a few more things now and do the rest later. I need to focus on the festival."

"You can let a mover do the rest. Call me impatient, but I want our lives back together fully."

"I do, too."

He cups my head and rests his forehead against mine. "We adopt." He pulls back to look at me. "Or we just get more horses."

"You have a lot of horses."

"*We* have a lot of horses."

I smile. "We. *We* sounds good."

"Let's go eat with Jason and Jessica, and after, we'll swing by your apartment."

"Actually, I need to buy a car. A rental isn't cost-effective."

"Do you know what you want?"

"I have no idea."

"We have an extra vehicle. You want to drive it while you decide?"

We. I will never get tired of that word. "Yes. That sounds perfect."

He laces the fingers of one of my hands with his and kisses my knuckles. "Then, that's what we'll do."

We share a smile, and a few minutes later, when

we walk into the restaurant downstairs hand in hand to a table filled with Jessica, Jason, Ruth, and Martha, they stand up and clap, and I blush, but it's one heck of a happy blush.

• • •

Roarke…

Breakfast wraps up, and Jason motions for me to join him in the hotel lobby. We walk underneath the winding stairs leading to the second level and claim two chairs against the wall. "The party was good. You two okay?"

"Better when I get this family stuff out." I scrub my jaw. "You're sure we can make this happen? Because I'm not waiting to tell her to have it blow up in my face."

"How can buying the property from the government and returning it to her family blow up in your face?"

Here is a man who gave up his baseball career when his parents died to take over his family's struggling ranch and to protect the families depending on it, rather than filing for bankruptcy. He barely blinked when I told him that his father was willing to sell it off and put them all out on the street and our horses with them. Instead of dwelling on his father's part in the family feud, he was all about "How do we fix this for you and Hannah?"

"Seriously, man," he says. "This is going to work out."

"I've tried to buy that property for Hannah. *For years.*"

"And now you've told me, and I'm in the unique position of knowing a lot of powerful people. The team owner is on this. He'll make it happen."

"Have you told Jessica about this? Does she think waiting to tell Hannah when I can hand her the property deed is the right move?"

"I haven't told her, but talk to her when we get back. If she disagrees with our plan, then weigh your own feelings, and do what's right."

"What I want is to put a ring on Hannah's finger and marry her before this explodes in my face, but that's selfish and wrong. I need to open this wound and throw medicine on it, and this feels like the way, but she brought up me not going after her again. It's killing me not to explain why." I shake my head. "Maybe I just won't tell her that her parents sent the video."

"It will always be there between you and her if you don't. I think she needs to know. Not only that, but one of the reasons you didn't go after her was because you knew how it would affect her with her parents."

"Which is why I still don't want to say more than I have to," I argue.

He leans in closer. "Why didn't you go after her? How do you make that right?"

I don't try to explain to him how betrayed I felt in the days after what happened. I don't try to explain that right when I would have gone after her, this shit with our parents exploded. When I did call, when I got drunk enough to say *screw our parents*, her number was already changed. But I have to say it all to Jessica.

"Hell," Jason adds. "I think you need a female's opinion. Talk to Jessica."

"And propose before or after I give her the property?"

"Oh yeah." He slaps his knees. "You need Jessica. In the meantime, I'm going to get that property." He pats my shoulder, and we stand up, walking together back to the lobby, where we find Jessica and Hannah standing together. The two fast friends are in deep conversation, but I only see one of them. The beautiful brunette I want to be my wife. She must feel my attention because her gaze lifts and turns, colliding with mine.

She smiles this stunning smile and rushes toward me, pushing to her toes to kiss me. "The hotel's delivering the flowers to the children's hospital. See? You did something special twice with those flowers."

I cup her head and kiss her firmly on the mouth before I say, "You're something special. I'm not letting you get away."

"Stop saying that. It makes it seem like I'm trying to leave again. I'm not going anywhere."

No. She's not. I'm going to find a way to heal our families. I'm going to be the damn Sweetwater Whisperer if it kills me. Because I have to. I love her too damn much to accept any other answer.

CHAPTER THIRTY-NINE

Hannah…

Roarke and I arrive at my little apartment, and I stop him before we head inside. "This place isn't fancy, but I'm launching a business. I got a lump sum payout from my boss when he let me go, and I'm investing that in my business, not a place to live." His hands come down on my shoulders, and he pulls me to him. "I know you were successful in L.A. I followed your photographer to follow you."

"You did?"

"Yeah, Han, I did. I told you. I never got over you."

"But you dated. You had to have someone—"

"No one who mattered, but there were times when I wanted to find someone. I wanted you to stop controlling my life, but there was no chance of that happening. What about you?"

"Same. Exactly the same."

"No hot model or Hollywood star sweeping you off your feet?"

"I never got over you, and how can anyone compare to the Horse Wrangler?"

"Don't do that. Don't put me up on some pedestal, Han. I'm right here with you, and I'm no one without you."

"I know that. I was young, too young maybe. I hadn't found my own footing, my own confidence.

Now, we're the same but different. I think that's good."

"Then why are we standing out here? The apartment doesn't matter."

"No," I say, smiling. "It doesn't." I push to my toes and kiss him. "I love you, Horse Wrangler, and yes, I'm calling you that. It's very sexy."

He arches a dark brow. "Is that right?"

"Yes. It is." I twist in his arms and decide I know the perfect way to say goodbye to this apartment. I unlock the door, grab his belt, and tug. "Come inside, *Horse Wrangler*."

• • •

After spending a few hours at my apartment, Roarke and I finally pack up everything we can fit in the car, and I run back inside for my favorite camera. I'm just walking down the stairs when a kid runs up them, smacks into me, and sends my camera flying. I cry out for my baby and dive for it, but it's too late. It crashes to the ground. Roarke rounds the steps, obviously responding to my cry out. I glance over my shoulder, and the kid is gone.

"What happened?" he asks, picking up the camera pack for me.

"A kid knocked it out of my hands. I don't even want to know if it's damaged right now. Let's just get out of here before I cry."

He wraps his arm around my shoulders, and we start down the stairs. "We'll buy a new one if it's broken."

"It's six grand, Roarke. It was my first big

purchase when my career took off."

"We have money, Hannah." We pause at the bottom of the steps, and he kisses me. "We'll get another camera if you need it."

The funny thing about Roarke is that I know he wants to take care of me, but I don't feel owned or controlled. He's never been that way. He's just so damn perfect. Money doesn't matter to him, and therefore, he's generous with what he has, which I know because I've seen it firsthand. Those retired horses cost money to support, lots of money. So it's not the offer of a camera that makes me love him all the more right now; it's the reminder of his generosity and the way he's already made us one.

• • •

I call Linda once we're on the road. "What's happening?" she asks. "You're moving in with Roarke? What about Cindy? Wait. Is he right there with you?"

"Yes," I say tightly.

"Okay, I'll talk. Did he do it?"

"No."

"Are you sure?" she presses. "Really sure?"

"Yes and yes." We talk a few more minutes and disconnect. I glance at Roarke. "How much did you hear?"

"All of it."

Of course he did. "And?" I prod. "Say what you're thinking."

"I hope you really are sure."

"I am, or I wouldn't be moving in with you."

"Good." He glances over at me. "Because I love you, Han."

"I love you, too, so stop talking about this. Let's talk about the festival."

And so we do. We talk about the festival and horses and my photography. We talk about everything and anything, and it feels good and right. We talk so much that there isn't a moment of silence the entire ride back to Sweetwater, and when we arrive there, the town feels like home. Our path leads us right past my old family property when I spy that deer again. "Stop, Roarke."

He halts the truck, and I point to the deer. "I saw it the other day when I stopped by and then again at your house." I glance over at him. "She felt like a sign of hope. It feels special that she's here now, while we drive home together." Two baby deer dart out of the bushes, and I suck in air.

Roarke turns to me and catches my arms. "We have babies. A bunch of them waiting a mile up the road for you to sing to them."

"I know." I touch the strong line of his jaw. "You'd make beautiful babies."

"We'd make beautiful babies. We'll get a surrogate if we need to, Han. We'll do what we need to do if that's what we decide is right for us."

"I never thought of that idea."

"That's why we figure these things out together, baby. We're better together." He kisses my hand. "Let's go home."

We settle back into our seats, and a few minutes later, we've just gotten the suitcases and boxes in the house when Javier rushes up the steps and meets us on the porch. "We have an emergency horse being flown in now. This one is in your wheelhouse. I was about to call you."

"How far out?" Roarke asks.

"Twenty minutes."

"We'll meet you at the hospital," Roarke replies.

He nods and then gives me a mock salute before he heads down the stairs while Roarke turns to me. "We got back at just the right time. Thank God."

His response isn't, *oh God, we just got home*, but *good timing*. "Yes," I agree. "Good timing."

"Let me get your things upstairs, and then we can head over there."

"I'll get everything out of the doorway. You go get ready for surgery, get up to speed on the case. I'll be there in a few minutes."

His eyes warm with my understanding of where he needs to be focused right now. He grabs me, kisses me, and starts a jog toward the hospital. I get both our overnight bags upstairs and unpacked so that if this surgery runs late, Roarke can just pass out and rest. I'm just about to head back downstairs when I spy the boots on the chair. The boots that hold my ring. I walk over to the chair and pick them up, resolutely carrying them back to the bed, kneeling beside it where I stick the boots back underneath. That's where they belong until Roarke pulls them out. We were meant to find each other again, and we did. We found each other. The rest will work out this time. Nothing is going to tear us apart. I truly believe that.

CHAPTER FORTY

Roarke...

It's a few nights after our return to Sweetwater, and Hannah and I are at Jason's. The women are all inspecting brochures for the festival and making plans. Jason is in the mix of it all with them, so I head out onto the porch. The door opens behind me, and Jessica steps outside, joining me at the railing, shivering due to a chilly breeze, which is a hint of our version of a mild winter.

"I hear you might want to talk to me."

I turn to face her, and she does the same to me. "What do you know?"

"Pretty much everything. I can't believe her parents did all that they did. It's going to hurt her. She talks about them a lot. She's trying to get them here for the festival."

"Should I tell her now?"

"I think handing her the deed to the land gives her something positive to focus on in the middle of the negative you're going to share with her. And Jason says he really thinks he can make that happen for you."

"But it's weeks out," I say. "It's killing me not to just tell her. It's killing me not to just propose, but I feel like I need to deal with this first."

"Are you ready to propose?"

"I never wanted her to take the ring off. Hell

yes, I'm ready. I was thinking Thanksgiving, though, just to give her time to feel how damn much I love her."

"That's perfect. You should have the deed by then, or at least, that's how Jason makes it sound, but honestly, I think you should propose before you tell her, and hear me out. The family rivalry will take away from what should be untarnished and special. Give her a chance to enjoy that moment with nothing to tear it apart."

"I have to tell her about this. It's eating me alive."

"Propose and then let her enjoy the success of the festival, the one she's worked hard to make perfect. Then, tell her well before Christmas, so it doesn't screw up Christmas."

I take in her suggestions, and they sit well. "It's a good plan. I'll propose on Thanksgiving."

"Do you have a ring?"

"Her old ring, but I took it in yesterday to have it turned into a necklace. I picked a new ring. A new us. A new ring."

"Is it bigger than the last one?" She holds up her hands. "Not that it matters."

I laugh. "Yes. It's bigger."

"Can I see it when you pick it up?" she prods.

"You can see it when Hannah puts it on her finger," I say, vowing to keep this one on her finger.

CHAPTER FORTY-ONE

Hannah...

In the month following me moving in with Roarke, we grow closer than I'd ever imagined possible, and I'd thought we were close the first go-around. But this time, it's as if we value us all the more because we know how easily we could lose each other.

Easily, as if it's natural, I start doing what I've always loved doing: photographing nature and the animals, in particular the horses and even the Horse Wrangler himself. Secretly, at first, I submit my shots to magazines, contests, and my agent, who is glad to see me active again. After seeing my recent shots, she coordinates a gallery showing for me in Dallas in January, and this news not only has me excited, it earns me more lilies from Roarke, who shares in my joy. He knows what this means to me, I feel that in him, and that's easy to do, considering we spend every moment possible together and without interruption thus far. That is, until the weekend before Thanksgiving, when we wake to an emergency call for Roarke that will take him to Tennessee.

"I can't go," I say as he throws the blankets off our bed. "The festival is only a week away."

"I know, baby," he says, meeting me at the end of the bed. "You can't always be with me, no matter how much I wish you could. You take care of the festival." He strokes my hair and kisses me, before setting me aside to hurry to the shower.

I pull on leggings and a tank top and rush downstairs, fighting a wave of weird queasiness as I make him coffee and then fill a thermos with it blended just the way he likes it. It's not long before we're at the chopper pickup site with me behind the wheel of the Jeep I've been driving and loving for the past few weeks. "After this festival," he says, "I want you to come with me on these trips. You can bring your camera."

"I'd love that," I say, because as much as I've enjoyed planning the festival, my camera is loving my new direction, and it's given new life to my photography.

I watch as he rushes away and the helicopter lifts off, disappearing into the horizon. Once I'm back at the house, I hurry upstairs to shower and change when I have a sudden realization. I haven't started my period. I grab the bathroom sink, stunned. I can't get pregnant. Or I can, but it's like a five percent chance. That basically means I can't get pregnant. And if I did, by some odd, freak chance, have that happen, we aren't ready for that. Roarke hasn't said a word about marriage. Not a word. Not that it matters. We're happy. We are, but we're still new to this second chance we're giving ourselves. I press my hands to my face. I have so many feelings right now. I drop my hands. I need to take a test, but I can't get one in this town without word getting out.

I glance at the clock. Jessica will be here soon. We're headed into town because holiday lights are being installed, right along with a massive tree to be lit at the festival. Grabbing my phone, I call her now, thankful for the friend she's become. "I can't believe I'm asking this. You wouldn't have a random pregnancy test lying around, would you?"

"Wait. What? I thought you couldn't—"

"I can't, but I didn't start my period, and I just need peace of mind that isn't town news."

"Well, it just so happens," she says, "that I had a scare a month back. I might have one test left. I kept repeating just to be sure."

"But you weren't pregnant?"

"No. The doctor said it happens sometimes. We aren't ready yet, you know? We want kids, and if it happened, we wouldn't be upset, but we want to plan. Anyway, I'll grab the suitcase I think it's in. We were traveling during my panic attack."

"At least that kept it from being town gossip."

"Amen to that," she says. "I'll see you soon."

We disconnect, and I quickly shower and then dress in black jeans and a red sweater. We are, after all, decorating for the holidays today. I've just filled up a cup with coffee when Jessica walks into my kitchen, also wearing a red sweater. "Aren't we cute?" she asks, joining me at the island and whispering. "Where's Roarke? Does he know?"

"He flew out to handle an emergency. And no, he doesn't know."

She sets the test in front of me. "Let's go take it."

I pick up the kit. "I can't believe I'm doing this to myself. I can't even get pregnant. I've told you the story."

"It would be a special miracle, since you want kids. Go. Take the test."

I pant out a breath, and we both hurry upstairs. I walk into the bathroom, pee on the stick, and leave it on top of the trash can to join Jessica in the bedroom. "It's going to be a fast result, and I can't look. If I am pregnant, I don't even know if I can carry to term. I don't want a miscarriage to shake me and Roarke up right now. I don't."

"Why are you thinking about miscarriages, woman? Stop working yourself up. You and Roarke are strong. You will be fine. The baby will be a miracle and wonderfully full-term and healthy. You want me to look at the results?"

"Yes. Please. I feel sick." Literally, actually. I sit down on the bed and watch her disappear into the bathroom. She exits in thirty seconds, her eyes alight with joy. "It's positive. You're pregnant."

I stand up. "What? Really? I am?"

"Yes, honey. *You are.*"

I rush past her and stare down at the test. I throw it in the trash and turn to face Jessica, who is now in the doorway. "Roarke hasn't even asked me to marry him. What if he isn't ready? And what if I can't carry a baby? I need to see a doctor. I need to see one before I tell him."

"You need to tell him, and then you both go see the doctor." She stops in front of me, her hands on my shoulders steadying me. "You're a team. Be a team. Tell him. There is no other answer."

"Right. Right. You're right. I'll tell him. I'll tell him on Thanksgiving. That gives him time to get back and for me to decide how to tell him. It's a gift, right? I know he'll feel like it's a reason to be truly thankful on Thanksgiving."

"Yes. Exactly. Tell him. That's what matters."

"Thanksgiving it is." I don't know why I'm letting this be an issue with Roarke. I'm not going to doubt him. He wants this, too, but nevertheless, my world is spinning. I'm afraid of believing this can be real only to have it fall apart.

CHAPTER FORTY-TWO

Roarke…

It's the day before Thanksgiving when I land at Dallas Love Field to have Jason pick me up. "How does it look?"

"The ring or the real estate deal?" He hands me the bag he picked up at the jewelers. "The ring is huge, the biggest damn diamond heart you can get, I imagine. The necklace set in a stallion—clever, man. The real estate deal is going to take another week."

I curse. "What the hell? I thought today was the day. That's why I flew in here to sign the papers. And I'm proposing tomorrow."

"And you'll give her the deed well before Christmas."

I grimace, already feeling really damn uncomfortable with the time that's passed. "I'm on borrowed time here. Her parents could tell her before I can."

"First of all," he says, pulling out of the parking area, "you told me yourself that her parents have gone silent on her. They hate that she's in Sweetwater. They don't want her to know what shits they were to your family and the horses. Greed got them in trouble, not you. Secondly, even if they did tell her, I've got your back. I know what you're trying to do for her. Stick to the plan. It's a damn good one."

Stick to the plan, he says, but I don't know how I feel about that anymore. So much so that I spend most of the drive thinking about this, and by the time we're pulling into Sweetwater, I'm convinced I'm doing this all wrong. I need to tell her everything bad and get it over with. I'll give her the deed, let her digest the mess of the family war, and then end with the good. I'll propose at Christmas and hope she still says yes.

Beside me, Jason's phone rings, and he answers with, "Hey, babe." He listens a minute and then hands me the phone. "Jessica."

Here we go. I get to tell her there will be a wait on the proposal. "Do you have the ring?" she asks excitedly.

"I do," I say, "but I'm going to wait until Christmas. I need to have everything on the table when I ask her. I need her to know there are no secrets."

"You need to propose now, like tonight or at midnight to make it Thanksgiving or whatever."

"Jessica—"

"I'm telling you that you need to do this, as a friend. Listen to me."

I go cold inside. "Is she thinking about leaving me?"

"Oh God no, but you'll understand soon. Just please do this for you and her."

"Look," I say. "I really want to tell her everything first. It's eating me alive, keeping this from her."

"Don't tell her now. Propose."

"No. I don't want the proposal muddied by this. And I want her to hold that deed in her hands when I tell her about our family feud. That's not today. I'm sure Jason told you that—"

"Roarke. *Propose.* Screw the title. Screw the family feud. *Please* listen to me."

My brows dip, and I glance at Jason as I ask, "What the hell is going on, Jessica?"

Jason shakes his head, telling me he's clueless while Jessica says, "Friendship. My friendship with both of you. She wants you to propose, and she believes something special is happening on Thanksgiving. Don't let her be disappointed."

I'm officially irritated. "Did you tell her?"

"No! No. She told me. She feels that Thanksgiving is a big day for you two. I swear to you that I didn't tell her that you're proposing."

"Did the damn jewelers call her?"

"I don't know anything about that," she says. "Just don't let her feel the hit of disappointment."

"Right." My lips thin. "Thanks, Jessica." I hand the phone back to Jason.

Holy hell! I can't wait now, and the truth is, I don't want to wait. The two things that stick with me from that call with Jessica is that Hannah wants me to propose and that I can't let Hannah down. I don't ever want to let her down.

By the time Jason disconnects the line, we're at my house, and I've pulled the necklace from the bag, inspected it, and stuck it in the pocket of the jacket I'm wearing. I grab the ring box next, open it, pleased with how it turned out. It goes in the other pocket.

"You doing this now?" Jason asks.

"Seems I am," I say, popping open the door.

"Good luck, man."

"My good luck was when she came back." I exit into a chilly afternoon and eye the Jeep by the door, which means Hannah is home. Home. She's home. That punches me in the gut in all kinds of ways. This is where she belongs. I can't let any of this go south. I grab my suitcase and head inside.

"Hannah!"

Silence greets me, and I know what that means. She's in the stables. I exit the house and walk toward a gated area where two horses that we ride often are running free. Once I'm in the stable behind the house, the one that I use for our personal horses, I saddle them up, complete with the Christmas saddle pads that Hannah bought for the festival, and then text Hannah where to meet me. In all of four minutes, she's in front of me, wrapping her arms around me.

"I'm so glad you're home," she says, and there is so much genuine joy in her that I vow to never make her feel anything but happy to see me.

I cup her head and kiss her. "Let's go take a ride."

"Now?"

"Now." I smack her jean-clad backside. "We'll go sit in our favorite spot, and I'll tell you a little story."

"A story." She smiles. "You tell me a story, and I'll tell you one."

"Deal," I say, and in a few minutes, we're riding, taking the fifteen-minute trip to the river, where we secure the horses. While we do so, Hannah starts singing, stroking her horse, Carrie's nose, while my horse, Mercy, nuzzles her neck. I laugh as she makes up lyrics to "Rumor" to include Mercy's name, and then I pull her with me under the tree. "About that rumor."

"They're willing to live large and let everyone talk."

"I was talking about the one about you and me."

She laughs that sweet, sexy laugh of hers that I want to hear every day for the rest of my life. "I'm pretty sure we've ended those rumors. Everyone knows that I'm living with you again."

"Not all the rumors," I say as I go down on my knee.

CHAPTER FORTY-THREE

Roarke...

"Marry me, Hannah. Be my wife. Do it for real this time." I pull out the ring case and open it.

"Roarke," she whispers, tears pooling in her eyes. "Roarke, oh God. I—"

"A new ring for a new start." The diamond heart that is a full carat larger than the prior version glistens against the velvet.

She gasps. "You got me a new ring? I mean, I know you said you did and you did, but oh my God. Roarke. It's stunning, and I can't believe you did this. I didn't know if you would and—"

"Say yes, Han. You're killing me here."

"Yes!" She smiles and laughs and smiles all over. "Of course, yes. Did you really doubt my yes?"

Relief that I shouldn't need to feel, but I do, washes over me. I pull the ring out of the velvet and slide it on her finger before casting her a hopeful look. "You like it?"

"I love it, but I didn't need a new ring. It's so—big and beautiful, but I know this was expensive."

"I really wanted you to have a new ring for a new us. I have one more thing for you." I stand up and reach into my opposite pocket. "You still have your old ring." I open the bag and the heart inside the stallion is a glistening diamond. She gasps and tears up.

"It's amazing. It's perfect. It's so very special."

I step into her and cup her face. "*You're* so very special." My voice is low, rough, laden with emotions no one but Hannah stirs in me. "You're everything to me. I love you, Hannah."

"I love you, too. Can I put on the necklace?"

"Of course you can. I'll put it on you."

She turns around, and I help her settle it at her neck, and when she turns back around, she's tearing up. "This was your story you had to tell me?" she asks, touching the stallion with her fingers.

"*Our* story," I amend. "This is our story."

"Actually, our story is a little bigger than you might think."

My brows furrow. "What does that mean?"

"It's means—God, I hope you're good with this, and I don't know if it will stick or how it's possible but—"

I know. Somehow I know what's coming, and that call with Jessica makes sense. "You're pregnant."

"Yes," she breathes out. "I missed my period, and I took a test, and I'm scared because what if I can't carry a baby to term? And what if—"

I don't let her finish that sentence. I kiss her, driving away the bad, vowing to always drive away the bad, before I say, "Don't be scared, Han," choosing my words carefully, ensuring that she knows that this pregnancy is special, but it's not our beginning or our end. "Whatever is meant to be will be, and we will do it together. I need you. We need each other. That doesn't change."

"But you do want this? You do, right? It's not just me."

"You know I do, but only because it's us, baby. *Only* because it's a part of us. If it doesn't happen, we have a world to explore together."

"I know. I do. I really do, but I want this. I know you know I want this. But I'm afraid to even talk about it right now. I have an appointment booked with a doctor in Abilene."

"*We* have an appointment," I say. "When?"

"We," she agrees. "The day before the festival, which is horrible timing, but I don't want to put this off. That was the only time I could get in anywhere because of the holidays."

"We'll make it work."

Her hand settles on my chest, heavier than I might expect. "I don't want anyone to know until we feel like this is going to last."

"Whatever feels right to you, Han," I say, really damn glad I didn't tell her about the family feud before now. The last thing she needs right now, while trying to carry our child through these early stages, is that kind of stress.

"So tell me," I say, "when do you want to get married and where? Because tomorrow works just fine for me."

She laughs. "Tomorrow?"

"Today?"

"How about—" She motions to the tree hanging low around us, our willow tree. "Here," she says. "This is our special place."

"When? And for the record, in case I didn't make

myself clear, tomorrow isn't soon enough for me."

"How about Christmas Eve? Just a small wedding, a few friends, and my red boots?"

"Your red boots, baby. And a red tie for me if I remember correctly?"

"Yes," she approves. "A red tie for you. And if it's only you and me, Jessica and Jason, I'm happy. And your father. And Linda. That's all."

"What about your parents?"

"I think I'll call them right before the wedding. I don't want them turning negative on me. I want to enjoy this time and all the planning. I'll tell them I have a surprise and insist on them showing up."

I know then that the sooner I hand her that deed the better, but it can't be until after her doctor's appointment. Christmas Eve is going to be special. I cup her head and lean in to kiss her. "Christmas Eve, I get to marry my best friend." I kiss her, and we sit down under the tree and talk about the wedding for hours.

When we finally head home, it's with a detour to see Jason's house, where my grandmother and Ruth are hanging out as well. Hannah shows off her ring and necklace, and joy erupts around us. Jessica slips back from the chaos to nudge me. "Everything great?"

"She told me. And you were right. I don't want to stress her out."

"Are you happy?"

"Elated, but I don't want to say that to her. I don't want her to feel like a loss means I'm no longer satisfied."

She squeezes my arm. "Good call. Oh, what the

heck." She hugs me and whispers, "You two are perfect together," before she releases me.

She's right. We are perfect together, and somehow, some way, I need to make her parents see that, too. For Hannah, because she's what matters.

CHAPTER FORTY-FOUR

Hannah...

Thanksgiving Day at Jason and Jessica's with Martha cooking is pretty special. It's a time filled with laughter and family. I come through for Nick, too. He joins us and starts eating the minute he comes in the door. Roarke's father even shows up with his new woman on his arm, and watching Roarke's joy over this surprise is an amazing thing to behold. His dad's girlfriend, Becca, is lovely, inside and out, with an abundance of red hair.

His father takes one look at my ring and hugs me so tightly, I can't breathe. "About damn time you two got this thing moving." He pulls back to look at me, and he looks good, healthy, happy. "When's the big day?"

"Christmas Eve," I say. "This just happened. We haven't even had time to tell anyone."

"I'll be here," he replies, glancing at Roarke. "You bet I will."

He doesn't ask about my parents, which sits a little odd with me, but then they've been gone a long time, and it seems they left quite bitter. It has to hurt Roarke's father to be shut out by lifelong friends. It hurts me for him.

By evening, the two of them are on the porch talking for hours on end while I'm in the stables brushing Snowflake. "You'll have your baby soon, girl," I say. "If all goes well, we'll be mamas together."

I want to call my parents and tell them all my news, but they're so negative about me being back in Sweetwater that I want to tell them in person. Thankfully, Roarke approves. If they don't show up to the festival, then we'll travel to them right away, to give them time to plan for a Sweetwater wedding and a grandbaby.

• • •

On the morning of my doctor's appointment, I step onto the porch to find that deer standing at the bottom of the steps staring at me. It's a magical moment, truly magical. Roarke joins me, and it doesn't even dart away. "Hope," he says, knowing what that deer means to me. "This appointment will be good news."

It's the perfect thing to say, but I ruin it by hanging over the porch and throwing up.

"You're nervous," Roarke insists. "About the appointment and the festival. That's making your morning sickness worse."

This after we've been on the road half an hour, and I've been talking to Jessica the whole way, only to hang up quickly and make Roarke pull over so I can dry heave on the side of the road. "You know what I read this morning?" Roarke asks.

"That pregnant sick women are emotional and cry a lot? Because I feel like I might cry."

He smiles. "That sickness is a sign of a healthy pregnancy." He strokes my cheek. "It's going to be good news. I feel it." He squeezes my hand and adds, "Remember the deer, Han."

A few minutes later, we step into the doctor's office, and I'm so nervous that my hands shake, and Roarke has to fill out my paperwork for me. It takes me a minute to even remember that I have insurance that I'm now glad I've had in place for years. I'm also happy to learn that my records have arrived from my prior doctors. It's a good half hour later when I'm weighed, poked with a needle, and sitting in a doctor's office with Roarke by my side. The doctor is a jolly old man, who reminds me of Santa Claus, and who delivers the best gift of all.

"Your chances of conception were next to impossible, but you are, in fact, pregnant," he says. "Your risks during pregnancy are no different than anyone else's. Is this good news?"

Roarke stands up next to me where I sit on the table, wraps his arms around me, and leans in close. "It's amazing news," he murmurs before kissing me.

• • •

The morning of the festival arrives with a rush of famous people in and out of our house and Jason and Jessica's. It's craziness, but it's so much fun, with Christmas decorations on every store and window in the town. The Adeline High School marching band even does an early-morning show in the town square to launch the event. Linda and her team hit the town in time to take lots of photos of the event, and it's not long before she's at Jason's house with all of us, with donuts in hand that

Martha immediately throws away. I laugh as Linda complains right up until the moment that Martha hands her a homemade cinnamon roll that she devours. Someone else is at Jason's house, too. Max the mad catcher, and soon, he and Linda are teaming up to help the town get ready for the scavenger hunt.

Midday, parking lots are filled and so are the streets. There are booths with games for the kids in town and at Jason and Jessica's ranch. At our place, kids ride horses, visit a petting zoo, and parents watch the action. It's all-day fun with a choir, baseball players tossing balls with kids, and lots of food that Martha coordinated with care. There are also television cameras that I control with the security I've hired, but it's still a challenge. This little town has a lot of famous people in one tiny place, and it's almost too much for the media to handle.

By evening, Sweetwater is a twinkling cheerful display of Christmas lights, and the town square awaits the auction and tree lighting, with well-placed heaters that may not even be needed. The temperature is in the seventies, a Texas-style holiday celebration for sure. We have horses with ribbons and holiday saddles, and the ranch is decorated. Nathan and Allison, as well as about another ten more staff members, are present, allowing guests to visit the retired horses. Luke is in charge of the auction, and he even makes up with Roarke, not that they were really fighting in the first place. Everything is perfect, except, of course, my parents' refusal to join us, but Roarke and I plan to take matters into our own hands. We have plane tickets to leave to visit them in a few days.

I watch as Roarke steps onto a stage in town square that's decorated with white lights. Tonight he'll be auctioned off with ten other volunteers, after which the tree will be lit. The auction begins, and Linda cracks me up with her bids on Max. She pays five thousand dollars for him, but I suspect that Max might have donated that money. She hugs me when she wins and rushes to the stage.

Roarke, who isn't even offering a date, but rather a tour of the ranch and a chance to ride with him, goes for just as high. Ruth also bids on a retired fireman from one town over. She doesn't win, but the way those two look at each other, I think she'll get her date anyway.

The auction is just wrapping up when a hand comes down on my arm. I turn in shock to find my father there. "Dad?"

"Come with me right now. We need to talk."

Fear fills me. "What's wrong? What's going on?"

He doesn't answer. He bulldozes me through the crowd and to the side of a mustang statue on the opposite side of the town square, where I find my mother. "What's wrong?" She looks thin and worried, her dark hair in disarray. She grabs my hand. "It's true. You're engaged to him."

"I was coming to surprise you in Pennsylvania to tell you," I say. "Next week."

My father steps to her side, and he looks weathered and older than I remember but still fit. He's not missing meals like my mother. "Roarke's family drove us into bankruptcy. We've been trying to get our property back ever since. And now we can't. We were informed that it's being purchased. Roarke and Jason are buying it. He doesn't want to marry you. You came to town, and you were a threat. He was buying time to get the property."

My hand instantly goes to my belly, and I feel sick, not figuratively, either. I'm going to be sick.

CHAPTER FORTY-FIVE

Roarke…

As soon as I step off the stage, Jason steps in front of me, and he doesn't look happy. "Hannah's parents are here, and they just pulled her aside. It didn't look like a good thing, either. Sorry, man. We'll get that deed. Soon. Next week. I'll make it happen."

I curse. "This isn't on you. Where are they?"

"Mustang statue."

I start to turn, but he catches my arm. "The property—"

"I don't care about the damn property," I say, pulling my arm free. "Right now, all I care about is how this affects Hannah." I rotate, and I'm already walking, thinking about every move I've made to protect her and now her pregnancy, our baby. I'm trying to protect our baby, and now this.

I don't want her upset. I don't want her to find out about our families' feud this way, and I pray that's not what this is about. I pray her parents actually came here to put all that shit aside and to just see their daughter. I clear the crowd and come up behind the statue as Hannah's voice lifts in the air. I'm just about to round it when something tells me to wait, to stop and listen.

"I'm fine," Hannah says, her voice raised. "I'm fine. I was sick. It's over for now, but you know why I'm sick?" she demands, not giving them time to reply. "Because I'm pregnant with Roarke's child. *We're* pregnant. We're getting married."

"You're pregnant?" her mother exclaims. "I didn't think you could get pregnant. Are you sure?"

"I'm positive," she says. "And I'm happy. I can't believe you both can't just be happy for us."

"Does he know?" her father asks.

"Of course he knows," Hannah says. "Why would I keep this from him?"

"He's using you and you got pregnant," her father snaps. "He's buying time with you to secure that land, Hannah," he adds, and right when I think I've had enough, when I'm about to step into this, Hannah snaps back at him.

"If Roarke's buying our old place, good. We need more room to help more animals."

I couldn't hope for a better response from her, but it doesn't back her father off. "And you don't know about it?" he challenges. "Isn't that strange?"

"I didn't know about the ring before he gave it to me, either," she argues. "Or the six dozen flowers he had waiting for me on my birthday. Or the surprise birthday party. He's *good* to me. I love him, Dad. And I'm back to repeating myself here: why can't you just be happy for me?"

"He cheated on you," he says. "That video—"

"What video?" she demands, and I can almost feel her fury beating at them and at me. "I never told you about a video."

"You sure as hell did tell me," her father bites out.

"What video?" her mother asks. "What is this about?"

"The one Dad sent me to make me think Roarke cheated on me," Hannah says. "You did it, didn't you, Dad? No. Don't answer. I can't stomach the reply. I'm leaving. I'm going to be with the father of my unborn child and my future husband. I hope you both enjoy the festival. Try the cookies. The baby and I recommend them."

"Hannah!" her mother shouts, making it clear that Hannah is walking away.

"Not now, Mother," Hannah calls out, close to me now.

"Let her go," Hannah's father says to her mother, and then suddenly, Hannah's rounding the statue and running smack into me. I catch her arms.

"Roarke," she gasps. "Oh God. You're here."

"Yes," I say, blown away at the way she just stood up for me, for us. "And I always will be."

"I need out of here right now. Can we go somewhere, please?"

I don't hesitate. I don't ask questions. I link the fingers of one of her hands with mine, and I lead her away from the statue, with no real direction besides *away.* Two blocks down, I spy one of the horse-drawn carriages decorated for the event and donated by our ranch parked nearby. "This way," I say, leading her in that direction and then helping her inside the carriage. Once we're settled into the cushioned seat, I pull the blanket over her and wave the driver onward.

My hand finds her hand, and we look at each other, a world of history and emotion between us. "Did you hear it all?" she asks, and her voice is trembling; really, her entire body is trembling despite the mild night that can barely be called winter.

Aware that emotions and adrenaline have her, I pull the blanket around her shoulders. “I heard it all. You okay?”

“Are you?”

“Han, baby, you said yes to marrying me again. I’m more okay than I have been in years. It’s you I’m worried about.”

“My father sent that video.”

“I know that. I knew before tonight.”

“You knew?” She twists around to face me. “You didn’t tell me? When did you find out?”

“Right after you left for L.A. and changed your number. I didn’t know how to reach you, and that felt like a clear message to stay away.”

“You didn’t try very hard or you would have found a way.” She twists in the other direction, trying to get away from me.

I hold onto her hand.

“Let go,” she orders.

“Let me tell the story. Then, if you still want your hand back, I’ll give it back. Please. Make that deal with me?”

Her jaw tenses. “Fine,” she says. “Tell the story, but I want my hand back.”

I’d let her go and that’s where I went wrong. I let her go before, but I don’t think that’s what she needs from me now. “Right after you left, my father let me in on what was going on.”

“Which was what?”

“A highway was coming through town, right across our properties. All the animals would be displaced and you know that, at any given time, there are animals with us that can't survive a move, including the retirees. It's not something that can be done quickly on someone else's terms. Your family and Jason's seemed to understand. They agreed not to sell, but your father worked a side deal to give up part of his land. That move would have allowed the highway to cut in front of the property, right in front of the enclosures for the horses."

"Why would he do that?"

"Money. A million dollars. He convinced Jason's dad to sell, too. My father fought back. He hired someone who found an endangered insect on all of our properties. There are laws to protect endangered species of any kind. Those laws killed the highway."

"My parents did that?"

"I think it was mostly your father, but yes."

"I don't understand. How did that drive my family into bankruptcy? Was my family in financial trouble? Did they need the sale to stay alive? Was he so panicked over debt that it affected his judgment?"

"My father does think that's the case, which is why he offered them help, which they rejected. What ultimately sent your parents into bankruptcy was spending the advance they got from the state. The deal had a small print clause. If the deal died in sixty days or less, they had to pay back the money. They didn't wait. They spent the money, and when they couldn't pay it back, they were foreclosed on."

"And Jason's parents?"

"They never got paid, and thank God for it, or he might have ended up the same." I lean in closer. "I didn't tell you about the highway because as far as I knew, you hated me. You thought I cheated, and I loved you enough not to want to hurt you any more than you were already hurting. I knew the animals mattered to you. I knew your parents playing the games they played with their safety would upset you. What end did that give me but making you angry at them? That would have seemed like I was viciously attacking them. That would have hurt you all over again."

Her lashes lower and then lift, torment etched in her beautiful face, brushed by moonlight.

"And the video? Why did he send that video? And why was she all over you?"

"Interesting story there. I was trying to get out off the elevator and she stepped in front of me and wrapped herself around me. Later, looking back, it felt like a setup."

"He didn't want me with you because he hated your father."

"He told my father that we'd never get married. A week later, you were sent that video."

"In other words, we lost years of ours lives over a highway."

"We're here now," I say, squeezing her hand. "That's what matters."

"What was he talking about you buying the land?" she asks, and there isn't an accusation in her voice. None. Not even a hint of her doubting me, a realization that speaks volumes about how far we've come.

"I've been trying to buy it for years," I explain, "but it's been locked down. When you came back, I knew I had to make that happen. I knew there was really only one person who could help. That's when I finally told Jason the whole story."

Her eyes go wide. "He didn't know?"

"No. He was off playing ball when all this went down, and I didn't see any reason to tell him that his father was willing to sell out the animals and the people who worked for him. Especially after Jason all but lost everything trying to save that ranch when his father died. Once he knew, though, all he saw was the need to help you and me. He went to his team's owner, and he pulled strings. The idea was to tell you the history and then hand you the deed."

"You were buying the land for me?"

"Yes, Han. For you. That was always my intent. It felt like a way back to you. We'll have the deed next week. You can give it to your parents."

She shakes her head. "No," she says adamantly. "I'm not giving it to my parents. I'm giving it to the animals we can save with that extra land."

"It's your decision. That was how I always intended it to be. That's how it *will* be. It's yours."

Her expression softens. "You amaze me with your generosity, Roarke. With the animals. With the people around you. *With me.*"

"Does that mean that I can keep holding onto your hand?"

"It means you better keep holding on. Don't ever save me again if it means dividing us. Promise."

"I won't," I say, cupping her head. "I told you, Han, I'm not letting you go again. I'm not letting you go again, Han. Ever."

She leans in and presses her lips to mine. "I love you."

"And I love you."

We share a spontaneous smile, and her trembling is gone. She sinks against me, and I pull her under my arm, holding her close, the way I plan to hold her for the rest of her life. For several minutes, we ride in silence before she asks, "What do you think of the name Hope if it's a girl?"

I smile and nuzzle her hair. "I love the name Hope."

"And Matthew for a boy? It means God's gift."

"I love the name Matthew," I say, because the truth is the name doesn't matter. Hannah and the joy of sharing this life, of creating life with her, is what matters. That's the gift.

CHAPTER FORTY-SIX

Hannah…

I wake the morning after the Christmas festival without feeling sick, which is a miracle, but then I'm snuggled into Roarke, and he's pretty good medicine. So much so that I don't want to get out of bed, but I have no choice. Today is festival cleanup, and we have to supervise a hired crew to make it all happen. With that in mind, it's not long before Roarke and I are dressed in tees, boots, and jeans, ready for a workday, when Jessica and Jason show up, eager to talk about the festival's massive success and worried about my encounter with my parents.

Considering they're the only two people who know I'm pregnant, it's good to share coffee and hear their thoughts. We talk about my parents and all that happened in the past but move on to the festival. "We don't have the final totals," Jessica says, "but the money we brought in tops six figures. It's amazing. The auction was the big ticket. It was huge money."

We're all celebrating this news when a truck I don't recognize pulls up in front of our house. "I'll see who it is," Roarke offers, giving me a kiss as he heads out of the kitchen.

Jessica launches into talk about the camp waiting list last night created, but Roarke doesn't return quickly, which bothers me. His extended departure has me concerned there might be an emergency animal arriving. "Let me go check on him," I say, hurrying through the house. As I step out onto the porch, I find Roarke talking to my father.

The minute my father's eyes land on me, his expression softens. "I'm sorry. I don't know what else I can say. I'm sorry. Your mother gave me a thrashing last night and talked some sense into me. She made me see that I'm destroying you and our family. You two, you and Roarke, you're the new generation. I forget that sometimes. I don't want to miss out on my daughter's life or my grandbaby's. Please don't let me lose you and that baby."

I don't miss how his voice cracks, nor do I miss how bloodshot his eyes are, but it just feels like too little, too late. He could have brought me and Roarke back together. He could have spared us years apart. "You still think Roarke was trying to trick me and use me?"

"No," he says. "I was just angry and lashing out. Roarke explained the situation with the land. He's a better man than me, generous. I'm stubborn. I hold grudges. You know this about me."

"Why would you do something that would hurt the animals, Dad? Why? You know Roarke and his father needed to protect them. They had to protect them."

He scrubs his jaw and looks away before meeting my stare, his eyes redder now. "I thought we could all become millionaires. I thought I was helping Roarke's dad get more money to help the animals. His refusal to take the money made no sense to me at the time. I wanted to force him to take it."

"The animals can't just be moved," I say, my voice lifting, "and finding a suitable place is no easy task."

"Roarke's father called me Thanksgiving Day," he says. "I heard what he said. It made sense, but when I found out Roarke was buying the property—"

"For you," I say. "He told me I could give it to you, but I'm not doing it. We need it for the animals. You have a new life. And you know what? You showed up when you got pissed, but you couldn't show up for me when I asked you to show up." I try to turn away.

Roarke catches my arm. "Easy, baby. It's time to put this behind us. Let's put it behind us."

"How can you just let this go, Roarke?" I demand softly. "He hurt us."

"How about inviting your mother and me in for coffee?" my father asks, and when I glance over at him, he waves behind him. "For your mother. She needs to see you. I'll make this up to you."

The door to my parents' truck opens, and my mother climbs out. The next thing I know, she comes rushing forward. "Hi, honey! Hi!"

"She's been so upset over these secrets," my father says, his voice low, taut. "She won't eat. I'm worried about her. She wanted this out in the open. I fought her on it, but she needs you, Hannah," he adds. "We need you."

"You made me think Roarke cheated," I hiss.

"I was a fool in a desperate, angry mode," he

says. "I didn't want you with him because of his father. I can't undo the past, Hannah, but I'm standing here begging for another chance. I'd love to have that coffee with my daughter and her future husband."

I glance up at Roarke, and he pulls me under his arm, next to him. "Say yes," he says, when I'm not feeling eager to agree at all. *He made me think Roarke cheated*. He drove us apart for years. Roarke leans in and whispers, "Life is short, too damn short. Think about Jason's parents. Think about my father."

That statement hits me hard, so I do. I think about his father, and I know why Roarke wants me in that headspace. The stroke. It's about his father's stroke and suddenly facing reality here; how easily it could have been one of my parents. How easily it still could be one day. "You're right," I say to Roarke and nod with my approval. "Yes."

Roarke's eyes warm on me, lingering a moment, confirming, I think, that I'm really okay with this. He turns his attention to my father and says, "We'd love to have coffee."

My mother sobs and then launches herself at me, all but dragging me from Roarke's arms to pull me into hers.

Half an hour later, it's not just me and Roarke with my parents but Jessica, Jason, Martha, and Ruth. Somehow, despite all the pain around the island of our kitchen, there's healing, there's family. My parents even volunteer to help with the festival cleanup.

Many hours later, Roarke and I stand on our

porch watching the sun set on the horizon, his arm around me. "I did coffee, but I don't know how to just put this thing with my father behind us. I don't know how to fully forgive him."

He turns me to face him. "Go slow. Talk to him on the phone. Invite him to the wedding."

My heart starts racing with that idea. "You want a man who tried to destroy us at the wedding."

"He's the only father you will ever have," he says. "The day you say goodbye to him forever shouldn't be filled with regrets."

I swallow hard. "I know. I know. I do. That's why I let him in for coffee. I'll get there with him, ironically because of you, the man he treated horribly."

"We'll get there together, Han. Together always. This is the end of the day but the beginning of a new family, our family." He lowers his forehead to mine, and we stand there, just living in the moment, the two of us who will soon be three. And perhaps in that and the reconnection to family, we have more than the hope that deer brought me. We have a holiday miracle.

EPILOGUE

Hannah…

December 5th…

My morning starts with a call from my father. He's trying. He really is, but I have yet to send him a wedding invitation. I'm closer, though. After lots of long talks with Roarke about forgiveness and life being short, I'm closer. The holiday helps, too. It's about family and friends, and today has really proven that to be true. It's been a fun day of planning that included picking out my first real Christmas tree in years.

Roarke and I currently stand in the living room decorating that tree, a giant Christmas tree actually, that I had to have, despite Roarke and Jason swearing it would kill them to get it into the house. I actually did think at one point it might take them both out, but they came through, brawny men that they are. It's perfect in our living room, too. The night really couldn't be more perfect. We even have a fire in the fireplace while we fill the limbs with bulbs, thanks to one of those Texas one-day-long cold fronts. We have company, too. A border collie who was deserted at a rest stop and brought to us that I've named Shirley, despite Roarke's mock protests. Shirley is adorable and sweet. Roarke doesn't know yet, but I'm not letting her go.

When we finish decorating, we sit down on the couch, me snuggled close to Roarke as we enjoy the twinkling wonder of the lights on our tree. Shirley hops on the couch and settles her head on Roarke's lap, and he gives her a good stroke and glances at me. "She thinks she's staying."

"Because she is," I assure him, and he laughs.

Roarke arches a brow in my direction, those brown eyes as warm as the fire. "Is she now?"

"She is. Any objection?"

"Not even a small one," he says, kissing me, as Shirley decides to kiss him, leaving us both smiling our way closer to our wedding and Christmas.

• • •

December 15th…

I stand in the Dallas bridal shop staring at myself in the mirror wearing the red dress that I want to wear for my wedding with Jessica by my side. "Red dress," she says. "Red boots. I love it. The skirt flaring at the bottom is my favorite. Or maybe the lace at the bodice that makes the dress so darn perfect."

"It's not traditional," I say, running my hands through the lace at my waist, which thankfully isn't showing my pregnancy yet.

"It's not about traditional or nontraditional," Jessica says. "It's about you loving it. It's about you and Roarke being in love. And who wants to be about everyone else's expectations anyway? How many white-dressed brides did you photograph in the fashion world?"

My cellphone rings, and I grab it to find my father, who is almost going overboard with daily calls. I answer the line. “What if my wedding dress isn’t white?”

“It depends,” he says. “Do I get to come see you get married?”

My chest tightens. “Christmas Eve. Are you busy?”

“Now I am. And so is your mother. What color is the dress?”

“Red.”

He laughs. “It reminds me of the red princess gown you wore around the house for a year when you were ten. I think red is perfect. And it is a Christmas wedding.”

I laugh. “I remember that dress, and yes, it is a Christmas wedding. Thanks, Dad. I have to go buy the dress.”

“I love you, honey.”

“I love you, too.”

We disconnect and I inspect myself in the mirror before I smile. “This is the dress!”

The attendant behind us starts to clap and so do we. I’m marrying the love of my life in less than two weeks.

• • •

December 20th…

“What can I do to help?” my mother asks. “We’ll be there tomorrow. I can do anything you need.”

“All I need is for you to be here,” I assure her. “And to be nice to Roarke’s father.”

"We've been talking with him," she surprises me by saying.

"You have?"

"Don't sound so surprised. We were friends much longer than enemies."

"Then you've given me the best wedding gift ever," I say. "Because I want us all to be family."

"That boy was like a son to me growing up, honey. I love Roarke. He's a good catch, but don't forget, so are you."

So am I. "I know," I say, and I mean it this time. The time apart hurt, but perhaps it's how we came together now, stronger than ever. I'm stronger. I'm more confident, and in that, I feel that I can love and be loved on a much deeper level.

All things happen as they should, and I now believe that's the case with me and Roarke, past and present.

• • •

December 22nd…

Roarke and I are in surgery on a stallion who just arrived, and I can't seem to help him the way I normally would. The blood is just too much for me and my delicate stomach these days, as is the metallic smell. Somehow, though, I stand there next to him without leaving the room because I will not allow him to be distracted. But he knows. I don't know how he knows, but he does. He leans close and whispers, "Go get some air, Han. I'm good."

"I'll help," Allison offers, moving to my side. "Go, honey."

"I'm fine," I argue, but her lips purse.

"You're turning green. Go get some air."

I listen. I have no choice. Once I'm outside, I sit down on a step, and Shirley is right there with me, giving me kisses. Slowly, I start to feel better, and thankfully, when my phone rings, I'm able to answer, especially since it's my agent.

"Good news. I sent some of your work to Hamiltons in London to be considered for a rising stars event. They're in love. They're featuring you next summer." Hamiltons is one of the most famous photography galleries in the world. "You're on your way, honey!" she says. "You are a rising star."

I stand up and shout with excitement. "What photos?"

"All horses with their Horse Wrangler. Seems you and your future husband know how to make magic together."

"Yes," I say, teary-eyed with joy. "Yes, we do."

Later, much later, Roarke and I celebrate with sparkling cider and cucumbers with ranch dressing, which might seem like an odd combination, but it's what the baby wants. And Roarke doesn't even blink. He eats cucumbers and ranch dressing while drinking sparkling cider.

• • •

Roarke…

December 24th…

I've never been so damn nervous in my life.

I stand under the tree where I proposed to

Hannah in a tuxedo with a red tie, as per Hannah's directions, with Shirley by my side and our personal horses grazing nearby. Her parents, my father, and Becca are in the crowd that has morphed into one hundred as the surrounding areas got word that we were finally doing this. Linda is all over the crowd, shooting photos, while Max has tagged along with her, trading in his pitching glove to help control the crowd.

The preacher, a man who has known Hannah and me since we were in diapers, is in front of me, smiling at my nerves while Jason is by my side in the role of my best man and the best damn friend anyone could ask for. Jessica, the bridesmaid, is somewhere with Hannah, in the trailer setup, I think. It doesn't matter where. Hannah's not here with me yet. Finally, the song "God Gave Me You" by Blake Shelton starts to play, and Hannah appears on the lily-and-rose-lined walkway set up between chairs, stunning in a red dress. I step to the end of the walkway, and we stand there, staring at each other before we both break into smiles.

She starts walking toward me, her long brown hair lifting in a light breeze off the river running beside the ceremony.

The closer she comes, the more impatient I feel. I want to run down the aisle and pick her up, but I stay where I'm at. The moment she's in front of me, Shirley barks with excitement, and when I take her hand, my heart thunders in my chest, the emotion I feel for this woman something I can't even put into words.

"I love you, Han," I whisper softly, walking her

to me. "You look beautiful."

"I love you, too," she whispers.

"What do you say we get married?" I ask.

She laughs. "Yes. Let's get married."

And so we do. We stand before the town of Sweetwater, and we say "I do," and with those words to the rest of the world, I vow to love and cherish Hannah, but silently there is so much more for me to add. I will listen to her. I will talk to her. I will never allow us to be divided by insecurities or other people's wars ever again.

I will hold on and love her, and our child, for the rest of our lives.

• • •

Roarke…

Eight months later…

Hannah screams with the final push of labor while I hold onto her hand. "It's a girl!" the doctor shouts, which we knew, of course, but hearing it damn near knocks me over. We have a girl. I'm a father. We're parents. It's almost too much to comprehend, and yet it's also everything I could ever want: the complement to a perfect life with Hannah.

I stroke Hannah's face. "A girl, Han. Hope is here."

"Hope," she whispers, tears in her eyes. "She will never understand that name the way we do, the way we will every moment with her. Can I hold her?"

The doctor bundles her up and sets her in

Hannah's arms, and when Hannah starts to cry, really cry this time, my heart swells with love for my wife and our new daughter. "I'm in trouble," I tease. "You and a little you to team up on me."

She laughs. "Yes. You're definitely in trouble."

But it's the best trouble I could ever hope for. Hannah and Hope, my perfect family. My everything.

Continue reading to discover
SANTA, BABY, a Christmas novel
by Lisa Renee Jones

Sometimes a good girl needs to be naughty. When bookshop owner Caron Avery dresses up as Marilyn Monroe for a charity ball, she decides that for once in her life she'll let her inhibitions go. Before she knows it, Caron is living a night of fantasy with sexy millionaire Baxter Remington in hot pursuit. And what a night it is.

Sizzling, red-hot, and sensual, Baxter can't believe he's fallen under the adorable blonde's...er...brunette's spell. But with the scandal going on in his life, he knows he should let her go before she gets caught up in it, too. Then again, maybe one more night (or eight!) of mind-blowing passion will help them both forget.

SANTA, BABY

This book is a work of fiction. Names, characters, places, and incidents are the product of the author's imagination or are used fictitiously. Any resemblance to actual events, locales, or persons, living or dead, is coincidental.

Interior design by Toni Kerr

Manufactured in the United States of America

SANTA, BABY

NEW YORK TIMES BESTSELLING AUTHOR

Lisa Renee Jones

CHAPTER ONE

She woke from a restless slumber, warm with awareness, sensing that she was not alone, sensing that he was there, that he had once again come to her. Anticipation thrummed through her limbs, and she pushed herself to a sitting position, leaning against the padded headboard behind her, eyes drawn to the balcony, to the billowing curtains dancing in the midnight air. Hungrily, her gaze lingered there, riveted to the shadows beyond the white lace fabric, her thighs pressed together against the heated desire burning a path up their length.

Movement scattered the shadows, and sent her heart racing. Her breath lodged in her throat as he stepped forward, his fair hair lifting with the wind and falling around broad, leather-clad shoulders. Crystal blue eyes touched hers, eyes so deeply colored, they reached across the small space and swept her into their scorching depths. In the distance, a drum played.

No. She frowned. Not a drum. A knock. A knock on the door.

Oh! Caron Avery snapped back to the present, her gaze shifting from the romance novel in her hand to her office door inside the Book Nook, her San Francisco bookstore. She'd used her savings and a loan from her grandmother to purchase the bookstore two years before. A daring move she still couldn't believe she'd made.

Another knock sounded at the door. "Just a minute!" she called, opening a desk drawer and shoving the book inside, next to the tropical cruise brochure she'd been fantasizing over for her upcoming thirtieth birthday. She slammed the drawer shut, telling herself she had nothing to hide. She was just doing research, learning about the product offerings of her store.

After all, her recent decision to take her eccentric little store in a more distinctive direction and begin catering to women's fiction had paid off big-time. Sales had ramped up in a major way. She'd even managed to hire some staff. Well, one person. But that was better than being on her own. Soon, the whole upstairs of the store would be converted entirely to women's interests, filled with books, candles, and gifts—a special place for women to privately explore their hearts' desires, from inspirational reads to sizzling red-hot page-turners. A successful decision, indeed.

So much so, that she had almost paid her grandmother back every dime she'd borrowed sooner than she thought. Even sooner as Christmas was only a few weeks away, and sales were booming. An amazingly wonderful feeling considering a plane crash had stolen her parents from her at age five. But her grandmother had always been there for her, no questions asked—quickly offering her the cash to chase her dream.

Caron tucked a wisp of unruly brunette hair back into the confines of her neatly groomed bun and squeezed her thighs together, feeling the lingering fire of her fantasy taunting her. No doubt, her lack of a social life was catching up to her.

"Come in!" she called, lacing her fingers together on the desk and returning to her prim and proper librarian persona. The one that was real, not fantasy. The one she wished she had the courage to discard, but feared she never would.

The door swung open and her assistant manager, Kasey Washington, darted into the office, excitement lighting her youthful features, her cute little blonde bob bouncing as she rushed toward the desk.

"Oh, my gosh!" Kasey exclaimed. "I have big, big news." She plopped down in the worn, cloth-covered chair Caron had bought at a secondhand store. "Big news?" Caron pursed her lips. To Kasey, a new flavor at Starbucks constituted big news. Kasey grinned and continued, "One of our new romance customers is upstairs looking around. I don't know if you remember her? Ruth Parker."

Caron shook her head. "Doesn't sound familiar."

"She said you helped her pick out a couple of books last week and she really liked you."

Okay. "That's great to hear," Caron said, and silently added, *But hardly big, big news!*

"She works for the Cancer Society, and she's on the committee that is sponsoring that big charity event going on a week from Friday, the old Hollywood-style gala they've been advertising for weeks. Well"—her eyes lit—"one of the ladies in the runway show had an emergency and can't make it. She needs someone to play Audrey Hepburn and she wants you!" She squealed. "How cool is that? You're going to be on television."

Caron's jaw dropped. "What?" She shook her head. "Oh, no. I'm not getting up in front of all those people dressed in a costume. And I am not going on television!"

"You have to!" Kasey insisted. "It's fun. It's exciting. It's a once in a lifetime opportunity. You said you wanted to do something out of the ordinary, to let loose a little."

Caron didn't do public speaking, let alone walk across a stage in front of a bunch of society people *and* on television. "By taking a cruise! Not going on television. No. This is not fun to me."

"The store will be in television commercials, in every brochure handed out, and in publicity after the event. And for free. She isn't even asking for a donation because the spot is paid for already. This is free publicity for the store and perfect to launch our new romance section and it's the first Friday of December, right smack in the midst of holiday shopping. Talk about a last-minute chance to boost Christmas sales. It's perfect! Go be Audrey for a night. Have fun." She wiggled an eyebrow. "There will be lots of hot, rich men there. In fact, now that I think about it, you have to take me. *We* have to do this. You have to do it. For the store, Caron. Do it for the store. You know we need the exposure. It could mean lots of business."

Leaning back in her chair, Caron scowled at her assistant. Because Kasey was right. They needed the exposure. And exposure equaled business, which equaled paying her grandmother back the rest of the money she owed her. Suddenly, this wasn't about stepping outside her comfort zone and doing something that felt awkward. This was about responsibility and what was right.

"She's here now?" Caron asked. "Waiting to talk with me?"

"Right outside the door," Kasey agreed. "Your ticket to adventure and great sales. I can feel it."

Caron rolled her chair back from her desk. "I can't believe I am going to do this," she murmured.

Kasey hopped to her feet. "Yes! This is going to be so much fun. Just wait and see. You are going to have a blast. A night of pure fantasy. Did I mention you get a celebrity stylist and hours of being pampered before the show? You are going to be in heaven. You are going to be Audrey Hepburn for a night. To live a fantasy. I'm so excited for you, but jealous. Really jealous."

Right. Fantasy. Audrey Hepburn. Maybe that might be okay. If she could forget the crowds. Right. Forget. The. Crowds. Forget falling down on stage during her high school graduation. She'd never quite gotten over that, but she'd better get over it now. Audrey Hepburn wouldn't fall down, after all. And they wanted *her*—Caron Avery—to be Audrey for a night.

• • •

Friday night came far too quickly, especially in the midst of a busy work schedule that did nothing to abate her nerves. At five o'clock, Caron had been headed toward the gala for professional primping done by experts, when she'd received the news—the toilet had overflowed in the bookstore. Immediately detouring, she'd rushed back to the store, unable to leave Kasey to such ugliness on her own. An argument with the plumber had ensued over his outrageous fees, and she'd fired him in favor of someone she could afford to pay. The result—toilet fixed but she was late for her appointment with makeup and hair. Almost two hours late. Terribly, horribly late. And since there was absolutely no parking to be found in the hotel parking garage, any relief she had found in finally arriving at the five-star downtown Hyatt was quickly fading. Could this get any more embarrassing?

Caron's little red Volkswagen sputtered on the third go-round in the parking lot, and one look at the gas gauge said, yes, it could get worse. Her car was on empty. She blew strands of dark hair from her eyes. This was not exactly the makings of a Cinderella fantasy night.

Desperate times required desperate measures. She lightly pedaled the accelerator, ever aware of her fuel gauge, and turned toward the front door of the hotel. Mini Christmas trees flickering with white lights lined the entryway, and she pulled up behind a line of cars waiting for the valet. Wow! Already people in fancy dresses and tuxes were speckled along the sidewalk and entryway. This was beyond late. This was downright cringe-worthy.

Desperate times, she reminded herself. She shifted into park and killed the engine. She slid out of the car despite being more than a little self-conscious about her pink sweatpants and butterfly-print T-shirt. Her face was bare of makeup, her hair piled on top of her head. A wilted flower amongst the glamorous roses in glittery dresses. Nevertheless, the fastest path to the entrance, and the parking of her car, was right there, in front of her. She slammed the car door shut and tried to think of the bright side. Instead, she thought how little time the stylist had to transform her into runway-ready. At least she didn't have time for nerves. There was a light at the end of the long, twisting, black tunnel called this day.

Spotting a doorman, she rushed forward, ignoring the horns honking as several cars pulled forward and her Volkswagen remained in place. She half ran to the uniformed attendant, hoping to reach him ahead of a lady in an elegant white formal suit. She hated to be rude, but she had to get into that hotel.

Caron held out her keys, panting a bit breathlessly. "I'm in the show, and I'm very, very late." A gorgeous brunette in a red satin gown walked by, and Caron cringed, her pink sweats feeling dingier by the minute. "Make that three verys. I have to get into costume and I can't find a parking spot and—"

"Miss. I have cars ahead of you. I can't just move you ahead."

This was the part where she needed money that she didn't have. The part where someone rich hands cash to the naysayer and makes them a yeah-sayer. Sometimes she really hated the way money made the world go round.

She plunged onward in her argument. "Again," she said. "I'm in the show. I'm one of the Hollywood starlets—Audrey Hepburn. They can't start without me." He gave her a quick inspection that said he'd believe that the day hell froze over. She frowned. "I'm aware I don't look the role at the moment. I missed my appointment with hair and makeup. The toilet at my store…"

He snatched her keys. "I'll take care of it," he said grudgingly.

Apparently, the mention of a toilet was almost as good as cash. It sure scored her a parking spot. Whatever worked. Now if she could get a ticket to claim her car and disappear. And she almost wished she could just disappear. Unfortunately, it looked as if she'd need that cruise to get her fantasy escape. Tonight was turning into one big flop.

On that note, she accepted the ticket from the valet and whirled toward the door and right into the hard, tuxedo-clad chest of a man. His hands came out to steady her—strong hands—warm hands that sent a shock wave of awareness through her body.

She blinked up into the amber gaze of a handsome face framed with dark hair, a hint of gray sprinkled at the temples. Very George Clooney—Ocean's Thirteen sexy with a strong, square jaw, and firm, nice lips. Oh, God. Don't look at his lips. Back to those amber eyes. Eyes that inspected her pink butterfly shirt with a lifted eyebrow. She swallowed. She'd made it to the fantasy but managed to do it in pink sweats and tennis shoes.

This was so *her* life, not Cinderella's.

• • •

She had blue eyes. That was the first thought that came to his mind as he stared down at the heart-shaped face of the woman who'd unwittingly become his prey. Sky-blue, deep, almost navy with a hint of yellow. He'd guessed green from a distance, a contrast to her dark brown hair. But he liked the blue. He hadn't been on the hunt in a long time; and on this night, certainly, he hadn't expected to be. But there was no denying the demand within him for this woman—the primal hunger she'd taken from dormant to downright raging. The minute he'd seen the pink sweat suit in the midst of the clingy silk gowns, he'd stood at attention.

"I am so sorry." The woman apologized for running into him, her voice as adorable as her pointed chin and cute button nose. "I am sort of in a rush. The makeup people are going to kill me. I…sorry."

"I'm not," he replied, reluctantly letting go of her petite shoulders when everything male inside him roared with demand. A demand to pull her close. No. He wasn't sorry at all. In fact, he'd put himself in her path for a reason. To meet her. "I'm Baxter Remington. You are?"

She swallowed hard. She had a slender neck, a neck meant for kissing. "Baxter Remington," she repeated. "As in the Baxter Remington who owns Remington's? With coffee bars all over the United States?"

And Canada, but he didn't say that. It still amazed him that his father's little dream was launching into a global enterprise. "You know our coffee?"

"Of course," she said. "The shops are everywhere." She crinkled her nose. "It's a little pricey for me, though." Her eyes flared, as if she realized she'd misspoken. She quickly added, "But worth it.

I just can't afford...I mean..." She obviously cringed. "I'm late. I need to go. Sorry again." She started to leave.

"Wait!" he called out before he could stop himself.

"Sir?" The valet was standing beside Baxter, offering service for Baxter's 911 Porsche sitting a few steps from the curb.

Baxter held up an impatient hand and focused on the female turning back to him with surprise on her face, as if she hadn't expected him to continue their conversation. Certainly, she hadn't lured him to call after her as most of the women he knew would. Was that what intrigued him? Her unassuming nature? And yet she sent fire through his veins. She wasn't his normal blonde, blue-eyed, big-breasted, thirty-second distraction, then back to work. She was brunette, and wore no makeup. There were no plastic bells and whistles, either, just pure, natural woman. Pretty, earthy, genuine.

"How do I find you later?" he asked.

Her lips parted in hesitation, and then a slow smile lit her features. "Look for Audrey Hepburn." And then she turned and rushed away.

Baxter stared after her; the thrum of carnal desire burned through his body. To think he'd almost skipped this event, since there was more than coffee brewing right now at Remington. He was hot in the midst of allegations about his VP's supposed insider trading, which he hoped like hell weren't true. A good reason to hide from the press. Seems little Miss Audrey Hepburn had given him a reason to come out and play.

CHAPTER TWO

Caron was still reeling from her encounter with the ultrasexy Baxter Remington when she hit the backstage area of the show. All around her women were fretting in front of mirrors, while stylists attended to last-minute touch-ups to hair and makeup. The nervous energy in the room was so darn electric, it was contagious. It rushed over Caron and set alight the idea of embracing her persona as Audrey Hepburn for the night.

Her mind raced as she searched for the lead stylist, Betsy, to announce her arrival. Illicit thoughts of living out a fantasy—with Baxter Remington in the starring male role, and she, the sophisticated starlet—took root. She almost laughed at that. She'd met the man in a sweat suit, with no makeup on—a guise that wasn't uncommon on her days off. It was comfortable. And men like Baxter Remington did not *do* women like her. Not that she wanted to do him. Or him to do her, rather. She grimaced. Okay. Maybe she did. If she was going to live a fantasy, why not *do* a man as hot as Baxter? That highly sensual, quite entertaining idea lasted all of two seconds before being smashed nice and flat as she found Betsy.

"I'm here," she announced, and smiled nervously. "Just in time, right?"

"We already replaced you." Betsy delivered the message with all the brassy personality that her red hair and bodacious curves suggested. Did so while still managing to stick some bobby pins in the wig of what appeared to be a business owner representing Elizabeth Taylor.

Disappointment washed over Caron, and she whispered, "Replaced me?"

"What'd you expect me to do, sugar?" Betsy challenged. A hand went to her robust hip. "You're hours late. Not one hour. *Hours late*. As in plural." She raked fingers through a mess of wild red curls. "I had to turn one of the makeup girls into Audrey, and that wasn't an easy task." She grimaced. "Suzie barely fit her size-eight body into your size-four dress. I worked miracles, I tell you. Miracles."

"I really loved that dress," Caron half-whispered to herself.

"*You* weren't here," Betsy countered.

"I know," Caron admitted, feeling the heat of embarrassment and disappointment rush to her cheeks. "I left a message. I had a plumbing problem."

"And I was in poo up to my neck," Betsy spat. "This event is televised, and my job is to fill these dresses with starlet look-alikes before those cameras roll." She motioned to all the craziness around her. "And do I look like I could check messages? I have a show to put on."

"And a problem to solve," came a male voice.

Caron, Betsy, and Elizabeth Taylor all turned to find Reginald, Betsy's assistant, holding a blonde wig. Betsy grabbed Elizabeth Taylor's shoulder, and Elizabeth yelped. Betsy quickly apologized, dropping her hand but not the grimace on her face.

"Why are you holding Marilyn's hair?" she asked, her face redder than Caron's felt.

Reginald was a tall, black, effeminate man, with better grooming than a lot of the women she knew. "Because," he said, lips pursed, "*Marilyn* doesn't like high heels and never wears them, thus, how she fell down the stairs and broke her ankle. She's out. No show for her."

"Come again?" Betsy asked, blinking as if she didn't believe what she'd heard.

"She's out, Betsy. We lost our star!" Reginald was losing his cool.

Betsy turned slowly, and fixed her attention on Caron. "You'll be Marilyn."

Caron's eyes went wide. "Are you nuts? I don't look anything like Marilyn."

"The dress will swallow her whole," Reginald interjected.

"Turn Suzie into Marilyn," Caron suggested. "Let me have my Audrey dress back."

"Listen," Betsy commanded, "I sewed her into that thing. She's not coming out anytime soon. You're Marilyn, honey. You owe me for being so late." She waved at Reginald. "Get the dress, and let me work my miracles."

Caron looked down at her B-cup chest. "I don't have the equipment."

"It's time for you to learn the miracles of the pushup gel bra. You'll never again leave home without one."

Reginald reappeared with a figure-hugging white dress, and Caron's mouth went dry. "Are we doing this?" he asked.

"I need you, Caron," Betsy said.

It had taken her all week to embrace her walk down the runway as the demure, sophisticated Audrey Hepburn. She had all of thirty seconds to decide on a very different role—the sexy, sensational Marilyn Monroe. Did she dare? Caron inhaled, thinking of paying back her grandmother, of the exposure this event would deliver to her store and her future. And yes, the adventure she'd been craving came to mind, as well. Responsibility and adventure—an enticing combination. She made her decision. Yes—she dared.

• • •

FBI Agent Sarah Walker slid a hand over her silver satin-covered hip and sashayed into action, speaking low into her invisible mic. "I have Baxter Remington in view. Repeat, target in view."

Her assignment was simple, direct—get up close and personal with Baxter Remington. Find out what Baxter knew about his now-missing VP's insider trading activities, and the missing man's current location.

Considering Baxter's affinity for blondes with curves, she was the perfect agent for the job. Considering he was James Bond debonair, the assignment wasn't totally unappealing. Not that she was anything but professional. That said, Baxter's appeal did nothing to change how much she despised being used for her looks. She always paid the price later—less respect from a partner who had barely offered her any to start with. That really ticked her off.

She was good at her job, top of her class at the academy, promoted long before many of her peers. And she wanted another promotion, far away from this place and her partner's abuse. Baxter Remington was her ticket to that promotion. Snag him and his VP, and she'd snag opportunity and an exit from hell.

Time for action—she stepped around a Christmas tree decorated with brilliant, albeit costume, diamonds and pearls, and intercepted a waiter. Perfectly timed, Sarah managed to reach for the champagne tray at the same moment Baxter did. Their hands collided and she laughed, low, sexy.

"Sorry about that," she said, casting him an interested look.

He gave her a half smile. It lacked the returned interest she'd hoped for. "Ladies first," he offered, motioning to the tray.

She accepted a glass from the waiter and watched as Baxter did the same. Expectantly, she waited for the server to leave, waited for Baxter's affinity for flirtation to kick in. Instead, she found him turning away, watching the stage.

Fred, her partner and the agent in her earpiece, spoke. "Sarah, honey, you are going to have to do better than that." Fred hated female agents. Or maybe he just hated her. She wanted to tell him what she thought of him, but professionally, this was not the time, or the place.

Sarah blew a long lock of silvery blonde hair out of her eyes. She'd sprayed it with just enough silver sparkle to bring attention to her dress and her ample cleavage. She'd really put herself out to look like Baxter's ideal fantasy. Baxter had a thing for blondes; it was well-known. As a favorite of the local press, he was often photographed with a blonde flavor-of-the-month dangling from his arm.

The announcer came to the stage. The runway show was starting. A reporter appeared in front of Baxter, drilling him over the accusations of his VP's insider trading activities. Sneaky bastard had managed to snag an invitation to the party. *He should be working for the Feds*, she thought. Sarah flagged another waiter and told him to call security, quickly easing her way to Baxter's side and bringing his conversation with the reporter within hearing range.

"Mr. Remington," the reporter said. "I find it hard to believe that your VP is your closest friend and yet you knew nothing of his actions."

"Frankly," Baxter stated, "I don't give a rat's ass what you believe."

Sarah smoothly linked her arm to his. "Security is on its way, sugar," she said, glaring at the reporter, who cursed and searched the crowd. Sure enough, a pair of security guards were rushing in their direction. The reporter darted away.

She glanced up at Baxter, saw the heaviness of his stare, the disinterest. Damn. What did it take to get this man hot?

"I'm Sarah," she said, leaning into him so that her breast brushed his arm. She used her real name as often as possible. It was easier to avoid screwups that way. "I gather you're Baxter Remington."

He stared down at her, no sign of emotion, an

indecipherable mask on his handsome face. He disengaged his arm from hers. "Thanks for the save, Sarah. Now, if you'll excuse me. I don't want to miss the show."

The first model was taking the stage, and just like that, he walked away. She watched him weave through the crowd, edging closer to the stage.

Sarah's efforts at seduction had been fruitless.

"I guess he doesn't prefer all blondes, babe," Fred said into the mike.

"Jerk," she hissed, working her way through the crowd toward an empty spot at the food table, where she could speak more freely.

"Save the sweet talk for later, honey," Fred said. "Right now, we need someone close to Baxter Remington. Since you can't do it, we'd better hope one of the other ladies in that joint can. And when she does, we'll snag her, and convince her to help us."

"I'm not your honey or your sweetie," she replied. Unfortunately, she wasn't Baxter's, either.

"Yeah, well—"

She set her plate down and reached up and flipped off her mike, tired of Fred's mouth. Turning to the room, Sarah took in the glitter and glam, and hoped like hell some lucky girl would score with Baxter, as Sarah had not. Because that lady's score would be Sarah's score, as well. They'd both get their man.

And then Sarah could get rid of Fred.

• • •

After that distasteful encounter with the reporter, all that kept Baxter from leaving the charity event was the prospect of another glimpse of the mystery woman wearing the pink sweats. As for the blonde's blatant flirtation, she might not be a reporter, though he wouldn't rule it out. An opportunist of some type, regardless. Been there, done that, not interested.

Impatient, staring at the stage, Baxter's mind flickered to the questions the reporter had flung in his direction. He was sick and tired of the accusations directed at his personal character, tainting the reputation of a company he had worked into a solid success. A company that he'd committed to the mission of giving back to the community at every opportunity. Yet, now, thanks to a trusted employee, he was seeing that reputation, that foundation he'd fought so hard for, smashed into oblivion.

"And as Audrey Hepburn, we have the lovely owner of the Book Nook, Caron Avery."

With that announcement, Baxter's eyes riveted to the stage; all thoughts of the reporter, of the scandal haunting him, slid away. Caron Avery was the mystery woman, and she owned a bookstore. He found that charming for reasons he didn't understand, any more than he understood the overwhelmingly complete way the woman had taken him by storm. When was the last time his gut had twisted with anticipation over seeing a woman? The fact that Caron Avery had excited such a response had become the reason he was still here.

His heart raced as the brunette at the end of the runway appeared; his limbs heated. What would she look like transformed into a starlet? But then he was quite partial to that little pink sweat suit for reasons he couldn't begin to understand. A smile lifted the corners of his mouth as he thought of the way it hugged her cute, firm backside with delicious precision. Okay, maybe he did know what he liked about it.

A female appeared at the edge of the runway and began to sashay toward the crowd. Baxter inhaled, savoring the moment, anticipating the thrum of fire in his veins. The fire that never came. He frowned. This wasn't the woman he'd met at the valet podium. He knew it with the same certainty that he knew those pink sweats had made him hot. The woman on the runway was taller than his mystery woman; she walked with heavier steps, her hips and breasts fuller.

Baxter cursed under his breath, disappointment curling in his gut. Disappointment that was no more explainable, no more logical, than the over-the-top interest that a chance meeting with a stranger had created in him.

"Correction, ladies and gentlemen," the announcer said. "Caron Avery will be with us later in the show. We've had some last-minute costume changes due to a missing model. In the role of Audrey Hepburn is Suzie Cantu, one of the staffers from the event. What a trouper she is. Whisked onto the runway with no warning!"

The tension in Baxter's shoulders slid away. A waiter appeared and offered him a glass of champagne, and he decided to indulge—that glass of bubbly wasn't the only thing he planned to indulge in. There was a woman on his mind, a woman who had his attention, a woman he had to have. Instinctively, he knew she wasn't a woman for casual bedroom encounters—the only thing his life allowed at the moment. She might want him, but he was certain she would hesitate to act. He would simply have to convince her of the value, the pleasure, of a night of sensual escape. She would be a challenge, a provocative chase he couldn't wait to get underway.

• • •

"Time to head to the stage, honey." The brassy yell came from behind her as Betsy appeared in the mirror behind Caron and whistled. "I do declare, missy. You make a damn good Marilyn Monroe."

Did she? Caron wasn't sure. The transformation had happened so quickly, her mind was spinning. She stared at herself in the mirror, amazed at what she saw, amazed at herself. The woman in the reflection wasn't her—but yet, it was. She would never have thought that blonde hair would suit her coloring, but with the right makeup and the ruby-red lipstick, she had to admit it appeared she could pull it off.

Then there was her clingy sparkling gown that somehow seemed to create curves that weren't there before, hugging her waist, and caressing her hips. As for her breasts—well, gel bras were, indeed, the true miracle bras. And the low cut of the gown showed plenty of cleavage. Too much. Oh, yeah, too much. How could she walk out on the stage with so much chest showing?

She whirled around and motioned to her chest. "I can't go out there like this."

"Looking sexy?" Betsy asked. "Of course you can!"

Her hands covered her breasts. "They are so exposed."

Betsy laughed. "They are not," she scoffed, one hand on a cocked hip. "You look *elegant* sexy, not slutty sexy. You, darlin', are the show in this showcase. You look amazing."

This was not going as planned. "I was supposed to wear the other dress. The one with the high neckline."

"You wilted in that dress," Betsy said. "You shine in this one."

Oh, God. Her neckline concerns slid away as a new worry took their place. "What if I fall?"

"You won't fall!"

Her stomach rolled. "I fell during high school graduation. People laughed. They laughed a long time. And loud."

Betsy paled, clearly rattled, but it didn't keep her from pushing onward. "Think of this as a challenge. Take over the room like you do your business. Just go out there and forget the crowd, and be Marilyn!"

Betsy really did not understand. "Unless there is a list I can check off and a plan I can follow, I don't do challenge. I do planning, organization. Structure. High necklines." Caron shook her head. "No. No, I don't do last-minute, daring things. It's not me." She waved her hand over the dress again, pointing at her exposed chest. "I. Don't. Do. This." She was starting to hyperventilate. She hadn't done that since college. Not since she'd tried hypnosis. "I can't. I—"

"You can," Betsy argued.

"Can't…breathe," Caron wheezed. "I can't… breathe."

"Step aside! Step aside! She's hyperventilating." Reginald rushed forward with a bag. He started to hold it to her mouth and hesitated. "Watch the lipstick." She grabbed the bag, and he said, "That's it, breathe."

"We have three minutes," Betsy announced, and now she sounded as if *she* might hyperventilate. "If we don't get her out there, *I* am going to need that bag."

Reginald held up a hand. "Wait," he murmured, and focused on Caron. He dropped the bag, put his hands on Caron's shoulders. "My therapist, also known as my older sister, taught me a trick. Imagine—"

She could breathe just enough to cut him off. "Don't say 'the audience in their underwear' or I'll scream."

He pursed his lips and ignored the interruption, as if it did not justify a response. "Shut your eyes." She hesitated and he grimaced and put some authority into his voice. "Snap. Them. Shut. We're out of time."

She grimaced right back, but did as he said. It was better than going out on that stage.

"Now," he said. "I want you to imagine yourself inside a red glowing circle. A protective circle."

Her eyes went wide. This wasn't unfamiliar. "You've done hypnosis."

He pursed his lips. "Snap those eyes shut and imagine the circle."

She inhaled a heavy breath and did as he said.

"Inside your circle is your safe zone. No one can hurt you, no one can laugh, and you cannot and will not fall down. You can be anything you want, *do* anything you want. You can be Marilyn. You can be daring, be challenged. You can live the fantasy."

She repeated his words in her mind, not about the damn red circle, but about how silly she must seem right now. As if a red circle would help her? Please. Hypnosis hadn't done nearly as much for her as the idea of needing it had.

Shoot. Why did she freak out like this? Why couldn't she be Marilyn for a night? Why couldn't she live the fantasy? She opened her eyes. She *could* live the fantasy! She would live the fantasy. She was going to walk that runway, and meet any challenge that came her way that night with bold daring.

Baxter Remington and everyone else in that room—beware! Marilyn Monroe aka Caron Avery was headed their way.

CHAPTER THREE

Hours after Caron had walked out on that stage, she prudently nursed her second glass of champagne, the sparkling liquid tickling her tongue, the party around her abuzz with food, friends, and chatter. Caron herself was abuzz with a titillating game of cat and mouse, which had ensued shortly after her surprisingly successful walk down that stage. A game of Hunter and Huntress, with Caron and Baxter Remington exchanging heated stares, connecting with an electricity that defied reason. There was no conversation, no attempts at contact, the anticipation heightening with each glance. It excited, it entranced. It promised pleasure long overdue.

She wanted him. The steamy looks he'd cast her way, the heavy-lidded stares, said he wanted her, too. No doubt, he had no idea she was the woman in those pink sweats. She barely knew that woman herself right now. Didn't want to know her. That woman would be logical and prim; that woman would not blatantly flirt with Baxter Remington, even from a distance, as she had done often this evening.

"The economy is not improving. I think…"

Caron blinked, realizing she was involved in a conversation she had forgotten. A short, balding man named Lou, a commercial real estate agent of some sort, was rambling on about office space rates.

She nodded, made a lame comment, her gaze flickering again to the man standing at the bar in the corner, to the Hunter. God, the man was hot. Tall. Dark. Suave in all ways, masculine and sexy.

Her eyes locked with his, her body heating, skin tingling. She could feel her nipples pebble beneath the sheer fabric. Another time, another day, she would have covered herself and been shy rather than boldly female. But she had become the game, become Marilyn. And she was loving every second, embracing the freedom, the power of being "woman."

The flirtation had become an alluring distraction, as had the game of control. She was having fun with the sexy bombshell image that she would leave at the door at the end of the enchanting evening. For now, she reveled in the freedom that came with the role she was playing. Once she'd pressed past her nerves, once she'd embraced Marilyn, she'd found the experience quite absorbing, found it alluringly sexy. But the most alluring part of all was knowing *he* was watching. Knowing she had the ability to make him watch.

A tiny ache budded between her thighs with a discomfort that demanded attention. Caron sipped her champagne, the bubbles floating down her throat. She had a buzz that delivered courage. A buzz that sizzled with a cry for satisfaction. That called out for action. It was time to escalate this flirtation, to find out exactly how far it would travel.

She shifted her attention to the conversation, nodded and exchanged a few words before excusing herself. She didn't look toward her Hunter. Didn't have to. She could feel him staring at her, feel him as surely as she could the tingling of her skin, the sizzle of her sensitized nerve endings. How long had it been since she had felt the touch of a man's hand, felt the pleasure of intimately joined bodies? She needed that feeling, needed it as surely as she needed her next breath.

Caron weaved through the thinning crowd; the hour was growing late, near midnight. Her destination was the courtyard at the rear of the elegant entertainment room, as she murmured a few greetings along the way.

She pushed open the double-paned doors and exited, the cool air sweeping her hot skin, enveloping her with temporary relief. Fancy stone benches and fragrant sweet flowers lined the red brick trail, ground lights illuminating the colors of red, yellow, and white. Caron didn't linger, pressing forward, down the path, into the shadows. The click of the door sounded behind her, and a shiver tingled its way down her spine. *He* was there. He followed.

• • •

Baxter stepped into the night air, the wind lifting around him, his eyes catching on the silky swirl of material a second before it disappeared down the fork to the left, hidden by decorative foliage. He smiled, the Hunter in him on the prowl. For her, his little contradiction. The woman beneath the seductive Marilyn Monroe persona, who was also his little brunette butterfly. Innocence and seduction. The contrast intrigued him. But what really intrigued him was what he felt deep in his gut when he peered across the room at her, the deep swirl of desire that tightened his groin and maddened him with need.

He inhaled, took in the night air, tasted it—savoring the flavor of passion and perfume thick on his tongue—her perfume, her passion. He stepped forward, tension in his muscles, desire in his blood. Long strides took him down the path—slow, steady strides that defied the urgency pulsing within his groin. Control was a talent, a game-winning tool in all aspects of life, certainly in the art of pleasure. The more anticipation, the more wanting, the more relish in the ultimate moment of release.

He turned the corner, cut back through the darkness illuminated with little lights dangling above the brick path, teetering on black steel poles. His nostrils flared as the sweet smell of floral-scented passion thickened. One more step, two. Three. And then he paused at the end of the path, the vision before him breathtaking. A glorious view of the San Francisco Bridge opened up to him, the moon shining in the deep black sky, framing a vision of one single, blonde goddess.

She leaned against the railing, the breeze gently blowing, exposing creamy white skin. Would it be as soft as he thought it would be? Would she taste of sugar or spice? Would she purr like a kitten or scream like a cat? A kitten, he thought. He couldn't wait to find out for sure. Still, he didn't rush, didn't push forward. Baxter lingered to enjoy the vision of pure female loveliness before him. Enjoyed considering all the erotic possibilities the two of them could share. Enjoyed trailing his eyes along the zipper of her dress, imagining drawing it downward, moments before he tugged away the silky material. Moments before he exposed bare skin and full, high breasts. His eyes traveled the long line of her silhouette one last time, the tapered, tiny waist, the curves of her lush hips. She didn't turn, didn't move, yet somehow he felt her awareness of his presence.

His lips lifted slightly, the thrum of excitement roused by the coyness of her keeping her back to him. With slow precision, he closed the distance between himself and the blonde seductress, his pace a part of retaining his mandatory, ironclad control—control that defied the demands of his body. Just as slowly, Caron turned and faced him, presenting him with further reason for urgency. He stopped mere steps from touching her. His gaze rasped along the low-cut dress, caressing her breasts, noting the taut nipples pressed against the thin, white silk.

His eyes lifted to her full, red lips, parted with anticipation, with invitation. The bright color contrasted with her pale skin as perfectly as did her dark, full lashes. He wanted to kiss those lips. He wanted to taste her, to please her. He wanted to tell her everything he longed to do to her, intended to do to her. But something in her eyes kept him from speaking. A flash of fear, a split second where she was a doe in the headlights. Insecure. Nervous. He didn't remember the last time he'd seen such things in a woman. Had he ever? Those things touched him deeply, aroused him profoundly.

Silence became his weapon of seduction. Silence held no demands; it came without questions, without consequence, without reasons to think rather than to feel. He could see those needs in her eyes, see that she was acting out of character, acting out the fantasy of the costume, against the more sensible decisions of her true self. And the fact that she'd chosen to step outside her own personal boundaries and do so with him only served to ignite a primal possessiveness in him. A desire to make her his—if only for one night. A desire that urged him to reach for her, but he did not, yet.

Instinct told him he had a choice to make. He could wait and allow her to act—but did he dare risk her running, risk her darting away? Perhaps he should press forward, take what he wanted—take her pleasure and take her passion—take her on a ride to satisfaction she would never forget. He considered a moment, the deep thrum of desire pulsing through his veins, primal fire pumping with each beat of his heart.

The hunt was over but the game had only just begun.

• • •

Caron had set the stage for the courtyard seduction, yet she could barely breathe as Baxter Remington leaned on the railing next to her, smelling like cinnamon and spice, and oh, yes, everything nice. The man simply oozed sex appeal, the confident playboy and millionaire. "Caron logic" said she was way over her head, a lamb playing a wolf's game. The buzz of champagne, gel bra, and a successful walk down that runway, said she was empowered, living a fantasy where she owned the game.

"It's a city made for lovers," he said softly, the heaviness of his attentive stare caressing her bare skin as she slid into position beside him, her hands dangling over the railing.

"And a night made for fantasies," she replied, staring out at the magnificence of the San Francisco Bridge, its structure seeming to float atop the endless mass of dark water. She tilted her chin to her left, met Baxter's expression, the depths of passion she found there stripping away any and all barriers in a tantalizingly sensual way.

"Is that what this is?" he asked, facing her, casually leaning on the rail, though there was nothing casual about the tension crackling in the air, nor the lavish promise of pleasure that lifted in the midst of that crackle. "A fantasy?"

Caron eased around to face him, the moon and the stars shadowing the chiseled angles of his face, adding mystery to his suave allure. Her mouth watered as she took in his hotness factor. He was one of those rare men who made a tux sexy, rather than the opposite.

"You have a problem with fantasies?" she challenged softly, her voice somewhere between confident and uncertain.

His lips lifted in a barely perceivable, ultrasexy way. "No problem with fantasies whatsoever."

"Good," she said and ran her teeth over her

bottom lip, nerve endings she didn't know existed, raw and tingling. "Because I'm— "

A gust of wind blew through the thin material of her dress, and Caron lost her thought, curling into herself, and shivering in the process.

As would be expected of a gallant knight in a fantasy—and Baxter was most certainly that—he quickly shrugged out of his jacket and wrapped it around her shoulders, using the lapels to pull her close. His body sheltered her, warmed her in intimate places.

"A city made for lovers," he said, repeating his earlier words. "Sometimes I think it's alive. That it lives and breathes romance and seduction. That well-timed breeze did, after all, give me the perfect excuse to pull you closer."

A new shiver chased a path down her spine, and this one had nothing to do with the cool night. "I wouldn't think a man like Baxter Remington needs an excuse to take what he wants."

He arched a brow. "And why is that?"

"Rich, successful owner of a major coffee company," she replied without hesitation—after all, she was stating pure fact. "You didn't get there by waiting for an excuse to act."

Sultry, attentive eyes met hers. Oh, yes. She wanted to lick this man from head to toe. She swallowed hard, realizing how out of character her thinking was. Actually, she should expect Baxter to do the licking, not the opposite. Maybe there would be time for both? She bit her lip. Perhaps she should settle for another glass of champagne. Yes. That was probably the more appropriate response than licking him. All over. Right. Champagne.

She blinked up at him, realizing Baxter had said something, and tried to disguise the blatant desire, no doubt ablaze in her eyes. "I'm sorry. What?"

Amusement lit his handsome features, as if he knew she'd been in naughty fantasyland instead of listening. He gently tugged the lapels of his coat with enough force to insist she step closer. So close they were almost touching. Their legs, their hips. Her chin tilted upward, seeking confirmation that he felt the charge tingling along her nerve endings. Her attention focused on his mouth. Firm. Sexy. She wanted to kiss him.

"It hardly seems fair that you know so much more about me than I know about you," he commented softly.

It was an obvious nudge to reveal the woman beneath the costume, but Caron wasn't a fool. She recognized that too much Caron in this equation meant bye-bye fantasy and a chance to enjoy this hunk of a man. Caron wasn't letting that happen. She smiled coyly.

"I like it that way," she replied, flattening her hand on the warm, solid wall of his chest to keep from melting against him. Muscles flexed beneath her fingers. Somehow she managed to find her voice again. "Yes," she murmured, repeating her words. "I like it that way. Me knowing more about you than you about me."

His hand covered hers, holding her palm over his heart. "Is that so?"

She nodded slowly. "It is," she assured him. "After all, tonight I'm Cinderella, or rather Marilyn.

It's my fantasy, which means I set the rules."

"And who says it's your fantasy?" he asked, a hint of amusement in his tone. "Why can't it be mine?"

"I'm the one in costume," she quickly reminded him. "If you go put on a nice pirate costume, I'll let it be your fantasy."

A sexy rumble of deep laughter followed. "I'll keep that in mind for future reference," he said. "But for the record, I have a variety of fantasies forming that I might well feel compelled to make come true—none of which involve a pirate's costume." His lips lifted. "Though I'm not ruling out anything." His eyes danced with mischief. "But in light of these fantasies, I'll have to request you be up-front about my boundaries—'the rules,' as you called them," his seductive voice whispered. "That way I don't forget myself and say...kiss you, when you might prefer I simply do this." He slid his hands to her waist and began nuzzling her neck. "Hmm," he murmured next to her ear. "You smell like roses." His hands caressed a path up her back.

Caron embraced the solid wall of muscle in a tidal wave of sensation.

"Kissing me would definitely be out of line." She pressed her hands to his powerful shoulders, and slid them slowly downward, absorbing every flex and line with slow intent. "I can't have my lipstick messed up when I have to go back inside."

He smiled against her neck. "We couldn't have that, now could we?"

"Excuse me, Miss, well, Ms. Monroe," came a gentle female voice that jerked Caron backward as her gaze skittered and landed on a petite brunette she recognized as one of the event organizers.

"Hi," Caron replied, more than a little flustered. She started to push away from Baxter but quickly caught herself. What had happened to her confidence, her allure? She'd just been caught with the sexiest man in the building. Instead of fleeing, she rotated in Baxter's arms, held the jacket in place, while he wrapped a possessive arm around her waist beneath it. "Did you need me?"

Appearing nervous, the woman's gaze skittered from Baxter to Caron. "I do apologize for the interruption and for not having your given name handy," the woman said, wringing her fingers together. "But the last dance of the night is about to start and it's televised. There's quite the panic to find you."

Caron offered a reassuring smile. "I'll be there in a minute."

The woman nodded and rushed away in a frenzied half run. Baxter returned to nuzzling Caron's neck, the touch of his lips on the sensitive flesh. She pressed her hands on his chest, to put at least some distance between them. She wasn't about to be an easy catch, no matter how much she longed for this man. This wasn't about falling at this guy's feet. She could do that any day. This was about the high of having him fall at hers. About enjoying the power of her newfound sexuality before this night ended.

She peered up at him through her lashes, those sultry bedroom eyes inviting her back into a world of silk sheets and naked bodies—their naked bodies. "The final dance of the night is always the best, you know," she said, hardly believing what she was about to say. Did she dare?

One dark brow arched. "And why exactly is that?"

Caron's throat thickened at the cue for her reply and silently inhaled, channeling her new persona and forcefully shoving aside her nerves. *Be daring, Caron*, she told herself. She ran her hands down his tie—she liked that he'd chosen a conventional tie over a bow tie. Liked the sprinkle of gray at his sideburns. She liked a lot about this man, she thought.

Finally she said, "Everyone knows the guy who gets the last dance takes the girl home." Her voice was soft, sexy. The challenge in the words unfamiliar, yet surprisingly comfortable. She rather enjoyed the freedom to say what she was thinking.

Baxter rewarded her lack of reserve by tugging her closer, thighs aligned with hers, warmth radiating through her limbs despite a sudden gust of evening wind.

"Sweetheart," he said. "As honored as I would be to be your last dance, the last thing you want is to be photographed as my latest conquest and splashed all over the papers."

Caron's eyes went wide at the unexpected, and not-so-satisfying bite of those words. She was no born Marilyn, but she was woman enough to know Baxter Remington had just earned himself a justified smack-down in the name of every woman in this place. And she intended to give it to him.

A slow, confident smile slid onto red-painted lips. "Ah now, darling," she purred. "The only one in danger of being a conquest this night is you." She pushed to her toes and brought her lips a breath from his, teasing him with the potential kiss. "And that is still up for debate."

She pulled back, denying him her mouth, pleased at the stunned look gracing his chiseled features. She slid off his coat and pressed it into his hands, leaning into him as she did and allowing a nice view of her gel-induced, ogleworthy cleavage, while she still had it.

"Thanks for the jacket," she told him, her lips pursing ever so slightly. "And the company." Desire flared in his eyes, and he reached for her. She took a fast step backward, then two.

"Final dance to attend," she reminded him, wiggling her fingers in a sultry wave, and then she turned and started walking—no, strutting—just as she had on the runway. A sexy, empowered sort of walk she'd never even attempted before tonight but found to be liberating.

Caron could feel the heat of Baxter's stare, the way he watched every sway of her hips, every slow, calculated step. Oh, yeah. She'd taught him a lesson. He was going to have to work to be her arm candy. And she had no doubt he would. She'd seen the shocked look on his face, the flare of renewed desire that had followed—she would be seeing more of Baxter Remington before this night of Marilyn ended.

CHAPTER FOUR

Calling Caron a conquest had been a slip of the tongue brought on by the bitter taste of media hell, a hell that he couldn't drag her into for just a night of fantasy. A slip that she was making him pay for, and pay well.

Thirty minutes after being left alone in that courtyard, wishing he could pull back his slight, Baxter was propped against a bar near the dance floor, nursing a barely touched scotch, and pretending nonchalance he didn't feel. He sipped the amber-colored liquor and watched as Rich Reynolds, the CEO of a major telecom—a man known for running through women as fast as he did board members—danced with Caron in far too intimate an embrace, the damn Dean Martin holiday tune apparently never coming to an end.

That he fought a possessive desire to interrupt Caron's dance and claim it as his own, despite the media frenzy sure to follow, spoke volumes about how completely this woman had taken him by storm. Caron and Marilyn had successfully seduced him—one woman, in two completely different ways. And if that one woman had been anyone but Caron, he'd think she was playing him, and playing him like a pro. But he'd seen Caron in her natural form, experienced the pure honesty that slid from her lush little mouth, regardless of consequence, as she'd rambled adorably on about toilets and *his* high-priced coffee. Leading him to the firm belief that her Marilyn persona had not been the one to put him in his place. The response had been too natural, too quick. It had been the real Caron, the natural woman.

She'd put him in his place, and let him know that as easily as she had invited him into her fantasy, she could set him aside. Well. He had no intention of being set aside. So he was biding his time, waiting until the right moment to approach her again—knowing she expected as much and being remarkably okay with that.

He sipped his drink, watched with agitation as Rich slowly brushed the top of Caron's lush backside. He ground his teeth. "Oh, hell." Before Baxter could stop himself, he charged toward the dance floor and made his way to Caron's side. He tapped Rich's shoulder and leaned forward, "Cutting in."

Caron's eyes went wide, but lit with the hint of appreciation he'd hoped for. Rich, on the other hand, cast him a go-to-hell look. "Sorry, bud," Rich retorted. "Last dance is a complete dance."

"Let's let the lady decide," Baxter argued, standing his ground.

Both men's eyes fell on Caron, and she visibly swallowed hard. Then, motioned toward Baxter. "I did promise you the last dance," she offered and shrugged out of Rich's arms, graciously adding, "Thank you for the dance, Rich."

Rich had the nerve to look as if he might refuse to step aside, which sat none too well with Baxter. He quickly slid his arm around Caron's waist and directed her toward the center of the dance floor, away from the disgruntled CEO.

Caron laughed, her expression lighting with a spontaneous, engaging, smile. "That was rude," she chided. "And I thought you couldn't dance with me because of the media frenzy?"

"I shouldn't be," he agreed, molding her closer. She was a petite package of softness and curves. Even in her stilettos, her head barely reached his shoulders. "But I wasn't about to leave his hand on your lovely backside." His own hand rested dangerously close on her lower back. He wanted her naked, that ass firmly in his palms.

"It seems to me your hand is in the exact same spot," she challenged with a lift of her chin and enough uncertainty in her eyes to tell him she was struggling to act her role. His groin tightened. Why did that vulnerability in her turn him on so?

"But you want my hand there," he countered gently, cautiously taking the bait, no desire to scare her off.

She blushed despite her sexy persona but managed to keep him on his toes with a challenge. "So another man's hand is enough to make you forget your media phobia?"

"Apparently," he told her, the soft scent of woman flaring in his nostrils. "And considering the scandal my company is going through, that's not an easy task."

She fixed him with a suspicious look. "What scandal?"

His eyes held hers, welcoming her to see the honesty there. "Nothing you'd wish to be a part of," he assured her, their hips swaying in a slow rhythm, legs intimately entwined. He wanted them naked and entwined. "Believe me, I wanted nothing more than to share your last dance. I was trying to protect you." He pressed his cheek to hers, lips near her ear. "What man wouldn't want to be Marilyn Monroe's public conquest?"

She shivered in his arms—so damn responsive it drove him wild. Her hand flattened on his chest as she inched backward and challenged, "I thought *I* was the conquest?"

"I was thinking it would be rather fun to compete for that honor," he suggested. "Privately."

She considered that and then motioned toward the table not far away. "See the feisty redhead yelling at the tall, thin man?"

His gaze took in the woman with a tape measure and sewing kit of some sort around her neck. "The one who looks like she's about to blow a gasket?" he asked, curiosity piqued at the odd shift in conversation.

Caron's hands settled on his upper arms, framing her cleavage in a deliciously inviting way as she said, "She's waiting to strip away Marilyn as soon as this dance ends."

Baxter's gaze narrowed on Caron, searching her lovely features for confirmation of what he believed he understood—she didn't want anyone but him to strip away Marilyn. "We can't have that, now can we?"

She drew a discreet breath that he didn't miss, a sign of nerves he vowed to pleasure away. "What do you propose?"

He wiggled a brow. "The great escape, of course," he offered. "You game?"

A slow smile slid onto her face. "Lead the way."

• • •

Before Caron understood what was happening, Baxter was weaving through the crowd, sidestepping one attempt at communication after another until he pulled her down a hallway and into a stairwell. The next thing she knew, they were cutting through the kitchen, and approaching one of the busboys. Her eyes went wide as she realized Baxter was speaking to him in Spanish—damn, could the man get any sexier? A second later, he handed the man cash, and then whisked her into the staff elevator and pushed the button for the basement level.

Caron laughed as Baxter leaned against the wall, tugged her against his long, hard body and settled one hand on her lower back as he had done several times before, fingers barely brushing her backside. Again, nerves clamored within her, but Caron was living on the high of the moment, fears forgotten. "I can't believe you got us out of there so fast. What did you say to the busboy?"

"A limo is picking us up in the basement."

Her jaw dropped. "Limo?"

His finger trailed over her lower lip and goose bumps chased a path along her spine. "Nothing less for Marilyn, right? And it will throw at least a few people off our trail."

Before Caron could process this announcement,

the elevator opened on the basement parking level. Caron turned in Baxter's arms to find the limo ready and waiting, back door open. Her heart raced, all the nerves she'd combated this night suddenly colliding in an instant of panic. She couldn't do this! What the heck was she thinking?

How could she compare to the women of his past? Of his future? Her. Little Caron Avery, whose college boyfriend had been more interested in books than sex, and when he'd gotten around to the sex part—well, the books had been better. The few other men—improvements, but still nothing grand.

Walking a runway without falling down did not make her a seductress ready to take on a man like Baxter Remington, no matter how fancy the costume. She started to bolt, to seek escape, but warm, powerful arms wrapped around her from behind. "Does the car meet your satisfaction?"

Caron swallowed hard, Baxter's breath tickling her ear, her neck. "Oh, yes," she whispered, thinking more than the car met her satisfaction. The man did, too. Because no man had ever affected her like Baxter. A look, a touch, a simple word spoken in that deep baritone voice, and she was ready to give herself to him. The reaction he created in her was both terrifying and thrilling in the same breath.

"That's what I was hoping you would say," Baxter replied, and walked her forward, toward the car, that big, delicious body still draped around hers.

She was getting in that limo with him, she realized, and not because he wanted her to. Because she wanted to, because she'd come so far tonight—too far to toss away the ultimate reward—and that reward was not Baxter. He was simply the man who fit the fantasy, and that fantasy was about being daring. Daring to let go of her inhibitions, if only for one night. And even better, a night that came with benefits to her business. This night wasn't self-indulgent. It was about a better future, a better bookstore, a more confident self.

Caron was taking the fantasy to a whole new level.

• • •

The minute the limo pulled away, Sarah exited from the shadows and crossed to a van parked in the dark corner spot, lights out. The back doors popped open—Fred had obviously noted her approach—and she lifted her skirt to awkwardly climb inside, not missing the raised eyebrow Fred cast her way as she flashed him, her legs embarrassingly wide at the time. Of course, he wasn't about to let it go, either, non-gentleman that he was.

"Easy now, darlin'," he taunted. "I'm not the target."

"Just tell me you've got the background on Marilyn," Sarah grumbled, turning away to shut the door so he wouldn't see the flush of her cheeks. She had no idea why she let the man get to her, but he did. And in his normal irritating refusal to be dismissed, he appeared by her side and pulled the other door shut, their hands colliding in an awkward charge of electricity.

For just an instant, she blinked at those big brown eyes framed by a few strands of light brown hair slipped free from the tie at the back of his neck, and like always, she felt that familiar punch in her gut. The one that made her want to punch him in the gut for making her feel such a thing. He was everything she hated in the agency, a man who made being a female agent feel as if her presence was breaking the rules, as if she didn't belong.

"I could have gotten inside fine by myself," she said foully, distancing herself with as much grace as she could, yet managing to stick her ass right in his incredibly not handsome, though somehow ruggedly alluring, face. She looked over her shoulder as he lifted his big hand to have a smack.

"Don't you dare," she said, jerking around to sit in the chair in front of a monitor—exactly where he should be focused, instead of giving her hell.

A low, baritone chuckle escaped his lips. "You really are in a foul mood," he said, claiming the chair next to her, the rip in his faded denim jeans displaying a light sprinkle of brown hair probably the same color as the hair on his chest.

Why was she thinking about his chest hair? "Damn it," Sarah murmured, jerking her gaze to the closed notebook computer in front of her and opening it.

Fred frowned. "Your computer crash again?"

"No," she ground out between her teeth. "We do have a man on that limo, right?"

He pointed to a monitor on the far left. "The limo service will be calling us with the drop-off location."

Good, she thought. "What about Marilyn? You have anything on her yet?"

"I had it the minute Baxter made it clear he had eyes for no one but her, hours ago," he said, as he punched a few keys and sent data to her computer. "And she's as squeaky clean as they come." He punched another few keys. "Caron Avery owns a bookstore on the corner of Anchor and 2nd Street. Workaholic. Barely dates. Before her store, she worked for Barnes & Noble. She visits her grandmother in Sonoma every other week. Has no living parents. No siblings. Doesn't own a pet, though has been known to volunteer at the local animal shelter. Doesn't even have a parking ticket. Not one. Ever. In her life."

"Look harder. There has to be something we can use to motivate her to help." Sarah tabbed through the file. "What about a friend in trouble we can help as a reward for her assistance?"

He shook his head. "A small list, carefully selected," he replied. "They're all as shiny and nice as she is." He ran big hands down his thighs and leaned back in the metal chair. "It's all there. Check me if you like."

"I will," she said, scanning the screen.

"There's no guarantee this will go beyond tonight," he said. "I say wait until tomorrow and see what happens."

"Unless something goes drastically wrong tonight, he'll be back."

"You can't know that."

"I saw up close and personal how he looked at her."

"You mean how he didn't look at you."

Sarah ignored his remark. "What about employees? Anything we can use there?"

"She has one and she's college age and never been in a lick of trouble. We have zilch to motivate her to help." Lick. He used that word just to get at her. She hated it. She'd told him so. Sarah ignored it this time, too rattled by her personal failure with Baxter to keep up with Fred. "Just her duty to help us as an upstanding, good citizen, which it sounds like she takes seriously."

Fred snorted. "You're wasting your time with this chick. Strip away the costume and she loses the security blanket. She'll wilt into a wallflower."

Instantly, Sarah stiffened. How many women had been made to feel like either a wallflower or trophy, compliments of some man? She frowned.

"A costume does not make a woman," she argued. "Confidence does." *And experience*, Sarah thought, but Caron would have that after tonight. "Caron Avery can handle Baxter Remington if she puts her mind to it." She hoped.

CHAPTER FIVE

Caron settled on the limo seat, when, much to her dismay, the front slit split wide, exposing leg all the way to the top of the lacy thigh-highs. She sucked in a breath and fumbled for her skirt, struggling. Baxter bent down and pulled the silk material together, his touch gentle yet insistent.

He smiled, gentle, playful. "Having trouble?"

She blushed. "Nothing you don't seem to have under control."

His eyes lit. "I aim to please."

Oh, wow, what did she say to that? The man was making her wet just talking. How was she supposed to think? Talking. Right. That worked.

"Talk is cheap, *Mr. Remington*," she taunted in a remarkably hot voice. She didn't know she could sound like that. She liked it.

He chuckled and gave the driver directions, before scooting her farther inside the car with him following, one long, muscular leg plastered to hers.

A moment later, his hand framed her face, his lips lingering above hers. Good. No talking. She didn't do so well in that category. Right to the kisses. To the pleasure. But he didn't kiss her. His breath tickled her lips, teasing her with the kiss she'd longed for since the moment she'd set eyes on him. He waited, lingered. Teased her. Somehow one of her legs rested across his, their bodies melded intimately. Caron was breathing hard, her chest rising and falling against his, her breasts aching for his touch. Her core tightened with need, her panties wet with the desire that had been building over the past few hours for this man—now unleashed.

Never before had Caron forgotten her environment, her control. Never had she wanted a kiss to the point of taking it, and she told herself to wait, to make him come to her. To make him beg.

Suddenly, she didn't care. Caron laced her fingers into his dark, tousled hair and brought his lips to hers. He rewarded her with a long slide of delicious tongue that had her begging for more. Hungrily, she kissed him, hungrily she took his tongue, his mouth. Clung to him when he tore his mouth from hers, blinking in disorientation.

He slid her to a sitting position in the seat, him on one knee in front of her, another seat behind him. He shoved open the front slit of her skirt, exposing her legs again all the way to the lace of her thigh-highs.

Their eyes held and locked, and Caron could barely breathe for the potency of that connection. "Do you know why I stopped kissing you?"

No, but she wanted to. "Why?" she asked, staring into his light brown eyes, unable to look away. It was like indulging in a creamy mixture of melted chocolate, silky smooth and full of pleasure.

"Because," he said, the one word lingering in the air as she reached for the words to follow. "You never told me the rules. I wouldn't want to overstep my boundaries."

She sat back slightly. Oh, yeah. Damn. That had sounded good at the time. But she kind of liked the "no thinking" part of a few moments before. Yep. Really wanted to go back to the lost in abandonment, no thinking, no nerves kind of kissing. "I'll, um, let you know if you're out of line. So far you're doing very well."

He shook his head, those dark, dreamy eyes taking on a dangerously seductive quality. "A smart man learns his boundaries up front." He looked up at her with devilish innocence, his dark hair mussed and begging for her fingers as he said, "So—tell me, *Marilyn*. Can I touch you?"

Could he hear her heart racing, because she was pretty darn certain it was loud enough to reach the driver's distant ears. Where? Where did he want to touch her? She wanted to ask but she wasn't sure how she'd handle his answer. She settled for, "Yes." The one-word reply barely qualified as a whisper.

"Here?" he asked. His palms settled gently on her knees and shot little darts of fire up her thighs.

She squeezed them together, embarrassed by how easily she was aroused. "Yes."

His hand trailed over her calves, leaving goose bumps in their wake before soothing them away as he caressed back up to her knees. Then his palms moved up her thighs until his fingers traced the lace of her thigh-highs, his gaze on the tight V of her body. He skimmed back to her knees and fixed her in a heavy-lidded stare.

"Open for me," he ordered.

She squeezed the tiny gap that his prodding had inadvertently created. She instantly felt the pleasure and fear of his gentle demand. She was excited. She was terrified. She didn't know how to respond. She didn't have to. He was kissing her knees, running his hands down her calves and making her forget words. She shivered with the touch, hungered for more.

"Open baby. I've been thinking about how sweet you'd taste all night."

She barely contained a gasp at the words. No one had ever said something so bold to her before. It scared her how much it turned her on, how out of control she felt. How under his control. Her hands settled on top of his where they rested on her knees, stilling his actions before she forgot to stop him.

He seemed to sense her panic, leaning back on his ankles, his hands sliding away, leaving her wishing for them back. "It's your fantasy, your rules. Tell me what you want."

She bit her bottom lip. She wanted his hands back. She wanted… She knew what she wanted and, damn it, she would not be afraid to ask for it. She lifted her hips before she lost her courage, and slid her panties off, then reached for his hand and pressed them into his palm. "You forgot to take these off first," she stated, amazed and pleased at the confident, sexy voice she issued the reprimand in.

Hunger—deep, dark and profoundly male—slid across his face, and she reveled at her achievement of having put it there. She shifted her skirt aside and opened her knees. "Now, where were we?"

With a look of pure, primal lust etching his chiseled face, he eased out of his jacket and tossed it aside. A slow, sensual smile slid onto his firm lips.

"The part where I become your conquest, I believe."

He wasted no time getting to work on her pleasure. His palms pressed a path up her legs, his thumbs teasing her sensitive inner thighs.

His body followed the path his hands were taking, his hips spreading her wider. She welcomed him closer, welcomed his warmth, her arms wrapping around his neck. His mouth found hers at the same instant his thumbs brushed her swollen nub. Caron gasped with shock, and he swallowed it with a slow drag of his mouth across hers. Then another.

His thumbs were replaced by long fingers sliding along the sleek, sensitive flesh of her core, and her hips jerked as one dipped inside her. "So wet, so hot," he murmured against her mouth. His fingers parted her farther, entered her deeper.

"Do these lips taste as good as these?" he said, his teeth nipping at her mouth, his fingers doing something absolutely too good to be described before he added, "Why don't I find out? Yes?"

At her boldest she would not have thought she would answer that question, yet she heard herself say, "Yes."

He leaned back, stared down at her, that pure male hunger she'd seen when she handed him her panties back again. Apparently, he liked it when she asked for things. She'd have to remember that for later.

With satisfaction, she watched as he settled between her legs, the warm heat of his mouth closing down over her clit. Caron felt as if every nerve ending in her body exploded with that contact. Her back arched, her hips lifted, chest thrust in the air. And when her legs were suddenly over his shoulders—little pants of pleasure coming uncontrollably from her lips—she decided this asking-for-what-she-wanted thing was working out pretty nicely for her, as well.

He lapped at her, licking, suckling, teasing. Far more easily than she would have ever imagined, Caron found herself shivering into mindless bliss. She didn't want him to stop. She grabbed for the back of the seat, stared down at his head between her legs. Moaned at the erotic sight it made. He suckled her clit into his mouth and slid a finger inside her, then another. She felt them search her inner wall, caressing, then pumping. Her eyes were heavy, her limbs weightless. Pumping against his hand, his mouth. She didn't want him to stop.

Her hand went to his head but she bit her lip, forced herself not to cling. But that tongue. It was magic. It was…Her fingers laced into his hair. She couldn't help herself. And hung on tight. She was afraid he would stop before she was ready. He couldn't stop. Not yet. Something about the way he lavished her with long, silky strokes was just too good to end. She could feel that little bite of ache that had to be answered, and she pumped against his tongue, against his hand, panting with need. Soon, she shattered; the hard spasms rocked her with so much pleasure that her entire body shook.

With slow perfection, Baxter eased her body into relaxation, soothing her with slower strokes of his tongue, caressed her down to complete, utter satisfaction, and then, and only then, did he slide his fingers from inside her. He brought her knees together and then settled his hands on top of them, and Caron found herself embarrassed by the intensity of her response to this man.

"Even sweeter than I imagined," he said softly. His words only intensified the heat rushing to her cheeks. Her lashes fluttered, lifted, and she fumbled for the right reply. Should she say thank you? She didn't know. She'd never been given a mind-blowing orgasm like this one, let alone in a public place. "It was, um, nice."

"Nice?" he asked, his features darkening instantly. "Did you just say it was 'nice'?" He wasn't pleased.

Okay. Try again. "Thank you?"

He lifted a brow. "Thank you?"

His eyes darkened, narrowed, and then he moved, his hands pressing into the leather on either side of her knees.

"*Nice* is how you describe the guy you're fixing a friend up with. *Nice* is the guy you went out with and never want to see again. Was it nice?"

Okay. Bad choice of words. She shook her head, swallowed hard. Decided to say to heck with the Marilyn-style slyness and just speak her mind. "Mind-blowing," she said. "It was mind-blowing. Couldn't you tell?"

With a half-veiled look he studied her intently, then moved toward her to brush that firm mouth across hers. "Do you know what I want to do right now?"

Strip her naked and make love to her? "Tell

me," she whispered.

"Take you inside my apartment and make you come in so many mind-blowing ways, you forget the word 'nice' ever existed."

She didn't even know they had started driving, let alone arrived at his apartment. But it didn't matter. His words—their meaning—were very clear.

"Oh." She mouthed the word, realizing she'd just received her second lesson of the night. Lesson number one had been: tell him what she wanted and he would give it to her. Lesson number two: compliment him after a grand orgasm and he would give her more. Check. Not likely to forget that one.

"Just one special request," he said.

Her heart fluttered, excitement spurring it into erratic action. What did he want? The return of pleasure? Here? Now? "Request?"

"Don't ever use the word *nice* again." And then he kissed her.

• • •

Baxter kicked the door of his twentieth-floor apartment shut. Lust, raw and heavy, settled in his gut as he watched Caron step to the edge of the shiny stairwell of six steps leading down to the grand-sized, open room of sleek black leather decor. His gaze swept that heart-shaped perky little ass and his groin tightened, expanding uncomfortably against the steel of his zipper. She was his now. They were alone. A back entrance to the building and well-trained staff had allowed a silent entry into the elite Financial District building. The manned security desk offered extra assurance that no one would reach them from there.

He busied himself with the security panel, reining in his passion, aware she was on unfamiliar ground. If he'd read her right—and he was pretty damn certain he had—she'd need a minute to feel in control. But that control would be as much a facade as her costume. This was his domain, his world, and that was why he'd brought her here despite his policy of never bringing women home. Here he could allow her all the freedom she wanted, without the concern that she'd bolt at any minute.

He took a step toward her and she darted forward, out of reach.

"Nice place you have here," she said, cautiously lifting her skirt as she took the stairs.

Baxter's lips twisted with amusement, his cock thickening with the thrill of the chase as he sauntered down the stairs in willing pursuit. "Glad you approve," he said, aware that bringing her here satisfied the deep possessive burn she created in him.

She stopped in the center of his living room beside the marble coffee table, the marble fireplace behind her adorned with family pictures. A corner wine display was to her right. A few sentimental trinkets were displayed in various locations. She took them all in, held her delicate hands by her sides. "Needs books, though."

He smiled, amused, charmed—hungry to get his hands on her. "Says the librarian." He stepped toward her.

She stepped backward, hit the bar, recovered by leaning back and resting her elbows on the granite surface. The action thrust her chest forward, offering him a lush view of her cleavage. His gaze stalled on her full, ripe breasts.

She kept talking. "Books are sexy," she said, her voice hoarser now, affected by his inspection. "They make you smart. Smart is sexy."

Baxter closed in on her, pressed one hand on the counter beside her. Inhaling the scent of aroused woman, every muscle in his body tensed with the need he felt for this woman.

"Sexy is you in that dress," he said, a finger trailing the valley between her breasts. He could feel her heart racing beneath his touch, and it pleased him. "Sexier is you out of this dress."

CHAPTER SIX

Sexier is you out of this dress.

Caron cringed as she replayed those words in her mind—Baxter's words—a sudden panic overtaking her. The idea of baring her cleavage had seemed grand, sexy, daring, until she had a realization. When the dress came off, so did the gel bra. Her mind raced. She had to keep the dress on or leave. And judging from her experience with Baxter, if he made any real persuasive effort, she'd be out of this dress.

Intent on escaping, she tried to duck under his arm. He moved, captured her, his big legs pinning hers. His hands palmed her breasts, pushing them together. She looked down, studied her own amazing cleavage in awe and disbelief. If only they were real. His fingers rasped over the bare skin exposed by her skimpy top, the pleasure immense. He felt so damn good, his body, his hands, those lips. She tried to shake off the lusty fog. Desperately, she reached up and covered his hands with hers.

He kissed her, long, deep, and her body warmed. Her hands fell away from his and pressed to his chest, fingers sprawled out in wanton exploration. He was so hard, so strong, so unbelievably wonderful to touch.

Every nerve ending she owned was alive, aware, as his hands slowly traveled over her waist, slid along the curve of her backside. Slowly…as if he were savoring the touch, savoring her. It was amazingly sexy, overwhelmingly hot. He skimmed a path over her ribs before returning to her breasts. He shoved down the lace there, shamelessly exposing her nipples, and tugged them between his fingers before she could object. She moaned into the kiss, forgetting the bra, forgetting everything but how good the touch felt. His gentle touch turned a bit rough, rasping her nipples with calloused fingers and tight little tugs that had her core spasming.

He tore his mouth from hers, leaving her panting for more, as he stared down at the stiff peaks. "Beautiful," he said. "I want to kiss them."

Oh, please, yes. She wet her lips. "O…kay." She squeezed her eyes shut at the ridiculous response. Where was her inner vixen when she needed her? How did anyone play coy when they wanted their nipples kissed?

But he didn't kiss her nipples. Instead, he turned her around, leaned across her body, the hard proof of his arousal nuzzled beneath her backside. He drew down the zipper.

Panic anew arose inside her. She had no idea what to do. "Wait!" His palms slid beneath the open zipper, warm against her midsection, and she pressed into him, the straps of her dress falling down her shoulders.

His hands slid to her stomach as he tugged her gently to him, his lips near her ear. "I can't wait."

She didn't want to wait, either. She didn't want to care about the damn bra. She wished she'd never put it on so she wouldn't be worried about taking it off. Her head fell back against his shoulder. She blinked up at him, distracted by his mouth. Wishing for a taste, for more than a taste. That thought fueled her vixen confidence.

"Prove it," she challenged, asking for what she really wanted. Him naked. How had she gone this long without ripping this man's clothes off? She rotated in his arms to face him, tugged on his shirt. "Take it off," she ordered. "My rules, remember? No clothes for you." Her clit throbbed just thinking about him naked, about him inside her. She was swollen, achy. Wanton in a way she'd never been in her life. And it felt good. So good.

"And you?" he rebutted, the raw desire etched across his features almost enough to make her strip right here and now. Almost. He was going first.

She lifted her chin defiantly. "After you," she said, leaning against the bar to watch him undress, gown now back in place. It was his turn to be a little exposed, and she planned to enjoy every minute.

His pupils darkened, fierce with arousal, rich with a hunger that said he wanted to eat her alive, and she flashed back to the limo, to the intimate way he'd pleasured her, the brazen way she'd writhed in response.

He reached up and loosened his tie, quickly tossing it aside. Next came his shirt. A few buttons undone, then he pulled it over his head, as if he was as impatient as she.

Caron surveyed all that tawny skin, so taut over a spectacular chest sprinkled with dark hair, just begging for her hands. A six-pack of abdominal muscles intended for her mouth. And when, in one easy move, he dropped his pants and underwear, Caron was reminded quite clearly why a gel bra was not a good enough reason to miss this. Not by a long shot, not even close. Baxter was not to be missed.

He stood there, aroused, in all his magnificent, naked glory, all eight inches plus jutting out in front of him, and for the first time in her life, she wanted to go down on her knees. Wanted to. Not because she felt obligated, not because it seemed to be the thing to do. Wanted to take him in her mouth, to lick him up and down. To hear him moan and know she'd made it happen.

He held up a condom. "Care to do the honors." Oh, yeah, she did, and she didn't have to be asked twice. Nerves clamored in her stomach but they were secondary now, her desire to explore this man's body far outreaching any fear of making a fool of herself. Tomorrow this was over. If she let fear win, she'd wake up with regrets.

She pushed off the counter and let the dress slide off her shoulders, suddenly finding it a cumbersome restraint better done away with. That left her with the bra, the hose, the shoes. She'd lost her panties in the limo.

Baxter's hot stare seemed to drink her in with arousing detail. She flushed under the attention, a bit embarrassed, a lot aroused.

Caron went to him then, slid the condom from his hand. She'd never actually put a condom on a man, but she confidently wrapped her hand around his erection, enjoyed the feel of his width in her palm.

Easing to her knees, she touched the pool of

liquid hovering on the tip of his swollen head with her tongue. He moaned, his hips jerking slightly. She smiled, enjoying this power she had over him. Her tongue explored the ridge of his erection before she closed her lips around him. The more she took of him, the more he responded, and the more she wanted him inside more than her mouth. The more her legs spread. The wetter she became. Responding to the needs of her body, Caron tore her mouth from his erection, ripped open the condom and rolled it down his steely length. She'd barely completed the task, when he picked her up and carried her to the couch.

A second later, he was sitting on the couch and she was straddling him, sliding down the long, hard reach of his cock until he was buried deep inside her.

He gently pulled at her wig. "It's falling off," he said. She tried to fix it, and he stopped her. "Get rid of it."

She blinked, not sure what to do. That wig was her persona, the diva who'd allowed her to come there tonight. For just a moment, they sat there, bodies intimately merged, staring at one another. And she felt something in that moment, something intense, something that burned with erotic intensity, yet stripped away the need for emotional inhibition. She neither understood it, nor tried. It simply released her to freedom, pleasure.

Caron reached up and loosened the pins holding the wig, and tossed it onto the couch. Baxter pulled the clip holding her own hair on top of her head. She shook it out.

"I like you like this," he said, twining his fingers in her hair and joining his lips to hers.

She didn't know if he meant the words, didn't even have time to consider the unveiling of Caron, the destruction of Marilyn. Because this was a kiss like none he had given her to this point, a kiss that consumed, as if he literally breathed her in, as if they were merging, becoming one. She felt him thicken inside her, felt the pulse of his arousal. Felt the first thrust of his hips as they began to sway together, rocking with a slow, sultry rhythm. They devoured one another, drank one another, absorbed one another.

Somewhere along the line, she lost her bra and she didn't care. He stared at her breasts as if they were beautiful, touched them with hot, needy hands. Caron forgot Marilyn, she forgot fear. She moved sensually with passion, with the ultimate hunt for that place of no return—where she exploded in a rush of frenzied action and clung to him as he shook with his own release.

Long minutes later, she buried her face in his shoulder, satisfied, reconnecting with herself. Which was when she started worrying about what came next.

As if he sensed her unease, Baxter stole her moment of fear, framing her face with his hands as he studied her. "Do you remember what you called that orgasm I gave you in the limousine?"

Her brows dipped. Was this a trick question? "Nice?"

His expression darkened. "That's what I was afraid of. We have more work to do." He stood up, her body still wrapped around his.

"What?" she asked. "Where are we going?"

"To the bedroom," he said, holding her as if she were featherlight. "I told you I was going to make you come until you forget that word, and I meant it."

Caron laughed in disbelief. This might be a long night, because she wasn't giving up on the word 'nice' until she was darn good and ready.

• • •

Caron lay nuzzled under Baxter's shoulder, her hand on his chest as he slept. She stared across the room, through the open patio window, to the moon hovering low, threatening to be replaced by sunlight. She couldn't sleep, and she didn't want to wake up to be stuffed into an awkward Marilyn costume, trying to navigate an equally awkward morning-after. The question was—how did she get out of here without Baxter waking up? And what to do when she did? She had no purse, no money. Considering she had to leave dressed as Marilyn, the sooner the better. She didn't need unwanted attention. Flexing her fingers on his chest, Caron inhaled one last breath of Baxter's scrumptious male scent, and then gently eased away from him. Or tried.

He lifted his head, tightened his arm around her. "Where are you going?"

"Bathroom," she murmured.

"Hurry back," he replied sleepily, patting her on the ass.

Caron's heart fluttered. He liked her ass, he'd

made that clear. She'd liked that he liked it. But it was done, over. Baxter appeared unworried about an awkward morning-after. He was Baxter Remington, and even Caron, reader of romance, not newspapers, knew his reputation. A new woman every time he was photographed. Maybe he was just so used to morning-afters, they weren't weird to him anymore.

Caron scooted off the bed, naked, aware of feeling exposed for the first time in hours. Sadness pitted in her stomach. Her Cinderella night was over. She tiptoed toward the bedroom door, ignoring the bathroom, though she could darn sure use a little detour in that direction. Looked as if she'd be squeezing her legs closed upon exiting Baxter's apartment just as she had entered, but this time the reason wouldn't be quite so joyful.

She snagged her shoes on departure, one by the bed, one by the door—not sure how that had happened. The thigh-highs, she wasn't even going to try to find. Quietly, she rounded up her clothes and dressed, leaving the wig on the couch. The sexy dress was enough zing and bling to draw watchful gazes on its own—she didn't need the blonde Marilyn thing going on along with it.

Dressed but for the shoes—which she planned to carry for the sake of quietness—she began the hunt for a pen, to leave a note. It seemed wrong not to. Problem was, the apartment was so darn neat, free of any signs of real living, let alone anything useful, like that pen.

A snakelike, steel stairwell in the far corner of the room led to a loftlike area above. Why hadn't she noticed that before? Right. Why? She knew why. Because all she'd cared about last night was Baxter's naked body. She frowned. Was it an office? Yes. It looked like an office.

Shoes dangling from her fingers, she tiptoed up the stairwell and then stood in awe at what she found. It was a library. A library! Full of books. Fiction, history, business. Big fluffy chairs with lamps and tables beside them. Windows offering a dreamy view. It was the most wonderful room. A room she had always longed to have in her own home. And she'd accused him of having no books. Who would have thought? She sighed. She liked Baxter. Too much. His playfulness. The way he made her laugh and forget nerves and inhibitions. Regret curled inside her at never seeing him again, and she shook herself. She had to get moving.

Her bare feet sank into plush carpeting as she moved to the corner desk by the window and found a pen and paper. She studied the blank page, unsure what to say, but certain she was out of time. Baxter would discover her absence soon. A mischievous smile slid onto her lips and she started scribbling. "Thanks for a 'nice' night." Pleased with herself, she retopped the pen and set it down.

She rushed to the stairs and hurried back to the lower level, thankful all was still peaceful there. In a quick dart, she made it to the door and exited, sticking the piece of paper in the door. Now, to creatively figure out how to pay for a cab with no wallet. This should be interesting.

After twenty minutes of trying, and the early-morning sky blossoming with oranges and yellows,

Caron accepted she wasn't getting a cab with the promise of payment on the other end of the ride, and she simply wasn't willing to charge Baxter's account. So she started walking, the breeze from the nearby water turning sixty degrees into fifty. And she had no coat and a slinky dress on. Thankfully she was in a good area of town, and the sun was fast rising. It was an idea that lasted a block. She was freezing. She had to go back, to charge Baxter's account. She'd send him the money later that day. She turned to retreat and found a petite blonde approaching in slim black jeans and a turtleneck, a businesslike look on her chiseled face.

"Caron Avery?"

A badge flashed in front of Caron and she frowned. "FBI?"

"Agent Sarah Walker. You are Caron Avery, correct?"

"I am," Caron agreed cautiously. "Did I do something wrong?" Concern prickled. "Oh, God. Is something wrong at my store? Was I robbed?"

"Your store is fine, Ms. Avery," she quickly assured, though her tone was serious. "I'm here about Baxter Remington." A dark sedan pulled up beside them. "Why don't you let us give you a ride home, Ms. Avery, and I'll explain?"

Alarm bells went off in her head. "I'm all about respecting the law, Ms...."

"Agent Walker."

"Agent Walker," Caron amended, hugging herself against the chilly air that darn near had her teeth chattering. "But I'm not getting into a car with you just because you flash a badge. How do I know it's real?"

The woman raised a brow in surprise before a look of appreciation settled on it. Several cabs pulled up to the red light at the corner, and Agent Walker rushed to the edge of the sidewalk, signaling for one's attention. One of the cabs backed up and parked in front of the sedan.

Agent Walker yanked open the back door and called to Caron. "I'll spring for the ride to your apartment."

Caron's indecision lasted all of ten seconds before she dashed toward the cab. She was too cold to turn down a cab, and it seemed as safe, or safer, than walking. In the backseat of the car, Caron tried to subdue her shivers, offering the driver her address.

Agent Walker was quick to join her, wasting no time getting to her point. "We need your help, Ms. Avery." Her voice was low, for Caron's ears only. "Baxter Remington's partner is being investigated for securities fraud and he's gone MIA. He has ties to a certain investor who miraculously knew the exact moment to unload his Remington stock. We believe Baxter knows where his partner is."

Now she understood what Baxter meant by scandal, and why he'd wanted to protect her from the press. It appeared that the FBI wasn't so easily avoided. "Maybe he doesn't know anything. And what does that have to do with me?"

"We need you to use whatever bond you have with Baxter to find out exactly what he does know."

A disbelieving laugh bubbled from Caron's lips. "Me?" she asked. "I have nothing to do with Baxter

Remington. You've got the wrong girl."

"Weren't you with him tonight?"

"That has nothing—"

"Then you're the right girl. You can do this. You *have* to do this. It's your duty as a citizen to use the opportunity you have to get close to this man and stop any wrongdoing."

Okay, now Caron was getting mad. "Duty?" she asked. "How is it my duty when I don't even know this man?"

"Then why are you leaving his apartment at the crack of dawn?"

Caron opened her mouth and shut it. Bit her tongue and processed, flustered. This was none of their business. "I won't be seeing him again," she finally ground out. "Period. End of story. No forwarding number or address left."

"It's your duty as a good citizen to see him again. You have a chance to stop someone from getting away with a crime."

Caron shook the cobwebs from her head. "Let me get this straight. Baxter isn't being accused of any wrongdoing, but you want me to manipulate him to catch someone who is? And you're calling that my duty?"

"We don't know what Mr. Remington's role in all of this is, but aiding and abetting a wanted man is a felony, Ms. Avery. So yes, Mr. Remington could very well be in a great deal of trouble."

"But all you want to do is question Baxter's partner," she pointed out. "He's not charged with a crime. I don't know the law all that well, yet that does seem relevant."

"He'll be charged," the agent assured her. "And so will your lover boy if he's not careful."

Anger began to curl in Caron's belly at what was nothing more than a manipulative threat. "Clearly, you have no proof Baxter knows where his partner is. I mean, surely you've done your surveillance on him and found nothing damning or you wouldn't be talking to me right now." She gave a little snort. "Because I have to tell you that thinking I can get answers from Baxter Remington is putting you in the pretty desperate category. As I told you." The cab pulled up to Caron's building, and she quickly opened the door. "I can't help you, Agent Walker."

"Can't or won't?"

"Both," Caron stated, and tried to get out of the cab. She'd always had instincts about people, and Baxter wasn't a felon. A bit arrogant, a lot playboy, but not a felon. She wouldn't be party to manipulating innocent people. Not that she had any influence over Baxter in the first place.

Agent Walker gently shackled her arm. "You can do this. I saw the way he looked at you at that party. You have his attention."

"You saw the way he looked at a dolled-up fantasy. That's not me."

Agent Walker seemed as if she would insist further, but she didn't. She dropped her hold on Caron. "Think about it, Ms. Avery. I'll be in touch."

Caron climbed out of the car, and it sped away. She turned and looked at her building and cringed. She didn't have her keys. They were in her purse. It seemed her fantasy night had started with the toilet and ended there, too. Maybe she should have stayed for that awkward morning-after. A hunk of a hot man and a warm bed sounded pretty darn "nice" right now.

CHAPTER SEVEN

Monday morning, Baxter stood at the window of the conference room. His weekend rendezvous with Marilyn was not forgotten, but the day had started with the grim depiction of Remington Coffee's tumbling stocks. He now listened to a group of five employees as they debated "image management" and ways to increase sales, while the PR person he'd hired, Katie Kelley, nixed one idea after the other.

Baxter scanned the oceanfront horizon. Doing so reminded him of how he'd spent far too much time this weekend staring at that damn note Caron had left him. Her message "thanks for a 'nice' night" had taunted him. It wasn't like him to be so easily distracted, and certainly not in the midst of a crisis, but he couldn't stop the burn to want to find Caron and prove how much better than "nice" their night had been. But he'd restrained himself. This unfamiliar need to prove something to a woman served no purpose, and would most certainly drag her into his present hell. But that hadn't stopped him from sending Caron a little goodbye of his own by way of his assistant, to arrive at her bookstore this morning.

"What do you think, Mr. Remington?" Katie asked, referring to a suggestion for a "Remington for Kids" fun time at select coffee shops every weekend. A portion of all sales during the event would be donated to charity. "With Christmas only a few short weeks away, we could use the holiday as a launching platform. The program will appear motivated by the holiday, not the scandal."

Baxter turned to the group sitting around the rectangular mahogany table and dismissed the idea. "We've never made our charity events self-serving."

"It's well-timed charity, Mr. Baxter," Katie countered. "The public needs something to talk about other than the scandal. Because, speaking frankly, there is a natural human tendency to cling to the scandalous."

Reluctantly, Baxter agreed. And a vice president accused of insider trading, now gone missing, was pretty scandalous. And damning where investors were concerned.

She continued, "We must counteract the negative media attention, flood the memory banks with positive. And remember that staying strong in their eyes allows you to continue to give back in such a generous way while securing your employees' futures, as well."

Baxter felt a steely punch in his gut for the people Jett had put in jeopardy, guilty or not, by fleeing. Everything his father, his family, had built was in jeopardy.

"I find your points valid, Ms. Kelley," he conceded. "However, there are those who will spin whatever we do into something corrupt right now. We must tread carefully." Strategic, rapid action—that's what his father had preached and what Baxter lived.

"If I may," offered Dan Moore, VP of marketing,

clearing his throat. He was thirty-something, ambitious, full of good ideas with action to back them up. "Why not roll out a program that's threefold and appeals to more than one type of consumer." He ticked the three areas off on his fingers. "Discounts, charity, new product."

The debate continued for another hour until Baxter finally found a comfort level and agreed to the three-pronged approach, sending Katie, Dan, and the rest of his staff on their way to make it all happen—preferably yesterday. Finding his way back to his office, he passed in front of his secretary's desk as she juggled a delivery person and several phone calls.

At sixty, Lorraine had been with his father before working for him. Not only slender and elegant, she had enough style and snap to teach a few of the much younger up-and-comers around the office the meaning of the word "professional." Baxter couldn't live without her.

He'd barely settled behind his desk when Lorraine poked her head in his office.

"How are you holding up?"

He waved her forward. "Better than I would be without you," he countered, not as a compliment, but the simple truth.

Lorraine shut the door behind her and then perched on the edge of the chair in front of his desk, pad of paper and messages in hand. "Your father called from Europe. He's—"

"Worried," Baxter said, as he pressed his fingers to the bridge of his nose and then let go. "I know. And let me guess. My mother called. She's worried."

"And wants to remind you about your sister's thirty-fifth birthday on Saturday. You're headed out of town for the rest of the week. It's likely to be busy when you return. I thought you might want me to pick up a gift."

"No," he said. "I'll go today." Maybe he'd go to Caron's store and look for a gift. But he left that part out, adding, "Thirty-five is a big birthday. I want it to be special." He and Becky were only two years apart, him being the oldest; they'd grown up close and remained that way. He wanted her gift to be special. "Remind me again why I thought this Texas trip was a good idea?"

"You wanted to be sure the new stores meet company standards and rally the troops," she answered, as if he didn't know his own reasons. "Why not cancel?"

He nixed that as quickly as Katie had rejected a dozen ideas. "A cancellation might rattle the staff. I don't want them thinking that trouble is keeping me away."

"Well, there is one positive to an absence," she commented. "The FBI can't camp on your doorstep." She slid a pile of messages to his desk. "The top three are all from Agent Sarah Walker, who would like you to call her, apparently right away since she won't stop calling."

He scrubbed his jaw. "What else?"

"Confirmation the package you wanted delivered was received," she said, setting the slip on his desk, showing that the courier had, indeed, left Caron his little package.

"Oh, my," Lorraine laughed. "I wish I'd looked

inside that package. I'd like to know what put that expression on your face."

Baxter blinked. "I have no idea what you're talking about."

"I've known you since you were a kid, Baxter Remington," she scolded. "I know a look when I see one."

Having no intention of opening the door to speculation, he pushed to his feet. He didn't know why Caron wouldn't get out of his head, but it was time to find out. "I'll grab that gift before my next series of meetings begins."

Lorraine stood, as well. "Did I mention you don't need to call back that FBI agent?"

His brow lifted and she continued, "She's in the lobby waiting for you." She shrugged. "I figured as many of these meetings as you've endured, she could wait until we were done."

Baxter would have laughed at Lorraine's tactics if it wasn't for the dread he had of yet another FBI meeting. He'd been cooperative above and beyond what his attorney had advised.

"I'll tell her goodbye on my way out the door," he quipped, crossing the room. He exited to the lobby.

A petite blonde sprang to her feet from a lobby chair, and Baxter barely spared her a glance. He punched the elevator button as she rushed to his side.

"If you have something to ask me, do it on the ride down," he scolded, punching the elevator button again.

"I'd think you'd prefer these matters private,"

the woman said, reaching his side.

The familiar female voice grated a nerve. Baxter knew her. The woman from the party, the one he'd suspected of being with the press. He sliced her a chilling look. "Do you often try and seduce the men you're trying to question?"

"I don't remember ever being given the chance to identify myself," she countered. "We need answers, Mr. Remington."

He shook his head. The elevator opened and he walked inside, hovering in the doorway to block her entry. "On second thought," he told her, "I'll take this ride down on my own. Call my attorney. I think he'll have a word or two more to say this time." He stepped back inside the car and let the door shut.

He realized then one of the reasons why Caron appealed so much to him. Even in that Marilyn Monroe costume, she'd been real, one-hundred-percent pure honesty. One of the few people he'd met who was so purely human, with flaws, opinions, and personality. No games that weren't shared fun.

She was a breath of fresh air in the midst of secrets and lies. And he couldn't seem to fight the urge to see her just one more time. Besides, who was he kidding? He knew he was going to see her when he'd sent that package. That note she'd left him had all but been a challenge—and he'd never been one to walk away from a challenge.

• • •

Apparently being Marilyn came with more perks than just Baxter Remington for a night. By midmorning Monday, The Book Nook had not only debuted its new romance loft, but done so with a rush of Christmas shoppers.

Things were so crazy that, in a panic, Kasey had called her roommate, Alice, to ask her to come in and run the register. And though Caron didn't fool herself into thinking things would remain this busy—after all, there had been coupons and special deals announced at the charity event—even a small portion of this traffic would do a world of good toward paying back her grandmother.

Standing behind the front counter, half supervising Alice, Caron finished preparing the "Romance in a Bag" special advertised at the charity show, which included a candle, a bookmark, a pen, and a book of choice from the loft. Alice wished a customer a good day and seemed to be doing well. Kasey had the other customers handled. Things were finally calming down. Caron finished arranging the display she had set up by the front door with the romance bags, and then started for her office.

"Oh, wait!" Alice called out. "This came for you a few minutes ago."

Caron frowned and accepted the shoe-box-sized delivery with no return address, wondering at the funny flutter in her stomach that seemed some sort of premonition. Brushing off the feeling, she weighed the package with her hands—it was light, maybe the silk scarves she'd ordered.

A few moments later, she sat at her desk, the flutter in her stomach back again as she cut open the box. Tissue paper covered the contents; a note card sat on top of the paper. She flipped open the card, a few slashes of masculine writing on the simple white page.

You never know when you might find an occasion to wear it again. But I kept the panties. I didn't get a goodbye. You owed me a keepsake.

There was no signature.

Caron lifted the tissue and then shoved it back down, her heart thundering against her rib cage. It was her wig. Oh, God. Baxter had sent her the wig. And kept her *panties!* She reread the note; her heart raced some more—as erratically as three drums playing to different tunes. *You never know when you might find an occasion to wear it again.* As in, with him? No. That was insane. She was so not his kind of woman. He was not her kind of guy, not that she really knew what kind of guy *was* her kind of guy. But not Baxter. Not a filthy rich playboy who controlled everyone and everything around him. He'd sure controlled her. And well… that had been rather pleasurable, but just for a night. A fizzle of excitement lifted the corners of her lips. Of course, she'd done a good deal of controlling, too. And making that man moan had been so erotic.

"The toilet is stopped up again," Kasey announced, appearing in Caron's office doorway and blasting away her fantasy with a hard knock of bitter reality. "I sealed the door and, ah, well, sprayed some of the perfume samples."

Caron slammed the box top shut, taking in the announcement with painful disbelief. "Oh, please, no," Caron said, her hand pressing to her rolling stomach. "Not today." The bathroom was in the romance loft, of all places.

Kasey gave a stop motion with her hands. “Before you freak out,” she said, “I called the plumber and screamed, so *you* don’t have to. He said he’d be here in thirty minutes and that was fifteen minutes ago. It took me that long to get away from a customer to come tell you. And as much as I hate to show this to you,” she said as she set a piece of paper on the desk, “you need to see it before he gets here.”

Caron studied the plumber’s bill from Friday night and about fell over. “Five hundred dollars!” she exclaimed. “Is he *insane?* And it’s broken again on top of that?”

Kasey nodded, her expression saying she knew the plumber was going to be sorry for both—the bill and the broken toilet.

“There are people everywhere,” came the blurted announcement from Alice as she appeared in the doorway. “I need help.” She lowered her voice, “And, oh, my God, there is this really hot guy who just came in and all the women are panting. Me included.” She disappeared again.

Kasey cleared her throat. “Sounds like the situation requires attention.” She disappeared.

On another occasion, recognizing that Kasey’s urgency translated to “I really have to go see this guy, if he’s that hot,” Caron might have laughed at the youthful folly. As for Caron, there were only two men on her mind right now and both had her in knots. The plumber who had her pipes clogged and her temper hot. And Baxter, who also had her hot, but in a totally different way.

She grabbed the box and held it over the trash can, telling herself to stop thinking about the man, but she couldn't make herself drop the package. With a heavy sigh, she shoved the box under her desk. She should return the wig to the costume shop, as Betsy had requested when Caron had picked up her purse and dropped off the dress. She bit her lip. Or just pay for the wig. Make it her keepsake, as Baxter did her panties.

She squeezed her eyes shut. He had her *panties*. It means nothing, she told herself. He was just paying her back for her little "nice" note, which had clearly been a mistake. No doubt, a man such as Baxter had to end things on his terms. Which really irritated her because part of what had made that night so spectacular was the way he'd shared the power, the way he'd made her laugh, and feel as if they were sharing more than their bodies.

Power plays didn't sit well with Caron, and this felt like that to her. His way of making it clear who had seduced who. Her note had been a joke, a funny memory of their night together. And damn it, he didn't seduce her. She'd seduced him. Or maybe they'd seduced each other. She grimaced. *This* was why she kept to the real world, her fantasies between the pages of books. "Except for Friday night," she whispered.

"He's here!" Kasey yelled from down the hall. "He's here, Caron!"

Caron rounded her desk, ready for a battle. She charged down the hall and cut a fast right to the stairwell, her focus onefold now—the plumber and his ridiculous bill were getting a whack of her attention. She exploded on him in the bathroom to find him packing up his bag to leave.

"It's fixed?" she demanded, bringing into view the same cranky fifty-something plumber from Friday night. He shot her an irritated look that said he wasn't answering a stupid question. Picking up his bag, he casually tossed it over one shoulder. "Wait!" she demanded, walking to the edge of the toilet to inspect his work. "For real, this time?"

"Old pipes, lady," he said. "Replace the entire system or use this." He handed her a plunger and another bill. "That'll save you some money next time." He started walking toward the door.

Caron gaped down at the invoice for two hundred dollars and whirled in pursuit, but stopped dead in her tracks to avoid running into the man now blocking the exit.

"Baxter?" she whispered, shocked to find him here, looking every bit as scrumptious in a dark suit as he had in a tuxedo.

Amusement danced in his dark eyes as he glanced at the plunger in her hand before returning his gaze to her face. "Problem?"

Heat rushed to Caron's cheeks as she realized how far from her Friday-night fantasy she must look—brown hair twisted neatly at the back of her head, a prim black suit, and, well, the damn plunger in her hand.

She shook off the embarrassment. Unwilling to let the plumber escape, she thrust the plunger at Baxter. "Hold this," she said and started forward but rethought her rash rudeness. "Please. And thank you." With an inhaled breath, and no time to lose, she squeezed past Baxter, an instant charge darting through her body.

Caron rushed down the stairs, liquid fire shimmering through her limbs, memories of intimate, shared moments with Baxter fluttering through her mind, of being naked and entwined. She couldn't believe he was here, in her store, and instead of challenging him over the meaning of that package he'd sent, she was chasing after the plumber. She had to deal with one man and his mischief at a time. But Baxter's turn was coming.

CHAPTER EIGHT

Baxter stood in that bathroom doorway and shook his head, a low chuckle sliding from his lips. Never in his life would he have imagined his efforts to seduce a woman would result in him holding a toilet plunger, nor would he have ever believed he would actually find himself in pursuit of the woman who'd given it to him.

Disposing of the plunger, Baxter followed in Caron's wake as she pursued the plumber, a path that took him to a hallway leading to a back door.

"I am not paying seven hundred dollars for a plunger!" she hollered to the back of the guy's head as the back door slammed shut.

Caron threw her hands up in the air and then pressed her hand to her face, turning to blink Baxter into focus. "Oh," she said. "I'm sorry. I—it's just that…I'm having plumbing problems."

"I remember that from Friday night," he offered, biting back a smile.

She frowned, a cute dimple forming between her brows. "Friday night? I don't remember telling you about my plumbing problems. No. I didn't. I wouldn't do that."

Did she really think he didn't remember her from the front door of the hotel? "You told the doorman." He lowered his voice, though the hallway curved away from the store, away from the ears and eyes of potential eavesdroppers. "I liked the pink sweat suit almost as much as the dress. I didn't go looking for Marilyn. Or for Audrey. I went looking for the woman in that pink sweat suit."

She looked surprised, her gaze shifting to the store—ensuring they weren't being overheard, he assumed. Then, "I didn't know you knew that was me. I..." She stopped, sealed her lips. Then, drew herself up straight. "Why are you here?" she demanded.

He laughed. There was the Caron he'd found so adorable—equally flustered, direct and to the point. It was her way of hiding vulnerability but it didn't work. Not with him.

"I need a birthday gift for my sister. Kasey seemed to believe you could help. She said you have a knack for picking the perfect gifts."

She looked as if she might refuse, but Kasey quickly nixed that idea by appearing.

"Oh, good," she said to Caron. "He found you. I told him you'd have a better idea than me about a gift for his sister." She glanced at Baxter. "Again, I'm sorry I wasn't more help. It's crazy busy, and Caron is better at picking gifts than me anyway. I don't want to steer you wrong for such an important occasion." She glanced at Caron. "It's his sister's thirty-fifth birthday. She likes to travel, and she considers herself an amateur chef, right?"

"Thank you, Kasey," he said, offering a nod, and Kasey's face filled with a schoolgirl flush, before she quickly excused herself.

Baxter fixed Caron with an expectant look, his brow arched. "So?" he asked. "Will you come to the rescue and help me find the perfect gift?"

• • •

Caron lost herself in Baxter's dark, probing stare—a stare that intimately stroked her into such a frenzy of awareness that she wanted to run away. Or run to him. Maybe bury her nose in his jacket for just a tiny minute and inhale that delicious spicy scent of his. A dangerous proposition that said she needed to expedite his departure before she went and did something like sleep with the man again. He didn't want her. She didn't care if he claimed he wanted the girl in the pink sweats—he'd been enthralled with the fantasy. Now he wanted the fantasy woman in the wig and a chance to end things on his terms. She wanted no part of being used. The man had her panties; he wasn't getting anything else. She had to take this situation and get it under control. Put him in his place, not the opposite, which she was certain was his intention.

"You came for a gift," she said flatly, her disbelief meant to be obvious.

His eyes held mischief and mayhem, proving he was not at all affected by her directness. A sound rich and masculine escaped his lips—lips she knew to be firm but gentle.

"I really *do* need a gift," he said, his hands held up in defense. "My sister's birthday is Saturday, and I'm headed out of town tomorrow for the rest of the week."

"Don't you have an assistant who does that sort of thing for you?"

He gave her a knowing look—as if he knew she

was trying to turn him into the bad guy. And she was. If he were the bad guy, then ignoring his hot body and charming smile would be oh-so-much easier. "I'd never allow anyone else to pick out a gift for my sister."

She wasn't letting him off that easily. Tilting her chin up, she fixed him in a steady stare and walked toward him, pausing next to him. "So, just by coincidence, you happened to end up in my store to buy it."

"No coincidence," he promised in a low, velvety voice. "I came here for you, Caron."

Caron's breath hitched in her throat at that announcement, her body betraying her decision to resist. *I came here for you, Caron*. No. She rejected that claim. He came for a game of cat and mouse, and control. A game she feared would only end badly. She liked Baxter, liked him far too much to delve any deeper into this thing, this whatever-it-was going on between them. She'd get hurt. He'd simply walk away without a glance back.

She opened her mouth to tell him in no uncertain terms she wasn't interested, but found herself cut short when Alice's voice cut through the air.

"Caron! Kasey! Someone. Help, please!"

Caron inhaled and turned to find her new helper struggling with the cash register, which was known for jamming, while three customers patiently waited to check out.

"She's new," Caron murmured to Baxter, more than a little happy for a quick retreat to gain some composure. "I'll be right back."

She scurried away, aware of every step taken

under his watchful regard. Her skin prickled. A few punched keys, and Alice was set. Kasey appeared, as well, with a customer in tow, her eyes alight with as much mischief as Baxter's. Mischief that said she'd intentionally brought Baxter to Caron—no doubt, playing matchmaker. Little did Kasey know, the match had been made, and with a blonde bombshell packing a gel bra—a temporary persona that was apparently more successful with the opposite sex than the real her. That costume had empowered her and allowed her to escape her inhibitions, even when it had been discarded. Morning had come and she'd gone back to her simple reality where her seduction prowess was a big whopping zero. That realization sat uncomfortably. She knew she had to deal with Baxter and be done with this.

Caron found Baxter patiently leaning against a wall, still watching her—inspecting her with an attentive, heavy-lidded stare that explained the heated flush of her skin that refused to cool.

"This way," she said, motioning to the back of the store, where bookshelves lined walls and came together in a far too secluded corner. A narrow, round table sat in the center of the snug aisle to allow customers to sit and study their potential purchases. And though privacy with a man like Baxter could easily prove dangerous to a girl's willpower, Caron decided it had its merits right about now, offering a chance for confrontation.

The instant they were out of sight of the rest of the store, Caron whirled around to confront Baxter. She found him closer than expected. So close. Too close.

"Why are you really here?" she demanded, intending to get the obvious out in the open and, therefore, end this awkward torture of the unspoken between them.

"I needed a gift. I *wanted* to see you." His attention flickered over her lips, before he prodded, "Aren't you even a little pleased to see me?"

No. Yes. She was. She didn't want to be, but she was. That was why she wasn't about to answer that question, "This is about my note, isn't it? You took it as some kind of challenge."

The air crackled with instant challenge. "Was it?"

"No!" she hissed in a whisper, his question telling her that he did, indeed, see it as a challenge. This was not about her, but his male ego. "It was a joke. Over. Done with. A way to say goodbye." Wasn't it? Had she subconsciously wanted to challenge him? No! She shook off that idea, refusing to analyze herself.

Find the gift and get some distance, she told herself. She redirected the conversation. "Kasey said your sister loves to travel and cook?"

He didn't immediately answer, his expression indecipherable but for a tiny hint of calculation ticking away in his dark eyes. Then finally, his expression shifted, softened, and he said, "She's a high school teacher, world history, and world culture is her obsession. She thinks experiencing other cultures makes her a better teacher. That includes learning about the food and trying to re-create it for her classes. Right now, Russia is her obsession. I thought maybe something that would feed that interest."

There was genuine thoughtfulness behind his words, in his expression. He really needed a gift, she admitted, and not only that, he cared about making it special for his sister. "I think that's a wonderful idea."

"I'm probably too late for this, but I don't suppose you would have a cookbook that has Russian cuisine?"

"No," she said. "Typically, smaller stores don't stock something so customized to a small niche market, especially with the internet so readily accessible."

He grimaced. "I should have planned ahead. I don't want to show up with some generic, meaningless gift."

She thought of the FBI agents, and noted Baxter had his own little "plumbing" problems going on. She considered telling him about the agent who'd approached her but decided it might be better left alone.

"No worries," she replied, sympathizing with the hell he must be going through. "I can special order something that will fit the bill and have it delivered to wherever you'd like in time for her birthday. But," Caron said, and held up a finger, "I have an idea." She bent down to the bottom row of a shelf and removed a large, glossy book.

Baxter stood above her, his hand gliding down one of the shelves. "You have a unique selection of books. Travel. History. A little of everything."

"I try to carry unique, special choices in every genre since I can't carry the variety that a bigger store can." She pushed to her feet, the heaviness of the oversize book a bit of a struggle. Baxter clearly noticed as much, reaching out to offer aid. Their hands collided; electricity darted up her arm, her eyes riveting on his. "Thank you," she whispered, allowing him to fully take the weight from her and set the book on the table.

Their eyes held, a magnetic pull of awareness, of memories of intimate touches shared. A connection that made her heart flutter and chest tighten. A connection that made her forget the wig and the costume, and remember the sultry touches and mind-drugging kisses.

He reached out and plucked a wayward strand of her hair. "Do you know how badly I want to pull those pins free and then kiss you?"

She reached up and swiped the hair out of his reach. "Behave," she whispered.

A low rumble of laughter escaped his lips. "But you like it when I misbehave."

"You're trying to get a reaction," she said, calling him on his motive. "And we both know it."

"Is it working?"

"Yes," she answered. "So stop."

He leaned against the bookshelf. "Are you always so direct?"

"You have a problem with direct?" she countered.

"I prefer it," he said and motioned toward the book. "So tell me why you chose this one." He straightened to study her selection.

Caron ran her hand over the gorgeous collage of exotic locations on the cover. "Besides being a gorgeous display piece for her home, it features an array of wonderful travel locations with pictorials and recipes for each region." She turned it around to offer him a chance to glance through it, watching as he studied the selection.

"It's perfect," he said, flipping through a few pages with a satisfied look on his face. "She'll love it. Is there time to order that cookbook, as well?"

"Of course," she said. "I can email you some choices and let you pick."

"From what I've seen, I'm safe trusting you. Especially since I'll be traveling." He turned and scanned a wall of rare history books with approval. "Once my sister finds your store—and she will once she opens her gift—she'll spend hours here. And most likely you'll end up with her entire class visiting with her one day."

"We'd be thrilled to have her class," Caron said, pleased by the sincerity she sensed in him. She'd put a lot of heart and soul into the store, and she was proud of it. "I'll order the cookbook today and then have everything wrapped and delivered by Friday to whatever address you leave."

"My home," he said. "I won't be back till Friday night. The front desk will hold the packages for me."

His home. Where they'd made love too many times to count. She cleared her throat, straightened. "Let me jot down that address in my office."

She reached for the book.

He snagged it first. "I'll carry it."

She gave a quick nod and passed him, leading him to her office, but not without a quick pause to accept praise from a customer who adored the new romance loft. Baxter waited patiently and then cast her an interested look as the fifty-something woman rushed to the register to make her purchase. Caron motioned him toward the hall and her office.

"You're a hit," he commented. "All you need now is a Remington coffee shop inside the store."

She laughed. "Is that right?"

"Everything's better with a cup of Remington coffee," he teased. "Didn't you know that?"

"Way too extravagant for my budget," she said quickly and then blushed, pausing in front of her office door. "Oh, no." She waved a hand. Once again she was insulting the prices of his coffee without meaning to. "That came out wrong. I didn't mean your coffee was too extravagant. I mean having a coffee bar in the store is."

His lips twitched. "That's not what you said the other night," he reminded her.

Heat slid up her neck. "That doesn't mean I don't like it," she quickly inserted. The truth was, she'd often dreamed of having a coffee shop in the store, but it was simply too costly an endeavor to consider.

Eager to change the subject, she motioned him inside her office, and she quickly darted behind the protective shield of her simple wooden desk. It was a tiny office, made smaller by his dominating presence, and, no doubt, no comparison to his executive-flavored world or expensive leather furnishings. There was no brass and glass, no money dripping from the walls. Just bookshelves much like those lining the walls of the store, with her personal collection of books and knickknacks.

She slid a piece of paper and a pen across the wooden surface of her desk. "If you can jot down that address. I can include the bill in the package if you like?"

"That would be excellent," he said agreeably, and then with easy male grace, crossed the small distance between the door and her desk. He reached for the paper and pen, scribbled his address with that powerful male writing of his and then looked up at her. "And please include a gift certificate for a hundred dollars."

His cell phone buzzed and he glanced down at the screen, a furrow forming in his brow. "Business never stops." He slid the note toward her. "The first address is for the package." His eyes darkened, turned intimate, as did his voice. The room seemed to shrink even smaller. "The second address is the private dinner club I'll be at tonight. Ten o'clock. Alone."

He gave her no time to respond. Turning away, he sauntered toward the door, his casual composure holding her as spellbound as the invitation, free of the demand for an immediate answer, free of pressure, and she was glad for it. He'd handed her the power as he had many times Friday night. But Caron wasn't sure she knew how to deal with him outside of the freedom of the glitz, glamour, and costumes.

"I thought you were worried about the press?" she called to him, reaching for anything that might convince her to walk away from this before she did something silly, like fall for Baxter Remington instead of simply falling into bed with him.

He turned and winked. "That's what the wig is for," he said, and then departed, leaving Caron with an office filled with his spicy male cologne and temptation.

He wanted her to wear the wig. Caron stared after him, wrestling with a kaleidoscope of emotions. He'd given her back the power of the costume, the veil of a seductress. Why did that bother her so much?

• • •

Caron sat in the back of a Yellow Cab on the way to the address Baxter had left her and pressed her fingers to her mouth. Coming here had been a tormenting choice. But ultimately, Friday night's lovemaking was still so vivid, she could almost taste Baxter on her lips. Depriving herself of such pleasure seemed ridiculous. She was a grown woman with needs and desires. A woman who deserved to have those needs fulfilled. And Baxter had proven he knew how to deliver—why go elsewhere? Besides, she'd worn the wig, like a veil, or a shield... Yes, a shield. A shield that allowed her to explore her sexuality, let her be the seductress of Friday night. She hoped.

The driver pulled the car to a stop in front of a corner lot, a fancy brick building with valet parking and doormen—her destination. Caron paid the driver, and then drew a deep breath, before opening the car door. She slid out, tugging at the black skirt that rode just above the knee. She wore a sheer black silk blouse and knee-high boots. She'd added a velvet blazer for warmth, which she tugged more snuggly around her, the wind whipping as fiercely as her stomach rolled. The wind calmed a moment later; her stomach did not.

She approached the doormen, found herself dropping Baxter's name—her…dropping names. This was insane. So not her world. But sure as she said his name, she was swept inside, treated like a princess. She liked it, too. She didn't want to like it. Why start liking something you couldn't have? *Live the fantasy, Caron*, she told herself. But she'd never been good at the whole window-shopping kind of thing. If she couldn't have something, why taunt herself?

Dim lights and elegance greeted her, the entry adorned with a gorgeous crystal chandelier dangling above a mahogany table. And the red and white floral arrangement, the largest that Caron had ever seen, sat as a centerpiece—fake no doubt. No one could afford to have that many flowers delivered every day. Or maybe they could, but Caron didn't even want to think about the price tag. And that only proved how out of her element she truly was. She couldn't enjoy the decor without thinking about how much it cost.

A man in his late forties appeared in front of her, his salt-and-pepper hair sleek and perfectly groomed. He wore a tuxedo and waved her toward the stairs. "This way, miss."

Caron followed him up a marble stairway lined with an Oriental rug in a delicate floral design of rich burgundy and black. An ornate wooden railing steadied her as she navigated up the winding path.

More dim lighting greeted her at the top level, candles flickering through etched brass holders that cast lovely designs on the shadowy walls. Velvet curtains stood in various positions of opened and closed, with private supper booths behind each, or rather—as it seemed to Caron—private compartments, almost as one might expect inside a train.

She wasn't led to one of these booths, but down another hall to several doors, each a different color and each displaying a sign: RED ROOM, BLUE ROOM, GREEN ROOM. The gentleman attending Caron indicated a door.

"You will be dining in the Red Room this evening," he stated, turning the brass doorknob and motioning her inside.

Caron walked in front of him, a tiny hallway before her, the walls flickering with more candle-induced shadows. The air was laced with the soft scent of jasmine, a sensual tune floating through ceiling speakers. Behind her, the sound of the door gently closing sent a wave of anticipation climbing up Caron's spine.

Suddenly, strong arms wrapped around her from behind, proving Baxter had followed her into the hallway without her knowing.

"You're late," he purred in a whiskey-smooth voice near her ear.

"I wasn't sure I was coming," she said, her voice shuddering with the feeling of his legs and hips settling against hers, molding her close.

"Then why did you?"

Her mind raced with the proper way to answer. "I have to send the wig back tomorrow. You're leaving tomorrow. It was now or never."

He chuckled, low and inviting, and turned her in his arms. His tie was gone, his shirt unbuttoned—a tiny sprinkling of dark hair peeked through the top. "So it's all about the wig, is it?"

"Isn't it?" she challenged, holding her breath as she waited for his answer.

"The wig was for the press," he promised, tugging at the pins and tossing them aside. The wig came next. "You're for me."

Caron barely kept herself from holding the wig in place, as he removed it. She used her fingers to shake her natural hair free.

"You have no idea how badly I wanted to do that in the store today." He took her hand. "Come. Drink some wine with me."

He led her toward the table and Caron willed her heart to stop racing. Because whatever happened tonight, there was no bombshell image to hide behind.

CHAPTER NINE

What Caron did to him, well, it had him in knots, had him burning with the need to do so much more than simply shove her skirt to her waist and bury himself inside her body—though that sounded damn good right now.

Relentless desire tightened his groin as Baxter held Caron's chair out, his gaze flickering across the subtle glimpse of thigh as she settled into the seat. The hard thrum of lust pumped through his veins, his mind filled with illicit fantasies the private room allowed. In the back of his mind, he told himself to act on those things, take Caron now, forget dinner. After all, this was about sex—about a fantasy. And sex was sex, plain and simple. A way to relieve a little tension, fulfill that deep primal need all men accepted as a part of living, and then refocus on the performance pressure of running Remington—the pressure to come through for family, for stockholders, for his employees. Or at least that's how it had always been in the past. Until Caron. Suddenly, plain and simple wasn't so simple.

Clamping down on his male urges, Baxter managed a facade of nonchalance as he claimed the seat across from Caron and studied her, trying to connect with what it was about her that had him practically shaking with desire. And normally he didn't shake. Not for a woman. Not in business. He had to know why he did for her.

She blinked at him, then her lashes fluttered closed, dark half circles on pale skin, relaying that quality of genuine vulnerability he'd found himself drawn to. Vulnerability that contrasted with the inner strength and confidence she also managed quite magnificently. Qualities that said she wouldn't let fear defeat her—that she could, and would, survive whatever life threw at her.

Eager to draw her into conversation, to learn more about her, Baxter opened a menu. "Everything is excellent. Steaks, fish, pasta."

"Allergic to fish," she said. "So better pass on that. I, ah, swell up kind of like a blowfish." He laughed and she flushed. "Too much information," she quickly added. "Really don't want you picturing that right about now. But anyway, ah, never loved the taste or the smell of seafood anyway, so it's no real loss." She crinkled her nose. "The smell especially."

He chuckled at her adorable rambling, already quite familiar with that being her way of dealing with stress, nerves, anything spinning out of control. "Not fond of the taste or smell myself," he said, surprised at that parallel in their lives. "Not many people understand that, here in San Fran." He pointed to a section of the menu. "So on that note, let me recommend the chicken."

She grinned her appreciation. "Chicken sounds good."

They went on to debate several food choices before both deciding on two orders of chicken Marsala, which he could personally recommend. Once decided, Baxter hit the buzzer on the table and ordered their meal.

Caron scanned the elegantly decorated Red Room. “Private themed rooms. Ordering over an intercom.” Her eyes widened. “I’ve never seen anything like this place.”

“They cater to a crowd that prefers discretion in both business and pleasure,” he said, filling her glass with wine. “They do it well.”

Caron picked up her glass and inhaled. “Smells wonderful.”

“It’s Jordan Cabernet from a local vineyard,” he supplied. “One of my favorites.”

She sipped, her lips stained the same red from Friday night. He stared at that lovely mouth, his groin tightening as he thought of kissing her. Of tasting her sweetness one more time.

“It’s wonderful,” she murmured. “I do love a good red wine.” She set her glass down. “My grandmother retired from the state library this past year and moved to the Sonoma area. It’s a great excuse to do some local wine sampling but with the demands of the store, I’m always rushing there for a visit and then rushing right back.”

“I guess her career explains your love for books as easily as my father’s explains mine for coffee,” he commented.

“Oh, yes. My mother was a librarian. It’s in the blood, I think. I guess that goes for you, as well, considering you run the family business.”

“It does for me but not my three sisters. They want nothing to do with coffee. Two of them are teachers like my mother. The youngest is in law school at the University of Texas in Austin.”

"So it's been all you, then, running the show."

"Oh, no," he said. "I'd do a disservice to my father to claim any of this success was about me. I simply learned from the best and grabbed the reins when he retired. This was his dream and his hard work. He opened the first store right here in the city before I was even born. The only store until I was almost ten."

"Really?" she said. "There must be hundreds of locations now."

"Thousands," he amended, unable to stop the pride simmering in his voice. "But it was a struggle, and a lot of years, to get here. He used what little savings we had and commuted from Oakland daily and still had moments when he was certain he'd failed."

Surprise flickered across her face. "And here I thought you were born with a silver spoon in your mouth," she teased.

He snorted at that, thinking of the harder times in his youth. "Plastic is more like it," he amended. "And we washed those for multiple uses for a lot of years. My father struggled to compete against bigger name brands."

"That's how I feel about the big bookstores," she said, her elbows settling on the table, her chin on her hands, genuine interest in her expression. "So what turned it around?"

"He finally broke down and brought in a private investor, which meant letting go of some stock but it also gave him the cash to compete. A year later he was managing stores in several malls and another inside Turnball's department store. From there, things skyrocketed."

"And coffee lovers around the world rejoiced," she chimed in, applauding softly before resting her hands on the edge of the table as if hiring herself back to reality. "One successful store will be enough for me, though, I believe."

He'd seen her in that store today, the special touches so clearly her own, and he believed her. Ruling the world was not on her agenda. Nor was using him to do it. "And what would make your store a success in your mind?" he asked, exceedingly interested in her goals and dreams.

"Paying my grandmother back the money she loaned me to open the store, for starters." Her answer was quick, certain. "That's huge to me. She not only raised me, but she's always believed in me. I want her to know it was for a good reason." She ran her fingers down the etched stem of her glass. "Funny thing—or not so funny really—I don't remember much about my mother, but she loved books. She and my grandmother dreamed of opening a bookstore together. Now, my grandmother says she's living vicariously through me."

She only had her grandmother. He wondered if that wasn't part of that vulnerability he sensed in her. "Why vicariously?"

Her eyes sparkled and she leaned forward as if sharing a secret. "She seems to have another interest now. I think the retired fireman who pops into the library she's volunteering at might have a thing or two to do with it. I can hardly believe how smitten she is." Caron eased back into her chair again. "My grandma! Unbelievable. I mean

Grandpa passed a good thirty years ago, and this is the first time I've ever seen her take to another man. It's actually pretty fun to watch."

"My parents have been married forty-five years," he said with pride, but his mind was on a burning question he couldn't hold back. "Can I ask what happened to your parents?"

Solemnly, but without hesitation, she answered. "I lost them a long time ago—when I was five. My father was an architect who'd been invited to bid on a project in China. It was a rare, unique opportunity, and he took my mother along for the preliminary evaluation. I, of course, being so young, stayed home with my grandmother." A bit wearily, she inhaled and then exhaled. "While they were there, they chartered a plane from one location to another and, well, that was how it ended."

His gut twisted with that news. Five and no parents. "It must have been hard growing up without them," he commented, prodding gently for more insight into this woman who drew his interest more with each passing word.

Staring at the wineglass, her eyes turned down, she stroked the stem a bit more. His gaze caught on her long, delicate fingers. Everything about her intrigued him. "I think maybe it's easier at that age than being older and losing your parents. There is an emptiness inside me, yes, but not the kind of pain that comes with vividly remembering someone you've loved and lost. It's more indefinable." She let out a brittle, humorless laugh. "But then, as sure as I say that, I feel guilty for the absence of emotion—they are the people who brought me into this world." Emotion laced her next confession, "Sometimes that freaks me out a little. Not being able to clearly recall their faces. It sends me rushing to the photo album, trying to picture them in my mind again." She studied him carefully. "Again, probably way more than you wanted to know." She swirled her wine gently. "I blame the wine for making my tongue waggle."

"Then I'm glad for the wine," he said, lifting his glass in a mock salute, a moment before their eyes locked and held. The room seemed to heat, shared intimacy wrapping around them just as a blanket might. Then, he gently, seductively teased, "I find myself wanting to understand more about you than your inability to properly define the word 'nice.'" His pulse pounded in his temples, desire rocketing through his body. He leaned back in his chair before he caved to his desire, reached around the table, and pulled her onto his lap.

More and more, he knew he wasn't going to be fair to her. She created a burn in him, a burn that wasn't going to be sated anytime soon. All he would do is drag her into the mess he was going through. She was just so damn *real*. He needed that right now. Needed it in a way that made it hard to do what was right. Which was walk away. Maybe he could make her do it for him. "You should run from me right now, Caron. Get far away from me before I've got you into something you don't want to be part of."

She tilted her head to one side. "Because of the accusations made against your VP?"

His lips thinned. "You've seen the papers, I presume?"

"Not before Friday night," she assured him. "But since then…yes…I was curious enough to look you up."

Again, her honesty. No coyness. No games. "Then you know why I worried about that dance Friday night. Why I've tried to keep you from the press."

"It must be difficult," she said, not directly commenting on his statement. "Trying to seem impervious to onlookers, even those close to you who trust you to make it all turn out okay."

"The hardest damn thing I've ever done in my life," he found himself admitting, despite the warning in his head telling him to stay silent. But the truth was, he had no one to talk to but Caron. Everyone else did expect him to be the steel behind the crisis. "My father is taking the entire thing far more smoothly than I am, but then he's in Europe on vacation—rather removed from it all. And Jett is someone I've considered a friend. That makes this more difficult to swallow."

"Jett," she said. "That's the VP accused of securities fraud."

He gave a quick nod. "I would have sworn he was innocent."

"Would have?"

"His absence is pretty damning," he said, repeating what he'd only said in his head until this point. "Why run if you're innocent?"

She dismissed that immediately. "Fear and stupidity don't equal guilt. And fear makes people do stupid things."

He paused to consider her and then laughed.

"You just say whatever you think, don't you?"

"Every time I've ever tried not to, it's backfired. If my foot is going to end up in my mouth, I, at least, want to be speaking the truth when it lands there."

"I guess that makes sense," Baxter said, smiling yet again as he sipped his wine.

Caron did the same and then said, "It sure beats that bitter champagne from the party Friday." She sniffed. "Though I very uncharacteristically did it more justice than it deserved."

"And why was that?"

"Are you kidding me?" she asked, giving him a disbelieving look. "It was hard enough to walk down that runway with all those people watching. But I wasn't exactly expecting to be Marilyn Monroe that night." She sipped her wine. "And I can blame my plumbing for that one. I was late and they gave my Audrey costume away, which was why I told you to look for Audrey when we met. Then the woman scheduled to be Marilyn broke her ankle, and next thing I knew—poof. I was blonde and wearing a dress with cleavage to the waist. I was terrified."

"Speaking from close observation," he said, "you owned the runway and the costume. You certainly got my attention."

"I thought it was the sweat suit," she countered.

"Oh, it was," he assured her. "That and the way you told the doorman about your plumbing problems."

She grimaced. "He didn't seem to understand my urgent parking situation."

The buzzer on the table went off, and Baxter hit a button. The door to the room opened, and their food was served.

As they began their meal, to his surprise, he found himself thoroughly engaged in conversation, forgetting all the reasons to keep Caron at a distance. Debates arose over politics, the state of the city council, and even who made the better James Bond. He couldn't remember a dinner that he had enjoyed more in recent times, if ever. And for the second time in two weeks, both occasions in Caron's company, Baxter found himself relaxing.

A good hour after dinner was served, Baxter and Caron relocated to a sitting room attached to the dining area where they sat on a plush red couch that faced huge double-paned windows overlooking the ocean. Slices of chocolate cake and cups of coffee sat untouched on the rectangular table before them, the magnetic pull of their attraction darn near combustible.

He turned to her, their knees touching. "I did bring you here to prove a point, you know?"

She smiled. "I know."

"Are you going to give me that opportunity?"

"I'm still deciding," she said. "Perhaps you should give me a reason."

"Friday night was—"

"Memorable," she provided, the glint in her eyes saying she knew he wouldn't like that description any more than the *nice* orgasm.

His hand slid around her neck, his mouth lowering to linger above hers; a soft floral scent flared in his nostrils. A silky strand of hair fell gently to his cheek. "You enjoy teasing me, don't you?"

"I believe I do," she replied, leaning into him, fingers pressing into his chest, promising sultry caresses to follow.

He laughed, so damn taken with her frankness, with the sweetness that was so purely Caron. "Do you know that a Red Door is symbolic of passion to many—to others, a sanctuary?" He didn't intend for her to answer, didn't give her a chance. "That's why I chose the Red Room. So it could be our little sanctuary." His lips feathered over hers. "I'm going to make love to you, Caron," he whispered. "And there isn't going to be anything *nice* about it."

"Promises, promises," she whispered just before he slanted his mouth over hers, his tongue pressing past her teeth with a hungry kiss that answered her teasing with more than a promise—it answered with proof.

CHAPTER TEN

It was official. Caron had become a wanton vixen, and she should immediately cease to act so brazenly. And she would. Right after she kissed Baxter just a little bit longer. Just a kiss—a nice, deep, sensual kiss. With lots of serious tongue. No one would know. There was that red door protecting her from exposure. Oh, yes. She liked that red door. And she liked Baxter. So much. Too much.

And just as she'd hoped, long, deep strokes of Baxter's tongue delivered the promised kiss, working her over, reason slipping further from the forefront of her mind. His hand slid up her thigh, under her dress, and Caron felt her legs inch apart, boldly encouraging him to move higher. She didn't know what had happened to her since she donned that blonde wig, or maybe she did—Baxter had happened. He had swept into her life and taken her on a roller-coaster ride of passion sure to end with her being heartbroken. But somehow she couldn't seem to care. Nor did she think twice when his lips, and then his hands, lured her to his lap, her legs spread wide, dress hiked to her waist as she straddled him. He was hard, his erection straining against the zipper of his slacks, the thin material doing nothing to disguise the thick ridge of his impressive bulge. That didn't help her muster any willpower, considering she knew just how impressive his cock was. She pressed against him, fought the urge to rock, but found it nearly impossible. She was losing her mind with need, losing herself to desire.

Suddenly, the buzzer on the door sounded with warning. Caron tore her lips from Baxter's. "Oh, God." She tried to escape his lap. But his hands settled on her waist, held her in place.

"They won't come in unless I hit the remote entry button."

Her eyes were wide, her heart fluttering wildly in her chest. "What? Where?"

"On the same remote I ordered dinner from."

"You're sure?"

"Positive," he assured her, his hands gliding up and down her sides to create a soothing sensation. Slowly, she eased into him, allowed him to lure her lips to his.

And then the buzzer went off again. A voice sounded through the mike on the remote control. "There's an urgent call for you, Mr. Remington."

Baxter sighed in defeat and pressed his forehead to hers. "I'm sorry."

Something in his voice reached out to her, told of something more than regret. She leaned back, searched his chiseled features, his furrowed brow. Exhaustion haunted the depths of his eyes, the kind born from far too much stress.

Her fingers curved his jaw. "It's okay." She grabbed the remote from the coffee table and handed it to him. "Talk to whoever you have to talk to and get it over with." She offered a soft smile. "Then we can eat that chocolate cake."

He brought her fingers to his lips and smiled in

return, but it didn't quite reach his eyes. "That sounds perfect." Caron slid off his lap; she quickly tugged her clothing back into place as he hit the speaker on the remote and said, "What line?"

"The caller said he would ring again in exactly ten minutes," came the response. "That was three minutes ago, sir. I'll put him through to your room when he calls if that meets your satisfaction?"

"It does," Baxter said, his brows furrowing all over again.

Caron gave him a keen inspection. "What's troubling you?"

He scrubbed his jaw, then rested his elbows on his knees. "Anyone who I'd want to talk to would call my cell phone."

Caron tucked her hair behind her ears and made the obvious assumption. "Reporters?"

"Or the damn FBI," he grumbled. "No matter how many times I tell them I don't know where Jett is, they insist I do."

Caron swallowed her guilt. She should tell him about being approached. She would tell him. However, this moment didn't seem exactly right.

The phone mounted on the far left wall near the window rang. Baxter pushed to his feet, and Caron stood, as well, thinking he might want privacy. "I'll go to the ladies' room," she told him.

He gave her a quick, appreciative nod—she had no doubt he was embarrassed by all of this. By the time she reached the door, Caron heard him answer the line, and then the muffled, "Where the hell have you been?"

Jett, she thought. Caron's stomach churned with

this knowledge, with the fact that she might know something she didn't want to know. She wasn't certain, and she didn't want to be. The truth was, she liked Baxter, probably far more than she should. Maybe she wasn't fully objective anymore. The less she knew, the better.

Exiting to the hallway, Caron found it empty, flickering with those candles that could be sexy or spooky, depending on the moment, and right now, spooky seemed more like it. Where the heck was everyone? All behind closed doors, she thought, and doing naughty things, like the things she and Baxter were about to do.

Oh, wow! She stopped dead in her tracks. Was Dinner Club a translation for Sex Club? Suddenly, Caron felt nauseated.

Quickly she rushed toward the double-pillar archway that seemed a logical restroom entrance. Up ahead, a woman in a conservative business suit walked through the pillars, a briefcase and purse in hand. Male voices sounded, and Caron paused as the woman greeted three men, their legal chatter beginning almost instantly. Attorneys here on business, she surmised quickly.

Caron let out a relieved breath. This was not a sex club. Good grief, that Agent Walker and then that phone call had her paranoid. Of course Baxter had not brought her to a sex club!

Marginally less tense, Caron found the ladies' room and entered the marble-tiled sitting room finished in blues and grays that adjoined several restroom stalls. Caron claimed the edge of a soft love seat and let her face fall into her hands. How did she end up in this ritzy place, with a rich, sought-after guy, who incidentally happened to be involved in a nasty legal scandal? She should run away, as he said. Do so quickly and decisively—leave—do not pass go, do not collect two hundred dollars, which in this case translated to, do not collect another orgasm.

"Seems you weren't completely honest with me, Ms. Avery."

Caron jumped at the unexpected female voice, her hands going to the edge of the seat. To her utter dismay, as if conjured up by her thoughts, Agent Walker stood before her. And she was looking far more intimidating in a black pantsuit, her hair twisted in a knot at the back of her head, than she had in her blouse and jeans in their previous encounter.

Caron's mouth went dry, her throat tight. "I thought this was a private club."

Agent Walker shoved her jacket aside to indicate the badge hooked to her belt. "I've got the ultimate entry pass," she boasted and then added drily, "Bet you wish I didn't, right about now." She crossed her arms in front of her ample bosom and tapped a high-heeled foot. "Don't play me for a fool," she said. "You weren't going to see Baxter Remington again, but yet here you are."

A defensive, rushed response flew from her lips. "I didn't plan to. I didn't. He came—" She bit back the rest of the words. This was not the FBI's business. She owed them no explanation of her personal life. She might not be a pushy witch like this woman, but her grandmother had not raised a *pushover*, either. "I've done nothing wrong. Going to dinner with this man does not make me a felon nor does anything I've heard from you, or the media, indicate he's a criminal. This is harassment."

Agent Walker cast her a dubious stare and then sat down on the love seat. She sighed, ran her hands down her legs. "Okay. I'm forgetting my badge for a minute and talking woman to woman. Baxter Remington is hot. I get that. He's rich. I get that, too."

"I don't care about his money!" Caron objected, offended.

Agent Walker held her hands up stop-sign fashion. "Sorry. My point is simply that a man like Baxter can lead a girl to the wrong place. I know, believe me. I've had my Baxter, and I don't want to go for that ride ever again."

Caron pursed her lips. "He's not leading me anywhere."

"Good," she said with enough bite to the reply to seem as if she really meant it. "Don't let him. Many a good person has fallen for the wrong person and regretted the outcome. Don't let that be you. Remember this—if you find out Baxter is involved in any illegal activity, or even that he knows where his VP is...and you don't say something...then you've crossed a line of guilt yourself." She fixed Caron in a steady stare. "Don't cross that line. Come to me. Let me help." She handed Caron a card, pressed it into her hand. "Call me any time of the day or night. I'm not the enemy. I'm a friend."

Without another word, Agent Walker pushed to

her feet, her high heels clicking a taunting rhythm on the tiled floor as she departed.

Caron sat there, nails digging into the velvet cloth of the seat, and willed herself to think logically, not to panic. She wasn't going to get in trouble because she'd done nothing wrong. Right now, the only thing she was a part of was a two-night stand. Baxter was going out of town, and most likely that would be the end of their little adventure. Which was good. Because that kept her out of this FBI trouble for one thing. And it kept her from doing something crazy, like falling for him.

Her gaze traveled to the expensive painting on the lounge wall. Right. He wasn't right for her anyway. The man lived in a world where the bathroom decorations cost more than the plumbing bill she couldn't afford to pay. So what if he was funny, charming, and kissed like Don Juan—or the way she assumed Don Juan must have kissed.

Caron pushed off the seat and once again found herself straightening her clothes but with the full intention of seeing them messed up again. She had been Baxter's Marilyn; he'd just have to be her Don Juan tonight. And then she'd end their short acquaintance with a delicious memory-worthy kiss before saying goodbye.

• • •

"I'm not going to jail for something I didn't do," Jett hissed through the phone line at Baxter. "The Feds manufactured their so-called proof. They want me to go down."

That accusation didn't sit well with Baxter. He'd believed Jett innocent but doubts were forming. "And why would they want that?"

"You tell me," he growled. "The corrupt bastards are obviously covering something up."

Baxter clamped down on the budding anger threatening to surface. "Your attorney will deal with it. Running isn't the answer. Aside from shaking up your family and friends, it's made Remington's stockholders uneasy." His lips thinned. "And that is putting employees' jobs on the line."

"Fuck the stockholders! I *am not* going to jail."

"Then why are you calling?" he said. "What do you want from me?"

"I can't get to my funds right now," he said. "I need help. I need money."

Money. He wanted money? Not a chance in hell. Baxter ground his teeth and issued an undeserved warning. "If you haven't turned yourself in by Monday, I'm going to the FBI myself."

"You don't know anything to tell the FBI," he blasted back. "What happened to friendship, Remington? Or is that reserved for only those lining your pockets at the time?"

"Friendship and my dire need to believe in you," Baxter replied in a steely voice, "are the only reasons I'm giving you until Monday."

"Don't hold your breath," he spout out. The line went dead.

"Damn it," Baxter cursed, his hand holding the receiver in a death grip. "Damn it."

He replaced the phone on the cradle. Ran a hand through his hair and stood, feet rooted into the carpet, pulse pounding in a fierce beat, his temple throbbing.

Baxter was loyal to those he trusted, loyal to those who counted on him. But he expected the same loyalty in return. He'd given that loyalty to Jett. A decision that was fast appearing to be a bad one, a decision that had hurt other people—his family, his employees, those people who'd believed their company a worthy investment. And he had no one to blame but himself. He'd hired Jett, vetted him through a process that had left only himself as the final decision-maker. Trusted Jett to make decisions in the best interest of the company, and its stakeholders, not his own interests.

Tension balled in his muscles and he started pacing. It felt like the world was caving in on him. Night after night, day after day, he had bled for this company, worked tirelessly to build success—so many times with Jett by his side. Had it all been a lie? A setup for ultimate betrayal? Or had Jett simply found trouble and not known how to get out of it? Not that it really mattered either way—Jett had chosen the wrong path regardless. And Baxter knew in his core that Jett wasn't going to turn himself in. Baxter would be forced to turn on Jett.

A knock sounded and his head jerked toward the door. Caron. He'd forgotten to give her the remote. He inhaled the soft scent of her perfume, still lingering on his skin. The sweet taste of her lips still flavoring his tongue. Meeting her had been the only escape he'd found from all of this; she was the only person who'd made him smile, made him forget. And he needed to forget now. He needed to get lost in Caron. He hit the remote, a primal, wild burn pulsing through his veins as he charged toward the door.

• • •

Caron barely crossed the threshold of the Red Room before she found herself wrapped in Baxter's embrace and drawn into a long, drugging kiss. One of his hands laced roughly through her hair, the other wrapped around her hips and then curved along her backside. It was a hungry, desperate kiss laden with emotion. He pressed her against the wall, tugged her leg to his waist. Pressed the long, hard length of his erection between her thighs. Caron moaned with the intimacy of it.

His lips brushed her ear. "I want you, Caron," he murmured hotly, one hand cupping her breast, unmercifully caressing her nipple.

Another moan escaped her lips, but she sensed the wildness in him, the shift in emotion to something dark and out of control. This was not the man she'd left minutes before.

"Baxter," she gasped. Her hands pressed into his shoulders, her chin tilted upward as she searched his face. She noted the tortured look in his eyes for a flash before he kissed her again, his tongue relentlessly demanding.

Caron fought the meltdown overtaking her, the fast tumble into passion quickly destroying her will to resist. She stopped kissing him. "Baxter! Wait. Please. Are you okay? You seem—"

"I will be once I'm inside you," he murmured hoarsely, reaching between her legs and sliding a finger beneath her panties to stroke her sensitive flesh. "Ah, so wet."

She gasped with the intimate invasion, panting as he slid a long finger inside her. Yes, she was wet. Embarrassingly so, considering she'd barely walked in the door, and they were both still fully clothed.

"Baxt—" A hot, primal kiss swallowed her intention to object, though she wasn't quite sure why she felt the need to do so. Except there was something different about him, something wild, unleashed—dark. But she had no will to fight, no will to debate the difference in one pleasure over the other. Caron whimpered helplessly into the possessive kiss, the invasion hot, demanding—the licks, nips, and strokes taking her to the shadows of all-consuming passion.

She barely knew when he picked her up, scooped up her backside with his hands and carried her to the couch. Willingly she straddled him, her skirt hiked to her upper thighs as his heavy-lidded stare dropped to the red silk panties she wore, his thick lashes lowered. His fingers formed a V around her clit, the wet silk of her panties shoved aside as he teased the sensitive nub.

His gaze lifted to hers, held her spellbound, touched her in a way that his hands, and even his mouth, could not. It made her shiver from the inside out with the depth of passion radiating between them. A second later, it was as if their connection snapped. Moving as one, their mouths slanted together in a crazy, hot kiss, hands desperately traveling each other's bodies.

Baxter's pants were soon unzipped, his thick erection shoving aside her panties, the steely hard length sliding along the slick, swollen lips of her core. Caron writhed against him, burning to feel him inside her. That was all she could think. Get. Him. Inside her.

And so she made it happen, slipping his silky head past her sensitive lips, and pulling him into the depths of her body.

"Condom," he half whispered, half moaned, and she took him deeper.

"Pill," she panted and then had a moment of clarity that drew embarrassment. Her hands went to his shoulders. Her eyes latched on to his. "I'm not on it to have sex. I mean—it's not because I do this all the time." She didn't want him thinking she had some disease. "I don't. It's because—" He covered her mouth with his, and she never finished the explanation.

Wild kisses and long, hard strokes of his cock followed. Their bodies melded, hips rocked. Wild. So wild. Caron had never felt so hot and out of control. They moaned into a fast, hard rhythm that had her pumping her hips, had him thrusting his. Had her leaning back to find that perfect spot that delivered a new surge of energy. That spot that said release was in sight, that it was one more swivel of her hips…just one more. Or maybe one more. That feeling that drove her to keep going, to keep reaching.

"Oh, yeah, baby," Baxter moaned, and her body

spasmed around the hard length of him, buried oh-so-deliciously deep inside her—pulling at him, taking and taking.

He thrust again and again, then exploded inside her, hips lifting her, hands pressing her hard against him. Caron buried her face in his neck, clung to him as their bodies climbed to release. Her body melted against that rock-hard chest, melted into those powerful arms as they closed around her.

For a long while afterward, they lay there as one, unmoving, satisfied, a wonderfully comfortable silence between them. His hand stroked through her hair.

Reality slowly seeped into Caron's mind, and she sensed a heaviness in Baxter's emotions. Seeking confirmation, she shifted, searching his face. One look into his turbulent eyes, and she whispered, "Are you okay?"

"It was Jett." A stark quality touched his low voice. "On the phone."

Her stomach knotted. There was the information she didn't want to know. Didn't need to know. But now she did. Now there was no place to go but into the fire. "And?"

A muscle in his jaw jumped. "I gave him until Monday to turn himself in or I'll go to the authorities."

Relief washed over her. He was the man she'd sensed. A man of honor who would do the right thing. "What did he say?"

He grimaced. "In short. That I'm a self-serving bastard." The betrayal he felt etched his face.

She touched his cheek. "You're doing the right

thing. Don't let him get to you."

He drew her hand into his, examined her expression. "You should stay away from me." The words were spoken as if he felt he had to say them. As if he didn't want to say them.

"I know," she whispered, wishing it weren't true, knowing it was.

"I could drag you into something you don't want any part of. Probably already have."

She nodded. "I know that, too."

His hand caressed her waist. "I want you to come home with me, Caron. Tell me, no."

"No," she murmured, their eyes locking, the magnetic pull of their attraction crackling in the air because they both knew 'no' meant 'yes'. And that Caron was already in the fire, already burning with the heat of a bad position that felt too good to deny. At least tonight. Tomorrow, she told herself, was a new day. Tomorrow she'd say 'no' and mean 'no.'

But not today.

CHAPTER ELEVEN

After a decadent night of lovemaking, conversation, and more lovemaking, morning arrived far too early—especially considering Caron had to be at work, and Baxter had to catch a flight to Texas. Just before eight a.m., wearing only Baxter's T-shirt, Caron fumbled her way around his barren kitchen cabinets and managed to find two mugs. She filled them with the piping hot coffee she'd brewed and then mixed in some vanilla creamer before heading back to the bathroom where she'd left Baxter to shave. It seemed coffee supplies were the only plentiful thing in Baxter's kitchen.

"Coffee is served," she said, finding Baxter at the bathroom sink with shaving cream slathered over his jaw, looking sexier than sin in nothing but boxers. Blue. With little black checks on them. Her gaze traveled his long, muscular legs brushed with dark hair. She really liked his legs. But then, she liked a lot about Baxter.

She set the cup next to him on the marble countertop and then claimed a seat on the tiled step leading to the gorgeous sunken tub, tucking the T-shirt under her backside. "A few hours from now, you are going to hate me for keeping you up all night," she said, her palms wrapped around the mug, the warmth heating her chilly hands. "What time did you say your flight is?"

"Eleven o'clock." He stopped shaving long

enough to cast her a look in the mirror. "And you were well worth some lost sleep."

Her eyes met his and the spark of that connection sent a warm flush over her skin. "We'll see if you say that a few hours from now," she teased.

"I'll be fine," he insisted, refocusing on the task of shaving. "I'll sleep on the plane."

For several seconds, Caron was spellbound by the way he moved, the way he held the razor. She'd never known a man so powerfully male—so dominantly present in every room he entered—yet, still so gentle and unassuming in all the right ways.

"I've never liked sleeping on planes," she said finally, trying to snap herself out of this lusty longing for more Baxter, when the goodbyes were about to come. The final goodbyes. "I always worry about doing something silly in my sleep like snoring. Not that I snore, but what if I chose a public place to start? Or what if I drool?" She shuddered.

He cast her an amused glance and chuckled. "You've given this some thought, I see."

"I flew to one of my suppliers' distribution centers a few months back and did so with very little sleep. My eyes kept trying to shut on the plane but, needless to say, I managed to stay awake." She sipped her coffee. "Hmm," she said. "Remington coffee is pretty darn good."

"But expensive," he said, reminding her again of her verbal faux pas when they'd first met.

"Way, way expensive," she joked, glad to take his bait. "You should have a day a week that is some sort of budget promotion for people like me."

He snagged the towel on the rack and wiped his

face, turning to study her with a thoughtful expression on his face. "That's not a bad idea. Not bad at all." Absentmindedly, he ran light fingers over his cleanly shaven jaw, checking his work. "I've been looking for ways to bring positive attention instead of negative, and get my stockholders excited again. This might fit into that agenda." He homed in on her. "That is, if you don't mind me stealing your idea?"

"I'd be thrilled if you used it." Her mind started to race, and she set her cup on the edge of the tub and straightened. "You could do it in a way that generates revenue for you, too, which logically would please stockholders. Pick the time of day you sell the least coffee and offer incentives during those times. It's affordable for people with less money and you generate revenue you wouldn't normally generate without cutting into your expected sales. Maybe some sort of catchy saying that you use to promote it—'The Remington two-dollar, two-hour dash.'" She cringed. "Okay. Forget I said that. Something better, but snappy."

He reached for her and pulled her to her feet, lifting her and setting her on the sink, slicking a strand of her hair behind one ear. "It's adorable, just like you."

Adorable. She had never liked 'adorable.' 'Cute' was even worse. Her stomach started to roll. Who was she fooling? Baxter wanted a bombshell. Why else had he sent her that package? "I guess I have to put the wig back on to be sexy?"

His finger slid under her chin, his eyes held hers. "You're adorable *and* sexy," he said, his voice a bit smoky, a bit aroused. She liked aroused and liked when he added, "It's a perfect combination."

She wanted to believe he meant that, but she was afraid to. "So suave," she rebutted, her fingers threading through the soft dark hair of his chest, despite the ache in her heart. "You must be very good with the ladies."

"Just one, I hope," he promised, and slid a hand around her neck, fingers tickling her with sensation as they caressed, but he offered no more reassurances. Both his expression and his tone sobered as he said, "I'm worried about you getting out of here unnoticed. The press has been stalking me. When I leave, I'll make sure I'm seen so they think hanging around here is unnecessary. But your safest exit is to wait awhile, stay here and get some rest if you want. I can have a car on standby for you in the basement, and you should be able to slip out unnoticed."

Surprised, she asked, "You want me to stay in your apartment when you leave?" She wasn't sure she understood correctly. Surely not.

"That's right," he told her. "Make yourself at home. Sleep. Take a bath. Explore the library upstairs and make sure I meet your book quota for a home." His lips lifted with that last suggestion. "Whatever pleases you. I'd feel better if you waited awhile to leave."

"But I have to open the store."

"I know this is an imposition, and I feel like a selfish bastard for bringing you here." He slid his hands to her face. "But I can't say I'm sorry because it would be a lie. Worried about you—yes. Sorry you came—no. Kasey seemed like a nice, responsible girl. Can't she open for you?"

He was probably right, but she felt awkward staying here when he was gone. "Aren't you worried I'll snoop around? And what about locking up?"

"You have my permission to snoop," he said, amusement dancing in his eyes. "And I'll give you a key to lock up. I trust you to get it back to me. After all, you owe me a birthday gift for my sister, who incidentally is the ultimate snooper and does not have a key, so be sure to keep the key separate from the gift. If she gets her hands on it, she'd rearrange everything I own, and fill my kitchen with groceries that will go bad and that I'll end up throwing out. She thinks I live on coffee and takeout."

Caron laughed at that. He talked about his family a lot. She wondered if he knew how much. "Do you?"

"Yes, but I'd never admit that to her, and certainly not to my mother. Say yes to staying, Caron." His hands settled on her waist. "I need to know I didn't turn your life upside down."

Smooth like whiskey, his voice was a gentle caress, coaxing her into easy submission. "Okay," she whispered. "I'll stay." She could always leave once he'd gone.

A smile touched those sensual lips before he kissed her, a kiss that led to one last wonderful round of pleasure. A kiss that almost made her feel she really was his bombshell. At least for a little while longer.

An hour later, her body sated, her stomach knotted, Caron stood in the foyer of the apartment, with Baxter by the door preparing to depart. Dressed in a black pin-striped suit, he looked good enough to eat, a picture-perfect, hunky image to remember. Her chest tightened, fearful of the final, awkward goodbye she'd tried to avoid by leaving that first morning. But was it goodbye? Her mind kept going back to that key. Was it an excuse to see her again?

Contemplating that thought, she found herself wrapped in Baxter's arms, his spicy cologne teasing her nostrils. "I'll call you when I land and make sure you didn't have any trouble."

"You don't have to do that," she said, preferring that the end would just be the end. It was easier that way. "Really. It's not necessary."

"I know," he said, his hand lacing into her hair as he tugged her to him for a quick, but wonderful, kiss. And then he was gone; he'd turned away and walked out the door, leaving a trail of fine male-scented air in his wake. Leaving her to inhale that scent with bittersweet enjoyment, because he was gone, and all she had to look forward to was a bath in that big, wonderful tub—she wanted no part of sleep, no part of being in his bed without him in it with her.

• • •

The private car Baxter had arranged dropped Caron at the back door of her apartment near eleven o'clock, and thankfully, she'd found no sign of reporters. She'd quickly changed clothes and rushed to the bookstore.

Caron parked her Volkswagen at the rear entrance of the store near lunchtime and drew a deep breath, preparing to face the firing squad. Her bath had ended with a panicked call from Kasey; the store was swarming with more than customers. Apparently, several reporters were there, asking questions about Baxter. Seemed Caron's escape from the limelight had been no escape at all. Someone other than the FBI had placed them together.

Dressed in a conservative blue pin-striped pantsuit and high-heeled boots, she shoved open the door of the car and started for the store. Another car door opened and shut, and a man in slacks and casual jacket was by her side.

"Ms. Avery," he said, shoving a picture at her which Caron refused to look at even though she wanted to—badly. "I'm Troy Wilkins with the *Times*. Can you tell me what your relationship with Baxter Remington is?"

Avoidance seemed as if it would invite more questions so she stopped. "I have no idea what you are talking about."

He shoved another picture at her. "Is this you?"

Caron glanced at the photo of her and Baxter dancing Friday night. "Yeah. So?"

"And that's Baxter Remington. So what is your relationship with him?"

"The same as it was with every other guy I danced with that night. There is none. And I have no idea why you are asking this and why I am even answering. Please. I have to get to work."

"What do you say about this?" He flashed yet

another picture at her. Of her the night before, leaving the dinner, but thankfully her face wasn't showing. Just the blonde wig Baxter had insisted she put back on, along with a scarf the restaurant had managed to produce.

"The man has a thing for blondes," she said drily, a little punch in her gut at the truth behind those words…and the ones to follow. "As you can see," she continued, self-consciously touching the brunette knot tied at the back of her neck, "I don't fit that bill." She sidestepped the reporter and tried to close the short distance between where she stood and the door.

"You were blonde Friday night," he called after her. "Who says you weren't last night."

Caron's hand froze on the door, her teeth grinding. She whirled around and faced him. "Sounds like you need to write a story about your own kinky obsessions. I'm sure you've checked me out. I'm nothing but a good girl, through and through."

She gave him her back and yanked the door open but managed to hear his last snide remark, "The good girls are always the best at being bad."

Her heart sank at the realization that she'd failed to shut this guy down. In fact, if anything, she seemed to have given him an angle on a story. The press was on to her and no doubt the FBI would be calling again, as well. Rattled, her mind raced with turbulent thoughts. What if Agent Walker asked about Jett? She didn't want to get in trouble, but she didn't want to get Baxter in trouble, either.

"Oh, Caron!" Kasey exclaimed, charging down

the hall toward her, blonde bob bouncing with her rushed pace. "What is going on with you and Baxter Remington?"

Caron quickly entered her office and sat down behind her desk, wishing for a rock to climb under.

Relentless in her demand for answers, Kasey stood directly in front of her. "And don't say nothing," she warned. "I already figured out he's that hot guy who was in here yesterday."

Caron dropped her purse into her desk drawer. "Don't you have customers to attend?"

Kasey shoved her hands onto her hips. "You aren't talking, are you?"

"Nope," Caron agreed. "So you might as well turn around and go back to work."

"Will you reconsider later?" she asked hopefully.

Caron glared. "Not a chance."

"Would it help erase that angry look on your face if I told you I called the police on the reporters?" she asked.

"Yes."

"I'll go do that right now," she said, and quickly turned away.

Relief washed through Caron at her departure and her intended actions. The store phone rang on the edge of her desk, and Caron could see one of the lights was lit, indicating Kasey had already dialed the police.

Accepting the inevitable, Caron feigned a cheerful greeting, and answered, "Book Nook, can I help you?"

Static crackled on the line. "You made it to work,

I see," came the deep, sexy voice. Baxter. "Is everything okay?"

No, everything wasn't okay. Nothing was okay. More static. She avoided the loaded question. "Where are you?"

"Airport, between flights. Lots of bad weather and delays. I'm not getting good reception." More static. "Damn. It's bad here. Listen, sweetheart. I talked to our PR person about your idea. She loved it."

Sweetheart? "Really?" she asked, reasoning away the endearment as just casual guy talk and unable to be excited about his announcement. Any other time she would be. But the press, the FBI. She was trembling inside that she might say or do something wrong. "That's great, Baxter."

More static. "I can barely hear you, Caron. Give me your cell phone number, and I'll call you tonight when I get to a room."

She hesitated. Told herself not to. Found she had no willpower where he was concerned and rattled off her number. Twice, thanks to the static. Two times she had the chance to back down but she charged farther into the fire.

"It'll be late," he said. "Around ten."

"Have a safe flight," she said softly, emotions tightening her chest, but he was gone in a charge of static, the line disconnected.

Caron eased the phone back in the cradle and told herself she could not talk to him or see him again. What if the FBI came to her and asked about Jett? She knew he'd contacted Baxter. Caron could get Baxter in trouble. She could get herself in trouble. She had to stay away from him. But he was out of town, she reasoned. A call meant nothing.

So why was she worried? *A man like Baxter can lead a girl to the wrong place.* Agent Walker's words played in her head. Was Baxter leading her to a bad place? Had he already? Had all her will been destroyed? Because she was clearly falling for the man and falling hard. And even *he* had said "run away." Even he knew he was trouble.

She dropped her face into her hands. Taking his call tonight would not be smart, and she was a smart girl. Or she used to be. She wasn't sure anymore. Sadly, she realized she had no one to talk to. Her best friend had gotten married and moved to Europe the year before, and work had consumed Caron ever since. Her grandmother would go into protective mode. Kasey was too young, too naive. She'd tell Caron to jump back into bed and just enjoy. And why did she suddenly want to talk to Kasey?

"Caron," Kasey said, frowning in the doorway. "Did you call another plumber?"

"No," she replied, pushing to her feet. "I can't afford another plumber." She couldn't afford the last one.

"Well, there's a guy upstairs working on the toilet. Said he was instructed to fix it."

Caron rushed to the stairs, but not before noting the reporter from the parking lot in the store. She motioned to Kasey. "He's a reporter. Get him out of here."

"Okay, boss," she said. "And the police are on their way."

Standing in the doorway of the bathroom, Caron focused on the immediate issue of the plumber. "I didn't call you. I can't pay you," she blurted.

He glanced up at her. Flashed a badge that said Remington. "I'm on salary," he clarified. "I get paid no matter what. You need a new tank. I'll have you fixed up within the hour."

She couldn't believe Baxter was doing this. "I… How much is a tank?"

"My instructions were—this one's on the house."

Caron was blown away by this. Baxter was rich. She was poor. She wasn't overly sure how she felt about him taking care of this for her, although she couldn't deny that with her tight budget she was thankful.

Maybe it was nothing for him to flex some financial muscle for a woman. For her, it was a big deal. A really big deal. She was raised to believe you made it on your own; you didn't let someone do things for you. And all her life she and her grandmother had managed. It was scary thinking of leaning on someone else. Not that one toilet made for dependency, but Caron was confused. Her plumbing problems were fixed, though. It seemed everything else grew more complex by the minute. Including her feelings for Baxter.

• • •

Baxter settled onto the delayed flight and leaned back in his seat, a smile touching his lips as he thought of Caron's reasoning for not sleeping on a plane. His lips twitched, a smile barely contained.

Every bone in his body ached with tiredness, but Caron could still put a smile on his lips.

For the first time in his life, he couldn't get a woman off his mind, and that suited him fine. That was the crazy part. He liked this crazy feeling she provoked in him. He liked the way she made him laugh, the way she asked nothing but gave so much. Her way of thinking, her honesty. Her brains. God, he loved she had the brains and gumption to do her own thing. Her bookstore was unique; her idea for his stores, smart.

She didn't deserve to get drawn into this scandal of his, but he couldn't talk himself into walking away from her. It was stingy, selfish, and he knew it. Part of him hated himself for being so insensitive. But she was in his head. Hell, she was working her way to his heart if he was right about her. He couldn't not be with her. He just couldn't. Silently, he vowed to protect her, to take care of her and ensure none of this touched her life.

He frowned, thinking of Jett and his betrayal, thinking of how his father had always warned him to trust only family. He'd thought that was old-timer's thinking. Now, he wasn't so sure.

Already his attorney was plotting how Monday would go down, certain Jett wouldn't show. There would be negotiations, and, most likely, Baxter would be used to lure Jett into custody. Baxter's gut twisted and he clung to the hope that Jett would prove his innocence. He still couldn't accept he had been this wrong about the man.

He closed his eyes and rested his head on the seat, thinking of something far more pleasurable—

Caron. His mind replayed their lovemaking, her soft moans, and his cock hardened. There would definitely be no sleeping on this flight. Maybe none until he got back home to Caron.

CHAPTER TWELVE

Caron leaned against her cushioned headboard, snuggling under the white down comforter of her cushy quilt-top, queen-size bed, a bit before ten. Her cell phone rested on the white glossy nightstand nearby. She studied her tiny room, comparing it to the size of Baxter's master bathroom—thinking how different their worlds were. Sure, he came from nothing, but nothing for him was a long time ago. She lived in a world where her bed had been a rare splurge forced onto her when the springs of her old mattress had been popping out. The comforter was a gift from her grandmother. The books lining the shelves around her room, years of collecting. Her home wasn't fancy like Baxter's, but it was home—her home—and she didn't need the glitz of his world. But she did envy him the sense of security he must have—she longed for that and for the sense of achievement the store's long-term success would give her.

Beside her, the cell phone jangled and vibrated across the nightstand, and Caron knew without looking that it was Baxter. He was on time, dependable. Weren't playboys supposed to keep a girl hanging, make apologies for being late, and then win forgiveness with fancy dinners and amazing orgasms?

That is what she expected from playboys, but then, Baxter had yet to be anything she'd expected and so much more than she'd hoped. Not that dinners and orgasms rested in their future, so perhaps Baxter saw no reason to play games with her. All the more reason to simply stop talking to him. To avoid trouble.

But the man had sent her a plumber. How could she not take his call? Not thank him? And it wasn't as though the plumber or this call meant anything. It was simply his way of dealing with his guilt about fears that his media frenzy might touch her—and it had.

The phone stopped ringing. She inhaled and sank down beneath the covers. Okay. Done. Decision made for her. No conversation. She'd send him a thank-you note for the plumber with his sister's present and his key. So why did disappointment settle hard in her stomach? She willed it away, but it dug deeper, bit harder.

The ringing began again. Caron jumped and sat back up. Nervously, she answered the phone, not about to ignore it a second time. "Hello," and to her distress found her voice cracked.

"Hello, Caron," he said, his voice low, smooth, intimate. "You didn't answer. I was afraid with all the static earlier that I heard the number wrong."

"No. You heard right."

"But you didn't answer."

"No."

"Why not?"

"I answered," she argued.

"You weren't going to talk to me," he accused.

Oh, well, heck. "Okay," she said. "Fine. Since you clearly aren't going to let this go. You're right. I considered not talking to you."

"You didn't want to talk to me?"

"I did. I do. You confuse me, Baxter. We met one night. It was over. Then it was two nights. I'm never prepared for what comes next with you."

He laughed. "It's really good to hear your voice, Caron."

She had no idea what to say. Flirting had never been her thing, and she sort of thought they were flirting. Doing so over the phone was even less her thing. At least, seeing his face, she could read him better.

He seemed to read her hesitation and gave her a nudge, "This is where you are supposed to say—it is good to hear your voice, too, Baxter."

She could feel him smiling into the phone. "Oh," she said. "Of course. It is good to hear your voice, too, Baxter, and thank you for buying me a toilet."

"I bought you a toilet?" he asked, chuckling.

She loved that low rumbling chuckle. He did it often, and it always gave her a funny feeling in her stomach. "Yes," she said. "And it was quite the surprise. So was the plumber who showed up to install it."

"I've never bought a woman a toilet before. One of many firsts with you."

"That's good to hear because I have to tell you," she commented honestly, "if you went around buying women toilets, I'd be a little concerned. Though I do like mine."

He chuckled again, sending a shiver up her spine. "Not exactly the way to romance a girl. Next time, I'll make sure it's something far more romantic."

Next time? "You're trying to romance me?"

"What if I am?"

"Isn't it a little late for that?" she asked. "I mean—well, we kind of zoomed right past romance."

"Since when is making love all night long anything but romantic?" he disputed. "I'm sitting here in a downtown Austin hotel room, wishing I was there or you were here. I'm crazy about you, Caron."

She shook her head, rejected the heartache this was opening her up to. "You're crazy about the fantasy girl in a wig and gel bra. I'm not that girl, Baxter. I'm just a plain-Jane, hardworking girl whose bedroom is about the size of your shoe."

"Caron," he said softly, warmth reaching through the line and sliding along her skin. "There is nothing plain about you. Nothing. In fact, you are the most unique, dynamic person I think I've ever met. As for the fantasy—I found you in a pink sweat suit with no makeup on. That was the woman I wanted and still do."

Having a one- or two-night stand had been daring and out of character, but held limited risk. Falling for a guy like Baxter scared the heck out of her.

"I can't do this, Baxter," she said, thinking how easily he'd invaded her life, how easy it would be to get used to him being there. Then what happened when he was gone? "No. You're looking for an escape, and for whatever reason, you think I'm that. I'm not. And you aren't the one who'll get hurt. I will. I'm not up for that. I'm just not."

"I'm guilty as charged on at least one of your points, Caron, because you're right. I don't deny you're a welcome escape. You're genuine. What you see is what you get. I sat on that plane today and laughed as I thought about you talking about the possible mishaps of falling asleep while flying. You didn't even have to be with me to make me smile. Look, Caron. If you tell me to hang up the phone and never call again, so be it. But I don't want to. I want to stay on the line. I want to hear about your day. I want to hear about your life. Then, I want to come home to *you* and stay up all night long again, making love. Tell me you want that, too."

The emotions spoke to her more than the words. She was scared. Terrified. But she'd never let fear control her. "I do."

"Caron," he said softly. "You don't know how happy I am to hear that, and I swear to you," he said, "I'll do everything in my power to keep the press off your back."

"I know that." She spoke sincerely. "But we can kind of write that off as a done deal. They were waiting at my store today." She explained everything that had happened, including the police involvement. "They only have the wig shots, but it's just a matter of time before they are sure it's me."

"Come here with me," he offered. "Let me fly you out tomorrow morning where you can be close to me."

"I can't do that," she said. "I have a store to run. And I can't leave Kasey to deal with all of this. Besides. That would certainly tell them who I am."

"Sometimes coming out of hiding is best. After

all, reporters love a good mystery to uncover. And I have to warn you. I have some tough choices to make between now and Monday that are most likely only going to make the press worse."

"Has he called again?" she asked, referring to Jett, but somehow feeling uncomfortable saying his name.

"No," he answered solemnly, clearly knowing who she referred to. How could he not? "And he's not going to. I've already accepted that this doesn't have a happy ending."

"I'm sorry." She felt the pain in his words, and wished she could help. The only way she knew how to do that was to listen. "Do you want to talk about it?"

"Yes," he said without hesitation. "Later. In person. Right now, I just want to talk period, to hear your voice. Tell me something good about your day."

She didn't want to tell him any more about the nightmare that her day was, so she bit back her inhibitions, and started with what came to mind, "Talking to *you* right now," she said. "Your voice is very soothing." And yet so damn arousing, but she didn't add that part. "Tell me about your new coffee shops. How many stores do you have there?"

For a good hour, he told her about his travels, about Texas. Fifteen minutes into the call, Caron flipped on her space heater and shoved the covers aside to rest on her stomach and elbows. Much to her surprise, she learned that the Remington "Two-Hour Dash" was being discussed as a fast-launch program.

She was flattered, but fretful. "What if it doesn't work, Baxter? I'm going to feel horrible that I suggested this if it bombs. I should never have said anything. I was just rambling."

"Nothing is going to go wrong. We try new things all the time. Some work, some don't. There is no failure in this, Caron. Only potential success. You worry too much."

"Me?" she scoffed. "Look who's talking."

"We aren't talking about me," he reminded her all too quickly. "We're talking about you."

"The ole double standard," she accused.

"Exactly," he agreed. "And I'm going to take on the management of your stress as my personal priority, starting right now. I'm going to take you through some relaxation techniques."

"Now?" she queried, frowning. "You're in Texas, in case you forgot."

"That is a bit of a problem," he agreed, mischief lifting in his voice. "I'm afraid I'll have to ask for your assistance. I'll make it up to you later."

"Okay," she replied, smiling. "I'll bite. I have no idea where you are going with this, but what assistance do you require?"

"I'm going to need you to pretend I am right there with you," he explained. "And I'll do the same. So first off, where are you?"

She was grinning now. "In bed."

"Me, too," he said. "But I hate hotel beds, so let's be in your bed instead of mine. Describe yours to me."

Her jaw dropped. "You want me to describe my bed."

"I'd rather see it for myself, but due to my limited navigational abilities at present, I'll settle for the description."

"Description," she repeated. "Okay. It's soft. Cushion top. Queen-size. Really soft, white down comforter. White sheets."

"Are you under the blanket?"

"No," she said. "Are you under yours?"

"I'm with you—remember? On top of that soft down blanket."

"Oh." She thought of how wonderful that would be. How warm. How—

"What are you wearing?" he asked.

She looked down at her blue flannel pajamas and had a sudden realization. "Are we having phone sex?"

"Are we?" he asked, playfully. "What are you wearing, Caron?"

They *were* having phone sex! She glanced back down at her pjs. "A pink silk gown."

"I like pink," he murmured. "Tell me about it."

Tell him about it! "Pink."

"You said that," he said, almost laughing.

"Silk."

"You said that, too."

"Right."

"Long or short?" he asked, having sympathy and guiding her.

She looked down at her flannel-clad leg. "Short. Just above the knee. Spaghetti straps. Lacy bodice. I have my space heater on so I'll be warm." She hit her forehead. What a stupid thing to say.

"I'd rather keep you warm."

"That would be nice," she said. Nice! "I mean wonderful. That would be wonderful." They both started laughing.

"One day, I vow to erase that word from your vocabulary," he teased. "Now, back to getting me in that room with you right now. What color are your panties?"

She swallowed hard, thought of the white granny panties she usually wore with a nightie and lied, "Pink like the gown." Okay. Take control here, Caron. "What are *you* wearing?"

"What do you want me to be wearing?"

"Is this a trick question?"

"No trick. I'm right there with you. What would you want me to be wearing?"

"Though I do like your suits," she said slowly, "I'd hate for you to get one of them wrinkled. I think you better take it off. All of it. Go ahead and just get rid of the boxers, too."

"Let's keep the boxers," he said.

"Let's not," she countered.

He chuckled. "Okay. I'm naked. Now, let's work on getting you that way. Take off your gown, Caron. And the panties go, too."

She hesitated. "I've never done anything like this, Baxter."

"And that turns me on, Caron. It turns me on that I'll be the first."

"The first?" Her voice cracked, her throat suddenly dry.

"To make you come over the phone. You do want to come, don't you, baby?"

She melted. Good grief, melted like snow under

the hot sun. Went from icy cold nerves to a warm flush spreading over her skin. And she didn't like it. No. No. "I do," she whispered. "But Baxter. I can't do this without you here with me. Joking around and stuff was one thing. But I can't go beyond that without you here, looking into my eyes, and letting me know that you feel the same things I do. I need that. I guess it's more proof I'm not that daring bombshell you met Friday night. All I can be is me."

"All I want is you, Caron, and sooner or later, you're going to figure that out."

• • •

"What color are your panties?"

Sarah flipped the button to off on the van's control panel and set the audio to mute. Their phone tap was proving a little more provocative than expected, and Fred glanced at her with those smart-ass bedroom eyes and arched a brow.

"It's clear they're done talking about relevant information," she said. Sarah was not listening to phone sex with Fred. That was almost as good as having it themselves.

He rotated his chair around to face her, and she tried not to notice how close he was. "A good agent doesn't risk missing an important detail." His arms stretched toward the dial.

"Forget it," she said, covering the dial with her hand. "We are not listening to them have phone sex. And damn it, I am a good agent, no matter what you think of me."

"I never said you weren't a good agent."

"You make your opinions known."

"Or your own insecurity makes you read them how you see fit." His lips thinned, those piercing eyes narrowing in on her face. "That could have easily been you sweet-talking with Baxter," he said. "I would have been listening then, too. What's the difference?"

Then she wouldn't be listening with Fred, but she didn't say that. "Well, it's *not* me." She quickly trudged forward in hopes of redirecting the conversation. "From the moment Baxter set eyes on Caron, and we now know that was before she ever got into costume, he was completely absorbed with her. I think he might be falling for her. And that's a good thing. It's clear he's talking to her. If we keep listening, we're bound to get a nibble of something good."

"That's not what I meant and you know it," he said. "I meant you were willing to use yourself to get near Remington."

She turned to look at him. "To score the transfer I've asked for and get away from you and your superior attitude, I'd do that and more," she said. "You don't believe female agents have anything special to offer, but we do. And—"

To her utter shock, he leaned forward, elbows on his legs—his face, his body—so close, she could barely breathe. "You don't want to get away from me, and we both know it."

Fight or flight kicked in, and Sarah shifted away from him, intent on finding an exit. He gently shackled her arm, their knees colliding, heat ripping through her limbs, evil in its declaration of her desire for this man. The one she should hate. The one she did hate. "Let go."

He stared at her, unblinking, intense. "My sister was an agent."

"What?" she gasped, shocked at the declaration. "Was?" A bad feeling settled in her stomach.

"She died," he said. "The night before Christmas almost a year ago."

He let her go, recoiled away, and faced the blank television monitor.

She wanted to reach for him, started to and hesitated, her hand falling to her lap. "How?"

He scrubbed his jaw. "She was undercover, on a narcotics case, dating a guy high up in the organization. They delivered her body to the back door of the local FBI office with a note—'She was good, but not that good.'"

Sarah froze. "I'm sorry, Fred. I—I had no idea."

"She was all I had. She'd followed in my footsteps."

"It wasn't your fault," Sarah whispered, feeling the waves of pain washing off him.

He cut her a sharp, sideways look. "I'm your partner," he said, his tone angry, hard. "I can't stop you from making dangerous choices. Don't expect me to be agreeable when you do."

The attraction between them had always been obvious, but always before she'd discounted it because he was a jerk. Only now, he wasn't so much of a jerk. And she didn't know what to do about it. So she stuck to duty. "A good agent uses their assets to be successful."

"Because the job demands that they do so, not because the agent is trying to prove something."

Indignant, she objected, "I'm not trying to prove anything!" Though deep down, she knew she was. A detective father who'd wanted a son and got a daughter. A stepbrother who'd taken the place by his side that she should have had. A string of agents who'd made her feel second best.

She sensed Fred's piercing gaze seeping right into her soul, seeing the truth. "Yes. You are. About being a female and an agent. Just like my sister was. If you have something to prove, do it outside the job where you won't get one, or both of us killed." He didn't stay for a response. "I'm going out to smoke."

"I hate it when you smoke."

"Exactly why I'm going to do it."

She huffed and focused on the blank monitor. "Damn, the man," she murmured. She couldn't stand him. So why did she want to storm after him, stomp out his damn, stinky cigarette, and then kiss him until the pain she saw in his eyes disappeared?

She flipped on the audio, hoping like heck that the phone sex was over because she knew without a doubt that right now, she couldn't take hearing two people who were falling in wild, passionate love. Because they were. Baxter Remington and Caron Avery were falling in love. While she and Fred seemed to be falling apart.

"Happy Holidays, Sarah," she muttered.

The audio filled the room. "Good night, Caron."

"Good night, Baxter."

The line went dead. Caron's sigh followed, a

soft, satisfied sound that had Sarah wondering just how good that phone sex must have been. Her attention went to the van doors where Fred had exited. And she wondered just how good he would be. Wondered if she dared find out. Maybe she'd celebrate her transfer by finding out. But until then, he was her partner, and he was hands-off.

Maybe she'd have to find out sooner. Maybe Christmas. They'd both be alone. They'd both be in need of comfort, and she found herself wanting to give it to him, for reasons she didn't dare allow herself to consider. It would be one night. Only one night. And unlike Caron Avery, Sarah knew how to count. One night would be one night. No exceptions. No complications. Just pleasure.

CHAPTER THIRTEEN

It was ten o'clock on Friday morning when Caron settled into her office chair, smoothing her navy blue skirt over her knees, just above her boots. Her matching turtleneck was warm enough that she could shrug off her light jacket. She was eager to dig into last-minute prep for the weekend holiday sale. And despite the few hours of sleep—having stayed up talking on the phone with Baxter until three a.m.—she barely contained a smile. Especially considering it was one of several nights in a row they'd talked almost until dawn.

She'd never talked to a man on the phone for so long, but the time had flown by with Baxter. Hearing him talk about his past, his present, even his future hopes, intrigued her immensely. And when he'd prodded her into talking about her life, she'd found herself surprisingly willing. Perhaps because the more she learned of his family, the more she recognized their rise to the top hadn't been spun with silk and satin, but rather built with hammers and nails, like hers.

This evening, Baxter would return home, and though admittedly she had a fluttery nervous feeling in her stomach, she couldn't wait to see him. Another first for her because she didn't remember any man ever making her feel that way. But then, she hadn't really dated all that much. No one had really made her feel dating was much more than drama. Until Baxter.

Intent on a little caffeine boost, Caron headed for the kitchen, where she'd left the gorgeous gift basket, compliments of Baxter, filled with coffee, chocolate and all kinds of goodies from the Remington stores—a thank-you for the "Two-Hour Dash" idea, with a note saying he'd thank her "properly" in person.

Kasey appeared in the doorway of the kitchen about the time Caron filled her mug. At the same moment, her cell phone started to ring as it lay on the counter.

"Don't get that," Kasey ordered. "Not yet."

With a frown, Caron agreed, "Okay." She set her coffee down beside the demanding phone. A sense of something being wrong told her to steel herself for a jolt as she urged Kasey onward. "What's happening? What's wrong?"

Kasey hesitated and then asked, "Have you seen the paper?"

"No," Caron replied. "I didn't have time this morning." She'd slept in to compensate for being up so late on the phone.

Kasey pulled the paper from behind her back and dropped it on the counter. "Page twelve. There is a long piece about Baxter Remington's VP and Baxter's role in the whole mess. Then the article goes on to trash his personal life. They talk about you, Caron. They say he's dating you. That suddenly he's discarding his blonde bimbos for a 'good girl' and that the timing's quite the coincidence." She narrowed a knowing stare on Caron. "Never mind what the article says. That day he came in here…I told you, I saw how he was looking at you. This newspaper story means nothing. Baxter Remington digs you. The man is into you."

Caron's head was aching and her stomach wasn't much better. She grabbed the paper along with her other items. "I need a few minutes alone."

Kasey stepped aside, having the good sense to quickly clear the path for Caron's departure. Caron's cell phone started ringing again. She eyed the caller ID. Baxter. Of course. He'd read the paper. The whole world probably had, except her. And she didn't want to. She'd heard enough from Kasey.

Part of Caron wanted to take the call, to hear Baxter tell her the article was untrue, because hearing it from Kasey had soothed a tiny bit of the bite. Hearing it from Baxter would probably help more. Or would it? Another part of her felt hurt and betrayed, for probably illogical reasons, but still hurt and betrayed. It didn't matter that the press, not Baxter, had done this. It felt bad, whether that was fair to Baxter or not.

Caron entered her office, shut her door, and leaned against the wall, her attention fixed on the red-and-pink-wrapped package on the corner of her desk—the gift for Baxter's sister. She pushed off the wall and all but fell into her chair. Her cell phone rang again. And again.

When it finally stopped, Caron set it on the desk and pushed the voice-mail button: You have three unheard messages. Message number 1. *Caron. Call me, please. I need to talk to you.* Next message. *Caron. I keep calling, and you're not answering. I have to assume you saw the paper. Please, Caron.*

*Call me. Don't let this get to you. This is what the press does. This is—*Next message. *Caron. I'm crazy about you. I can't wait to see you tonight. Please. Don't let the press get to you. I have to hang up. I'm going through security at the airport. I'll call—*

Yes, she knew he'd call again soon and she had to decide what she was going to do about it. How to deal with the conflicted emotions eating her up inside. And she didn't have much time to think before that next call would come. He was taking an early-morning flight to St. Louis to do store inspections and then flying home later in the day. She knew all of this because he'd told her while he'd been planning their time together for this evening. Time that she wouldn't be sharing with him after all.

Caron squeezed her eyes shut. She couldn't do this. Everything was out of control. There was no way to plan, no way to structure it all so that it could be controlled and that included what she was feeling. She was falling for Baxter in a really big way, and she could tell she was going to get hurt. Or hurt him. Everyone wanted to use her against him.

She needed to get back on task—focus on her business, on paying back her grandmother. That needed to be her primary goal. Not wading around in the recesses of broken heart syndrome and earning bad press for the store and for Baxter. *People might feel sorry for you, Caron. Come and buy from you because you're so pathetic.* That thought was an absolutely depressing one.

She eyed the beautifully wrapped present and

knew she had to get it to Baxter. Using a delivery person would be smart and easy, but she quickly discarded that option. She wasn't about to allow a note to potentially end up in the wrong hands—like those of the press, or even the FBI. Taking the package herself gave her the opportunity to leave the key and a note, though it opened her up to being followed.

The timing for her and Baxter was horribly wrong. The world was spinning, and she had to make it stop.

• • •

As expected, Baxter had called her cell phone several more times throughout the day, but Caron didn't talk to him. She'd stuffed her phone in her purse and forced herself not to check the messages. And now, hours later, with the heavy birthday present pushed into a shopping bag for easy carrying and discretion, Caron headed down the hall toward Baxter's apartment. It was far too close to his arrival time to suit her comfort level, but the store had been swamped with customers and getting away had been difficult. It seemed every nosy female in the city, and quite a lot of men, wanted to know who Baxter's "good girl" was. Remarkably, all that curiosity had translated into a flood of purchases and praise for the store, and Alice had rushed in after class to help manage the register.

So finally, near eight, only an hour before Baxter was set to arrive home—having received a nod from security as being on some clearance list—Caron slid the key into his front door.

She made it unnoticed along the corridor and shut the door, the sound of holiday music touching her ears. Oh, God. Was Baxter home and she didn't know it? Why hadn't she listened to the messages? She turned to the door to exit. Turned back. No. She would not be a coward. Well, that had been the plan, but not now that she was here. Think. Okay. Right. Think.

Caron set the package on a foyer table of black glass. That seemed a start. Then she drew a breath and took the stairs before she chickened out, rounding the corner to bring the living room into view—and froze. Or her feet did. Her heart charged into a wild patter, adrenaline forced through her blood in a blast of shock at what she saw. Standing next to a Christmas tree that hadn't been there before was a blonde female, busily decorating it and humming to the "Winter Wonderland" song that was filling the air. And not just a blonde, but a bombshell in high heels with curves to die for, shown off under a snug red dress. Caron turned, this time in flight, and ran smack into the hard chest of Baxter.

"Oh, no," she said, her hands pressed to that impressive wall of muscle.

"Oh, yes," he rebutted. "Why haven't you been taking my calls? I was about to come to the store to get you."

Huh? Her gaze rocketed to his. "But you've had your hands a little *full*, I see. Or maybe a lot full! You jerk!"

"What?" he asked, his dark brows dipping. And damn him, he smelled all masculine and wonderful, and she hated him for it.

"You heard me," she blasted. "Jerk!"

"Is this Caron?"

The female voice came from behind her; she was stunned that the woman knew her name. "Did she just ask if I'm Caron?"

Baxter stared down at her, his eyes lighting with sudden understanding of her assumption. "Caron," he said softly. "Meet Rebecca. My *sister*."

"Your..." She couldn't seem to form the words. "Your...yo..."

"Sister."

Caron whirled around and took in the blonde bombshell. Baxter's hands settled possessively, warmly, on her shoulders. The woman was blonde. But Baxter had dark hair! Caron inwardly cringed. Marilyn wasn't really blonde, either. Damn. "Hi," Caron said, waving an awkward hand.

"I am Rebecca, Caron." She smiled a sly smile that said she knew what was going on. "And you're right. He can be a jerk every now and then. Make sure you keep calling him on it, too. Too few do." She rushed forward and offered her hand. "So nice to meet you."

Caron slipped her hand into Rebecca's, noting that same appealing sparkle in Rebecca's eyes that Baxter possessed. "Nice to meet you."

Rebecca waved her forward. "Come chat with me while I decorate."

Caron turned and glanced up at Baxter, warmth spreading through her limbs the minute her eyes met his. Her hand itching to reach up and touch the shadowy jaw that told of a long day of travel. His tie was gone, the top button of his dark blue shirt undone. He looked good, and being near him felt good. How could she simply walk away from this man?

His brow arched, dared her to decline his sister's invitation. Not that Caron really wanted to. Despite her earlier intention to leave his life, she was intrigued by Rebecca, and wanted a chance to learn more about Baxter.

Caron followed Rebecca to the corner near the fireplace, opposite the bar, memories flooding her mind about her and Baxter's lovemaking right there in that room.

"Baxter has been telling me all about your store," Rebecca said, reaching for an ornament as Caron joined her. "I can't wait to come by." Caron glanced at Baxter, who now sat on the couch, his arms stretched out across the leather pillows behind him. He'd been telling his sister about her? His eyes met hers, dark, warm with interest.

"I'd like that," Caron responded to Rebecca, reaching for an ornament to help her decorate. "I'm very proud of it. It doesn't compare with Remington Coffee, of course—"

Rebecca touched her arm. "We started small," she said and reached for another ornament. "And frankly, I'd never want to deal with something as big as Remington is now. I'm glad Baxter does it. But look at the junk he goes through in the process. No, thank you." She looked over her shoulder at her brother, before glancing back at Caron. "Which is why my fiancé surprised me with a trip to Russia for my birthday." She eyed Baxter. "Said Baxter urged him to get me out of town, away from all of this."

"Russia!" Caron exclaimed. "Baxter told me you've been wanting to go. How exciting."

"It's very exciting," she agreed. "But we leave Monday morning and won't be back until after the New Year. That's why I had to make sure he had a tree before I left. I know how he is. He'd have dismissed it as unimportant."

"The tree is an amazing thing for you to do." And Caron meant it. She'd always had a secret desire to have a sibling who would look out for her.

Rebecca smiled her appreciation and turned to Baxter. "She's absolutely charming." She laughed. "Not at all one of those blonde bimbos like me that the paper referred to." She made a face. "Good grief, you'd think if a woman is blonde, she can't have brains. I wanted to go kick that reporter and shove my Master's degree down his throat."

Caron blushed hot, fire touching her cheeks at the newspaper reference. "I didn't even think of that angle. He was really insulting to a lot of people."

"To women in general and certainly to my brother." Rebecca motioned Caron to the couch. "There's a certain breed of reporter who looks for anything that sells papers, and when they can't find it, they manufacture it. I know my brother. That reporter was way off base. You aren't some token 'good girl.' You wouldn't be standing here, in his home, talking to me right now, if he didn't think you were special."

"She's right," Baxter said softly, reaching for Caron's hand as she neared, pulling her to the spot right next to him. "And I would have said so myself today if you would have taken my calls."

Regret about her actions spiraled through Caron. There was a bond between her and Baxter, something she didn't doubt now that she was by his side, looking into his eyes. "I should have answered. I was upset. Admittedly, I wasn't feeling overly logical."

"Understandable," Rebecca stated, perching on the arm of the couch. "I was upset when I read the story and not just because of the way it blasted my brother's character so unfairly. I thought about being in your position and how you must feel."

"There was a bright side," Caron said, trying to shift the conversation away from an uncomfortable topic. "My store was bombarded with people. We sold books and gifts galore." She held up a finger. "Which reminds me." She glanced at Baxter and lowered her voice, "Her gift is by the door."

"I'll get it," he said, his eyes warm as they touched hers, but there was also a promise that they had to talk, to clear the air. And she wanted to. Wanted to badly.

The minute Baxter slipped away to retrieve the gift, Rebecca lowered her voice and said, "He never talks about women, but he told me about you, Caron, and I have a good feeling about you. Don't let this junk going on around him scare you away."

The truth was, it almost had, and Caron found herself sorry for that. She didn't believe Baxter was guilty of wrongdoing in his company, nor did she believe he was guilty of what the newspaper had insinuated, not now that she was with him again. Now that she could look into his eyes and feel their connection.

More and more, it was becoming clear, Baxter stood alone as he faced this thing with Jett. He'd shielded his family, worked to protect his employees. If he needed her, she wanted to be there for him.

That didn't change the fact that she was scared about opening herself up to him, about getting hurt. But being scared hadn't stopped her from opening her store, nor had it stopped her from walking down that runway. Baxter didn't fit into her carefully laid out plans, nor did the craziness that had ensued upon his appearance in her life. But she knew now that he was worth some risk, even if it wasn't calculated.

• • •

Baxter kissed his sister goodbye at the door not more than an hour after Caron arrived at his apartment. Though he regretted Rebecca's holiday departure, he knew she was happily on her way to her dream trip, and he couldn't help but be eager to have Caron alone.

The instant the door shut, he sought her out. He found her in the kitchen, where she'd just retrieved two wineglasses from the rack above the counter. Baxter closed the distance between them, pulled her into his arms, and kissed her. It was a punishing kiss, a kiss borne of hours and hours of frustration when Caron had shut him out, refused his calls.

"You were going to leave that gift and walk away," he accused when finally he pulled away from her. He was hot and hard, ready to take her to bed and make love to her, but not like this, not with so much still unspoken. "And don't tell me you weren't."

Her lashes lowered, dark semicircles on pale ivory perfection. "Yes," she admitted, meeting his gaze. "But I was suffering from temporary stress. I freak out when everything feels out of control."

The answer, the confirmation that he was right, punched him in the gut. She'd been ready to walk away when he couldn't possibly imagine doing so. What if she still was?

Shaken, Baxter released her, stepped back, and leaned his hands on the counter. "So you were going to walk away."

"No, I—"

"You just said you were," he countered, noting the dismay on her lovely face, his gaze drawn to the long, silky brunette strands of her hair, thinking of what it would be like to have them brush his face, his chest. Damn it. He ground his teeth, refocused. "I don't know what to say or do, Caron. You were going to walk away, yet when you saw my sister here, you were jealous."

"I was *not* jealous!" she objected indignantly, her hands balling by her sides. "I was angry. I was—okay, I was jealous." She made a tiny growling sound of frustration. "If I was really going to walk away, do you think I would have brought your sister's gift to you in person? I was rattled, Baxter. Really, really rattled. I've never dealt with press and investigations and stuff like that. I like structure, planning. I like to know what to expect and when to expect it. Since meeting you, that hasn't happened pretty much ever."

He didn't move, though he wanted to. But this was another one of those moments, he knew in his gut, when he had to give her space. "I can't control much of what is going on around me right now. I want to, Caron, but I can't. So you're right. My life won't allow structure and planning. Not until this is over. Can you deal with that?"

She waved her hands a bit helplessly before saying, "Obviously, I can, or I wouldn't be standing here."

"That's not true," he reminded her. "You planned to come and go before I arrived home. You didn't expect me to be here."

"I explained that."

"Explain again."

She inhaled. Let it out. "Baxter, I like you."

"I like you, too, Caron."

"No," she said. "I like you in that scary, I-think-about-you-way-too-often, I-can't-believe-I'm-admitting-this kind of way. I— "

For a second time, Baxter reached for her and held her in his arms. "I like you in the…you-make-me-crazy-for-too-many-reasons-to-name…kind of way," he said. "And I don't know what to do about it, but I do have a suggestion."

"What's that?" she asked.

"Let's make love all night and try to work each

other out of our systems."

"Didn't we try that already?" she asked, a bit breathlessly.

"Yes."

"And it didn't work."

"No," he said. "But we really enjoyed ourselves. I believe it merits one more dedicated effort."

She smiled. "I do like how you think."

CHAPTER FOURTEEN

It was after lunch on Sunday and rather than working in his office as usual, Baxter sat behind Caron's desk in her office, a slow Sunday afternoon weeding through the unimpressive financial reports for the prior week on his laptop. Normally, he'd be at his office, but having Caron nearby, attending her ever-flowing rush of customers, eased the pain of having to work. Actually, it made work enjoyable. There was a first. But then, there were a lot of unique things about his relationship with Caron.

After a weekend spent with her by his side, day and night, he only wanted her more. There was passion between them and not simply blazing hot sex—though there was plenty of that—but passion for shared interests, passion for conversation and healthy debate. More and more, it became clear—Caron was special. He wasn't willing to call it "love," not yet, but he wasn't willing to rule out the possibility that it might be headed there. In the most turbulent time of his life, she'd managed to be the calm in the storm, when he would have doubted anyone could be.

"I can't believe how busy it is." Caron had appeared in the office, little ringlets of dark hair fluttering around her face, the rest tucked neatly at the nape of her neck. "I guess the saying about how 'there is no such thing as bad press' is true."

"I don't know if I agree with that, considering

my current circumstances," he commented, but despite the slightly embittered tone of his remark, he felt his mood lighten as she walked around the desk and leaned on the wooden surface beside him.

He shoved the chair back and rotated to frame her body. "In your case, the charity event promotion was hefty and then followed up by the article. You were well-exposed. And not just to me," he teased, "though that was the best part in my book." His hand settled on her leg, her slim black skirt covering her knee beneath his palm. She had a classy, sleek way of dressing that he admired, though he was damn thankful today for his Sunday-casual jeans and shirt. "Seriously though. I'm happy your sales are up. You deserve to get something out of all of this. And even when the rush dies down, you'll maintain growth."

Her hand slid to his as she shyly said, "I am very happily exposed, thank you very much. To you, Baxter." There was no mischief, no sensual meaning, just the spontaneous honesty he'd come to expect from her. Too often she took him off guard as no other woman had managed to do, and the fact that she could, drove him further into the realm of no return. He wanted Caron in his life, shaking things up, making him crazy wondering when she would surprise him again.

He took her hand. "Caron—"

"Baxter," Kasey interrupted from the door. "There's a call on two for you. The guy refused to say who he was. Want me to get rid of him?"

His eyes met Caron's, the silent message that both were aware anyone calling him on the store phone wouldn't be good news. "Reporters," Caron ground out. "I wish they'd leave us alone."

She was probably right, but Baxter's instincts clamored with the promise of something more. "I'll take care of it, Kasey."

"Okay," Kasey said. "And Caron. I have a woman asking for ten of the romance bags, and we don't have them. Can you work some kind of magic and produce them or do I tell her no?"

Caron hesitated, obviously torn between finding out what the call was about and helping Kasey. He kissed her hand. "Go. Make the sale. I've got this."

Reluctantly, she nodded. "Let me know if there is trouble. I'll call the police."

"You just focus on your store," he said. "I'll deal with the trouble, if there is any."

Baxter grabbed the line as she exited the office and gave his standard greeting. "Baxter Remington."

Jett's muffled voice came through the line. "Pay phone at 5th and Levine in ten minutes." The phone went dead.

Baxter had expected him to call again, but not until the eleventh hour, sometime Monday. And he'd prepared for it. Things were simply moving a little faster than expected.

He quickly pushed to his feet, shut his computer and slid it into his briefcase. Baxter had a pretty good idea where this call was leading, and action would be required. Unwilling to expose Caron to any further nastiness until it was done and over, and knowing she wouldn't allow him to shelter her, he tore off a piece of paper from a nearby pad and grabbed a pen.

Taking care of a problem before it becomes bigger. I'll be away a few hours. Don't worry. Meet you at your place at eight. I'll bring dinner.

He set the note in the center of the desk, hating that he had to leave her like this, but knowing it was the right thing. He shoved his arms into the leather jacket he'd hung over the chair and gave the note another glance, unhappy with how abruptly it read. He grabbed the pen and added,

I'm crazy about you every second I'm with you, Caron.

And then, before he ended up having to explain things to her face-to-face, he made a fast exit out the back door and straight to the pay phone.

Baxter paced as he waited for the line to ring. He picked it up the minute it did, not bothering with hello, and heard, "Your VP ending up in prison isn't going to help the reputation of the company."

No more denials of guilt, Baxter noted and replied, "I've considered that." Less than a minute later, the call ended, and Baxter had an agreement in place with Jett—one that sat as easily as heavy bricks on his chest.

He started walking, pressing buttons on his cell. "It went down as planned."

The voice on the other end said, "I'll advise the necessary contacts and be in touch shortly."

• • •

It was well past dinnertime, and there was still no sign of Baxter. Caron sat on her navy blue well-worn couch and read the letter from Baxter for at least the tenth time. She'd long ago traded in her skirt for a sweat suit and bare feet, determined to go to bed unaffected by Baxter's absence. Right. Unaffected by Baxter was a joke.

Curling her legs onto the cushion, she didn't know if she should be mad or worried. She didn't want anything to be wrong with him, but she didn't want him to be an insensitive jerk who didn't deserve all the angst he'd created in her. She'd never been in a relationship that had twisted her in knots to the magnitude of this one, that made her feel the fear of rejection. It scared her.

Yet, when she was with Baxter, she felt happier than she'd ever imagined possible with a man. She'd always recognized the risk-and-reward aspect of dating, just never found anyone worth the risk. She didn't want today to be the day Baxter proved he had been a mistake. She didn't want that day to come—ever.

Determined to stop making herself crazy, Caron put the letter away and grabbed the television remote. She was about to punch the on button when a knock sounded on the door. More eager than she'd like to admit, even to herself, she discarded the remote and rushed toward the door, forgetting caution, and yanked it open.

There stood Baxter, his arm over his head, leaning on the door frame, his hair rumpled and sexy. His eyes dark, face etched with strain. "God, you look good," he said, and before she knew what was happening, he was in the foyer, wrapping powerful arms around her and walking her backward.

"Baxter—"

He kissed her, kicking the door shut at the same time, and drugging her with sensual strokes of his tongue. Somehow, she managed to drag her lips from his, her hands pressed to the solid wall of his chest. "I was worried."

Turbulent eyes met hers. "I couldn't call," he said. "I'll explain everything, I promise." His hands framed her face. "Right now—right now, I just need you, Caron."

The force of the emotion in his voice, etched in his face, in his eyes, set aside any hesitation in Caron. His hunger seeped through her resistance, tore a hole in her willpower. She believed him. Believed he would explain and believed he needed her. "I'm here," she whispered hoarsely, a moment before his mouth slanted over hers again.

She clung to him, realizing that the fear she'd felt had been about losing him, about never again feeling this wild burn that only he created in her. Afraid that he affected her more than she did him. But she knew better, knew in every inch of her body, every corner of her soul, that he felt what she felt. Something powerful was happening between them, and she didn't have the will to fight it.

He turned her, pressed her against the wall, her hands flat against the wooden surface. A wildness radiated from him, through his actions, that had her gasping for air, aroused to the point of panting. His hands slid over her hips, heavy, possessive. She could feel the warm, wet heat gathering in the V of her body, arousal thrumming a path through her limbs.

His breath touched her ear, his hand wrapping around her, covering her breasts and kneading. "Tell me you want me."

"You know I do," she assured him.

"Say it," he ordered, his hands sliding under her T-shirt—she was braless, her nipples throbbing even before his fingers tugged them with delicious insistence. "Say it."

"I want you," she gasped.

He rolled and tweaked her nipples. Pleasure shot through her limbs, darting to her core. She tried to shut her legs, tried to do anything to ease the ache there. Baxter was having no part of that, his knee holding her thighs apart, easing her wide again. His hands slid inside her sweatpants, and he took her off guard when he instantly tried to ease them down her hips.

Caron panicked, tried to turn. The idea of being naked in her tiny corridor with Baxter standing over her fully dressed was intimidating, despite all they had done together. But there was no turning, no resisting. Baxter held her easily. "You want me," he said against her ear. "But do you trust me?"

"Yes," she said. "I trust you."

His hands slid over her hips, over her backside. Her legs were weak. "Then just let go, Caron. Just be with me and forget everything else."

She closed her eyes shut, his words reaching inside her and touching her in places well beyond erotic. Just be with him. She wanted to. Yes. She wanted someone in her life she could simply be with, no need for barriers, no need for nerves or caution.

"I want that," she replied honestly. "I want that so much."

His lips brushed her ear again, nibbling. Skilled hands explored her body, touched her, caressed her, until he turned her to face him, lifting her and carrying her the few steps to her tiny kitchen before setting her on the counter.

His hands slid down her legs, spread them. He stepped closer and she wrapped her arms around his neck as he pressed his cock to the V of her body. He was thick with arousal and the wanton woman that she'd become since meeting him wanted to tear open his pants, impatient to have him inside her. Instead, she was drawn into a long, passionate kiss. And another.

They nipped, they tasted, licked. She wasn't sure who was wilder. Him or her. Wasn't sure which one of them decided her T-shirt would end up on the floor. Or which one decided his would follow. The not knowing was the part that felt so liberating. For once, she wasn't thinking. For once, all she knew was the lift of her hips as her pants came down, the erotic pleasure of him spreading her wide again and staring down at her with pure, white-hot lust.

He stepped back and reached for his pants, but his eyes were locked on her, hot as they slid over her naked body with so much unbridled passion, her nerve endings sizzled. By the time he toed off his shoes and disposed of his clothing, she was reaching for him, crazy hot with need. And it was with complete, utter spellbound lust that she watched as he pressed the head of his erection inside her. She could see the strain etched on his face, the desire to push into her, to take her. He was emotionally on edge, looking for a release. He was hard, so hard, and she wondered if she could take him, watching, feeling the thick width of his cock stretching her, the steely length of him inching deeper and deeper inside her. She widened her legs, wrapped them around his hips to pull him closer. He snapped with her response, as if she'd unleashed the wildness within him. The need, the burn.

He palmed her backside, tilted her hips. Caron pressed her hands into the counter, arching into him, and she knew in the past she would have clung to him, hiding her desire by burying her face in his neck. But she didn't hide. She lifted her hips, met his thrusts with pushes, her breasts bouncing with the action, his eyes scorching her with hot inspection. The feeling of being completely uninhibited, of animal lust that came from a sense of complete freedom, overcame her, aroused her. Pushed her to take more of him.

In response to her demands, his thrusts became tighter, faster, his jaw set with the desire etched in his face as he, too, strained for—more. She could see and feel how on edge he was, how close to coming, just as she herself was.

Biting her lip, Caron whispered, "More." Never before had she demanded anything during sex, but she found herself saying that word louder. "More, Baxter."

His gaze went to her, hot flames of lust blazing in the stare. He leaned over her, his hands by hers, his rock-hard, sweat-glistened body framing hers.

"Did I mention, I'm crazy about you?" he whispered, his voice low and seductive.

A second later, he thrust his tongue past her lips, ravishing her mouth as he buried his cock to the hilt, jolting her with the intensity of the connection. She shivered and shook, exploding into orgasm, her muscles grabbing at him, taking him deeper. Desperate to keep him there until the last spasm ended, her legs shackled him tight as he ground out one last pump of his hips and moaned with his release. He buried his head in her neck and Caron buried her fingers in the dark, silky strands of hair.

Long moments of pleasure passed as they clung to one another. Eventually, Baxter leaned away, looking at her, as if seeking her permission. "I want to tell you what happened."

She touched his jaw. "I want to hear."

• • •

An hour after arriving at Caron's apartment in a whirlwind of turbulent emotion, Baxter sat on the floor of Caron's living room, leaning on her couch, one of her legs stretched across his lap, a news talk show playing softly in the background. He'd tossed on his jeans and T-shirt, left his shoes somewhere near the front door. Chinese food take-out boxes sat open on the coffee table they'd used as their dining area.

"My head is spinning with everything you've told me," Caron said. "I still can't believe Jett called again. And that you're actually helping the FBI set him up. You were so resistant to the idea of him being guilty."

"I still am," he said, "but for the wrong reasons. Not because he's innocent but because I want him to be." He grimaced. "But he's not. He's not innocent."

Studying him, she asked, "When did you decide he was guilty, Baxter?"

"Wednesday night on the phone with you."

Surprise flickered across her face. "On the phone with me? How did I convince you Jett was guilty?"

"That first night talking about the plumber. You told me about that time you walked out of the store with a plunger in your hand and got to the car and realized you hadn't paid. So you walked back into the store, plunger in hand, and told them you needed to pay. Most people would have left, if for no other reason than embarrassment. But you knew that was wrong so you stayed."

She blushed. "Oh, yeah. I so wish I hadn't told you that story. Clearly, one of my rambling, saying-too-much—"

He squeezed her leg. "You didn't say too much. You said just enough. You reminded me that honest people do what's right, even when it's embarrassing or painful in some way."

"I'd hardly compare a two-dollar plunger to what Jett facing," she reminded him.

"I know that," he said. "But it made me think of little parts of Jett's personality that I should have noticed before. Ways he would cut corners at other people's expense. Plain and simple, Jett is not acting like an innocent man. He's calling me for money, not because he wants help clearing his name, but because something in his plan went wrong." The truth sat in his gut like acid. "And I did what I think is right. I called my attorney and prepared to take action."

"You were that sure Jett would call back?"

"Yeah," he said. "There was a desperate quality to his voice that night at the restaurant that seeped through his words. The more I replayed the call in my mind, the more I recognized it."

"But he didn't call until today," she pointed out. "That doesn't seem desperate."

"He might be desperate, but he didn't want to *seem* desperate. That was why I was surprised when he called when he did. I didn't think he'd call until tomorrow, the exact day of my deadline."

"This whole thing makes me nervous," she said. "Desperate people do desperate things. You don't know when or where you are meeting him, just that he will call, and you're supposed to give him money. What if he sees you as a risk—what if he lashes out at you in some way?"

Baxter kissed her hand. "I'll be fine." But damn it felt good to have her worry, to know he had someone here for him he could actually talk to about this. "The fact that the FBI is nervous means they'll be careful." Memories of a long afternoon with them came wearily to mind. "Believe me. After hours of being drilled and rehearsed for any possible outcome of tomorrow's call, I know how nervous they are and how careful."

"But are *you* nervous?"

"Real men don't get nervous," he said jokingly.

She shook her head. "I'm serious, Baxter. Are you nervous?"

"As hell," he admitted.

Seconds passed with her studying him, before she softly said, "I'm sorry about Jett."

He touched her cheek, brushed her hair behind her ears. "Life happens."

She quickly countered his dismissal, unwilling to let him hide from the emotions he'd tried to bury. Understanding what was going on inside him, she said, "Trusting him wasn't wrong."

"Tell my stockholders that." He snorted. "Tell my father that. He never had this kind of crap happen when *he* ran the company."

"I bet he did," she scoffed. "But like you, he shouldered it on his own. Let everyone believe he was *superhuman* when he was simply *human*. And you've never once mentioned him being upset. In fact, you've referred to how amazingly supportive of you he's been."

"He has been," Baxter agreed. "But I can't get rid of that gut-wrenching feeling, of being the one at the helm of his creation while it's stumbling."

"Good people do bad things, Baxter," she said, turning to lean against the coffee table to face him. "You have no idea what drove Jett to do this and may never know, but you didn't do this. He did. The stock will recover as soon as it's clear this is under control. And you're getting it under control."

Baxter felt everything inside him go utterly, completely still in the midst of one resounding thought. He trusted Caron. But he had trusted Jett, too, trusted him the way he trusted family. If she ever burned him, he didn't know what he would do.

Caron reached for a fortune cookie and handed it to him. "Open it. See what great things await tomorrow."

He laughed and cracked open the cookie, reading the tiny paper while Caron popped a piece of a cookie into her mouth. "'It takes more than a good memory to have good memories.'" He shook his head. "What the heck does that mean?"

Her expression lit with mischief. "There is only one way to interpret fortune cookies properly," she said, grinning, taking the paper and tossing it on the table with the broken cookie. "It's the simplest method any high-school-age student can tell you."

He quirked a brow. "And what would that be?"

"You add the words 'in bed' behind the statement. So—'It takes more than good memory to have good memories…'" Her eyes twinkled as she went on to say, "in bed."

"Leave it to you, Caron Avery," he said, reaching for her and tugging her snug against his side, "to find a way to make me smile. Shall we go try and make good memories?"

"My bed or yours?" she playfully asked. "Yours is bigger. Mine is closer. But all your clothes for an early day's work are at your place."

"I vote for both," he said. "That gives us an excuse to maybe double the memories." Caron was exactly what he needed the night before the storm that tomorrow was sure to hold.

CHAPTER FIFTEEN

A ringing sound broke through the warm, deep slumber in Baxter's bedroom where Caron slept. Snuggled next to him, she awoke abruptly, the jarring ring of his cell phone nearby. Caron lifted her head. Baxter didn't move. He was completely knocked out, exhausted after a night of sleepless worry that she'd done her best to eliminate. But he'd known the hammer was waiting to strike the next day, that he would wake and be forced to face the official loss of a man he'd thought was a friend.

Caron glanced at Baxter's alarm clock next to the phone. His cell stopped ringing as she blinked at the time. "Oh, my God!" Caron touched his chest, trying to wake him. "Baxter. We overslept. It's almost nine. The alarm didn't go off."

Groggily, he lifted his head. Turned to the clock and then scrambled to a sitting position, his hair mussed, eyes wild. "Sonofabitch! I'm supposed to be at my attorney's office in thirty minutes."

His cell started ringing again. Baxter grabbed it, looked at the ID. Answered. "Hello." The call lasted all of ten seconds before he ended it, reached for the remote control and scooted up against the headboard. He flipped on the television. The screen filled with a news report: a man being walked into a building, officials around him, cameras flashing.

Jett Alexander, vice president of worldwide

operations for Remington Coffee, who fled amidst charges of insider trading, and under the threat of federal prosecution, has turned himself in. This news comes with the unconfirmed reports that Alexander has a plea bargain to turn state's evidence against the president and CEO of Remington, Baxter Remington.

"Oh, my God," Caron whispered.

"Fuck!" Baxter hit the off button on the remote and flung the device to the end of the bed. His hands were in his hair as he tilted his head downward in a moment of frustration. "Fuck!"

Caron reached for him, but he threw the covers aside and got up before she could. In bare feet, pajama bottoms, and no shirt, he began pacing. He turned to her. "How *the hell* can this be happening? Do you know what this will do to our stock?"

"I do," she said, trying to sound calm when she felt anything but.

He motioned to the television, the set of his jaw hard, strain etched in his face. "Investors will react before they know the facts." The cordless house phone by his bed starting ringing again and he ignored it. "Like the fact that I am completely innocent. I cannot believe I would be accused of such a thing. That sorry, low-life bastard." The cordless stopped ringing and almost immediately started again. "My parents always call the home line. That has to be them. I don't even know what to say to my father."

"I'm sure they're worried," she said.

"I know. I know. I need to talk to them." He glanced at the cell phone ID as it began to ring, as well. Caron felt as if her ears were on permanent ring.

"My attorney," Baxter said. He answered, "What the hell is going on, Kevin?"

Caron couldn't feel more helpless. All she could do was sit and try to make out part of the conversation, which was short and apparently not so sweet. "I have to be at his office as soon as possible," he said, heading toward the shower.

The house phone rang again at the same time as his cell. "My family," he murmured. "On both lines, no doubt." He stared at his cell and confirmed. "Like I said. My family."

He stopped in the bathroom doorway and turned back to her. "Can you grab that call and tell them I'll call them back? I have to contact some critical staff members and still manage a shower." He didn't give her time to answer before disappearing inside the bathroom.

"You want me to talk to your family?" she squeaked. "I can't talk to your family!"

He poked his head back into the room. "Please, baby. Just tell them I'm not dead or in jail. That will hold them off a few hours."

She inhaled and let it out, reached for the cordless. "Okay." It stopped ringing. "It stopped ringing!" she called out.

"It'll start again," he yelled back just before the shower came on.

He was right. It started again. For the first time since she was about to walk down that runway, she thought she might hyperventilate. *Damn it, Caron, get it together. Baxter needs your help*. She punched the answer button on the cordless.

"Hello."

"Oh, thank goodness," came the female voice. "Caron, it's Rebecca. I'm at the airport, and I just saw the news broadcast here in the gate area. Baxter didn't answer his cell. Please tell me he's not in jail or something horrid like that."

"He's in the shower," Caron said, relieved at the familiar female voice. "Trying to get ready to go to the attorney's office. He's shaken, but okay."

"Tell him I'll meet him at the attorney's office," she said. "We're trying to get our luggage retrieved now."

"No!" Caron insisted quickly. "Please, Rebecca. Baxter will be devastated if you cancel your trip. This will get handled. By the time you land in Russia, it will be over. Please. I beg of you. Go on this trip." They went on to argue a minute or two.

Finally Rebecca said, "We fly through O'Hare. Give me your cell number, and if there isn't good news by the time I hit Chicago, I'm coming home."

Relieved, Caron offered her number and prayed there would, indeed, be good news by that time.

"My parents are going to be panicked. Can you make sure Baxter calls them?"

The other line had beeped several times. "I believe they're on the line now. I'll talk to them." And so Caron spoke to Baxter's mother and father. Both on the phone at once, on separate receivers. Rather than being resistant to some strange woman talking on Baxter's behalf, they acknowledged knowing her name, and thanked her for being there for Baxter. Assuring her they would be there, too, and soon.

She'd barely hung up the line when Baxter appeared in the doorway already dressed in a black suit, fitted to perfection.

She started with the good news. "I talked your sister into still going to Russia, though if she doesn't hear good news by the time they're in Chicago, she's coming back. I gave her my number and I'll handle it. Your father wants you to call him as soon as you get on the road." She swallowed hard and then gave him the bad news. "Baxter." She hated telling him this because she knew it would upset him. "He's on his way to the airport. He's coming home and he's bringing your mother."

He ran his hand over his face, weariness in his voice. "I guess I can't blame them." He sat down on the bed and reached for his watch on the night-stand. Caron crawled over the mattress and helped him put it on. He seemed content to accept her aid, as if it were one thing he didn't have to do himself. "So much for their Christmas in Paris, away from all of this," he added softly. "It's what, two weeks away?"

"I am hoping this will be over well before the holiday." Which was in eight days, not two weeks, but she didn't see any reason to point out the shorter time frame.

"We can only hope," he agreed, and turned more fully toward her. "Caron. Baby. I have to go. There's no way I can keep you out of this. The press is going to come after you."

"I know. I don't care."

He wrapped his hand around her neck and

kissed her. "I'll make all of this up to you when it's over. Take you away somewhere wonderful. We can take your grandmother, too." He tried to smile, but it didn't reach his eyes. "That is, if she likes me."

"She'll love you," Caron assured him, the strength of his nearness comforting in such an uncertain time. "I was actually going to ask you to spend Christmas with us."

"Looks like we'll be doing Christmas with my family and your grandma," he said, as if it was totally expected that they would be together.

His words rang in her ears. She was falling in love. Probably already had. And she worried for him, worried that Jett, a man so obviously devious, might have done more to destroy Baxter than he knew.

"Baxter," she said, her hand resting on his chest, over the thunder of his heart. "I know you have to put on a tough exterior for the rest of the world, for your stockholders and employees. But I want you to know, you don't have to for me. I'm here for you."

"I know, Caron. And it means more to me than I can possibly show you right now. But I will. I will."

His vow warmed her but not enough to erase the fear she felt for him, or about how this day was going to turn out.

• • •

It was nearly five, three hours into the FBI meeting he and his attorney had agreed to, when Baxter sat across from Agent Walker and her partner, Agent Ross, his nerves wearing thin.

"If you plan to arrest my client, then do it," his attorney, Kevin Hersh, stated flatly. "This is nothing more than a fishing expedition that is bordering on harassment. You have nothing more than Jett's accusations because there is nothing more to find. And you know that. You've looked. There's not one detrimental aspect to any of this that can be attached to my client." Clearly, Kevin's nerves weren't any better than Baxter's. That was good because one thing Baxter had learned working with Kevin these past five years was that the thirty-something attorney performed best in an agitated frame of mind. Point proven when Kevin added, "Therefore, this meeting is over."

Baxter silently said a "thank you." Yes. Please. Let this hell be over.

Agent Walker pursed her lips. The woman had a major chip on her shoulder that showed in her every expression.

"You have a problem with reasonable questions, Mr. Hersh?" she asked. "Or maybe your client does?" Her attentive inspection sharpened further. "Why would that be, I wonder?"

"Reasonable questions are fine," Hersh replied drily, his chiseled features schooled into an uncompromising mask, "but they've been asked and answered several times over. Reframing the same question does not make it a new question. And might I add, Ms. Walker, your methods of interrogation have proven not only ineffective, but unethical. We all know you meant to seduce him into some great confession that didn't exist."

"There is nothing unethical about being at the

same place as your client," she countered. "Unless your client has some reason to feel an aversion to the FBI."

"Give me a break, Agent Walker," Hersh stated. "You planned far more than a casual encounter with my client. You simply failed to garner his attention."

"We're done here," came the short, sharp response from Agent Ross, who'd spoken infrequently during the entire inquisition. "He can go."

Agent Ross's attention swung to Baxter, and Baxter looked straight into the depths of his stare and didn't like what he saw—the man had ghosts swimming in his eyes, deep dark secrets that told of hard times, and a harder soul.

"Don't leave town, Mr. Remington," he said. "I expect you to be available if we need you again. I'd hate for anyone else to suddenly go missing."

"I have no reason to run," Baxter said, his stare unwavering. "I've done nothing wrong."

"That's not what Jett Alexander says," Agent Walker interjected.

"We keep hearing that," Kevin rejoined. "Yet we see no proof." He leaned forward, as if he were sharing an inside secret. "You know what I think, Agent Walker? I think you jumped too soon, didn't dot your i's and cross your t's with Jett. You're afraid you don't have enough to charge him, either. Now you need someone to go down, so *you* don't." He shoved his chair back. "You have no evidence. When you get some, call us." He pushed to his feet, making the termination of the meeting final. "We're leaving."

Baxter eagerly stood, ready to run out of there.

"This isn't over," Agent Walker promised, leaning back in her seat as if they weren't worth the effort to stand.

Baxter followed his attorney out of the room, neither of them speaking until they had exited the front door of the building.

"This is all speculation on my part," Kevin said, his voice low, tight. "But experience leads me to certain conclusions." They stopped beside Kevin's BMW parked beside a meter, and he continued talking over the top of the roof. "I don't think Jett turned himself in. I think the Feds located him and brought him in. He most likely panicked under pressure and offered you on a silver platter."

"I don't see what that achieves," Baxter argued inside the car as he snapped his seat belt into place. "I'm innocent."

"Right now, all they're thinking is that losing Jett means someone's head's on the chopping block. Jett's attorneys will stall, which means the Feds' hands will be tied. They'll come at you hard and fast, trying to dig up dirt before I shut them down. But that'll be faster than they think." He glanced at his watch and turned on the car. "I'll be filing a restraining order and an injunction tonight. The courts won't let this harassment continue. You just keep a low profile, and I will make this go away."

"It's not enough to make it go away, Kevin," Baxter argued as Kevin pulled into traffic. "Everyone has to know I'm innocent or Remington is ruined." He scrubbed his jaw. "I have to appeal to the media and make myself visible." He didn't even want to know what the stock would close at today. "Do some of those high-profile interviews I've been offered. Tell my side of this."

"Going public is a weapon, but one that must be used with caution," he said. "In this case it serves us well to send the message that you aren't anywhere near intimidated by any of this. I will need to approve the format of any venue you undertake, as well as the questions asked and your answers, in advance."

"Understood," Baxter said, ready, willing, and able to fight back. It was time to shove back. Caron was right. Protecting himself did protect those he cared about, and she was one of those people. He wanted this over, and her in his arms, and he would do what he had to in order to see that happen.

• • •

"What the hell was that all about?" Sarah demanded, following Fred into his office where he was already sitting behind his desk, feet kicked up, as if he owned the world—or rather her career.

"We weren't getting anywhere in there. Baxter Remington has told the same story from day one. Nothing has changed."

She wanted to scream. She all but did. "You mean you didn't want to talk about me trying to seduce Baxter Remington for evidence," she accused. "I get that you don't like it when women use their bodies for duty, but men do it, too. Undercover agents do what they have to. That's the world we live in. If you can't deal with that, you shouldn't be an agent."

Furious, she turned to leave. Fred moved with stealthlike agility, and suddenly his body was framing hers, his hand on the door above her head, stopping her from opening it.

Sarah whirled around, her back against the wooden surface, forced to look up into his face. He was close. Too close. Her body betrayed her anger, uncomfortable feminine awareness shimmering across her skin.

"Get out of my way," she hissed. They'd pretended the conversation about his sister hadn't taken place, but it was there, though she'd tried to forget it. She didn't want to like Fred, didn't want to be attracted to him. And bullying behavior such as this only reminded her why she didn't respect him. "Move!"

"There is a time to push and a time to back off. It's time to back off. You're focused on getting away from *me*. It's clouding your judgment. It's the wrong reason to make a decision."

"Your ego is bigger than I thought if you believe this is all about you," she spat back, though guilt twisted in her gut. She did want to get away from Fred, away from him before he made her do something stupid and sleep with him. That would be the kiss of death for her career. "I want a transfer, yes, and a promotion. Early this week, I applied for entry into a special terrorist unit." It was where she'd get the special training to be seen as more than just a woman. "But they want a track record, Fred, and they want results. They're watching me on this one, and I have no doubt they expect me to clean up a mess and make it right. That means, cover my tail. I can't think he's innocent, I have to know he's innocent. And I can't do that with a partner who scoffs at every step I take and treats me like a little sister he has to protect." The instant the words were out, she regretted them. She'd never meant to refer to his sister. "Oh, God. Fred. I'm sorry. I didn't mean that."

He dropped his hand and stepped away from her. "I guess we finally agree on something. We can't work together. Good luck getting that promotion and Baxter Remington. It sure as hell won't be with me as your partner." He took another step backward, motioned her toward the door. "Feel free. I finally do. I won't stand in your way anymore."

Sarah's pulse raced, unexpected pain jabbing her in the heart. She grabbed the door and opened it, couldn't get away quick enough. Tears prickled her eyes. Tears! Agents didn't cry. Damn it, she didn't cry. This was why she needed to be away from that man. He confused her, made her nuts. She swiped at her cheeks.

In more ways than one, this all felt unfair. She could seduce a perp and be respected in the morning. Falling in bed with Fred was another story. Falling in love with him—well, that would be just plain crazy.

CHAPTER SIXTEEN

Three days after jett had suddenly reappeared and further shaken up Baxter's life—and Caron's along with it—Caron's grandmother was officially fretting. She'd seen the news and the papers, and despite Caron's reassurances that she was fine, her grandma was on the phone for the third time that day.

Standing in her store, behind the register, phone jammed between her shoulder and her ear, Caron straightened the display on the counter as her grandma expressed more worry. "Yes, Grandma, I'll be careful," Caron said, only to have her grandmother launch into more worry-driven fretting.

Caron raised an apologetic finger as a customer approached, one of the many despite the late eight o'clock hour—their normal closing time if not for the extended holiday hours. The well-advertised, unavoidable store schedule meant that she might not make it to Baxter's in time to watch the national news show in which Baxter would appear that night. At least, not in real time at his place, with him and his parents, as he had hoped. Meeting his parents had her distracted anyway. So did the outcome of this show—how it would affect his stockholders' confidence. They'd know tomorrow, when trading started, how well he was received.

Aware that her customer was staring at her, waiting patiently, Caron gently but firmly cut off her grandmother's musings. "I love you and I'm fine, Grandma. I have to take care of a customer. I'll call you in the morning." With an affectionate exchange of goodbyes, Caron replaced the receiver on the cradle and rang up her customer's purchases.

After wishing her customer goodbye, Caron glanced at the clock again, thinking Baxter should have landed about an hour ago, flying in from New York, and she wished he would call. On the other hand, she was comfortable that he would call when he could. She didn't feel out of control or scared with Baxter. She felt safe, secure.

Glancing around her store, adorned with flickering red lights and poinsettias, Caron smiled. She really was proud of her little shop. Decorating her apartment, too, had seemed a waste since she was always here or at Baxter's. Except last night, she thought longingly.

Despite his insistence that she go with him on his trip, she'd stayed behind to tend the store. Another sign Baxter was special, she thought. She wanted to be with him, but he didn't make her feel she ceased to exist without him. Simply that she was better with him.

Twenty minutes before closing, Caron stood at the register finishing paperwork, the keys dangling in the lock, ready for departure. Instinct made her look up a second before a gasp escaped her lips as Baxter pushed through the door. In a long coat and dark suit, he rounded the counter and reached for her. Caron all but fell into those warm, wonderful arms, amazed at how much she'd needed this.

"God, I missed you," he murmured, his chin brushing her hair.

She inhaled his yummy scent and wrapped her arms around his waist, smiling up at him. "I can't believe you're here." Her eyes searched his. "Your show. You won't make it home in time to watch it with your parents."

"Actually," he said. "I brought my parents with me."

Caron's eyes went wide. "What?" He brought his parents? She was meeting his parents. Now? Here?

"They're outside waiting," he said. "I thought you might want some warning. They knew I wanted to watch the show with you, so they picked me up at the airport, and we came straight to the store."

"Outside waiting is not a warning!" Caron's fingers closed around his jacket. "Why didn't you call and warn me?"

"That would have ruined the surprise."

"For future reference, since you clearly haven't figured this out—me and surprises—not really my thing. I like to *know*." She motioned to her new black pantsuit that had proven a wrinkle-grabbing disaster. "Look how I'm dressed!"

"Baxter?" The male voice came from behind and the door jingled.

Baxter quickly whispered, "You look beautiful." He released her as his parents entered the store, one of his hands resting protectively on her lower back. "Caron. Meet my parents, David and Linda Remington."

"Hello, Caron," David said, rushing forward and

offering Caron his hand. Caron was shocked at how much he and Baxter favored each other, although gray frosted his father's full, dark hair, and lines flavored his face. He smiled at her, friendly and engaging. "So nice to finally meet you."

Finally? "It is?" she asked, surprised.

He laughed and hugged her. "Don't act so surprised," he scoffed, patting her hand and studying her. "I'm glad you told my son to look out for himself in this mess. He's always worried about everyone else. It's the same damn thing I'd been telling him, but he wouldn't listen." He winked. "Next time I want him to listen to someone, I guess I'll call you."

Shocked at how readily Baxter's father accepted her, Caron glanced at Baxter, who simply looked amused and pleased with the interaction.

His mother stepped closer and extended her hand. "I'm Linda, Caron." She was a petite redhead who managed to be elegant despite barely reaching five feet tall. "I'm so glad we'll get to watch the show with you."

"Oh, yes!" Caron exclaimed, eyeing the clock and noting that several other customers still needed attention. "It starts in five minutes. We'd better go turn on the television." She focused on Baxter. "Can you take them to my office and get it set up while I lock up?"

Kasey appeared behind the register to help a customer. "I'll take care of things," she said to Caron. "You go watch the show."

"Thank you, sweetheart," Baxter's mother said. "That is so very wonderful of you." The words rang with sincerity and true appreciation. Kasey and Caron looked at one another, and Caron realized Kasey was thinking the same thing she was—that Linda Remington was a really classy woman.

"Thank you, Kasey," Caron said. "Are you sure?"

"Positive," she answered, a twinkle in her eyes as she glanced at Baxter and back at Caron.

Piled into Caron's office, the four of them watched Baxter's interview and shared comfortable conversation. He'd been firm but likable when he'd presented the FBI's approach to the securities investigation. He'd even rolled with the punches quite nicely when surprised by viewers' call-ins, and received overwhelming public support.

An hour after the show ended, the store was empty but for Caron and Baxter, his parents having left by private car. The two of them stood in Caron's office, Baxter's arms wrapped around her waist. "My parents loved you," he said.

That pleased Caron, not because she needed their approval, but because she had genuinely liked them. "I loved them, too," she said, her hands resting on his chest, his jacket long gone. Heat seeped through the white dress shirt to her palm, and before she could stop herself, she said, "I missed you, Baxter."

His hand slid down her hair. "I missed *you*, Caron." He carefully walked her toward her desk until she scooted on top of it to sit. He claimed the chair in front of her and rested his hands on her knees. "Did you know that my father is an excellent judge of character?" he asked, surprising her with the rather unexpected question. She'd expected something a little more naughty right about now.

Caron replied, "I can see that in him." She'd noted a shrewd intelligence in David Remington's eyes, in his observations.

Baxter's expression turned serious. "He never liked Jett."

The admission took her off guard, but it explained so much. "Why?"

"He said Jett would never look him in the eyes." Baxter laughed, bitter. "I thought Jett was simply intimidated by my father's success."

"You misjudged him," she said softly. "We're all human."

He stood up, stepped close, slid his hands into her hair. The air crackled with instant sensual tension. "What if I said I was falling in love with you, Caron?"

Her heart raced wildly, nerves charging through her body. "I'd say you better mean it because that would be a really horrible joke."

His lips lifted. "Wrong answer."

She ran her hand down his tie. "I never manage to say the right thing at moments like these, do I?" Her fingers brushed his jaw. "I'm pretty sure I'm already there, Baxter. I'm done falling. I'm—"

He kissed her then, long and passionate. Then he made love to her in her office, and not even her best romance novel–evoked fantasy came close to comparing or ever would again.

• • •

The next day, Caron learned the hard way that fantasies in romance novels were the only ones that came with perfectly happy endings. Her life was another story.

She arrived at work after the opening bell for trading; Remington stock was on the rise. And Baxter's attorney had said he felt the wheels were in motion now to end the mess. He had received indications that Jett Alexander had admitted he had nothing on Baxter. The bad news—Jett was likely to get off on a technicality, though his career would be over.

Caron was actually humming a Christmas tune, debating a Christmas gift for Baxter, when she walked into her office and stopped dead in her tracks. Leaning on her desk, right where Caron and Baxter had made love the night before, was Agent Walker, her long legs stretched out in front of her, crossed at the ankles, arms at her sides.

"You might want to shut that door, Caron," she said. "We have private matters to discuss."

"We have nothing to discuss," Caron countered, balling her fists by her side.

Agent Walker held up a small tape recorder. "I'd shut that door if I were you." She hit play and Caron's voice filled the room, "Has he called again?"

Outrage and panic overcame Caron at the sound of her private phone conversation with Baxter. "You bugged my telephone? I'll sue you. I'll—"

"You'll listen and listen well or end up in jail, Caron." She turned off the recorder. "We had court orders for everything we did, and obviously we now know that you were aware Baxter was communicating with Jett, and you didn't report him. Either you come forward and give me Baxter, or I plan to turn this on *you*."

"Me?" Caron exclaimed and then bit her tongue. She would not react. That was what this woman wanted. "I did nothing wrong," she added softly, vehemently.

Appearing almost bored, Agent Walker uncrossed her arms and legs. She set the recorder on the desk and rested her palms on the wooden surface. "Obstruction of justice, impeding a federal investigation..."

Caron was beyond angry, she was fuming, spitting mad. "Why do you want him so badly? Why?" She reined in her tone, but just barely. "You lost Jett and you need a conviction. Otherwise, you get in some kind of trouble. Well, press charges if you like. I have nothing to say to you that an attorney can't say for me and better."

Unmoving, Agent Walker said, "I like you, Caron. Don't let a guy screw up your life. You're better than that."

That was it. Caron opened the door. "Leave."

Agent Walker pushed to her feet, left the recorder. "I'll let you listen to that. Feel free to let your attorney listen, too. He or she should find it interesting." She stopped in front of Caron. "Tell me what I need to know."

"As I've told you several times before, Agent Walker—"

"Several times before?" It was Baxter, standing in the doorway, with roses in his arms, accusation burning dark in his eyes. "When have you talked to her before this, Caron?"

Caron's heart lurched. He looked handsome. Angry. One step from gone. Her mind raced, her throat froze. She would have told him all of this, but it had never seemed relevant, always like past history. Done before they were even started. Something else to worry him, over nothing. "Baxter—"

"You know what," he said, cutting her off with unfamiliar coldness and chilling her to the bone. "There isn't a good answer, Caron. Not one good answer you can give me. I trusted you—the woman who told me to protect myself and was stabbing me in the back at the same time. Well, I am protecting myself. By getting away from you."

"You really think that little of me?" she demanded, but he'd already turned away, tossing the flowers on the floor as he left.

He did think that little of her. He had no intention of hearing her out. Not now. Not ever. She'd lost him. And why did she want him if he thought she'd betrayed him? Caron fought the tears that threatened to overwhelm her. Because she did still want him, damn it; and with emotion about to strangle her, she couldn't begin to reason herself out of it.

"This changes nothing, Caron," Agent Walker said, reminding Caron the woman was still there.

"Leave!" she yelled, pointing toward the empty doorway. "Leave!" Actually yes, this changed something—it had changed everything.

Baxter was gone. Caron now faced the reality that her books had allowed her to escape—fairy tales *were* fiction.

CHAPTER SEVENTEEN

Sarah sat in her office in the San Francisco FBI hub late afternoon on Christmas Eve, a bottle of antacids on her desk that eased the knots in her stomach, but did nothing for her turbulent mood. Fred had been gone for days, having taken a leave of absence, and Jett would most likely be headed home before the night was out—free as a bird on a technicality.

Popping another milky pink tablet, Sarah stared at the manila envelope that had been delivered by a courier a few minutes earlier. Unless it gave her something to do besides go home alone, which was unlikely on Christmas Eve, she didn't want whatever was inside. Clinging to the hope that the contents might offer a needed distraction from her Christmas Eve blues, Sarah broke the seal and thumbed through the paperwork inside.

Stunned at what she'd found, Sarah sat back in her chair. "We got him. Finally, we got him."

"We" being her and Fred. Since it was Fred's hardheaded insistence that somewhere in Jett's background they'd find another misstep. Sure enough, before Jett had joined the Remington management staff, he'd played this same game of stock manipulation in another company. Jett couldn't be charged for his most recent activity, but he wouldn't walk on his past mistake.

Emotions charged at Sarah, fierce in their

intensity. The same emotions she'd been suppressing, the ones eating away at her stomach. She shoved away from her desk, took the envelope with her. She had to deal with Jett before she could deal with her own personal meltdown. She wasn't about to give him a chance to run again.

• • •

Night had fallen by the time Sarah pulled her Buick Skylark to a stop in front of the two-story apartment building that Fred called home. Noting his Jeep by the curb, she let out a shaky breath. He was home—like her, with no family, no holiday bliss to escape to.

But she didn't know what to say, what to do. Even why she'd come. Time ticked by as she sat there, a black hole spiraling around her as she ticked off all her mistakes these past few weeks, all the reasons she had to feel guilty. How long she sat in that car, she didn't know. Too long.

"Just go knock," she whispered, and shoved open the car door before she changed her mind.

Taking the stairs to Fred's floor, Sarah's pace was steady, rapid—with her decision made to move forward, she wasn't backing out. Nor did she hesitate at his door, knocking immediately. Almost instantly, it flew open and Fred stood in the doorway, shirtless, low-slung jeans showing off rippling, hard-earned muscles.

"Wondered how long you were going to sit in the car," he said drily.

Relief washed over her—relief that this man

was once again giving her shit. That he was here, and acting as if nothing had changed. Relief that triggered the emotional meltdown she'd held off for hours. Sarah fell into his arms and started to cry.

"I didn't mean to say that about your sister," she whispered into his chest. "I didn't mean to. I'm sorry."

"I know," he said, hugging her in the warm cocoon of his arms. Warm and wonderful, accepting not rejecting. She went blank for long minutes, tears shaking her body, her emotions so long contained. Quickly, she was inside his apartment, the door shut. Then she was on his couch, sitting snug against his side.

When finally she calmed, his fingers lightly brushed hair from her eyes. "Better now?" he asked gently, no sarcasm, no anger. No walls.

"We got Jett," she said. "Or you did. You were right. He had a past. A bad one."

"I thought that would be *good* news," he said, studying her. "Not something to cry about."

"You were right about my decisions, Fred. Right about so many things. I made the wrong choices for the wrong reasons. I didn't want the agency to think I was weak because I didn't go after Remington. I wasn't confident enough to just say I knew he was innocent. And I did, I do—I know he's innocent." She went on to tell Fred about the confrontation with Baxter and Caron. "See? I really screwed this all up. I destroyed their relationship. I destroyed our partnership. I've dropped my transfer request, Fred. Please come back. We are good together. We stopped Jett."

He stared down at her, didn't blink, didn't move. "Are you sure? What about your promotion?"

She didn't want it anymore. She'd wanted it for all the wrong reasons. "We make good partners," she repeated simply, and barely had the words out before Fred kissed her, a kiss that told of passion to come, passion barely restrained. But she couldn't allow herself the pleasure. Couldn't allow herself the peace.

Fred stopped abruptly, stared down at her. "What's wrong?"

"I destroyed their relationship," she whispered.

"Caron Avery and Baxter Remington?"

She nodded, emotion tightening her chest.

"Let's go," he said, pulling her to her feet and reaching for the T-shirt he'd flung over the edge of the couch, tugging it over his head.

"Where?"

"To see Baxter Remington." He wrapped his arm around her waist, leaned that hard body into hers. "Then we'll come back here, and you can be my Christmas present."

• • •

Standing in the den of his parents' waterfront home, Baxter stared into the crackling fire of their white-rock hearth, a glass of brandy in his hand, Caron on his mind, no matter how hard he tried to stop thinking about her. Though pleased that his middle sister had arrived an hour before, he'd been equally as pleased when she and his mother had retreated to the kitchen for girl talk. He needed the alone time to clear his head.

"I liked her, you know."

Baxter turned to see his father in the doorway. "I know you did," he said. Looking back, he now wished he had waited to introduce Caron to his parents. "That doesn't change what she did."

"Which was what?" David Remington asked, moving to stand next to his son, staring into the same fireplace.

Baxter cast him an incredulous look. "She should have told me about being approached."

"Perhaps," he agreed, and then peered at his son, clearly concerned. "But from what I understand, even from you yourself, she told them nothing."

"She didn't tell me, Dad," he argued, frustrated, running a hand through his hair. "Didn't. Tell. Me. What part of that rings okay with you?"

"The part where she endured a beating by the press and stuck by your side. The part where she encouraged you to protect yourself and apparently did so herself, as well. That earns her the benefit of the doubt in my mind. I thought it would for you, too. But then, maybe I was wrong, and these things don't matter."

"Wrong?" Baxter asked, glancing at his father, sensing he was being led into one of his father's all-too-knowing observations.

Shrewd eyes fixed on Baxter. "I thought you were in love with her."

Baxter inhaled a harsh breath at his father's directness. His statement touched on the core of the turmoil tearing him in two.

Baxter had been in love with Caron. Damn it,

he still was. But it didn't matter; he couldn't let it matter. "Secrets and lies do not equal love," he said, repeating what he had said to himself too many times to count. Jett had burned him. But finding out Caron had been talking to the FBI had cut like a knife.

"Honey."

His mother's voice had Baxter and David turning to the doorway, where she stood in her festive red velvet holiday dress. "Which honey?" Baxter's father joked.

Linda looked at him with mock reprimand. "You know I'm not talking to you, *darling*." She refocused on Baxter. "Agents Walker and Ross are here to see you." Baxter was about to tell her to send them away, when she added, "I really think you want to hear what they have to say."

Something in his mother's voice blasted away Baxter's refusal. He downed the brandy in his glass, and set it on the hearth. "Send them in."

Agents Walker and Ross appeared moments later, minus his mother, and Agent Walker quickly launched into conversation. It only took a few minutes before he learned that he was free and clear—no more visits from the FBI.

"Thank you for that good news," Baxter said.

Agent Walker hesitated. "I approached her the morning after you met," she said, not bothering with Caron's name. "I pressured her hard. Did my best to intimidate her. She gave me nothing. And I mean nothing. Shut me off faster than flipping a light switch. That day in her office, I even played a taped conversation that proved we had good reason to suspect that you had talked to Jett. I threatened to prosecute her. She was willing to risk that. She didn't even blink before she demanded I leave. Why didn't she tell you? I don't know. But I'd heard enough, and observed enough, to know that the woman was certain that every day of your relationship would be the last. That it was a fling, and you'd soon find a real blonde bombshell. Don't prove her right. I was an ass to you and to her. Don't *you* be a fool." She said nothing more, silently turning and leaving, Agent Ross by her side.

Baxter stood there, unable to breathe. Caron hadn't betrayed him and, indeed, he was a fool. He'd let Jett and his betrayal taint his objectivity. He was crazy about Caron. He was in love with Caron.

His father's hand came down on his shoulder. "Go get her, son."

"I plan to." Baxter was already on the move and in his car in a matter of seconds. He dialed the bookstore as he pulled onto the road, aware that Caron had stayed open late for last-minute shoppers and hoping to catch her. No answer. He dialed again. No answer. He considered calling her cell, but decided this was something better done face-to-face anyway.

He screeched into the parking lot but swore again when he found Caron's car absent. But Kasey's white Camry was there, and he rushed to the back door and pounded. Nothing.

"Kasey, it's Baxter." Damn. He ran around the building to the front. Knocked on the window over and over, until Kasey finally appeared.

She unlocked the door. "You just missed her. She's gone straight to Sonoma."

"What route?"

"She takes 101 to 37."

He was already walking away as Kasey called out, "It's about time you came to your senses."

Baxter waved a hand in understanding. She was right. It was about time. And he was more than willing to spend a lifetime making up for it.

• • •

With her heart heavy, Caron drove toward Sonoma, thankful the day was behind her. The store had been packed; the customers arriving one after another. And they had been godsends, distractions from the growing ache of hearing nothing from Baxter. There had been a few moments of weakness, when she'd considered calling him. At other times, she called him all right—a jerk, a rich, snotty, arrogant…well, the list went on. In the end, she didn't think he was any of those things, but she acknowledged it had felt good to lash out. In the end, he was simply a man betrayed by a close friend, fearful of being betrayed again. She should have told him, she supposed, about the FBI, but beating herself up about her logic didn't help matters.

For now, she simply wanted to get to her grandmother's place. To drink hot cocoa and eat her grandma's famous brownies—perhaps a few dozen or so would make her feel better. She began to fantasize about those sweet treats when the car behind her flashed its lights.

"Everyone is in a hurry," she mumbled, and changed lanes to let the car pass. But the car didn't pass—it flashed its lights again. Caron frowned.

She dug her cell from the empty drink holder where she'd stashed it, preparing to call for help—just in case. It started to ring. She didn't dare take her eyes off the road, punching the answer button. "Hello."

"It's Baxter, Caron."

Her heart jackknifed. "Baxter?"

"Pull over, baby. The sign says there's a rest stop at the next exit."

"That's you behind me?"

"Yeah," he said. "It's me."

Caron started shaking and tears pricked at her eyes. Emotion overcame her; that valued control she so loved, gone. Baxter was here? On the highway? She could barely drive the half mile it took to get to the rest stop and pull into a parking spot.

It was seconds before Baxter was at her open door, dropping to his knee on the ground beside her as she turned to face him, her feet on the pavement. His hands went to her knees in that familiar way he always touched her, the wind caressing his dark hair, her nostrils flaring with that spicy scent she so adored and thought she'd never smell again.

"I was a fool, Caron. A complete fool. Jett had let me down, and I was taken off guard when I heard about you talking to the FBI."

"I didn't—"

He touched her lips with his fingers, and shivers

raced down her spine with the intimate connection. "I know. You don't have to say another word except that you forgive me. I know we haven't known each other that long, but I know you're the one for me. I love you, Caron. I love you so much. Spend Christmas with me. Spend a lifetime with me."

"I love you, too," she said, tears spilling from her eyes as he hugged her and then kissed her—a long, loving kiss that promised passion would come later.

• • •

It was the day after Christmas when Caron finally had the opportunity to give Baxter the Christmas present she'd considered and reconsidered. Standing in Baxter's bathroom—soon to be hers since she was moving in with him—she surveyed her red dress and the now infamous blonde wig, with jitters in her stomach and a smile on her ruby-red lips. With a little thrill, she glanced at the emerald-cut white diamond sparkling on her finger. It had been her surprise Christmas gift.

She couldn't wait to see what he thought of her plan to seduce him Marilyn-style, and for once, she didn't think it was the bombshell, but Caron, that turned him on. She knew Baxter desired her, and that they could play a few bedroom games, without her feeling insecure. And *that* turned her on. She adored the idea of such freedom. Just as she adored Baxter.

He'd been wonderful with her grandmother,

who had surprised Caron by officially unveiling her own romance, just as Caron had suspected. And time spent with Baxter's family had only proven them more likable than ever. But now, home with Baxter, ready to celebrate alone—that was what she'd been waiting for.

Caron turned on the stereo built into the wall and popped in the CD. The music started and she opened the door to the bedroom and posed in the doorway. Baxter lay on the bed eagerly awaiting her surprise. With confidence she never thought possible, Caron began her sexy striptease to the music, "Santa Baby." A striptease that ended with the most passionate, wonderful lovemaking of her life.

Hours later, wrapped in Baxter's strong, protective arms, she twined her fingers in the dark, sexy hair on his chest. "I think I should send the wig back."

He lifted his head. "I like the wig."

She grinned. "Oh, I know. So do I. But what if I'm keeping some other girl from having the night of her life? I know I would never have wanted to miss mine."

"Send it back, then," he said, tightening his arms around her. "And I can only hope it turns out as lucky for the next guy as it did for me."

EPILOGUE

It was new year's eve and Josie stood behind the costume shop's counter, with her boss nearby, pressing her to stay longer than she'd wished. She was eager to get home and get ready for her night out with Tom.

She was busy adding the day's receipts when the door jingled and opened. To her happy surprise, Tom walked through the door, a package in his hand.

"Last delivery of the night," he said, winking as Josie's boss turned away. "Headed home to get ready for my hot date."

Josie grinned and waved as he left, wondering if the package was one of his "special deliveries." They'd been blissfully dating for over a month, and he often brought her packages. Flowers. Chocolates. Sexy lingerie. Seemed he preferred her costumes to be of the tiny silk and satin variety, and Josie was having fun experimenting with what turned him from hot to hottest.

With eagerness, Josie ripped open the package and found the blonde Marilyn wig. "What in the world?" She flipped open the enclosed card and read:

I considered keeping this, but decided not to be selfish. My night in the Marilyn costume turned into a lifetime of fantasy. Please make sure some other girl gets the same chance. Caron Avery.

Josie smiled, thinking about just how wonderful her night in the Marilyn costume had turned out as well, when she noticed the red envelope she hadn't seen at first. She bit her lip, a fizzle of excitement darting through her, certain it was from Tom. She slipped open the seal and pulled out the heart-covered card. Inside read:

My New Year's resolution is to spend every New Year with you, Josie. Forever.

Joy filled Josie. Happy New Year, indeed. And to all, a silk and satin good-night.

She was quite certain it would be for her.

ACKNOWLEDGMENTS

Thanks to the entire Entangled team for all the support and work that went into this book. Thanks to Louise Fury for always working so hard to be the "Fury" in my career. Thanks to Emily, my fearless, dedicated assistant. Thanks to Zita for proofing so many books over so many years, including this one. And finally, thank you to my readers, many of who follow me across genres and dive into my books just because I write them. I am forever honored!

A new heartwarming and humorous romance from USA Today *bestselling author Amy Andrews that is sure to have you in stitches.*

the trouble with christmas

by Amy Andrews

All Suzanne St. Michelle wants is an over-the-top, eggnog-induced holiday with her best friend in Credence, Colorado. But when her hoity-toity parents insist she come home for Christmas in New York, she blurts out that her sexy landlord is actually her boyfriend and she can't leave him—Joshy loves Christmas. The more twinkle lights the better.

Rancher Joshua Grady does not love Christmas. Or company, or chatty women. Unfortunately for him, the chattiest woman ever has rented the cottage on his ranch, invited her rich, art-scene parents, and now insists he play "fake rancher boyfriend" in a production of the Hokiest Christmas Ever. And somehow…she gets him to agree.

Apparently, he'll do anything to get his quiet life back. At least there's mistletoe every two feet—and kissing Suzy is surprisingly easy. But in the midst of acres of tinsel, far too many tacky Christmas sweaters, and a tree that can be seen from space, he's starting to want what he lost when he was a kid—a family. Too bad it's with a woman heading back to New York before the ball drops…

She's just one of the guys...until she's not in USA Today *bestselling author Cindi Madsen's unique take on weddings, small towns, and friends falling in love.*

Just One of the Groomsmen

by Cindi Madsen

Addison Murphy is the funny friend, the girl you grab a beer with—the girl voted most likely to start her own sweatshirt line. And now that one of her best guy friends is getting married, she'll add "groomsman" to that list, too. She'll get through this wedding if it's the last thing she does. Just don't ask her to dive for any bouquet.

When Tucker Crawford returns to his small hometown, he expects to see the same old people, feel comfort in the same old things. He certainly doesn't expect to see the nice pair of bare legs sticking out from under the hood of a broken-down car. Certainly doesn't expect to feel his heart beat faster when he realizes they belong to one of his best friends.

If he convinces Addie to give him a chance, they could be electric...or their break-up could split their tight-knit group in two.

Hiding the way he feels from the guys through bachelor parties, cake tastings, and rehearsals is one thing. But just asTucker realizes that Addie truly could be the perfect woman for him—he was just too stupid to realize it—now she's leaving to follow her own dreams. He's going to need to do a lot of compromising if he's going to convince her to take a shot at forever with him—on her terms this time.

How to Lose a Guy in 10 Days *meets* Accidentally on Purpose *by Jill Shalvis in this head-over-heels romantic comedy.*

the aussie next door

by *USA TODAY* bestselling author
Stefanie London

American Angie Donovan has never wanted much. When you grow up getting bounced from foster home to foster home, you learn not to become attached to anything, anyone, or any place. But it only took her two days to fall in love with Australia. With her visa clock ticking, surely she can fall in love with an Australian—and get hitched—in two months. Especially if he's as hot and funny as her next-door neighbor…

Jace Walters has never wanted much—except a bathroom he didn't have to share. The last cookie all to himself. And solitude. But when you grow up in a family of seven, you can kiss those things goodbye. He's *finally* living alone and working on his syndicated comic strip in privacy. Sure, his American neighbor is distractingly sexy and annoyingly nosy, but she'll be gone in a few months...

Except now she's determined to find her perfect match by checking out every eligible male in the town, and her choices are even more distracting. So why does it suddenly feel like he—and his obnoxious tight-knit family, and even these two wayward dogs—could be exactly what she needs?